Praise for *Tears o*

"A window into a world long-gone, *Tears of Pearl* delivers both interesting history and fast-action suspense—a winning combination for a great mystery read!"

—Borders' *Crime Scene* column

"[A] lush setting and beautiful details. . . . [Emily's] voice and the accurate historical details will keep the reader enthralled."

—*RT Book Reviews* (4 ½ stars)

Praise for *A Fatal Waltz*

"Alexander cleverly incorporates historical figures and events into a fictional story of European political intrigue, English society, Viennese culture, and plenty of genteel romantic chemistry."

—*Library Journal*

"Sparkling wit. . . . This is a captivating addition to the adventures of an irresistible Victorian iconoclast." —*Booklist*

"Delightful . . . superb storytelling." —*BookPage*

"A nineteenth-century amateur detective in a Worth gown . . . what's not to love?" —Karleen Koen, *New York Times* bestselling author of *Through a Glass Darkly*

Praise for *A Poisoned Season*

"Sometimes touching, sometimes funny, and always absorbing, this Victorian-era mystery hits all the right notes." —*RT Book Reviews*

"*A Poisoned Season* mixes spot-on dialogue, manners, and mores with a splash of erotic friction in a lively, delightful tale."

—Julie Spencer-Fleming, Edgar Award finalist
and author of *All Mortal Flesh*

Praise for *And Only to Deceive*

"Alexander excels in depicting the social mores of a society uncomfortable with the independence of women, and deftly allows the plot to develop in tandem with Emily's growth."

—*The Baltimore Sun*

"[C]harming . . . Alexander makes Emily light but sympathetic, and conveys period flavor without being ponderous. Her knowledge of the ethical dilemmas posed by Victorian etiquette is considerable; sexual chemistry in particular is handled with exquisite delicacy."

—*Publishers Weekly*

"Engagingly suspenseful and rich with period detail . . . Barrier-breaking sleuth Nancy Drew has nothing on Alexander's fearless and tenacious Lady Emily." —*BookPage*

Tears of Pearl

Tears of Pearl

A Novel of Suspense

Tasha Alexander

 Minotaur Books ⚓ New York

For my parents, who taught me to love books

TEARS OF PEARL. Copyright © 2009 by Tasha Alexander. All rights reserved. Printed in the United States of America. For information, address St. Martin's Press, 175 Fifth Avenue, New York, N.Y. 10010.

www.minotaurbooks.com

The Library of Congress has cataloged this hardcover edition as follows:

Alexander, Tasha, 1969–
    Tears of Pearl / Tasha Alexander. — 1st ed.
        p. cm.
    ISBN 978-0-312-38370-1
    1. British—Turkey—Fiction. 2. Murder—Fiction. 3. Turkey—History—Ottoman Empire, 1288–1918—Fiction. I. Title.
    PS3601.L3565T43 2009
    813'.6—dc22

                                                                    2009012726

ISBN 978-0-312-38380-0 (trade paperback)

First Minotaur Books Trade Paperback Edition: October 2010

10 9 8 7 6 5 4 3 2 1

Acknowledgments

Myriad thanks to . . .

Charlie Spicer, Allison Caplin, Andrew Martin, and Anne Hawkins, who guide, inspire, and make publishing more than a little fun.

Joyclyn Ellison, Kristy Kiernan, Elizabeth Letts, and Renee Rosen, whose talent and support are boundless.

Brett Battles, Laura Bradford, Rob Gregory Browne, Jon Clinch, Dusty Rhoades, and Dave White—tremendous writers and partners in crime.

Bill Cameron, who made me laugh pretty much every single day while I was writing this book and who is the master of status updates.

Christina Chen, Carrie Medders, and Missy Rightley—the best friends a girl could have.

Gary and Anastasia Gutting, for making me believe that the impossible is possible.

Acknowledgments

Andrew Grant, for changing everything.

Xander, who is, among many other things, an excellent gun consultant.

I fain would go, yet beauty calls me back.
To leave her so and not once say farewell
Were to transgress against all laws of love,
But if I use such ceremonious thanks
As parting friends accustom on the shore,
Her silver arms will coil me round about
And tears of pearl cry, "Stay, Aeneas, stay."
Each word she says will then contain a crown,
And every speech be ended with a kiss.
I may not 'dure this female drudgery.
To sea, Aeneas! Find out Italy!

—Christopher Marlowe, *Dido, Queen of Carthage*

Tears of Pearl

It is always a mistake to underestimate the possibilities of a train compartment. Some newly married couples might prefer luxurious, spacious suites at the Continental in Paris or rooms overlooking Lake Lucerne, but I shall never be convinced that one can find bliss more satisfactory than that to be had in a confined space with the company only of each other. Limitations lend themselves to creativity, and my spouse wasted no time in proving himself adept beyond imagination.

After the death of my first husband, a man I'd barely known, I hadn't expected that I, Lady Emily Ashton, would ever again agree to subject myself to the bonds of matrimony. I'd not believed there was a man alive capable of tempting me to give up even a shred of what I considered my hard-earned independence. More surprising than simply finding such an extraordinary individual was discovering that he was said late husband's best friend. Philip, the viscount Ashton, a dedicated hunter, had gone on safari immediately following our wedding trip, leaving me behind in London. He never returned.

Everyone initially accepted his death as natural—it appeared as if he'd fallen victim to fever—but I soon began to believe otherwise and spearheaded the ensuing investigation, suspecting early on that Colin Hargreaves had murdered the man who'd been like a brother to him.

Such are the follies of a novice detective, and in the end I was pleased to have been wholly incorrect about Colin's character. Far from a nefarious criminal, he instead turned out to be a gentleman of the highest morals who spent much of his time working for the Crown—investigating situations that, as he liked to say, required more than a modicum of discretion. This description was too modest. In fact, his services were indispensable to the British Empire, and he was one of Her Majesty's most trusted agents. I do not blame myself entirely for having been so wrong in my suspicions—a man who works in such mysterious ways ought to expect his actions to be, on occasion, misinterpreted.

And so, rather than seeing him off to prison, I fell in love with him, and after refusing his proposals twice, at last was convinced that matrimony was essential to my happiness. This decision came after I'd solved two more crimes in a fashion competent enough to earn Colin's praise and his suggestion that I begin to assist him in a more official capacity. Assuming, of course, his colleagues would agree to such an arrangement. A female investigator was not something much sought after in the halls of Buckingham Palace.

My decision to pursue such a line of work complemented nicely my other so-called eccentricities, in particular a propensity for academic pursuits that at present focused on the study of ancient Greek. All of this greatly vexed my mother, a staunch traditionalist, and strained our already tenuous relationship. When at last I agreed to be Colin's wife, she rejoiced (although she would have preferred for me to catch a duke), but her jovial attitude dissolved the instant she learned we had eloped on the Greek island of Santorini. Philip had left me a villa there, and it was the place to which I fled whenever I was overwhelmed or in need of escape. It also proved the perfect spot for an extremely private wedding.

Afterwards, we returned to England, where we passed an excruciating month with my parents at their estate in Kent. We felt it right to tell them our news in person and wanted to extend the proverbial olive branch. But only the most rare sort of mother could find it in her heart to welcome home a child who had deprived her of the pleasure of planning a society wedding, and Lady Catherine Bromley was not such a woman. The only bright spot in the visit was the fact that my dearest childhood friend, Ivy, in that happy condition that comes inevitably after marriage, was also there. My mother, upon learning that Ivy's parents were in India, had all but carried my friend into Kent, insisting that she needed special care during her confinement.

Much though Colin and I enjoyed seeing Ivy, it had become evident almost at once that escape was necessary. We longed to get away from everyone, to a place where our only pressing business would be to enjoy our honeymoon, and had planned a trip east to visit sites important to me because of my love of classical antiquities and literature. I wanted to see the ruins at Ephesus, and as student of Homer, craved a visit to Troy. Colin, proving himself husband extraordinaire from the first, did not need to be told any of this; he anticipated my every desire. And hence, we soon found ourselves speeding towards Constantinople on the *Orient Express*.

"I'm not sure your mother will ever forgive me all the way," Colin said as he guided me through narrow, mahogany-paneled corridors to the train's dining car. "I'd no idea how wild she and the queen had run with their wedding plans."

"Well, we did give up our opportunity to be wed in the chapel at Windsor Palace."

"Yes. With fireworks and our two thousand closest friends."

I laughed. "I confess I never thought she had it in her to be so fierce with you."

"Now that we're married, she considers me a safe mark. No more worries that I'll take my affections and my fortune elsewhere."

"Excellent point. But I'd hoped that her desire to charm you into eventually accepting a title from the queen would keep her better in line."

"She's quite amusing," he said.

"Spoken like a man who's never lived with her." A crisply uniformed steward pulled open a door for us, and we stepped into a dining room that, although small, was worthy of the best restaurants in Europe. Soft candles flickered with the gentle motion of the train, sending light undulating across crystal glasses, gold-rimmed porcelain, and damask tablecloths the color of bright moonlight, while the smell of perfectly roasted beef with a tangy claret sauce filled the air.

"Twenty-eight days was more than enough," Colin said.

"Was it only twenty-eight?" I asked.

"And a half. Why do you think I insisted we take the morning train to Paris?"

I slipped into a chair across from him at a table where a silver-haired gentleman was already settled. He'd risen and bowed to me—over me, more like, as his height was extraordinary—and then offered his hand to my husband. "Sir Richard St. Clare," he said, introducing himself with a stiff nod. Colin shook his hand and introduced us both. "Hargreaves, eh? I know of your work. Your reputation is sterling in diplomatic circles."

"The compliment is much appreciated," Colin said, sitting next to me.

"And much deserved. But we shan't bore your lovely wife with talk of business." He turned to me. "How far are you traveling?"

"All the way to Constantinople," I said, then leaned forward, a broad smile stretching across my face. "First real stop on our wedding trip."

"Excellent." He rubbed together thick-knuckled hands. "And where else shall you visit?"

"I've been promised Ephesus," I said, raising an eyebrow at Colin, who was a vision of handsome perfection in his evening kit.

"I'll take you to Philadelphia and Sardis as well," Colin said. "So long as you have clothing suitable for exploring ruins."

"You wouldn't have married me if I didn't," I said, wishing I could grab his knee under the table and feeling a hot rush of color flood my cheeks at this reference to a conversation we'd had nearly two years ago on the Pont Neuf in Paris, the night he'd fallen in love with me in spite of his erroneous belief I was not in possession of a wardrobe suitable for adventurous travel. The gown I was wearing now—of the palest pink silk embroidered with silver thread from which hung teardrop-shaped crystals—did not suggest I was a lady ready for the wilderness, but I was not the sort of woman who should be judged by her clothing. An appreciation for high fashion does not preclude possession of common sense.

"A rather wild agenda, isn't it?" Sir Richard asked. "You might find you'd prefer Rome for ruins. It's far safer."

"I was not aware of problems at Ephesus," Colin said, pointedly not looking at me as I raised an eyebrow.

"My son, Benjamin, is an archaeologist and spent some months with the team excavating there a year or so ago," Sir Richard said. "There's no longer the trouble they had there in the past, but I can't say it's a place I'd bring a new bride."

This line of thought did not surprise me in the least. It was precisely what I expected from an ordinary Englishman and precisely the sort of reaction I had grown accustomed to dismissing without reply. "What has induced you to visit the Ottomans, Sir Richard?" I asked.

"Constantinople is my home. I work at the embassy."

"Then you must tell us all the inside secrets of the city," Colin said. "The places we shouldn't miss."

"You might consider hiring a guide to keep track of you unless you plan on staying in the Westernized parts of the city."

"I'd much prefer an adventurous approach," I said. "I want to have no doubt in my mind that I'm far from England."

"You remind me of my wife. Not that she ever went to England— that she preferred adventure. An explorer like no other, my Assia."

"Will she be dining with us tonight?" I asked.

"I'm afraid I lost her many years ago."

"I'm so sorry," I said, a shard of grief piercing my stomach, bringing with it memories of Philip, whom I'd come to love only after he was gone. I owed my happiness with Colin in no small part to him. We would never have come to know each other were it not first for their friendship and second for Philip's murder. And this was a realization that carried with it a large dose of complicated and bittersweet emotion.

"It's a terrible thing to lose someone you love," Colin said.

"Quite," Sir Richard said, looking down and tapping a finger against the tines of his fork as an awkward silence enveloped us. I had thought of and rejected no fewer than fourteen ways to change the direction of the conversation before our dinner companion surprised me by continuing. "My son goes sour whenever the subject of his mother comes up—we lost her and his sister the same day. He was only eight years old and in ways has never fully recovered. Neither of us has, I suppose."

"Condolences are not enough," Colin said.

"But they are appreciated nonetheless," Sir Richard said, the words heavy with the sound of forced strength. "Assia was an Algerian Berber, and a more beautiful woman has never walked the earth. She had been educated in Paris—I imagine you, Lady Emily, would approve of the value placed on cultured women in Kabilya, the region in which she grew up. She loved adventure, and we traveled constantly. I took her to India and Egypt. After our children were born, we brought them with us."

"What a marvelous childhood," I said.

"I thought it would be." He squared his jaw. "Until bandits attacked our camp near the dig at Ephesus. This was twenty-odd years ago, soon after John Turtle Wood started excavating. He was plagued with problems—warned us not to come—but I would have none of it. I was a young fool."

"Redundant," Colin said, drawing a hard laugh from our visitor.

"Quite. We were in two tents. Ceyden, my daughter, had been sick, so Assia was sleeping next to her. I didn't know what was happening until I heard my wife screaming as they cut her throat. She'd struggled too much."

"I'm so sorry." I could not help reaching out to take his hand, but he pulled it from the table.

"I had to protect Benjamin. Helped him hide before I grabbed my rifle and went on the offensive, but at the first gunshot, the cowards started to retreat. They took Ceyden with them. She was a beauty, even at three years old. That striking red gold hair, blue eyes. Looked like her mother."

"You must have been frantic," I said. I considered the poor girl, terrified, torn from her family, and my heart ached at the thought of her carrying so much pain and such horrific images.

"I spent years and a fortune searching for her, but never uncovered a trace. All my efforts were futile. I've always assumed that she must have been sold into slavery. So you see, adventurous travel isn't all romance. You'd be better off, Hargreaves, keeping your wife safely in sight." He drained his wine, slammed the glass down with a thump, and laid his hands flat on the table.

"I of course appreciate the advice and shall heed it," Colin said. I resisted the urge to kick him under the table, restraining myself only out of respect for the tragedies suffered by Sir Richard.

"I'm afraid I've—I've quite ruined the mood of the evening. Apologies." His words sounded almost slurred as he reached for the half-empty bottle of wine in front of him, filled his glass, and took a long drink, sweat beading on his forehead. "I'm sure that between Topkapı Palace and . . . ah . . . yes, the Blue Mosque and the Grand Bazaar, you'll find yourselves quite well diverted. I'll see what I can do about arranging invitations to any parties in the diplomatic community as well as—"

His eyes rolled back in his head and he slumped over in his chair, still only for an instant before his body convulsed, sending him crashing to the floor.

The speed with which the ensuing chaos was calmed is a testament to the efficiency of the staff of La Compagnie Internationale des Wagons-

Lits. Within a quarter of an hour, Colin and I were crowded into the corridor outside the sleeping compartment, where a doctor, who had been traveling in the next car, was examining Sir Richard. The physician ducked out and took a short step towards Colin.

"May I talk to you privately?" He shot a glance at me. "I don't think it's appropriate— "

"You may speak freely in front of my wife," Colin said, his dark eyes serious.

The doctor clenched his jaw and scrunched his eyebrows together. "Sir Richard took an extremely high dose of chloral hydrate. A not uncommon occurrence among those dependent on the medication— it's given as a sleeping aid. I believe he'd mixed it in with his wine at dinner. He's lucky to be alive."

"Will he be all right?" I asked.

"There's not much to do but wait, and I'll sit with him as long as necessary. You need not stay."

Colin scribbled the number of our compartment on a piece of paper and handed it to the doctor. "Please alert us if the situation changes."

"Of course." He went back to Sir Richard, leaving us alone.

"I don't feel hungry anymore," I said as Colin and I started down the corridor.

"I've not the slightest interest in the dining car." He stopped walking and pressed me against the wall, kissing me.

"That's not what I meant. You're a beast to kiss me at a time like this," I said, twining my fingers through his. "Perhaps we should be doing more for him."

"A man who can't properly dose his own medicine has no right to interrupt our honeymoon."

"Could we contact his son?" I asked. "I don't feel right leaving him so alone."

"When we get to Constantinople. We're on a train, Emily."

"I had noticed that," I said.

"Perceptive girl." He kissed my forehead. "I do adore your compassion for Sir Richard. But right now, forgive me, I think you should direct it to me, your husband, who by unfortunate coincidence of seating arrangements has been forced to deal with doctors and train stewards all evening instead of being left to his violently elegant and relentlessly charming wife."

"Sounds delicious," I said. "I should have married you ages ago."

The two remaining days of our trip passed without further incident. We saw Sir Richard the following evening in the dining car. He was in fine health, full of apologies, and all easy charm for the rest of the trip—no more criticism of our itinerary or of my yearning for adventure. More important, no more signs that he was using too heavy a hand when dosing his medicine.

"Perhaps he's a changed man after his near brush with death," Colin said, gathering the few remaining books strewn about our compartment as the train pulled into the station at Constantinople.

"I don't believe in sudden transformations," I said.

"That's because you're so very cynical. It's one of your best qualities. You know . . ." He looked around. "I'm almost sorry to leave the train. It's effortless to lock this door and shut out the world. No house full of servants bothering us."

"Just overzealous stewards."

"Who were quick to learn that we wanted our privacy." He ran a hand through the thick, dark waves of his hair. "I think that's everything. Ready to have the Ottoman Empire at your feet?"

Excitement surged through me as we stepped onto the platform, and I looked around, eager to take in a culture so very foreign to me. Despite the fact that my guidebook told me it had been designed by a Prussian architect, the Müşir Ahmet Paşa Station, with its elaborately decorated façade, looked satisfyingly Oriental to me. Bright reddish pink bricks were arranged in rectangular patterns between wide stone borders along the lower portion of the building, the rest of the walls painted pink. Stained glass curved over the doors and long windows, above which there were more, these large and round, fashioned from leaded glass. The center of the structure was low, its sides anchored by taller sections, one with a flat roof edged with stone decoration, the other domed.

"Where shall we go first?" Colin asked.

"Meg is perfectly capable of seeing to it that our trunks get to the house. My plan is to get a spectacular view of the city, unless you've a mad desire to go to our quarters first." Meg, my maid, was traveling with us, despite my husband's protests that he'd prefer we be alone. I, too, liked very much the idea of privacy, but a lady must deal with hard realities, and there was simply no way my hair could be made presentable on a daily basis without skilled assistance. Furthermore, I'd spent a not inconsiderable effort to show her the merits of places beyond England. Her provincial attitude had begun to thaw in Paris more than a year ago, and I had every intention of continuing her enlightenment.

"If we go to the house first, you're not likely to see much of the city today." He pulled me close, his arm around my waist.

"I cannot tolerate that," I said, a delightful flash of heat shooting from toes to fingertips. I straightened my hat—a jaunty little thing, devoid of the ornamentation favored by many of my peers. So far as I was concerned, stuffed birds had no place in the world of fashion.

I was too eager in making the adjustment, and the tip of my hat pin jabbed into my scalp, causing me to jump, knocking into a gentleman walking behind me.

"Oh, Sir Richard, I'm so sorry," I said. "I didn't see you."

"I'm afraid I wasn't paying attention, either." A gruff edge cut through his already rough voice.

"Is something wrong?" I asked.

"Yes, actually. It appears I've been robbed. Nothing serious, just unsettling."

"What happened?" Colin stepped closer to me and began a methodical study of the area around us.

"I've no idea. When I was gathering my belongings to leave the train, I realized a sheaf of papers I was bringing from London to the embassy is gone."

"What sort of papers?" I asked.

Sir Richard narrowed his eyes, seeming to appraise my competence as I asked the question. "Standard diplomatic fare. Nothing of pressing confidentiality. More of a nuisance and embarrassment to lose them than anything else."

"Do you have any idea when they went missing?" I asked.

"Not at all," Sir Richard said. "I didn't need to deal with them during the trip and never pulled them out. It could have happened anytime."

"Who had access to your compartment?" I asked. "We should question the stewards at once and try to locate the physician who treated you. We know he was there."

"I assure you, there's no need, Lady Emily—"

I interrupted him. "Every possibility must be considered."

"Have you reported this to the local police?" Colin asked.

"No," Sir Richard said, shielding his eyes from the sun. "It's entirely unnecessary. This may be nothing more than a prank."

"I can't see that making any sense." I shook my head, harder than I ought to have, sending my already maligned hat off-kilter. "And if that were the case, wouldn't you have some idea who would do such a thing? Did you have any colleagues on the train? Did anyone even know you had the papers?"

"No. I saw none of my colleagues. But I'm a diplomat. It's reasonable to assume I'd be carrying papers. Someone—a Turk, perhaps—who's less than pleased with Britain could have done it to make a point."

"An awfully oblique point," I said, frowning. "We'd be happy to assist you—"

"Thank you, but that won't be necessary," he said. "As I said on the train, I know well your husband's reputation, but I assure you this is nothing more than an aggravating inconvenience and quite out of the sphere of his interest. I do, however, hope to be in touch soon with an invitation to something I think you'll both enjoy."

I watched, dissatisfied, as he walked away from us. "We are going back to the train, aren't we?" Sir Richard might refuse to investigate, but I could not do the same. My experience, while limited, had given me a taste for detecting.

Colin gave a short laugh. "This is not in the least what I want from a honeymoon, but I know you must be pacified."

"Yes, I must." I looped my arm through his and led him to the platform. He flashed some sort of identification, and within a short while we had conducted a quick but thorough interrogation of stewards and lingering passengers. Our efforts, however, were in vain: no suspicious characters, no overlooked clues, and certainly no breathless confession.

"I can't escape the feeling we've missed something," I said when, finished, we crossed back through the station.

"It's possible." Colin took my hand. "But there's no harm done, Emily. He might have mislaid the papers himself. There was no sign of forced entry into his compartment."

"He could have forgotten to lock the door."

"He's too competent to have done that."

"Doesn't it make you wonder about the chloral hydrate?" I asked. "Perhaps someone dosed his wine, knowing the subsequent commotion would provide an opportunity to snatch the papers."

"I understand the suspicion, my dear, but why would anyone go to so much trouble to take something that, by all accounts, is of no particular value?"

"Perhaps the papers were not the goal," I continued. "Perhaps harming Sir Richard was, and the theft was meant to set the investigation on the wrong course. We may be dealing with a matter entirely personal, not professional."

"We, my dear, are not at present dealing with any matter whatsoever other than enjoying our wedding trip."

"I just—"

"No, Emily. Let this go. Come. The Golden Horn awaits you."

Constantinople was like an exotic dream full of spice and music and beauty—the scent of cardamom blew through the streets like a fresh wind—but at the same time, it had a distinct and surprising European feel. The cobbled streets, winding at seemingly random angles through the city, teemed with gentlemen, as many wearing top hats as were in dark red fezzes. Stray cats darted in front of us with alarming frequency, slinking confidently in search of their next meal, while brazen shopkeepers called out, inviting us into stores brimming with Eastern treasures. Noise filled every inch of the air: seagulls crying, carts clattering, voices arguing in foreign tongues.

Before us, the choppy silver blue waters of the Golden Horn—the estuary slicing through the European section of the city—stood mere paces from the station. Boats tied too close knocked together down the length of battered docks, only the larger vessels meriting the space to stay safely untouched. One among them waited for us, but I did not pause to identify it, heading instead for the Galata Bridge, making my way through the crush of carriages in the road, Colin's

15

hand firm on my arm. We paused to pay the toll—a pittance—and walked until we reached the midpoint of the pontoon-supported structure.

"I like being able to see two continents," I said, watching Colin as his eyes swept the Asian shore far across the Bosphorus from us. "It gives an intrinsic satisfaction I've not before experienced."

"Seraglio Point, on the European side." Colin nodded towards the shore from which we'd come. "The spires of Topkapı Palace are there"—he pointed—"and farther this way, the Blue Mosque and Aya Sofya." The minarets of the holy buildings jutted into the crisp sky with mathematical precision, rising from the crowds of smaller stone structures. Gulls circled and dove, careening around the minarets and then pausing to coast on the air, as if catching their breath before darting off again. Trees surrounded the palace, its far-off buildings the only break in a sea of green.

"Topkapı looks marvelous, even from a distance," I said. "Perhaps I shall be kidnapped and given to the sultan and live out the rest of my years there." A few paces from me, a fisherman pulled up his line and dropped his flopping catch into an already full bucket. All around us, men were doing the same, and the air fell heavy with the oily, salty scent of their bounty.

"He should be so lucky." Our eyes met and lingered, and the most pleasant sort of warmth pulsed through me. "But you wouldn't be—the court is no longer at Topkapı. There's a new palace."

"I could stand here all day," I said. To our north, the neighborhoods of Pera stretched to the hills, and the Galata Tower, the last remnant of a fourteenth-century fort, stood tall above tier after tier of creamy rose-and-white houses.

"I've other plans for you." After bestowing upon me a deliciously discreet kiss that in an instant promised untold delights, Colin led me back to the docks, and in short order we had climbed aboard a small caïque rowed by two sturdy men. They moved with a grace I would not have expected from persons so muscular, pulling through water rough enough to make me wish for the stability of a large ship. As the Golden Horn opened to the wide expanse of the Bosphorus, I began to feel queasy bouncing up and down on erratic waves.

Houses packed the Asian shore as tightly as the European, but as we traveled north, they grew larger—*yalıs*, mansions built as summer homes for the city's elite. Some were spectacular, others in distressing states of disrepair, but all came right to the edge of the water, which lapped against terraces perfect for watching the light change as the sun set. Colin had rented one for us that was a vision of romantic perfection: bright white with a peaked red roof and elaborately delicate gingerbread trimwork on the myriad windows, pillars, and balconies gracing the eighteenth-century façade. I stepped, unsteady, off the boat, the fatigue of travel exacerbated by the rough crossing. Nonetheless, I was ready to explore the interior.

The rooms were leagues more refined and elegant than my villa in Greece and entirely different from the sort of luxury I was used to in England. Overstuffed pillows sheathed in silk covered low sofas, and the carpets were soft and spectacular, Anatolian, with designs of leaves and hyacinths twined together, their colors blending beneath an almost translucent sheen. Even pieces that at home would have been fashioned from simple wood were full of exquisite detail: every table inlaid with mother-of-pearl and ebony. An exotic retreat, full of delicious comforts. We collapsed, exhausted, and slept scandalously late the next morning.

"Mail at breakfast?" I asked, watching Meg hand Colin a stack of ivory envelopes as I dropped into a chair on our balcony. "It's as if we're still in England."

"Far from it," Colin said. I followed his gaze out to the water, where the sun danced across the Bosphorus. Scores of boats glided with breezy ease, showing no hint of the dangerous currents that had wreaked havoc on my stomach the previous day.

"Hmmm. I suppose you're right." As if the view were not enough to convince me, trays of decidedly un-English breakfast foods covered the table: thick yogurt drizzled with honey, pomegranate seeds, sliced fruits I did not recognize, sesame-seed-covered pastries filled with cheese and spinach. I cracked the shell of a hard-cooked egg and sprinkled salt over it. "What shall we do today?"

"Sir Richard has written to invite us to the palace this evening. Apparently the sultan is an opera fan. There's to be a production of *La Traviata* at his private theater. A Western score, perhaps, but dare I hope the possibility of being one of only a handful of European ladies to meet His Eminence and seeing the interior of Yıldız Palace might be enough to entice you?"

Entice me it did, and before the sun had set, we had made our way across the Bosphorus to the theater. Newly built for the sultan, it was gorgeous, though disappointingly European. European, that is, if one ignored the elaborately carved wooden screens that shielded members of the harem from the view of the rest of the audience. But if a person were to focus solely on the rich velvet curtain and ornately gilded boxes, it would be easy to imagine oneself at Covent Garden. Until, that is, the last act, when strains of Verdi succumbed to something wholly out of place.

"What on earth is this?" I leaned forward.

"Is it Gilbert and Sullivan?" Colin asked as the composer's tender notes were replaced by a melody far too cheerful for *La Traviata*. In tonight's production, Violetta did not die in her lover's arms after a heartbreaking separation and lengthy illness. Instead, her consumption vanished the moment she drank a potion handily supplied by an obliging physician. "Do you think anyone's told Verdi?"

"It's *The Mikado*." I leaned close and kept my voice low, breathing in the faint scent of tobacco lingering on his jacket as I tried to ignore a tremor in my core that was dangerously close to erupting in loud laughter.

"Of course. I recognize the song: 'Here's a how-de-do!' Appalling. They've usurped Verdi." Violetta, Alfredo, and this brilliant and mysterious man of science who had made their joy possible joined their voices in an ebullient trio, Mr. Gilbert's lyrics replaced with ones appropriate to the new and theoretically improved scene.

"Only think what we might accomplish had we access to this sort of miracle cure," I whispered, flipping my opera glasses closed.

Sir Richard, seated in the row behind us, leaned forward. "The sultan has no patience for unhappy endings. And when one who is the absolute ruler of an empire—a man claiming both secular and spiritual control over people who, technically, are little more than his slaves—has no patience for something, it is forbidden."

I bit back laughter and glanced across the spectacular theater to the royal box, where Abdül Hamit II sat, nodding, an enormous smile on his face. Next to him was Perestu, the valide sultan—the sultan's mother—the most powerful woman in the empire. Her petite body still showed signs of the beauty she'd possessed in her youth, and although many of the women in the harem were said to have adopted a Westernized sort of dress, Perestu clung to traditional outfits that were at once elegant and, to European eyes, exotic. Tonight she wore a long, slender dress fashioned from green silk, heavily embroidered with gold thread, wide sleeves hanging over her wrists to her fingertips, a short-sleeved, sheer black robe covering the gown. Her long dark hair hung in two braids down her back, and on her head sat a headdress, reminiscent of a small fez, draped in muslin, an enormous ruby pinned to its front. Rings graced each of the fingers on her henna-painted hands. Her regal bearing surpassed any I'd seen before. Behind the royal pair, four menacing guards stood against the back wall, their thick arms crossed, no hint of amusement on their faces.

"'Here's a pretty mess! / In a month, or less, / I must die without a wedding! / Let the bitter tears I'm shedding / Witness my distress,'" Colin sang under his breath as the applause faded after the curtain fell. "The proper words are much better."

"Agreed," I said, slipping my arm through his and dropping my head onto his shoulder as we made our way out of the theater. "I prefer Violetta's untimely demise to this happy ending."

"Bloody unromantic of you."

"I'm a beast, you know," I said.

"It's why I married you." We'd stepped outside, falling behind the sultan and his entourage. The night was warm for spring, the air heavy with humidity and the sweet scent of flowers. Above us, stars dangled, so dazzling bright that I felt certain they could compete with the moon. "Now, if we can just slip away before—"

A ragged, sharp cry pierced the night, and in an instant silence fell over the gay crowd on the theater steps. The garden around us seemed darker, and the stars lost all their brightness. The screaming continued, but now it was accompanied by the sound of slippers on gravel, and I turned to see a beautiful young woman, dark hair streaming behind her in a tangled mess, running towards us.

"Come! Help! Please!" she cried, pausing only long enough to speak, then running again. Before she had covered more than a few yards, two of the sultan's muscular guards stopped her. She struggled against them, and words that I could not hear were exchanged. Ab-dül Hamit stepped forward, and she flung herself onto the ground in front of him, all but grabbing his feet as the valide sultan watched. He muttered something, and the girl stood, shaking, not looking directly at him. His words appeared to soothe her, but before she could respond, a circle of guards surrounded him and the group disappeared into the night.

"Need to keep the sultan safe if there's trouble," came Sir Richard's voice from behind me. "He grows more paranoid with each passing day. There's no one in the empire he's not having watched."

"Should that make me feel safe or threatened?" I asked. Perestu had remained behind, taking the girl firmly by the arm and ordering the remaining guards to give her space as we all started down a path lit by a series of gilded torches. They obeyed at once. Colin dropped my arm and went towards them, catching up with a few long strides. I started to follow him, but Sir Richard stopped me.

"What do you think you're doing? If there's danger, we must get you back to your house at once."

"I can't imagine I'm in the slightest danger here," I said. "There are guards everywhere." I set off after Colin as quickly as my evening shoes would allow, frowning when a heel caught in the gravel and my ankle twisted fiercely. All the while I was fighting a stitch in my side caused, no doubt, by my tightly laced corset. I'd expected clothing to be an impediment to honeymoon bliss, but not like this.

Sir Richard caught up to me almost at once and gripped my wrist, a handful of sullen-looking men wearing fezzes trailing behind us. "I won't let you go alone," he said. "She's from the harem. One of the concubines." I strained to get a better look at the woman, ignoring the pain in my ankle, but she was too far ahead.

"How do you know?"

"It was obvious from her exchange with the sultan. She—" He stopped. We'd reached a small garden. Bright red bougainvillea cascaded from tall stone walls, and an elaborate fountain, carved in the shape of a fish, stood in the center of a smooth marble pavement. The pulse of falling water, soft but insistent, bounced off the walls and warded off the silence that descended upon us as we all froze, horrified at the sight before us.

A body was splayed on the ground, facedown, red gold hair shimmering in the torches' dancing light, a ghastly contrast to the inhuman stillness of the form. My throat burned and my stomach clenched, the sweet smell of the flowers now cloying. The valide sultan, who was standing next to the woman who'd brought us to this scene, took her hand and led her away, back towards the palace. No doubt she imagined the girl had seen enough. Colin bent down and brushed the hair away from the injured woman's neck, feeling for a pulse.

As he did this, Sir Richard came forward, unsteady on his feet. He knelt next to the body, his breath ragged, and pushed Colin out of the way.

"Sir Richard?" I followed and put a hand on his shoulder; he was trembling.

"No," he said. "No. It's not possible. It's not—" He gathered up her hair, twisting it gently off her neck, revealing alabaster white skin and a striking tattoo: a grid like that used to play noughts and crosses, but set at an angle with three letters beneath it. "Ceyden, my dear girl. No," he cried out, his voice sharp with pain.

He gingerly turned over the body and studied the girl's face, her deep blue eyes staring blankly at the night sky, a thin purple bruise spanning her throat. All emotion fell from his face, wrinkles smoothed, his skin blanched, as he cradled her lifeless head in his arms.

His voice broke and shattered. "She is the daughter who was stolen from me twenty years ago."

Sir Richard's response to this horrific scene scared me. He raged at those around him, unwilling to let anyone touch his daughter. Despite his thin frame, he pushed off the guards, who stood, awkward, casting uncertain glances at the growing crowd in the courtyard. Colin was speaking to the man in charge, and nearly everyone who'd been in the theater was now pushing into the garden, agitated murmurs and whispers dull replacements for the soothing sound of the fountain. A man in evening dress, his tie askew, hair rumpled, stepped forward and crossed to the largest of the guards.

"May I offer any assistance? I am an old friend." He faced Sir Richard, taking him by the shoulders and giving a soft shake. "I know your pain all too well. Lashing out will not help right now."

"How could I have so failed her?" Sir Richard said, shrugging him off and turning back to his daughter. He stood only for a moment before he collapsed, sobbing, over her body. I knelt beside him, knowing there were no words that could offer meaningful comfort. The guards began to clear out the area, demanding that everyone save the grieving father leave. I asked if I could stay with him, as did his friend—who introduced himself to me.

"Theodore Sutcliffe," he said, keeping his voice low as Sir Richard answered whatever questions the guards were asking. "I've known the old boy for years—we're both at the embassy."

"How lucky for him to find a friend near at such a moment," I said. "Are you close?"

"We've both lost children."

"I'm sorry. I—" I stumbled over the words, not sure how to deal with yet more tragedy. Colin interrupted before I was able to offer my condolences.

"Take him to the house," he said. "They're going to need to examine the body—I don't want him to witness that. I'll be along as soon as it's finished."

"Of course," I said. "Mr. Sutcliffe, would you come with us? It might comfort him to have you there as well."

"I shall be with him at every step. He won't be alone in his sad journey."

When we arrived at the *yalı*, I plied Sir Richard with hot orange blossom water—white coffee, a beverage the cook who came with the house insisted was a panacea—while Mr. Sutcliffe sat beside him, a quiet partner in sorrow.

"I wish I could offer you port," I said, pouring another cup of the pale, steaming liquid. Port was my own preferred beverage. I'd first tried it merely to make a point. After dinner, ladies were supposed to be herded out of the dining room, leaving the gentlemen to their liquor, cigars, and, most important, conversation deemed inappropriate for the gentle ears of the fairer sex. Knowing full well this was just the sort of talk I'd love to hear, I'd decided, while in mourning for Philip, to refuse to be exiled to the drawing room at a dinner party of my own. The discourse on that occasion was sadly limited, as my male guests were, on the whole, stunned, but the port seduced me at once. And gradually, the gentlemen of my acquaintance came to accept my eccentricity and welcomed me for the after-dinner ritual.

"I assure you, it makes no difference, Lady Emily," Sir Richard said. "The choice of beverage at such a moment is wholly irrelevant. Everything is useless now."

"Don't be hard on yourself," Mr. Sutcliffe said. "It was too late for you to have done anything."

"Had I only known she was here!"

"You couldn't have," his friend said. "The sultan himself wouldn't have known who she was. After all these years, there probably wasn't anything English left in her."

"She was my daughter, Theodore."

"I did not mean to offend. Only to say that even those close to her most likely had no idea of her heritage."

"They should have known! I had everyone in the empire on alert to find her."

"She was kidnapped, Richard," Mr. Sutcliffe said. "Undoubtedly her assailants waited until the furor had died down to . . . sell her."

"It's barbaric, all of it," I said, relieved to see Colin enter the room and save me from saying more on the subject. He nodded to me and shook our guests' hands.

"I've been to the embassy and arranged for a message to be sent to your son at once," he said, sitting across from Sir Richard. "He's sure to come as quickly as possible."

"Thank you." The older man placed the glass teacup on its bronze saucer. "Has there been an arrest?" Ottoman justice was swift. Even before we'd left the grounds of the palace, one of the eunuch guards from the harem had been fingered as the most likely suspect in the murder.

"I'm afraid so," Colin said. "He was standing sentry by her room—"

"She wasn't killed anywhere near her room," I said.

"Quite right." He refused the cup of white coffee I offered him.

"But that doesn't seem to factor into the charges against him. He was responsible for her safety. She's dead, and everyone seems to agree it's his fault."

"But is there any evidence?" I asked.

"None," Colin replied.

"He'll be executed," Sir Richard said. "And the brute who murdered my daughter will never be brought to justice."

"Now, now," Mr. Sutcliffe said. "The guard may well be guilty. Don't leap to conclusions. She shouldn't have been able to leave the harem, correct? Who let her out? Possibly the same person who killed her?"

"Sir Richard, are you quite certain it's Ceyden?" I hated asking the question; my skin felt stinging hot. "You haven't seen her since she was a child, and it's possible that—"

"There can be no doubt. All these years I've been here, in the same city, and never knew she was so close." He closed his eyes, rubbed a hand hard over them.

"Maybe it wasn't her," I said. "It's possible that—"

"No. It was Ceyden. When she'd fallen ill during our travels, Assia begged me to have her tattooed. It's common Berber practice, the medicinal use of tattoos. Half black magic, half ancient doctoring, I suppose. In the end, I decided it wouldn't hurt. Never was able to deny Assia anything. So I got her ink and needles and she did it herself."

"And you saw that tattoo tonight?" I asked.

"Yes. There's no doubt. Because when Assia had finished, I was so taken with the steadiness of her hand that I told her to add her initials, as if she were signing a painting. She didn't want to, but I convinced her. It was there, on her neck: ASC. There can be no mistake." He clasped his hands together, pulled them apart, rubbed his palms, then started again. "I need her murderer to be brought to justice, Hargreaves. Can I rely on you to help me?"

"I've already sought permission from our government and don't doubt that I'll receive it."

"Justice in such a case must be achieved at any cost. There is no crime more reprehensible than one that causes a person to lose his child," Mr. Sutcliffe said. "But will the sultan allow foreign intervention?"

"We should be able to persuade him to allow us at least a brief investigation," Colin said. "The girl was, after all, half English."

"I will have to count on you, Hargreaves," Sir Richard said.

"There's only one obstacle that I foresee," Colin said. "There's no chance I'll be allowed to interview anyone in the harem. I'll need the assistance of a lady."

"What luck you have," I said, meeting his eyes. "I believe you're well acquainted with someone quite capable of undertaking the task."

He smiled. "You'd be working in an official capacity, Emily. No running about doing whatever you wish. And I'll have to get approval—"

"Your wife is an investigator as well?" Mr. Sutcliffe's eyebrows shot upward.

"She's solved three murders," Colin said. His words were true, but I'd not before acted on behalf of the government. I'd only helped friends—and myself—in dire times when there was no other option. My stomach flipped, excitement competing with nerves for my attention. After the work I'd done in Vienna the previous winter, he'd spoken to his superiors at Buckingham Palace about me, and they'd agreed that my skills might prove useful to the government in the future—but only if I was partnering with my husband, and only if the job could not be done in the absence of feminine assistance. I'm quite certain they were convinced no such circumstance would ever come to pass.

"I'm not sure that I approve. Not that I doubt your talents, Lady Emily, but I cannot ask that you endanger yourself." The creases on Sir Richard's brow deepened. "But I suppose I have no choice but to graciously accept any assistance you can offer. I've now lost my daughter twice. I cannot let this insult go unpunished."

3 April 1892
Darnley House, Kent

My Dearest Emily,

I hope this letter finds you lost in the throes of connubial bliss. It was such a delight to see you and Colin—without question the best diversion I've had in months. Would that you'd been able to stay longer! I do, though, completely understand your desire to remove yourself from your parents' house, and I cannot be stern with you for having abandoned me. In fact, after the service you provided Robert and me in Vienna, I could hardly be stern with you on any subject. I'm not precisely sure what etiquette demands as the proper thanks for rescuing one's husband from prison and a charge of murder. Have you any suggestions?

I still can hardly believe Robert was ever suspected of such a crime— how anyone could think my dear husband would kill his own mentor is utterly beyond my comprehension. It was terrifying to see how quickly those around him abandoned him. If you hadn't been willing to pursue the investigation with such vigor, I'm quite certain I'd be swathed in mourning.

I must confess that at present it feels as if I'll never be able to leave your parents. Robert's business still keeps him in town, and your mother refuses to let me return alone to our estate. I appreciate her generous concern, but must admit that confinement with her is like being violently tamed by an unstoppable force of nature. I do fear for you, Emily, when your own time comes. There's not enough paper in England for me to list all she's doing to ensure I have a boy, but I can tell you that I'm quite tired of having beef broth forced on me six times a day.

Every corridor and nook in this house reminds me of the pleasant days you and I spent together as children. Just this morning I pried open that loose board in the solarium floor—the one we begged the butler not to have fixed—and found the box we'd hidden there long ago. Do you remember? In it there's a copy of Candide, a badly written statement pertaining to the outrage we felt at not being allowed to pursue employment as pirates, and a splendid collection of small rocks. All things considered, I do believe we've done well to abandon our thoughts of pirating.

Give Colin my best, and implore him to take care of you. I don't want to hear any stories of you being embroiled in intrigue while you're away.

I am, your most devoted friend, etc.,

Ivy Brandon

"Madam?" Meg opened our bedroom door a few inches after knocking. "An urgent message has come for you from the palace."

I pulled myself away from the perfect comfort of Colin's arms and sat up. The room was dark—tightly fit shutters keeping out the sun—and our silk quilted duvet and cotton blankets a perfect pool of soft warmth. The furniture, neither particularly Western nor Eastern, had simple, pleasing lines, and there were niches, lined with flower-painted tiles, cut out from the wall for candles on either side of the low mahogany bed. "The queen? Come in, Meg."

"No, madam. Not Buckingham Palace. Top—Top— Oh, I don't know that I could ever figure out how to say it." She shrugged and handed me an envelope heavy with the scent of lavender.

"Topkapı Sarayı." I leaned back as Colin raised a mountain of bright silk-covered pillows against the headboard. "A place undoubtedly full of exotic treasures, Meg. I'd love to see it, and you would, too."

"Oh, madam, I'm not sure I'd want to go there. There's a harem, you know. I might never come out."

"I shan't let the sultan claim you, Meg," Colin said. "Without you here, Emily might force me to do her hair."

"Thank you, sir." Meg blushed, not looking at him, still embarrassed at finding him in my room. "Is there anything else you need?"

"No. We'll be down for breakfast in another hour or so," Colin said. She dipped a curtsy and left the room, closing the door firmly behind her.

"That long?" I kissed him. "What if I'm hungry before then?"

"I'll try to keep you distracted."

"You'd better." I opened the envelope. "I can't imagine the sultan using fragranced paper."

"I can't imagine the sultan writing to a European woman."

"He's very cultured," I said. "And more Western than I'd expected. Surely you don't doubt I could charm him?"

"Quite the contrary. But though he may be cultured, he's a difficult man. Extremely paranoid—won't allow electricity in the city because when someone explained to him how it works, he mistook 'dynamo' for 'dynamite.'"

"Perhaps he's overwhelmed. He is, after all, ruling an empire in an advanced state of decay—a situation that's growing worse faster than expected. People accustomed to being in a position of strength often assume it will last. I often wonder about our own empire."

"Britain is not in a state of decay at the moment," he said. "But our way of life is a precarious one that must be protected with vigilance if we don't want it to slip away. All of Europe will be affected if Turkey becomes more unstable—instability has a way of being contagious."

"So we're witnessing the decline and fall of the Ottomans?"

"Due in large part to the excessive and obscene spending of Abdül Hamit's predecessors. They've done more palace building than prudent this century—and that went a long way to bankrupting the empire."

"Why would anyone with Topkapı Sarayı at his disposal want another palace? I've never heard such exotic descriptions of a place."

"It's ordinary to anyone who lives in it, I'd imagine."

"Not to the concubines when they first arrive and are prepared to meet the sultan. Only think how awestruck they must be to find themselves ensconced in such luxury."

"Your imagination is running quite wild, Emily. At any rate, the sultan now lives at Yıldız, not Topkapı."

I unfolded the paper I was holding. The letter was written in a confident, elegant hand. "This is from someone called Bezime. She says she's Abdül Aziz's mother. Who is Abdül Aziz?"

"He was sultan before Abdül Hamit's brother, Murat." Colin sat up, propping his pillows behind him. "And a master of excess, particularly after he visited Europe. I believe he had twenty-five hundred in his harem."

"Twenty-five hundred?" I asked.

"The number does include both slaves and eunuchs as well as the concubines, wives, and children. Murat followed him to the throne but ruled for only three months or so. He was mentally unstable, completely unfit to rule an empire, a raging alcoholic. So he was deposed, and Abdül Hamit the Second succeeded him and agreed to a constitutional monarchy. The Year of Three Sultans, they called it."

"When was this?" I asked, kissing his fingers as he spoke.

"1876. You're distracting me."

"Good," I said. "But a constitution? There's no parliament here, is there?"

"Not anymore. Abdül Hamit dissolved it years ago."

"What became of Murat? Nothing pleasant, I imagine."

"His brother let him live—although he did announce Murat's death in the papers. He's imprisoned in a palace somewhere in the city."

"Is he still ill?"

"Perhaps Bezime can enlighten you on that point. I've not the slightest idea."

"She writes to invite me to visit her at Topkapı Sarayı."

"Which is the old palace. Where discarded harem girls go to do whatever it is they do after they're discarded."

"It must be a dreadful life. Tedious." I sat up straight and turned to the window, my bare feet dangling off the edge of the bed.

"Tell me you're not thinking of opening the shutters," Colin said, scowling as I crossed the room. I flung them aside without answering him and pushed the tall windows out, a gush of watery air filling the room.

"It's a glorious day," I said. "Don't be so lazy."

"Lazy? No, my dear. Never lazy." He sprang up, swooped me off my feet, and dropped me back on the bed. "Stroke of genius, actually, letting in the light. I much prefer being able to see you."

I smiled. Breakfast would be more than late.

Within moments of arriving at the palace—the huge outer courtyard of which contained the Imperial Mint, the newly completed Archaeological Museum, and a bakery from whose windows wafted the most delicious yeasty smell of fresh bread—I decided that should I ever be discarded, I would be quite content to find this the site of my banishment, although I did momentarily reconsider this position as a guard led me past the Executioner's Fountain. I paused in front of it, imagining the men who, over hundreds of years, had washed in it their bloody hands and swords after public beheadings.

We reached the end of the courtyard's path and Topkapı Sarayı's Gate of Salutations—a tall structure with two pointed towers the likes of which I would have expected to find on a medieval European castle. My guide led me along a diagonal path, lined on both sides by tall, carefully shaped trees, through a second courtyard to the entrance of the harem, where he remanded me to the care of a tall, dark-skinned eunuch, the only sort of man other than the sultan who would ever be admitted to the harem.

"If you would follow me." He bobbed his head in what might be construed as a bow of sorts but did not meet my eyes. The rich voice with which he spoke was not at all what I'd expected, nothing like the stories I'd heard of the castrati, whose angelic sopranos had charmed all of Italy during the Baroque age. Although he sounded like an ordinary man, there was no trace of whiskers on his perfectly smooth face. "Her Highness has been waiting for you."

"It took me longer to get here than I expected," I said, moving more quickly to match his pace, my heels catching in the spaces between the smooth black and white pebbles formed as a mosaic to look like directional arrows down the center of an otherwise cobbled pavement.

"You should never be late when the valide sultan has summoned you."

I was not quite late, but I thought it best to restrain myself from pointing this out. "Valide sultan? I thought Perestu was valide sultan?"

He turned to look at me. "She is. But here it is Bezime who matters. It is unfortunate she lost her official position."

"Unfortunate, perhaps, but inevitable," I said. "Every sultan has his own mother."

"Abdül Hamit's mother died when he was young. Both Perestu and Bezime cared for him when he was a boy. This so-called inevitability was in fact a matter of choice."

"You speak very freely," I said, shocked to hear a servant give opinions—particularly opinions about the royal household—to a stranger.

"I am a favorite of many in the court, Bezime included, and have nothing to fear, no reason to hold my tongue." He stopped walking and faced me directly. "You are not used to educated slaves who wield their own power."

The flash in his black eyes made me suspect he was trying to shock me. Instead of registering the slightest surprise, I squared my shoulders and straightened my back. "No, I'm not. We don't have slaves of any sort in England. And I admire very much that you are educated."

"Everyone in the harem is educated."

"You mean the women?" I asked.

"Yes. Of course. You'll not find more cultured ladies anywhere. You think the sultan would want to surround himself with ignorant fools?"

"Many men have done worse." We were walking again, inside now, along a stone corridor that led through doorways above which hung passages painted in Arabic—I presumed from the Koran—gold paint on a green background. After passing through another outdoor courtyard, this one surrounded by buildings painted pink, we entered a small room whose every square inch was covered with tiles painted in blues and greens. "What is your name?" I asked as he paused to pull open a heavy wooden door, rich wood carved in a bold pattern of squares and rectangles.

"Jemal Kaan."

"I'm pleased to meet you."

He turned down the corners of his mouth and did not look at me. "Bezime is waiting."

The room into which we stepped had an enormously tall ceiling, domed at the top, with murals painted on the walls, landscapes that were leagues more Western than the rest of the tiled rooms I'd seen. Standing in the center of the square chamber was a table, inlaid, as were the cabinets built into the walls, with mother-of-pearl. Behind the table sat a woman, silver hair flowing down her back, the lines that etched her face somehow lending elegance to her appearance. She leaned forward on her elbows, then dropped back, puffing all the while on a long pipe.

"You've not seen a woman smoke a *çubuk*?" she asked, expertly blowing rings as she exhaled, fingering the pipe with hands whose long nails were dyed a rose color.

"I've never seen a *çubuk*," I said, sitting across from her, almost envious of the gorgeous gown she wore, a concoction of sky blue silk and tulle cinched at her tiny waist, puffed sleeves bursting from the fitted bodice. Only her hair kept her from looking like a perfect Western fashion plate.

"So you are Emily Hargreaves. *Lady* Emily Hargreaves?"

"Yes." I smiled. "And you are Bezime?"

She ignored my question. "I am not one to waste time on things lacking significance. You know of the murder that occurred last night?"

"Yes. I was there when—"

"Ceyden and I were close. I knew her when she first came to the harem. She was difficult then. Wouldn't speak to anyone."

"I can well imagine that. She must have been terrified. To have been stolen—"

"Sultans, Emily"—my name sounded exotic on her tongue, *"Aimahlee"*—"do not steal women. Yes, she was taken from her family and sold into slavery. But the noble Ottoman who bought her did her no harm. She wasn't well. He had her cared for, and when she was healthy, he gave her to the sultan as a gift. It is a great compliment for a girl."

"To be forced to live as a slave?" I asked.

"Do I look to you like a slave?" She narrowed her eyes and held up her arms, the heavy gold bangles on her wrists clanging together. "I have more freedom than my English counterparts."

I smiled. "You'll find I'm no proponent of the restrictions placed on my fellow Englishwomen. I'm well aware of the limitations of my society."

"I did not come to the harem as a child. I worked in a *hamam*—a bath—in the city. Mahmut—he was the sultan then, Mahmut the Second—saw me carrying linen from a laundry across the street. My beauty enchanted him." She drew deeply on her *çubuk*. "And I was brought to the harem, where I became his favorite, and I gave him a son. And when that son was made sultan, I was valide sultan, the most powerful woman in the empire." She leaned forward again. "Tell me, Emily Hargreaves, can an English girl, working for a living, aspire to someday marry the Prince of Wales and give birth to a future king?"

I pressed my lips together hard. "No. She could not."

"The lack of enlightenment in your country is unfortunate. I cannot see how women bother to live when they have no hope of advancing their positions."

"There's a certain amount of advancement possible, it's simply that—"

Before I could finish, she dismissed my statement with a wave of her hand. "What they can hope for is insignificant. And the loss of hope . . ." She turned away, then looked back at me, meeting my eyes. "There is nothing worse than the loss of hope."

"You're right." My skin prickled discomfort. "Why did you send for me? Because of Ceyden?"

"Yes. I am told that your husband will investigate the murder. But he will find no solutions outside of the harem."

"And he cannot come into the harem. We're well aware of that. It's why he sought—and received—permission for me to—"

She laughed. "Do you think, Emily, that I do not already know everything you do? You are to be set upon us, asking questions. That is not why I have summoned you here."

"Then why?"

"I have decided to offer you my allegiance. My support. Without which you will flail and accomplish nothing. Did you even know I was here? That this graveyard for the previous sultans' women existed?"

"No. I confess I did not."

"And do you know that Murat, the sultan's cast-aside brother, has a harem of his own at Çırağan Sarayı, the palace that is his prison on the shores of the Bosphorus? And that the dealings of the women in both these locations must be considered if we are to find and punish the person who ended Ceyden's life?"

"You speak as if you have an idea as to the identity of the guilty party," I said.

"Ideas, perhaps, but ideas are nothing but ephemeral."

"I did not expect my purpose to be a welcome one. I accept your assistance most gratefully. I promise I will not fail you."

"Of course you won't," she said. "I read your chart."

"My chart?"

"Know you nothing of astrology?"

". . . so she told me that I'm an Aries. Impulsive, bold, ruled by the planet Mars."

"Sounds dangerous," Colin said, raising his eyebrows, skepticism radiating from every inch of his face.

"Competitive—but you know that already." I took a fig from a bowl on the table and popped it in my mouth.

"All too well."

"I was thinking," I began, looking over the Bosphorus shining below us. "Perhaps we should have another bet. Bezime says it's impossible for you to solve this case. That all the keys lie in the harem."

"That may be. But we'll be sharing our information. I may put the story together before you. I've more experience."

"What did you learn today?" I asked.

"I spent the bulk of the afternoon at Çırağan Palace—where the sultan's brother is imprisoned. Nice digs, that," he said. "Far from a hotbed of political discontent, but there are several individuals who've aroused my suspicions."

"Who? What are they doing?"

"I've little to go on yet—primarily instinct. They're all men who lost power when Murat was deposed."

"I trust your instincts," I said. "Bezime suspects trouble is brewing there."

"I shan't dismiss her thoughts without further investigation. And you're quite right to trust my instincts. They will help me reach a solution before you."

"I don't think you will," I said.

"And?" His eyes narrowed.

"And if I'm right, I want you to swim the Bosphorus for me."

"Swim the Bosphorus? Don't be ridiculous."

"It's romantic." I picked up another fig. "Think of Hero and Leander. He crossed the sea every night to be with her."

"And drowned. After which Hero, if I remember correctly, flung herself off a tower to her own painful death."

"So you don't think you're a good enough swimmer?" I asked, a wicked smile creeping onto my face.

"I'm an excellent swimmer."

"Which is why you should swim the Bosphorus for me. I'll cheer you on from our balcony and receive you with open arms. Leander himself will never have had such a welcome."

Now he smiled, his dark eyes full of heat. "*If* you determine the identity of Ceyden's murderer before I do."

"Yes."

"And if you lose?" he asked.

"I don't ever lose our bets," I said.

"I shan't dignify that with a reply. What do I get if you lose?"

"You don't have to swim the Bosphorus."

"Not enough," he said. "If I win, you shall come to me dressed in Turkish robes and treat me like a sultan. Feed me peeled grapes. That sort of thing."

I laughed. "The harem is not at all what you think."

"Then I shall look forward to the disappointment to be found in victory," he said.

"What sort of robes, exactly?" I asked.

"I'll have to give the subject proper consideration. Diaphanous would be nice. Perhaps your new friend Bezime can guide you. I'd rather like to see you with a veil, if only so I can remove it."

"Pity you're making this a bet," I said. "I didn't have any plans for this evening."

4

"You are going to have to behave yourself. Do you understand?" Colin asked the next morning as he drained a glass of strong Turkish coffee before we started for the *yalı*'s dock. "No impulsive decisions, no walking into dangerous situations. The prime minister himself has approved your involvement in this case. You must remember at all times that you are working for the government."

"You've told me a thousand times," I said. "Am I so weak-minded that you think I'll require two thousand?"

"Of course not. I do wish . . ." He sighed, holding open the French doors that led to the terrace. "Eventually we may have to consider a way for you to protect yourself."

"Perhaps I need a pistol. A sword would be too heavy to drag about and particularly inconvenient when one is wearing evening dress."

"I'm not joking, Emily. You're very clever, and up to now have done an astonishing job relying on your wits alone. But there may come a time you need something more."

"A pistol." I must confess I rather liked the idea. "Maybe a Derringer?"

"How do you know about Derringers?" he asked.

"I read."

"It's not a bad idea."

"Can we get one here?" I asked.

"Probably, but you'd need to be trained before you could carry it. It would be more of a danger to you than a protection until you're fully competent using it."

"I'm sure I could learn."

"I shall teach you when we get back home," he said. "I'm something of an expert marksman."

"I didn't know that," I said, feeling my brow crease. "What other fascinating secrets are you hiding from me?"

"None that I can recall at present. For now, though, you'll have to be doubly diligent. Take no chances."

We'd reached the edge of the water, and I gripped his hand hard as I stepped into the vessel rocking violently before us, disappointed that my romantic notions of cruising the Bosphorus were being dashed on a daily basis by rough water that, so far as I was concerned, ought not to have troubled my stomach. Once we'd disembarked, it was into a carriage to take us the rest of the way through Pera, the section of Constantinople that housed not only the majority of foreign embassies and consulates, but also the Europeans who worked in them. Despite the preponderance of Western dress and more than one façade that looked straight out of London's Mayfair, the neighborhood did not lack flourishes of the exotic, from elaborately carved wooden buildings to veiled ladies ducking in and out of alleys.

Sir Richard's house, with its tall, Empire edifice, was a neoclassical vision, situated on the corner of a street near the British embassy. We were ushered inside by an English butler and served tea almost before we'd taken our seats in a drawing room furnished to showcase the eclectic mix of objects one would expect to find in the home of an international traveler. Serene-looking Isis, queen of the Egyptian gods, her arms outstretched, supported the cherry table on which a silver tea service was laid, and the heads of sphinxes decorated the chairs surrounding it.

"I'm having difficulty finalizing my daughter's funeral arrangements," Sir Richard said, his voice rough and tired. "Part of me wants to bring her to England, where, if I'd kept her in the first place, she'd still be alive. Sadly, though, that's a mistake it's far too late to correct. My initial—" He stopped speaking as the door swung open and a young man, his clothes encrusted with dried mud and his hair positively wild, staggered into the room, cringing as he put weight on his right foot. "Benjamin!" Sir Richard crossed the room and took him by the shoulders.

"Forgive me, Father," Benjamin said, his breath ragged. "I came as quickly as I could when I—I heard about Ceyden."

"What happened to you? You're a mess. Didn't you hire a special train?"

"The site's not far enough from here to require a train, Father. I rode."

"You shouldn't—"

Benjamin interrupted his father. "You're right, this time. I shouldn't have ridden alone. Bandits set on me. I managed to break away from them but did not escape entirely unscathed." He sat—collapsed, really—on a chair and motioned to his leg. "My ankle's giving me more than a little trouble."

"I'll send for the doctor at once," Sir Richard said.

"There's no need. If I rest—"

"No." Sir Richard pulled a heavily embroidered bell cord and dispatched the servant who appeared in short order to fetch a physician. "You will be treated by someone who knows the science of his profession."

The darkness that crossed Benjamin's face suggested he was far from agreement with his father, but he said nothing further on the topic, instead turning his red-rimmed gray eyes to Colin and me. "Who are your guests?" Sir Richard made speedy introductions that included our credentials as investigators while I poured a cup of tea for his son, who accepted it, dropped in three cubes of sugar, and stirred with a tiny silver spoon.

"Do you really think you can find my sister's murderer?" he asked, his face three shades paler than the porcelain cup in his hand.

"We'll do everything possible," Colin said. "And I have great hopes that we'll succeed. After all, we're dealing with a limited number of possible suspects. The killer has to be someone with access to the palace."

"Or someone wily enough to find his way in," Sir Richard said.

"No one could do that," Benjamin said, his words spilling on top of one another. "Yıldız is a veritable fortress. The walls are higher than those of prisons in England. We should not be careening in wild directions. Surely no one can doubt the murderer"—he seemed to choke on the word—"was someone from the harem. It may be that the right man is already in custody."

"There's no need for you to be thinking of any of this," Sir Richard said. "I want you focused only on recovering from this attack. You're safe now. I shan't let you come to any harm."

"I'm perfectly capable of taking care of myself." His father did not answer but pulled Colin towards a window, where they stood, heads bent together in earnest discussion.

I, however, could not help but smile at Benjamin's response. His words were old friends to my own lips, and I felt an immediate kinship with him. "I've no doubt of it," I said with a soft smile. "I'm so sorry about your sister."

"Thank you," he said, scooting his chair closer to mine. "My father takes overprotective to new heights." He kept his voice low.

"It's natural for a parent to worry about a child. But I understand how stifling it can be."

"He was bad before—and his friend Mr. Sutcliffe had been making it worse for as long as I can remember. They're both obsessed with having lost children."

"It's easy to sympathize," I said.

"I suppose so, but you cannot prevent every bad thing. Sutcliffe at least had begun to back off—he finally was accepting me as an adult and even went so far as to speak to my father about supporting my decision to work at the dig." He rubbed his forehead with the back of his hand, wincing as he moved his long legs. He'd inherited his father's height. "But now that Ceyden's dead, I'm wondering if I should put my father's mind at ease—go back to England. If only I could convince him to come with me."

"Would he leave?" I asked.

"Probably not. Especially when he's bent on getting justice for Ceyden." Tears hung heavy in his eyes. "There's no point in it, really. She's gone. There's no consolation to be found. I only wish—so desperately—that we'd known she was here."

"I know how difficult all this is," I said. "But I've no doubt that seeing your sister's killer in custody will bring more relief than you can imagine."

"Yes. Justice must be served." Benjamin looked at the ceiling, blinking to stop his tears. "I suppose there is no other way."

Colin and Sir Richard stepped back towards us and sat down. "Do you think . . ." I paused, studying the older man. "Could this in any way be connected to the theft of your papers on the train?"

"I can't dream up any relation between the two," Sir Richard said. "Especially as no one in Constantinople would have known Ceyden's true identity."

"Something in it all doesn't feel right. Your papers are stolen, your daughter murdered, your son attacked. All, coincidentally, in the space of a handful of days?" I was scrunching my forehead with such intensity, a pain had started between my eyebrows. "I'm finding it increasingly hard to believe that you took an incorrect dose of your sleeping draught. What if someone tried to poison you?"

"What is all this?" Benjamin asked.

"It's nothing for you to worry about," his father said, then turned to me. "I measured my chloral hydrate incorrectly and embarrassed myself at dinner on the train from Paris. I'd taken the dose before dinner and imagine the wine with the meal—wine that, if I remember correctly, tasted terrible—heightened the effect. That's all. What should be concerning us all right now is the fact that my son has been attacked."

"Did you notice anything unusual about the men who jumped you?" Colin asked.

Benjamin shook his head. "No. Not in the least."

"Was this the first time such a thing has happened?" I asked.

"No." Benjamin's voice was measured, even. "The site has suffered its share of raids."

"I thought those troubles had stopped." The firm edge in Sir

Richard's voice cut through the room, and his son looked at the floor as if he'd never seen something more fascinating than the soft carpet that covered it. "Benjamin!"

"Sir?"

"You have assured me repeatedly that you are in no danger working there." He pushed up hard on the arms of his chair and stood, towering over his son.

"It's as safe as anywhere—"

"That is not acceptable. Not when you've been the target so many times."

Colin stepped between them. "Target?"

"He's exaggerating," Benjamin said, standing. "The doctor will undoubtedly be here soon, and if it's not too much to ask, I'd prefer to speak to him in private. Excuse me." He hobbled as he walked, pushing away his father's outstretched arm and slamming the door behind him.

"What's this all about?" I asked.

"It was a few months ago," Sir Richard said. "There were a string of attacks at the excavation. Bandits. Appeared initially to be nothing out of the ordinary. But they never stole anything—never did anything to vandalize the site. Just hid up in the hills with their guns, aiming at no one but my son."

"You're quite certain?" I shot a pointed look at my husband. "It sounds like we should visit the camp."

Colin frowned. "It may be too dangerous for you. We shall have to see."

A surge of hot anger flashed through me, and I bit my tongue hard before responding. "We'll discuss the details later. I find myself in great sympathy with Benjamin and his sudden desire for privacy."

"I won't have you turning overprotective," I said to Colin after a sullen and silent trip back to our *yalı*.

"Suggesting that you stay away from a location riddled with bullets is hardly overprotective." Colin poured himself a glass of whiskey and drained it quickly. "Forgive me if I'm less than my usually enlightened self. I must confess I'm beginning to tire of nefarious distractions from what was supposed to be a honeymoon trip."

"We're not wholly distracted," I said, pushing away my anger and crossing the room to kiss him. He kissed me back, but the effort felt halfhearted.

"I'm trying very hard, Emily, to give you the freedom you need. But you know that when it comes to preserving your safety—"

"I know. No unnecessary risks. I've not the slightest problem with that. In this case, however, if it's safe for you to go—"

"I don't know that it is safe for me to go. There are circumstances in this line of work that are inherently dangerous. This time I ask that you let me act on my own."

"Will you ever let me do the same?" I asked.

"The time may come when it's required, and if it is, I shall of course support what you must do."

"It's not so simple for me either, you know," I said. "I don't like watching you walk—sprint—to danger."

"I'm well trained by experience to handle this particular situation."

"Can we compromise?" I asked. "We can both travel to whatever is the nearest town. You can go on to the site alone. If the person firing the shots is fixated on Benjamin, there's no reason to think anyone else is in danger. I trust you to determine if that's the case, and if it is, you can send for me."

"And if it's not?"

"I shall stay in town and content myself with reading," I said.

"How can I possibly count on you to stay and wait for my message?"

"I'm reliability itself. I give you my word."

He nodded. "All right. I'm willing to agree to that."

I kissed him. "Thank you. You won't regret it. Just think how tedious the trip would be without me."

"I do rather like you on trains, although Benjamin said it's not so far as to require that," he said. "Regardless, there are several avenues I want to pursue here in town first."

"Just don't forget you agreed to take me," I said, refilling his whiskey. "In the meantime, have you given any thought to taking up a swimming regimen? The Bosphorus is dangerous, and I can't have you drowning when you lose our bet."

"You've nothing to fear on that account." His smile made every nerve in my body tingle. "I'm meeting with Abdül Hamit tomorrow afternoon."

"You think he knows something?"

"We're to be joined by the members of his palace spy network. He's a paranoid man, our sultan —I've great hopes that at least one of his minions has seen something that can be of use to us."

"So you're trying to leap ahead of me?" I asked. "It won't work, you know."

"Do you know how to peel grapes, Emily? I'm told it's hard work."

"Is that so?" I gave him a quick kiss on each cheek. "Then I'm not sorry in the least I shall never have to learn how to do it."

5 April 1892
Darnley House, Kent

My dear daughter,

I hope that you and your husband are enjoying fine health and learning to adjust to the many challenges of married life. Your father and I are exceedingly happy for you, despite your unorthodox and, frankly, unacceptable wedding.

What's done is done, so I will say nothing further on the subject. Do not, however, expect the queen to offer the chapel at Windsor again. Your children will have to be baptized elsewhere.

On that subject, your friend Ivy has continued to prove a most agreeable houseguest, and I will confess to finding more pleasure in taking care of her during this time than I would have expected. I'll be more than ready to do the same for you when the time arrives—and I hope you are not impeding your husband's efforts to bring this about. A lady must graciously accept her duty.

Be careful of the food in Constantinople. I hear dreadful stories everywhere about it. Not to be trusted, these foreign locations.

I am, your most devoted mother,

C. Bromley

I woke before the sun, roused by the haunting and spiritually seductive voice coming from the nearest mosque. As the muezzin called the faithful to prayer, I lay, still and silent, absorbing the sound—at once comforting and eerie—as it trembled through my body. When it fell quiet, I stretched and reached for Colin, who was as eager as I to take full advantage of the myriad daily benefits of married life.

The time passed quickly, and too soon we were up and dressed, both of us headed for appointments. I'd applied to Perestu, the valide sultan, asking that I be allowed to come to the harem and begin interviewing Abdül Hamit's concubines, in particular Roxelana, who had discovered Ceyden's body. Although I knew well the dangers of assumption—of following baseless instinct—I could not help conjuring up any number of romantic scenarios surrounding the girl, namesake of the most famous—infamous—of harem women. In the sixteenth century, a stunning and intelligent concubine, Roxelana, had seduced, cajoled, and influenced Suleyman the Magnificent, eventually persuading him to take her as his wife. It was the first time a sultan had married; no one before had risen above the rank of favored concubine, and Roxelana wielded no small amount of power over her husband.

My Roxelana was an entirely different beast. She met me, waiting on a bridge made from rough-hewn logs in one of the gardens attached to the harem at Yıldız. Her burgundy gown was the latest Western fashion—high collar, fitted waist, skirts flowing gently over her hips—her dark hair upswept and held in place by a comb encrusted with rubies. Enormous pearls bobbed on her ears, and she parted her full lips, licking them to glistening perfection as she started to speak once I'd introduced myself.

"I don't see how I can be of any possible use." Her voice, thinner than her beauty suggested, shook as she spoke.

"I know well how awful what's happened has been for you," I said. "I lost a friend last year in Vienna. He was murdered and I found his body. It affects you in unimaginable ways, and I'm so terribly sorry you're suffering for it."

While working the previous winter to clear Robert Brandon in the death of Lord Fortescue, the most odious human I'd ever met, I'd become tenuous friends with a man who was both an asset to me and an adversary. Mutual enemies had brought us together, and he'd ended up aiding my investigation. Finding his brutalized body in Vienna's beautiful Stephansdom cathedral was worse than any nightmare, and I hoped never again to witness such a violent scene.

"Then you do understand," she said. "Everyone wants me to push the memory aside, but no matter what I do it comes back in my dreams."

"There are some things that never leave you entirely."

"I wish this would," she said. "I can't bear seeing it over and over."

I reached for her hand. "I know. There's no real comfort to be had, but perhaps helping us find Ceyden's murderer will bring some small measure of relief."

She pulled her hand away. "Nothing will make this better."

"I won't disagree," I said.

Her eyes were hard. "What do you want from me?"

"Tell me what you saw that night."

"The courtyard in which Ceyden was . . . that courtyard is one of my favorites. I like to read there on a comfortable bench near the fountain."

"Were you reading that night?"

"No. It was already dark. I only meant to say that it wasn't unusual for me to go there. That's all."

"Was Ceyden there when you arrived?" I asked.

"Of course she was."

"Did you see the attack?"

"No! Wouldn't I have told the sultan? Or the guards? Why would you ask such a thing?"

"You might have been afraid, Roxelana," I said. "It would be understandable."

She stared at me, her eyes still hard, but curves returning to her lips. "I nearly tripped over her."

"And she was dead?"

"I suppose so. I was scared and ran off screaming at once."

"Why?" I asked. "Why didn't you assume she'd fallen or fainted?"

"Everything about her pose looked wrong. Nothing seemed natural, and I could tell at once something terrible had happened."

"But you didn't know she was dead?"

"No." Her pupils were tiny dots. "Instinct told me it was bad—which is why I went for help."

"Was there anyone else in the courtyard?"

"Not that I saw," she said.

"But you're not certain?"

"It was dark. I imagine it's not impossible that someone was hiding in the shadows. Is that what you'd like me to say?"

"I'd like you to say the truth." I bit the inside of my cheek, frustration pushing against me. "Do you have a reason not to want to?"

"No one ever wants to tell the truth in the harem," she said. "But in this case, I've nothing to hide. I wish I'd seen something more."

"Do you have things to hide in other cases?"

"You know nothing about the harem, do you?"

"Not enough. Enlighten me."

She looked at me for a measured moment, then threw a short nod before starting to walk back towards the palace. "The sultan moved to Yıldız because he fears for his life and believes that Dolmabahçe was not secure." Dolmabahçe was one of the palaces Colin had cited as being partly responsible for the decline of the Ottoman treasury. Its elegant cut-stone façade with rows of vaulted windows on both floors rose above the Bosphorus, the waters lapping below gleaming white wrought-iron fences. Its interior, designed partially to impress Western diplomats and visitors, was ornate and luxurious, a perfect exercise in excess.

"Why is that?"

"Because he is seized with unfathomable paranoia, and the palace's location on the Bosphorus made him feel vulnerable. Of course, there is not much that does not make him feel vulnerable."

"Are you close to him?"

"I have been noticed," she said, turning away as hot color crept up her cheeks.

"Handkerchief dropped in front of you to alert you that you've been chosen for the night?" I had read more than my share of fantastical novels set in the seraglio and found the rituals of harem life fascinating.

"I hate to disappoint your Western romanticism, but that is not how it happens. Reality is much more prosaic. Most of us never have any contact with the sultan. We see him—from a safe distance—on formal occasions. It's not so easy to catch his attention, though. Some manage, of course, but it takes a not inconsiderable effort."

"How did you do it?"

"I didn't. The valide sultan selected me for him." I felt my face tighten as she spoke. "Barbaric, isn't it? But there's no handkerchief dropping. The *kızlar ağası*—chief black eunuch—informs you that you've been chosen, and you're off to the *hamam* to prepare. Generally the sultan sends a small gift."

"Had you never spoken to him before you were summoned to him?"

"I'd never even seen him. Had done all I could to keep from drawing attention to myself. If I must be here, I will have a quiet life of contemplation. You do not understand in the slightest how I am tormented."

"I'm so sorry," I said. I could not imagine the horror of being sent to the bed of a man I knew not at all. *Barbaric* did not even approach a strong enough word.

"Most of the time, no one pays attention to me. My religious beliefs have kept me from becoming close to those around me."

"You are not a Muslim?" I asked.

"And now, Lady Emily, you have discovered what it is that I need to hide. I'm a Christian. And every day—every night—that I spend with the sultan puts my soul in mortal danger. Have you any idea what it is to know that you are forced to live in sin?"

"Are you allowed—forgive me—to be Christian?" I asked.

"I do not speak of it to others. No one knows. I kneel in the direction of Mecca during times of prayer but recite my own words."

"As a fellow Christian, I can assure you that if you are forced to do things—"

"The martyrs had the strength to stand up for their beliefs. I am not so brave, nor so virtuous. Now that I've spent the night with the sultan and am a *gözde,* I have better quarters and more privacy. If I am elevated further and become an *ıkbal,* or *kadin*—an official consort—my position would be better still. But I ought not be tempted by privacy and should have refused to go to him in the first place, regardless of the consequences."

"What would the consequences have been?"

"I don't know, but can well guess. No one rejects the sultan. The punishment would be unspeakable."

"How did you come to your faith?"

"I have lots of time to myself here and fill most of my hours reading. One day I came upon a volume of Aquinas. . . ." She sighed. "No, I must be honest with you. I asked for it—one in a long list of books I requested. One of our maids is a Christian, and I've heard her speak of the comfort it brings her—a comfort for which I have great need."

"Why Aquinas?" I asked.

"She suggested his *Summa Theologica* to me. I devoured it and then moved on to every other of his works," she said. "'To convert somebody, go and take them by the hand and guide them.' It was as if he spoke to me and took my hand in his own. And now, lacking the courage to refuse my sin, I have no option but to flee. Perhaps years of penance will compensate for my weakness."

"You're too hard on yourself," I said.

"I will promise to aid your investigation in any way possible, but, please, please, Lady Emily—I implore that in exchange you help me find a way out of here." We had reached the harem building, where a eunuch guard pulled open a door to let us in. "We can say nothing further of it now. Everything spoken in these walls runs through channels you can't even imagine."

"Shall we return outside?"

"Not with that man watching us," she said. "Did you not see him in the trees?"

"No, I—"

The voice that interrupted me was not sharp, but startling regardless as it meandered, all soft bounces, through the stone corridor in which we stood.

"You would be in great danger were he not watching you." The valide sultan, in a golden kaftan over pink-and-silver billowing Turkish trousers held in place with a diamond-encrusted girdle, slipped out from a doorway and took Roxelana's arm, gripping with white knuckles. "It is time for you to go to the *hamam*. The sultan expects you tonight."

Roxelana blushed crimson, the sides of her eyes crinkling as tears welled. "Yes, madam."

"I have laid out clothing in your rooms. The servants will see to you in the *hamam*. Do not disappoint me."

If Bezime had intimidated me, Perestu terrified. Her face possessed the calm smoothness of marble as she watched Roxelana walk away from us, but something in her eyes—a shot of calculating manipulation—shook me, and a pervasive feeling of dislocation swam through as I considered the reality of what I'd just witnessed. Bezime might have had her share of power, could believe in hope, but nothing in the context of this world was better than a prison. A beautiful setting, servants, and fine clothing could not make up for freedom—real freedom. English society was full of restrictions, particularly for the fairer sex, but women were not forced into such reprehensible situations with no possibility of ever escaping. I recalled Bezime's claim that here, there was hope. She was right in her way, but that hope extended only to women whose goals fit into the most narrow of passages.

I was well acquainted with the difficulties faced when one's happiness depended upon living a life that did not fit into the standard view of what was acceptable. Roxelana's plight distressed me, and while I wished for an elegant and simple solution to her problems, I knew there was no such thing. The only sensible thing would be to dismiss the ideas mucking up my head. I could not assist her in any meaningful way, not so long as I was working for the Crown. But then again, it was not right—not moral—to leave her an unwilling slave. There had to be a way, subtle but radical, to save her.

"I am not certain of the best way to offer my aid to you." Perestu's voice sliced through my thoughts. "I will, of course, instruct the concubines to speak openly to you, but can make no promises that they will be forthcoming."

I did not much believe her. She was the valide sultan; surely the concubines would do whatever she told them. "If you could perhaps start by telling me everything possible about Ceyden," I said. "Was she a favorite of the sultan's?"

"No, no." She led me to a low sofa built along the outside wall of a charming room, stars painted on the ceiling. "Ceyden was not someone I thought fit for the sultan."

"And what of his opinion?"

"Men's opinions are often not worth considering."

I could not help but laugh at this. "Does he know you feel this way?"

"I make sure of it," she said. "For a very long time, the girl was not happy here. As a child, she was skittish and unpredictable. I understand this is to be explained by the violent manner in which she was taken from her parents, but we knew nothing of that until Sir Richard told her story after the murder. I am sorry for what she suffered, of course, but her inability to rise above it confirms I was correct about the flaws deep in her character."

"She saw her mother murdered and was then kidnapped."

"Yes. And was then taken extremely good care of and brought to the most spectacular palace to be found on earth. She was pampered, doted on, educated, given every luxury."

"Did she have any memory of what she'd been through?"

"Not at all. We think she was around five when she came to us—a gift from a noble family. They'd bought her from traders, I suppose, and had her in their household for at least two years. It is not unheard of to present the sultan with such a girl—it is an honor. She didn't speak English until Bezime taught her, and if I remember, she had a difficult time of it. It was strange—she seemed to have an affinity for languages, but English always troubled her. She all but refused to speak it."

I pressed my lips together hard, thinking of the little girl pulled away from her dying mother. "Surely that was because she remembered something of her past?"

"She was a proud girl and knew she hadn't mastered the language. It came as no surprise that she would avoid showcasing a weakness."

"Did she come to find a comfortable place here?"

"Eventually. As she got older, she began to enjoy the politics of the harem, and she did everything in her power to catch the notice of my son."

"Was she successful?"

"She was an accomplished artist, though a terrible musician. She could speak French fluently—something the sultan finds enchanting— and wrote maudlin poetry."

"Did he favor her at all?" I asked.

"He might have come to. But I kept her from him. The sultan cannot risk having children like her. It would threaten the very empire."

I opened my mouth to protest, having read scores of stories about the cages, as they were called, in which the crown princes grew up, not allowed to learn anything that might make them competent rulers—competence would threaten the sultan, compromise his political stability. This was a dynasty in which rulers for centuries had murdered their own brothers upon ascending to the throne in an attempt to secure their own positions. The immature behavior of a traumatized child paled in comparison.

"You are skeptical, I see," she said.

"I admit to feeling that it stretches credulity, but I've no reason to doubt your veracity."

"It is essential the sultan know that he can depend upon my judgment. I have in front of me scores of girls when you include the slaves in the harem as well as the wives and concubines. I choose for him the best. Ceyden was not that. You may not agree with my decision, but your opinion of the matter is irrelevant."

"Quite right. Please do not think I am questioning your actions." Alienating her would not benefit me in the least. "Did Ceyden know her situation was hopeless?"

Perestu shrugged. "I did not deliberately hide my feelings from her. But her persistence knew no bounds. The day she died she brought me a scarf embroidered with the most intricate detail I've ever seen—flowers and birds all in gold and silver thread against a red background. I collect such things."

"Did you feel she was insincere in her affection for you?"

"Affection? Her generosity was entirely self-serving, but there was a charm about her, a certain naïveté. She did not understand the art of bribery."

"Did she try to influence anyone else?"

"She had a friendship with Jemal that grew too close."

"I met him at Topkapı. Does he work at both palaces?"

"He was sent to Topkapı because of Ceyden. As I said, they'd become too close."

"Who forced him to move?"

"I am valide sultan," she said, smiling. "No one in the harem balks at my orders. It is as if they are law."

"Why did Ceyden's friendship with Jemal concern you?"

"Because I didn't trust either of them." I opened my mouth to ask why, but she did not let me speak. "And for now that is all there is to be said on the topic. It does not, I assure you, have any bearing on the matter at hand."

"Did Ceyden make any other attempts to circumvent you?"

"There would be no point."

"The sultan never makes a selection on his own?"

"He could, of course, but petty amusement is far from his top priority. He has an empire to run, Lady Emily. He already has children and their mothers to contend with."

I tried to squelch the judgment rising through me. Children and their mothers, yet still in need of petty amusement? For a moment,

I wished I could return to my romanticized view of the harem. Candor, I decided, was my only option. "Perestu, forgive me. This is all so very foreign. I cannot imagine sharing my husband."

"How long have you been married?"

"Only a few months."

"A short time, and you are very young. But this is not relevant."

"I suppose not. I'm only trying to better understand Ceyden's situation."

"The harem is a world of its own. She wanted to climb to the top of it. I would not let her."

"Are you glad she's dead?"

"Her existence made no difference to me. It was, occasionally, amusing to watch her unschooled attempts at seduction."

"I thought you said she wasn't close to the sultan?"

"No, only to Jemal. She loved him."

"But the eunuchs . . ." I was now full in territory that repelled, fascinated, and confused me.

"Are not true men," she finished for me. "Quite right, but some of them are men enough."

A thousand questions leapt to my lips, but I could not bring myself to ask a single one. "I didn't—"

"You are unused to this sort of openness. Such subjects are not forbidden to women here, Lady Emily. Ceyden was not entirely incapable of using her charms, limited though they were, to her advantage."

"Could Jemal wield influence with the sultan?"

"He would like to think he can influence me."

"Is he right?"

"Sometimes," she said.

"Who was watching Roxelana and me in the park? One of the guards?"

"We've covered quite enough for today." She gave me a narrow smile and left the room.

I spent the rest of the afternoon interviewing slaves and concubines, many of them stunning Circassians, the stuff of harem legend in Western tales. These women, brought from the Caucusus Mountains to be sold in Constantinople, were treasured for their beauty—pale, luminous skin, mesmerizing bright eyes, and lustrous hair, blond or dark. Everyone to whom I spoke agreed Ceyden had done whatever she could to gain Abdül Hamit's notice, but her lack of success in doing so kept her from threatening the positions, or desired positions, of her compatriots. The similarities not only in substance but in verbiage of what they told me made it apparent that someone had coached them, and well. Only a handful of them spoke much English, so Perestu translated for the rest. I had no idea whether she accurately reported to me what they said.

"Jemal must be subjected to extensive questioning," I said to Colin as we sat on the balcony outside our bedroom that evening. The view stretched nearly to Topkapı in the south, the hills of the city piling on top of one another as they rose from the Bosphorus. Houses and buildings formed a dense tapestry above the waterline, flat and peaked roofs obstructing all but more roofs behind them, as if each were vying for a superior view. Far to the north was the Black Sea, and a steady stream of ships—barges, feluccas, caïques, and yawls—moved towards it, well out of our sight. "As for the women, it's all too well organized, too orchestrated. I can't decide whether they're hiding something or just afraid."

"Afraid?" Colin asked.

"Whoever killed Ceyden could strike again. Perhaps the girls are afraid of drawing attention to themselves."

"They'd be better served by allowing you to gather as much information as possible. How else will this man ever be stopped?"

"How can you be sure it's a man?"

"It's difficult to strangle someone," Colin said. "More likely that a man would have the strength for it. I don't know that a woman could do such a thing with her bare hands."

"Hideous." Not wanting to dwell on the details, I mentally flipped through the catalog of women to whom I'd spoken and determined that each was far too delicate to pull off the task. "So we need a man in the harem."

"I'd say they could use several men in the harem."

"You're dreadful, and I'm going to ignore you." I let my eyes rest on his just long enough to fill my head with all sorts of visions about which I could do nothing at the moment.

"What of the other women?" Colin asked. "Did Ceyden have any particular friends?"

"None who will admit to it."

"They undoubtedly want to distance themselves from her, regardless. Avoid any guilt by association."

"Guilt?" I asked. "Ceyden is the victim in all this."

"True. But the status of these women depends entirely on their relationship with Perestu, and the sultan, if they're lucky enough to have won his favor. The reputation of her friends may have been tarnished by Ceyden's violent death."

I frowned. "Yes, but why not admit the relationship to me? Surely Perestu already knows. She keeps careful track of everything that happens in the harem."

"A harem that shelters no secrets?" He drew on his cigar. "I'd be thoroughly disappointed if I could bring myself to believe it even for an instant."

"Did you learn anything of use today?"

"I went back to Çırağan and spoke to Murat. Excellent prison, the palace."

"And is the former sultan discontented?" I asked.

"He did not seem so," Colin said. "Spends much of his time listening to music and watching plays. Enjoys his children. The stress of ruling did not agree with him. That does not, however, mean that those around him would not prefer to take a more active role in the government."

"Could they be plotting a coup?"

"It's unlikely. The sultan has a spy in the household—the chief black eunuch in Murat's harem. He's as thorough a man as I've ever met and isn't likely to miss something on that scale."

"What about something smaller?" I asked. "A plan that looks on the surface like nothing more than standard harem politics?"

"The discontent I felt comes from the men around Murat."

"You've not been in the harem."

"No, but the chief eunuch was adamant about there being no trouble there, and I believe him. Those women stand no chance at advancement, and there's surprisingly little intrigue other than petty gossip."

"You're certain?"

"I shall continue to press him for information, but my own efforts will be focused elsewhere in the palace." He rolled the cigar between the tips of his fingers. "And what about you? Will you search for concubines who were close to Ceyden?"

"Enemies, my darling man, are even more fascinating than friends, don't you think? I want to find out who despised her." I rose from my chair and stood in front of him. "Is there anything else we need to discuss?"

"Not that I can think of," he said.

"The sun's set. Shall we go inside?"

"The lights of Constantinople aren't enough to amuse you?"

"I adore the lights," I said. "But I much prefer you in the dark."

"Her Excellency cannot see you now." The smile on Jemal's face as he met me at the arched doorway that stood at the entrance to the harem at Topkapı was undoubtedly meant to irritate. "You're too early."

"Which is precisely what I wanted," I said, pulling down on the bottom of the jacket I wore, smoothing it over my fine wool corselet skirt. "I came now so as to have the opportunity to speak to you."

"I'm sure we have very little to say to each other."

"Tell me about your friendship with Ceyden."

"We were the most casual sort of acquaintances," he said. "And that only because our positions forced us to cross paths regularly."

"Why, Jemal, must you make this difficult? I know that you were sent here to be kept away from her."

"I was sent here because the sultan felt my talents better suited to Topkapı."

"That's not what Perestu told me."

"She does not have quite so much power as she likes to think," he said. "It's presumptuous to assume she'd even know what my mission is here."

"What is it?"

"Confidential."

"And it has nothing to do with Ceyden?"

"If it did, why would I still be here after her death?"

"I'm sure I don't know," I said. "Perhaps you could enlighten me."

"I do not approve of what you are doing, Lady Emily. There is nothing to be gained. Ceyden is dead and cannot be helped."

"Should she have no justice?"

"Sometimes justice brings only a worse pain."

"So we should seek solace in lies and half-truths instead?" I asked.

"I cannot have you drawing attention to my mistress."

"Does she have something to hide?"

"I suggested no such thing. I know only the risks of one's actions being misinterpreted. Leave Bezime out of your game."

"This isn't a game, Jemal," I said. "How could solving Ceyden's murder threaten her?"

"Digging into any court controversy can threaten her. It's not so long ago that the concubines of former sultans were drowned in the Bosphorus instead of being allowed a comfortable retirement."

"Abdül Hamit would never do such a thing to a woman he looked on once almost as a mother."

"But he stopped feeling that way for her, did he not? And why was that?"

"I couldn't begin to tell you."

He stood and began to pace in front of the doorway, the movement having a dizzying effect on me. "She is cut from all decisions, all events of importance. Is that not a precarious position?"

"Not necessarily," I said. "A lonely one, but not dangerous."

"She was closer to Ceyden than anyone else, raised her like a daughter. Groomed her to please the sultan."

"Only to have her efforts thwarted by Perestu."

"Precisely."

"But isn't that typical court behavior? Are not all the concubines competing for favor? It's hardly surprising that the valide sultan would refuse to aid the cause of the one woman who might have had the position she occupies. Perestu must know full well that the sultan could have named Bezime valide."

"I have said too much. It would be best for us all if you would cease your questions."

"Please—" A door in the corridor swung open, Bezime standing, arms crossed, on the other side.

"Go, Jemal," she said. "I will handle this."

The eunuch bowed deeply to her before disappearing. Bezime beckoned for me to come in, closing the door behind me with only the slightest click as the latch caught the edge of the frame.

"Come," she said. "I will take you to where it is safe to speak."

We wound our way through narrow corridors and series after series of connected rooms, until we were outside of the harem, in a courtyard. Then through an ornate gate, another courtyard, and into a tiled pavilion. She sat in the center of a low divan covered with buttery smooth crimson silk that ran the length of the wall and motioned for me to join her. Despite the sun streaking through the open windows, candles flickered in the tiled nooks that lined the walls, illuminating nothing but the space immediately around them.

"I must ask you about Jemal. He says—"

"I cannot speak of him right now." Her voice was a shredded whisper. "I'm being threatened."

"Threatened?"

She did not reply, but removed a small package from the folds of her skirt. With gentle hands, she untied the frayed purple bow wrapped around it, letting the well-worn fabric fall away from the object it encased, a dark blue velvet bag. From within that, she took a thin white cord. "Bowstrings like this were for uncountable years used by the *bostanji*, the sultan's most trusted guards and executioners. It was with these that anyone who threatened his throne—especially members of his family—was killed."

"Who would send you such a thing?"

"It must have come from Yıldız," she said, stretching the string in her hands, then laying it flat on the table in front of us. "No one elsewhere would presume to use such a thing."

"When did you receive it?"

"Not twenty minutes ago."

"Who at Yıldız would wish you harm?"

"That is no simple question to answer. Perestu, I suppose, is an obvious suspect."

"How so?"

"I used to be valide sultan. Perhaps that threatens her."

"Forgive me, but you're not any longer—surely she feels her role is secure."

"I'm still able to communicate directly with the sultan. She may not like that, particularly as she knows it is not difficult for a woman skilled in the mysterious arts to wield a certain amount of control over a man so full of fear."

I sat silent, skeptical of her claim of control, particularly as she'd been sent to Topkapı as an elegant banishment.

"You don't believe me?" she asked.

"What sort of official power did you have before coming here but after Perestu had been named valide sultan?"

"I had no title, if that's what you mean. But it is unusual for any concubine to be allowed to stay in the harem after her sultan no longer rules. I had the respect of every resident of the palace."

"Why did you come here?"

"I had no choice. Perestu wanted me to go."

"Which makes her an unlikely candidate to have sent the bowstring. She's got you where she wants you." I touched the silk, my fingers flinching at its cool smoothness. "Have you heard of anyone else receiving such a thing?"

"Never."

"Could it have to do with your connection to Ceyden?"

"You think the killer wants me next?"

"I don't know. Would there be a reason for him to?"

"Ceyden and I were close, as you already know. I did all I could when she was young to educate her, to train her to be everything that might please the sultan. She was a smart girl—eager to learn. Took to languages with no effort, except English. Her voice always had a seductive lilt to it—perhaps a hint of her lost British accent."

"I never thought of a British accent as seductive," I said.

"Here." She passed me her pipe. "You have not thought it so because to you it has nothing of the exotic. The ordinary cannot be inspiring."

"It is this knowledge, I imagine, that brought you to the center of attention in the harem." Surprised by its sweet taste, I drew smoke deep into my lungs—too deep—and was overwhelmed with a burst of coughing. Bezime laughed.

"You are unskilled in this art."

"Smoking? Yes," I said, still stuttering with continued coughs.

"Yes, that too." She took back the *çubuk*. "But I refer to the exotic. Seeking it, finding it, capturing it."

"We were talking about Ceyden."

"If you insist, we can return to that subject."

"I'm afraid we must."

"Then your lesson in the exotic must wait for another day. Your husband would not be pleased to know your priorities."

"Oh, he's perfectly pleased."

"You answer too fast," she said. "But I will allow you your misguided thoughts."

"I'm not sure I should thank you," I said, and watched her force a thin stream of silver smoke through lips stretched wide in a smile. "Back to Ceyden, though. Perestu made it exceedingly clear that she kept the girl away from the sultan. Am I correct to suspect you helped her gain access to him?"

"I did."

"And it caused a rift between you and Perestu?"

She shrugged. "There are so many rifts. We all fought for our survival in the harem."

"But what of your stories of freedom?"

"I was free to fight for it. Concubines who are successful must be able to charm both the sultan and the women around them. It is only once you've reached a high enough status—given birth to the sultan's child—that the necessity of alliance begins to fade. I do not think there is a man alive who would not have wanted Ceyden. But the other girls hated her."

"But you didn't?"

"No. I saw in her a brightness that appealed to me. And I was already old, had gained everything I wanted, stood to lose nothing by playing."

"Playing?"

"I wanted to see if I could circumvent Perestu and elevate Ceyden's status. Sadly, it did not work."

"When were you sent away from the harem?"

"Shortly after Ceyden spent the night with the sultan. Perestu did not appreciate my endeavor."

"Perestu seems to think Ceyden has never so much as spoken to Abdül Hamit."

Bezime laughed. "Well, perhaps they didn't speak." The scent of her tobacco filled the room. "But they did spend a night together."

I picked up the bowstring from the low table before us, fingering the soft cords. "If Perestu knows that, would it spur her to exact revenge on you?"

"If she's bored enough," Bezime said. "There's no better distraction from ennui than eliminating one's former rivals."

"I'm getting no candor from the concubines at Yıldız. What must I do to change this? How can I make them trust me?"

"It's impossible to force trust. There is, however, something you could try to earn it, but it may scare you too much."

"I never back down from a challenge."

She laughed. "Then tell Perestu you want to go to the *hamam* at Yıldız. You will find the women more likely to trust you if you bathe with them."

"Bathe with them?"

"It is our tradition. Everyone goes to the baths at least once a week—I told you I worked in one before the sultan found me. There is no better place to find out all the gossip, all the truth. Perestu will allow it because she will believe the experience will do nothing but horrify you."

"Horrify me?" She couldn't have been more right, but I had grown almost fond of bluffing people. "It sounds perfectly pleasant. I shall arrange to go as soon as possible."

The moment I left Topkapı, I directed my boatman to take me up the Bosphorus past Dolmabahçe to the dock closest to Yıldız, my stomach turning itself over and into knots. I clutched the side of the boat, the rough wood pressing hard against the bones in my hands, the faint fishy smell coming from the water tormenting me. Looking at the horizon, which Colin had insisted would help ward off seasickness, had the effect only of making me long to stand on the land at which I gazed. A man at the quay steadied me with a strong hand as I stepped off the rocking vessel, and I sat on a nearby bench, too queasy to walk to the palace. An obliging tree shaded me, and I stared across at the houses lining the Asian shore.

I was alarmed in no small way. I'd always considered myself of hearty constitution—seasickness was not something from which I'd previously suffered, although I'd not before been on small boats in such rough waters. More concerning—terrifying, in fact—was the thought that it might not be seasickness at all. Could I have already entered that phase of married life in which a lady's existence was forever altered in the most dramatic fashion? I bit my lip too hard and tasted salt on my tongue. Not that it would be a bad thing. It was inevitable, after all, and the inconvenience wouldn't be interminable. Nonetheless, I was filled with ambivalence and something darker, a thing I was not yet willing to face. I pulled myself up from the bench and started up the hill towards Yıldız, not wanting to be late for the appointment I'd scheduled to see the sultan.

The palace was not like most traditional royal houses. Instead of one massive building, it was formed by groupings of pavilions and kiosks overlooking a lake, all surrounded by high walls. Green lawns and well-tended gardens shared the grounds with more rugged wooded patches, and the scent of orange blossoms greeted me as I reached the gate.

The guards recognized me from my previous visit, and I was led into a formal reception room in the center of which stood a table big enough to seat twenty in comfort. It drew me in at once, and I reached out to touch the smooth, inlaid surface, feeling the thread-thin grooves between tortoiseshell and oak, mother-of-pearl and ebony. I had traced the entire circumference of the piece and still no one had come to me. I crossed to a window and pulled open the shutter, looking at the woods that stretched below me, dark evergreens blocking all but lacy cutouts of light.

"Lady Emily?" A eunuch poked his head around the open door. "His Imperial Majesty will see you."

He took me through corridor after corridor until we were outside, standing before a small building in which we found Abdül Hamit II, bent over a bench, rubbing a piece of sandpaper on a chair that lay on its back before him. He was not tall, though not strikingly short, but slim. Piercing dark eyes and a large, aquiline nose stood out from his black hair and neatly trimmed beard. His face was heavy with fatigue.

"It is my greatest pleasure to see you, Lady Emily," he said, bursting with youthful energy that I'd not expected from a man his age. His voice, however, was quiet in its exuberance, low, almost like a song. "My thanks to you for coming all this way." He swept his hand in front of his chest, gesturing to the space around him. "What do you think of my work?"

The room swam with the clean smell of fresh wood. Along the

walls stood cabinets, tables, chairs, and chests piled one in front of the other, all, I assumed, made by the sultan's own hands. "It's exquisite," I said, forgetting myself and walking away from him to inspect a tall bookcase fashioned from golden-stained cherry.

"I'm pleased you like it. There's little more satisfying than working with one's hands, yes?"

"I can imagine." Careful sanding had given the wood a smoothness that was at once firm and soft.

"Do you read?" he asked. "Anyone with such an appreciation for bookshelves must."

"Constantly," I said, not able to stop running my hands over the perfectly finished wood. "Sensational fiction. I've a terrible habit of reading the most lowbrow things you can imagine."

"Do you like detective novels?"

"Conan Doyle stuns me every time."

He nodded. "You are someone I could like very much. I have his novels translated into Turkish as soon as they are published. The chief of my wardrobe reads them to me, and I do not let him stop until the book is done."

"An admirable devotion to the written word."

"I would like very much to have the bookcases sent to your house in England. A gift for you."

"That's generous of you," I said. "Thank you. They will be adored."

"I would not give them to you otherwise. What else do you read?"

"I study Greek, so lots of Homer."

"Will you visit Troy while you are in my country?"

"I want to more than anything, if only to lie on the fields and weep for poor, slain Hector."

This drew a smile. "I will have the trip arranged for you when this ugly business in the harem is finished." He turned away from the piece on which he'd been working and walked to a pile of long boards, picking up one after another, running his fingertips along the length of each before selecting one to bring back to his bench.

"You're very kind," I said.

He pushed a yardstick against the board and began marking measurements with a chewed-up pencil. "I have a deep sympathy for Ceyden's father. I lost my first child, a daughter, when she was very young. She was burned after playing with matches. Her mother and I suffered immeasurably at the loss. She would be your age now."

"I'm so sorry."

"This is not, I think, the way you'd hoped to spend your wedding trip," he said.

"No one would anticipate such a thing, but I would never walk away from the opportunity to seek justice."

"Justice, Lady Emily, is not always so clear."

"Did you know Ceyden?"

"To a degree."

"Will you not tell me more?" I watched his face, searching for evidence that he was withholding something, but his countenance was calm, focused.

"You question the sultan?" He placed his palms flat against the board in front of him, and I expected anger to cloud his eyes. Instead, I saw laughter.

"Bad form?" I smiled at him.

"Terribly."

"It's not that I don't believe you," I said. "I'm merely trying to form as accurate a summation of the girl's life as I can."

"You'll find all you need to know in the harem."

"Your concubines have been less than forthcoming. It's almost as if their words are chosen for them."

"And this surprises you?"

"Yes, because I'd been led to believe you support my investigation. A word from you would surely—"

"It is not I you must convince, but my mother," he said.

"Does she not listen to you?"

"Does your mother listen to you?"

Laughter escaped my lips, and I felt my cheeks flushing hot. "Never."

"We are of one mind, then, at least in this regard. And if your mother is like mine"—he leaned closer to me—"the less said about it the better. Her spies are everywhere."

"But surely your own spies hold them at bay?"

"One can only hope."

He was warming to me. I felt we were on a course to getting along famously, and this brought me no small measure of pride. To have so quickly made an ally of the sultan himself! A slight tug of conscience made me almost wish Colin were standing behind me, reminding me of what, exactly, goes before a fall, but I dismissed the notion and beamed, ready to forward the rest of my agenda.

"There is something else I would like to discuss with you," I said. "I spoke with the young woman who found Ceyden's body. She's terribly upset."

"Understandable. Roxelana is a sensitive girl."

"I have heard that, on occasion, concubines are released from the harem and allowed to marry. Would you consider allowing her to do that?" It was not a perfectly satisfactory solution to Roxelana's plight, but better, I hoped, than nothing. I would much prefer to find a way to fully free her of her bonds, to let her rejoice in independence as I did, but fear of Colin's disapproval—particularly if my scheme was revealed to the British government—kept me from taking a more creative approach to her predicament. And this was something of which I was not proud in the least.

"There are times when such arrangements are made. Not, however, at the whim of the concubines. These marriages are careful political alliances, gestures of good faith to valued advisers from their sultan. It is a mark of the highest trust to be selected for a role like that."

"How so?"

"Wives can sometimes be in a position to observe much."

"They spy for you?"

"They ensure that I have staunch supporters in their husbands."

"I've no doubt Roxelana would serve you well." As I said the words, my throat clenched, and a chill of horror rippled through me. I hated negotiating as if the girl were some sort of chattel, hated even more the thought of marrying her off to some random and, undoubtedly, unsympathetic man. But so far as I could tell, there was no other way out of the harem.

He put down the pencil and flashed me a look full of power and disdain, his brow lined, his eyes narrow and strong. "No."

"No?"

"No. Is there anything else?"

"Could we not—"

"There will be no further discussion on this topic." He nodded sharply towards a dark corner of the room, and a tall eunuch appeared from the shadows. "He will escort you out. I did, Lady Emily, very much enjoy components of our conversation."

I opened my mouth to speak, but the eunuch's firm grip on my arm stopped the words. He all but dragged me, not easing the pressure of his fingers until he'd deposited me outside the palace gates, leaving me standing, dumbfounded, already feeling the beginnings of bruises.

6 April 1892

Emily, Emily, Emily:

I am writing this letter without giving you a single clue as to where I am. This is due entirely to the fact that I'm a dreadful and unredeemable human being who likes to torment her friends. You'll forgive me, though, in the end. I've embarked on a magnificent trip—one funded by my parents in exchange for letting them plan for me a wedding of the sort you so wisely avoided. Can you imagine what it would take to persuade me to accept such a thing? I need hardly tell you that I insist you and Colin come to New York for the hideous extravaganza.

My poor Mr. Michaels has no idea what he's in for. He's agreeable—as a fiancé ought to be—to anything so long as it doesn't interfere with his responsibilities at Oxford. The nuptials will be between terms, so we'll have only a brief honeymoon before he has to return to his academic duties. I confess to rather obscene excitement at the thought of watching him lecture and knowing that afterwards we'll return home together. Every nerve is full of the greatest anticipation. Can you imagine the breadth of our conversation? The perfect joining of mind and body? But of course I need not explain this to you—for at the moment you've a greater volume of experience than I and know well the pleasures of an intellectual marriage. How lucky we both are!

Not surprisingly, my dear parents insisted that I travel with a suitable companion, and she has already proven an incredible nuisance. Remember my mother's friend Mrs. Taylor? She recommended her daughters' former governess, and my mother snapped her up at once. I call her Medusa, as she's turned me to stone at least a dozen times since we left England.

Other than that, I've little of interest to report. Mr. Michaels has been sending me the most supremely ridiculous love letters every day. I'm sorry to say they're rather badly written—too scholarly—but the sentiments are heartily appreciated nonetheless.

I am, your most awful and debauched friend,

Margaret Seward

7

I'd refused to get out of bed that morning, insisting Meg bring my mail upstairs, where I burst out laughing more than once while reading Margaret's letter. My American friend, daughter of a fantastically wealthy railroad baron, was a kindred spirit whose love of the study of classics had brought us together while I was in mourning for my first husband. Although she was a Latinist (formally trained at Bryn Mawr) and I preferred Greek, our interests overlapped enough to provide for an intellectually stimulating friendship unlike any I'd known before. She'd become, in the span of a few years, as close to me as Ivy, though the two of them couldn't be more different. Margaret challenged me while Ivy offered comfort, and I couldn't imagine doing without either of them.

Margaret's modern thinking and passionate belief in the rights of women inspired me, and the way she managed to convince her parents to support her studies was impressive. She was an expert at negotiating trade-offs with them. A mere year ago, she'd agreed to a Season in London (with the theoretical goal of catching a titled husband) in exchange for a term at Oxford. In the process, she convinced everyone a duke (my dear friend Jeremy Sheffield) had mercilessly broken her heart and so completely won her parents' sympathies that they hardly balked when a few months later she'd accepted the proposal of a don at Oxford. She had admitted to being rather astonished at having agreed to marry anyone but said that some charms could not be resisted, and Mr. Michaels had them in abundance. It had all turned out brilliantly.

"I don't like it at all," Colin said, turning over and rubbing a gentle hand over the now blooming purple marks on my arm when I'd finished reading the letter. "How on earth did this happen?"

"It was entirely inadvertent," I said, not wanting to confess that I'd angered the sultan. "A guard was leading me out of the palace, and you know how steep the paths are at Yıldız. His grip was firm and I bruise easily."

"No one's grip is that fierce by accident."

"I'd never before considered the possibility of deliberately violent eunuchs." I folded the letter and tossed it aside, then scrunched the ends of my pillow and dropped my elbows in the center of it, resting my chin on my hands. "But perhaps that's precisely what he is."

"If only I'd been there to defend you."

"Rest assured I have no need of rescuing."

"I'm well aware of that." He pulled the pillow out from under me, rolled onto my back, and kissed my neck, the feeling of his legs against the backs of mine bliss itself. "But I do think, my dear, that you underestimate the value of being saved from dire circumstances. You might find it more than a little titillating."

"I promised you no unnecessary danger, and you must promise me no rescues."

"I wish you'd rescue me," he said, biting my ear.

"Stop. I'm being serious," I said.

"I'm all too aware of it. It's not so glamorous and invigorating as you think, necessary danger."

"When have you known me to yearn for glamour?"

"Every morning when you dress."

"Please, Colin, don't tease me," I said. "I need to know that you support what I'm doing."

"I do. But I can't say I'm without concern."

"I'm still waiting for my Derringer."

"It shall be our first order of business upon returning to England." He laughed, shook his head. "This is a conversation I never would have thought I'd have with my spouse."

"Would you prefer an ordinary wife?"

"Never," he said, kissing me until he could have had no doubt that all serious thoughts had taken flight from my brain. I was so carried away that I hardly noticed the door had creaked open, then slammed shut, then creaked again.

"Madam?" Meg's voice was low. "There's a Mr. Sutcliffe here to see Mr. Hargreaves. Says it's urgent."

"Tell him I'll be there as soon as I can," Colin said, heaving a sigh. As soon as she'd closed the door, he kissed me again. "We shall continue this later."

"I'm not sure I can wait."

"Which, first, makes me adore you all the more, and second, will make it that much better when we reconvene."

He pulled away, leaving me aching while he dressed, and I did not call for Meg to assist me with my own ablutions until after he'd gone downstairs. I submitted to her ministrations with little pleasure, wanting nothing but my husband. It did not help that she was severe with my hair—my scalp screamed in protest—and fought a valiant battle with my corset, pulling harder than usual to force my waist into submission. The end result pleased her but left me feeling a keen discomfort as I joined the gentlemen on the terrace.

"Good morning, Mr. Sutcliffe," I said. They were sitting at a table next to the water, a chessboard stretched between them. Colin had opened with the Queen's Gambit, two pawns moving to take control of the center of the board.

"A true pleasure to see you again, Lady Emily." Mr. Sutcliffe bent a silver gray head over my hand.

"I'm sorry to have interrupted your game." I studied the board. "I'd suggest you accept his gambit. It's not without risk. You'll lose control of the center, but if you play it right, you'll open yourself up to a greater freedom as the game goes on."

"Just who are you supporting in this match, my dear?" Colin asked.

"We had only just begun to pass the time until you arrived and would not dream of continuing now that you've joined us," Mr. Sutcliffe said. "I told your husband that, with his permission, I would like to speak to both of you, as it appears you're equally embroiled in this dreadful business at the palace. I'm concerned in the extreme about Sir Richard."

"We all are," I said.

"The loss of his daughter is a blow from which he may not recover. I've seen it too often—not just from my own experience, but in the charity work I do to support families whose children have succumbed to illness. Often poverty is a mitigating factor—bettering their situations may serve to prevent more loss. At least that's what I tell myself."

"An admirable position," Colin said.

"I cannot stand to see anyone suffer what I have. But when I think of Richard . . . Do you really think it wise to fuel his belief that the Ottomans have arrested the wrong man?"

"I've seen nothing that suggests he's guilty," Colin said. "And if he's not—"

Mr. Sutcliffe shook his head and held up a hand. "I want my friend to have peace, and I'm full of fear that this investigation will give him nothing but the opposite."

"How can he know peace until he finds out what happened to his daughter?" I asked.

"You think it's possible to determine that?"

"It's impossible to say at the moment," Colin said. "Best case would be finding some physical evidence that links a suspect to the crime."

"Wouldn't that already have been apparent? Surely the guards would have seen it that night?"

"Oversights are made with horrifying frequency," my husband said.

"So it's not too late?" Mr. Sutcliffe asked.

"Not necessarily," Colin replied, his voice all breezy confidence. "We're taking every possible measure."

"I can't see the old boy hurt further. This is the sort of pain that can ruin a man."

"I don't think he's verging on that territory," I said.

"No? He's coming completely unhinged and making more mistakes at his work than the ambassador will be able to tolerate for long. I assure you, Lady Emily, my concerns are well-founded. I'm doing all I can to help, but there are limits."

"You're a good friend," I said.

"I'm far too familiar with his pain," Mr. Sutcliffe said, "and hope that prolonging this investigation won't make it harder for him. He's been through quite enough."

"I couldn't agree more," I said. "And in an attempt to speed the process along, I'm afraid I must excuse myself. I'm expected at Yıldız."

"I wish you all luck," Mr. Sutcliffe said. "Physical evidence, Lady Emily. I'll be crossing fingers that you find some."

I thanked him, gave Colin a quick kiss, and stepped off the patio onto a waiting boat. Once again, the ride was interminable to my churning stomach, set in motion this time not only by the rough water, but by anxiety. I'd sent a note to Perestu, who had arranged for me to go to the *hamam*, agreeing that it might persuade the concubines I was someone they could trust. She'd promised to send English-speaking girls who knew Ceyden to talk to me. The prospect of bathing with untold numbers of total strangers was horrific, but I hoped to uncover some information of use.

Inside the harem, I followed a guard to the concubines' *hamam*, where I was handed off to a bath attendant, an elderly woman who spoke no English but managed to communicate to me that her name was Melek. She ushered me into a tiny dressing room, pantomiming actions that could only suggest I was to remove my clothing. In a matter of moments, she had whisked my dress over my head and turned her attentions to my corset. I was two shades from mortification, a condition not helped in the least when I realized that the towel—tiny and made from the thinnest-possible cotton—she was handing me would provide all the cover I was to get. She slipped wooden-soled clogs onto my feet and motioned for me to follow her.

Hobbling behind her, I focused on keeping my feet from sliding on the slick marble floor while at the same time gripping my toes lest the slippers fly off. She opened a wooden door and led me into a large, domed room made entirely of gray marble. The temperature was warmer than in the outer chamber, but not so hot as to be uncomfortable. Evenly spaced washbasins lined the perimeter, their faucets fashioned in elaborately patterned bronze. Marble benches ran continuously between the sinks, and on them sat more than a dozen women of the harem, all of them completely unclothed.

So shocked was I by this sight that I did not notice my attendant pulling my less than adequate towel away from me, leaving me in the same vulnerable state. I leapt for the nearest bench, falling onto it in a manner lacking any and all grace. Melek picked up a silver bowl, filled it in the basin, and dumped steaming water over my head. She repeated this several times before handing it to me and motioning for me to continue myself.

With a smile so weak as to be all but nonexistent, I dipped the bowl into the sink, sending water spilling over the sides. There were no drains. The water ran into a trough in the floor and disappeared beneath a wall, the sound of its travels dancing through echoes of the bouncing hum of the faucets. The warm stone felt good against my back, but there was no part of me finding even slim comfort in the situation. Other than the sound of water, the room appeared silent until I began to listen with focused attention. All around me, the women were whispering to one another, leaning forward to circumvent the basins, heads bent together as they spoke, coming apart when they lifted their bowls above them.

I looked at my arms, astonished to find that even my limbs had blushed crimson, and dropped my head back against the wall, ashamed of myself. Much though I wanted to throw myself into the local culture and behave nothing like the typical Englishwoman, I was failing miserably at the *hamam*. Still holding my now full bowl, I clenched my teeth and poured the water over my head. Bound and determined to enjoy myself, I dunked the bowl back into the sink and sloshed the contents onto my hair, which, thanks to Melek, was hanging loose down my back.

Meg would be beyond horrified when she saw me.

A petite blonde sat at the basin next to mine and began dousing herself. "I understand we are to be kind to you," she said. "An unusual directive."

"Is it?" I planted my elbows on my knees and rested my chin on them, trying to hide my body.

"You should relax." She tipped her head back and poured more water. I looked away, focusing on the floor. The marble, a superior grade, better than any I'd seen in England, shimmered in the soft light but was not enough to keep my attention. I tried the ceiling instead, counting the small circular windows cut into it and then analyzing the color of the sky, not quite cerulean. My neighbor's laughter floated into my false reverie. "Is it so taxing?"

"Taxing?" I asked, forcing myself to meet her clear eyes.

"I have heard stories of the West, of the European courts. Didn't believe them, but perhaps I should have. Is everyone in England so tense?"

This made me smile. "Yes, actually."

"Tedious." She pushed her hands against the bench, straightening her arms and arching her back.

"Different," I said. "But I don't know that tedious . . . yes, you're right. Tedious." We both laughed, and although I felt somewhat less exposed, my degree of anxiety dropped little more than the weight of a hummingbird.

"I would never go there," she said. "You know that Perestu sent only those whose English is good to speak to you today."

"I appreciate it. How long have you lived in the harem?"

"Since I was a girl. I can't imagine being anywhere else."

"You don't feel . . . restricted?"

"Of course not. Our options for amusement are endless."

"But you can't leave?"

"We take excursions whenever we want. I was shopping in Pera yesterday. Not everyone's as discontent as Roxelana."

"You know her?"

"Her room is near mine."

"Are you friends?"

"I wouldn't say that," she said. "Roxelana is very careful about her choice of confidantes. There's an air of superiority about her—she won't even pray with any of us. Furthermore, she prefers the friendship of men."

"In the harem?"

"The guards. Jemal is a favorite of hers."

"I'm surprised to learn that," I said.

"Who else are we to flirt with? Each other? Jemal is useful. Bezime may have no power anymore, but she can sometimes help us—and he arranges it."

"Help you how?" I asked, cataloging away in my head the fact that Roxelana and Jemal were friends.

"She practices the dark arts. Can tell our fortunes, read our charts. And she's something of a physician as well. There's no one I'd rather have prescribe a treatment for me when I fall ill."

"And Jemal tells you what she suggests?"

"He brings us her medicines."

"I understand he knew Ceyden well."

"Everyone knew her," she said. "She was impossible to escape."

"What can you tell me of their relationship?"

"It wasn't so unusual. As I said, we've no one to flirt with but the guards. Most of us have a favorite."

"Was she as close to him as Roxelana is?"

"Not at all. But Ceyden was less discreet and drew too much attention to them."

"Did he do anything to help her get the sultan's notice?" I asked.

"He let her believe he did, but I never saw anything that suggested he'd succeeded. Jemal's a pleasant enough distraction," she said. "But I wouldn't consider him reliable."

Melek had returned and motioned for me to follow her, putting a stop to our conversation with a sharp shake of her head. I stood, unsteady on the ill-fitting wooden clogs, and shuffled behind her to a large, octagonal marble platform in the middle of the room. Following the lead of the women who were already there, I lay down, resting my head on a small pillow, my heart racing.

Melek pulled a mohair mitt onto her hand and began scrubbing my skin with an earnest vigor, so hard that it almost hurt, leaving no inch unpolished, fingertips to toes, until I was tingling. I flipped onto my stomach and she continued with my back, pausing to show me the horrific amount of residue that had collected on the mitt. When she'd finished, she had me stand and soaked me with water before helping me to lie back down. Next came a gentle massage, another rinse, and another scrub. This time, instead of the mitt, she used a long, tail-like brush, which she rubbed with soap. As she moved it over my body, it left behind inches of fine lather. More rinsing followed, and now when I stood up, my self-consciousness had started to fade, but I kept my eyes closed, wanting neither to see the other women nor to notice them watching me.

I had to look, though, when she took my hand to lead me across the room to a small wooden door, through which she ushered me. The room beyond it was small, verging on claustrophobic, and radiated a heat that reminded me of the searing burn that accosted a person standing on the Acropolis in Athens on the hottest of summer days. I sat on the marble bench that lined the circumference of the space and leapt up almost at once, my delicate skin unable to stand the temperature. Laughter bounced off the walls.

"You are unused to the warmth?" Roxelana was stretched out on the other end of the bench.

"Warmth is not a strong enough word," I said, gingerly sitting back down and cringing at the result.

"It's marvelous when you're used to it. If you lie down, your weight will be more evenly distributed and you'll adjust with greater ease."

The thought of pressing the entire length of my body onto this instrument of torture did not appeal to me in the least, but Roxelana's suggestion made a certain amount of academic sense, so, with more than a dash of trepidation, I lowered myself.

She was correct; within minutes, the unbearable temperature had become a pleasant friend, and the marble cradled my limbs, lulling me into a trancelike state from which I had no desire to wake.

"I knew you would like it," she said.

I struggled to raise my head to look at her as I replied, "It's like nothing I've ever known."

"And you've relaxed enough that you've forgot you're naked."

At once I shot up, covering myself, and then laughed before dropping back onto the bench. "I suppose it makes no difference."

"Have the others poisoned you against me?"

"Far from it."

"They don't like me because of my religion."

"Are they aware of your beliefs?" I asked.

"No, but they can see I'm not a devout Muslim. It keeps me separate from the rest."

"Are they all faithful?"

"To a degree. Faithful enough to make me fear should I be caught with my rosary," she said. "I do hope you have the sense not to believe the things people here tell you."

"Including the things you tell me?"

"You can believe some of them. Dare I hope you've invented a plan to secure my freedom?"

"I don't know that it's even possible for me to do such a thing. I've discussed your situation with the sultan. He resisted, but I shall do all I can to convince him to release you," I said. "I am, in theory, opposed to arranged marriages, but it seems the only way to gain your release."

"I will not marry a man outside my faith," she said.

"You've no idea how I sympathize, and I wish there were another way. Marriage would at least serve to release you from this prison."

"Into another." Tears flashed in her liquid black eyes. "I thought I might find an ally in you—a woman who understood the need to fight for a life of her own, someone who was not bound by a prison of unfair and unjust rules. I see I was wrong."

The reappearance of Melek put an end to the conversation, but while I sat in front of her as she shampooed me, I couldn't stop the sting of Roxelana's words. She knew not how close they cut me. I'd risked much to pursue my own interests and wondered if I could embody the goals to which I aspired if I did nothing to free her from her cage. I felt sharp tears in my own eyes as Melek rinsed my hair and then left me, thoroughly clean, to relax on the warm marble until I was ready to dress. As the heat seduced me, wild scenarios for freeing Roxelana marched through my head, reminding me of the dangers of reading too much sensational fiction. I was beginning to approach a perilous place and already contemplating ways to avoid the British government being implicated should she escape. Uneasy, I was more than eager to seek out my clothes but thought I should lie down for another moment, long enough only to not appear rude. The inanity of this—relaxing by rule—made me smile, and the girl next to me rolled onto her stomach and propped her chin on a hand.

"It is much easier to talk in here, don't you think?"

"Is it?"

"No one's listening," she said. "Do you know yet about Ceyden and Jemal?"

"I've heard stories. What can you tell me?"

"There's more to it than a throwaway flirtation—" She stopped speaking, and her eyes left mine. I followed her gaze, turning my head to look behind me, where I saw Perestu, standing above us, fully clothed, not a drop of sweat on her face despite the heat.

"Have you enjoyed the *hamam*, Lady Emily?"

"More than I expected," I said, feeling once again wholly self-conscious and covering myself with my arms.

"Go dress. When you are ready, you will be brought to me."

As she left, I turned back to my neighbor, still sprawled on the warm marble. "There's not much to tell," she said, coming close to whisper to me. "It's just that sometimes there are ways to get to the sultan without earning Perestu's approval."

When I was dressed—expertly put back together by one of the harem maids—Perestu took me to Ceyden's room, a chamber with stone walls and almost no decoration that brought to mind a monk's cell. Her small bed was covered with heaping mounds of clothing—bright silks, embroidered fabrics, everything cut in current Western fashion. An armoire stood in the corner, doors open, nothing hanging inside, another pile of crumpled dresses lying on its floor.

I crossed to the only other piece of furniture in the room, a desk. On top of it were two books—a collection of Persian poetry translated into English and a copy of the Koran. The margins in the volume of poetry were full of scrawled notes, written in Greek. The Koran, though its spine was broken and the pages dog-eared, contained no annotations.

I pulled open each drawer in the desk. All were empty save one that contained a sewing kit wrapped in a beautifully embroidered cloth. "Who has had access to this room since the murder?" I asked.

"Anyone who wants to come in. You can see that her clothes have been pillaged. For all her faults, Ceyden did have a flair for fashion. If, that is, you like Western styles."

I shuddered at the thought of people digging through the dead girl's gowns, looking for something to wear. "You prefer another sort of fashion," I said. I'd never seen Perestu in anything other than traditional dresses and wide Turkish trousers. It set her apart from the other women and complemented her elegant bearing and petite figure.

"Yes, I do."

I began picking up gowns from the bed, shaking out each one before draping it over the desk. Aside from the occasional ripped hem, I noticed nothing out of the ordinary and moved to the armoire, where, beneath scarves and shawls and more dresses, I found something that could have been out of Perestu's wardrobe—a stunning Turkish-style gown fashioned from a rich blue-and-silver brocade. More fascinating than the beauty of the dress, however, was the fact that it was far too heavy for its yardage, its skirt bulky where it should have been smooth. The beginnings of excitement stirring in me, I spread out the garment on the floor and ran my hand over the cloth.

"There's something not right here," I said, flipping the dress inside out to reveal a cotton lining with neat seams stitched in it to form small, quilted squares of varying sizes. Anticipating me as she watched, Perestu took the sewing kit from the desk and handed me a slim, golden scissors. I cut the stitches and realized that it wasn't quilted—the squares were separate pieces of material. Once I'd removed two sides, I reached into what turned out to be a pocket and pulled out an emerald.

With a gasp, Perestu abandoned her regal bearing and dropped to her knees next to me. I opened another square and found three gold bracelets encrusted with rubies, and then another to reveal a pair of heavy diamond earrings.

"Are these her personal jewels?" I asked.

"No. She did not have the status to own such things."

I kept at my work, and in short order we had before us a glittering pile of gemstones and a slim gold dagger. I reached behind the last square and touched a stunning sapphire ring set in a diamond-encrusted bezel. I held it up to Perestu, who took it from my hand.

"This is mine," she said. "And I believe we've found quite enough, Lady Emily. I see Ceyden for who she was. My instincts about her were perfectly accurate, and we don't need to know anything else. I can no longer doubt that the guard was the one who killed her, most likely in an attempt to stop her from stealing anything else."

"That may not be the case, Your Highness," I said. "We should—"

"It's quite enough. The sultan will thank you for your services."

Standing in front of Aya Sofya, the former Byzantine church—now a mosque—I found it difficult to watch for my husband without being blinded by the sun. I adjusted my parasol, murmuring to myself the words of approval my mother would have spoken were she with me, and looked across the wide street, through a park filled with palm trees and green grass, in the direction of the Blue Mosque. Vendors pushed carts up and down the paths, selling cherry juice and sweets, calling with the hope of enticing passersby to sample their wares. It struck me to see the number of women on the street. Veils covered their faces, and the mystery drew me to them, the sparkle of kohl-rimmed dark eyes having a far greater effect than society women's diamonds and low-cut gowns. Sporadically, I would catch a glimpse of a hennaed hand peeking out from wide, long sleeves, and the sound of their frequent laughter seemed at odds with their restrictive clothing.

I had not expected to see women moving about the city with such freedom but had found almost as soon as we'd arrived that this was just another Western misconception. And as I watched them walk, crossing the street to greet friends or investigate the goods for sale piled on a cart, I contemplated the delicious possibility of going about without anyone recognizing who you were.

"Mrs. Hargreaves?" Mr. Sutcliffe bowed in front of me. "How delightful to see you."

"And you as well," I said, smiling. "You look full of purpose today." His eyes were focused and clear, his head high.

"That I am, although it's a difficult one." He shifted a bundle of packages in his arms. "I'm bringing clothes to a family in dire need. Their son, only eight years old, died from a fever last night. They're terrified it's contagious and are burning everything they own. I can give them new things, but such a deed pales when compared with their loss."

"How terrible. Is there anything I can do?"

"I should never turn down a donation, but would take nothing else. You do not need to put yourself in circumstances that might cause you harm. I can't have you falling ill—your husband would never forgive me. I must beg your leave, but hope to see you soon."

"Of course," I said. "And you may depend upon Mr. Hargreaves sending you a check."

"I am indebted to you both." With a nod, he stepped away. A gust of wind tugged at my parasol, spring reminding summer it was not yet ready to relinquish its crown, and I held the handle more tightly, squinting in the face of the bright sun.

"That's quite a scowl," Colin said, swooping in to kiss me. "Something wrong?"

"No, just the sun." I looped my arm through his and recounted my conversation with Mr. Sutcliffe.

"He's a dedicated man. Many in his position would be consumed with anger instead of compassion."

"I admire his ability to turn tragedy into an opportunity to lessen the pain of others," I said, adjusting my scarf to cover my head suitably for a mosque as we approached Aya Sofya. We walked a few paces before pausing to remove our shoes—a requirement before entering a Muslim holy building.

"Tell me about your morning," Colin said.

"I went to the *hamam* and then searched Ceyden's room. You won't believe what—"

"You went to the *hamam*? The baths? In the harem?"

"Yes, it was lovely." I adored the look in his eyes but was not going to be distracted. I tugged on his arm, pulling him inside, across a wide corridor, and into the domed center. The floors, built from marble in the Byzantine days, were now covered with thick carpets that muffled the sound of murmured prayers whispered by the faithful, their heads pressed to the ground. The old Christian mosaics had been hidden by painted plaster, but the space was beautiful, caught between two religions, a testament to the battles fought between them. Little light made its way through the windows, and the candles of the low-hanging chandeliers served only to cast flickering shadows, eerie in their elegance. "Ceyden was hiding a collection of—"

"I'm sorry," he said. "The baths?"

I could not help but grin. "This is precisely why I didn't tell you what I was doing at Yıldız before I left this morning. We'll discuss everything later. At the moment, we can't be distracted."

"Yes, we can. In fact, I'm fairly certain I'm already hopelessly distracted."

Now it was his turn to lead me, up a steep cobbled path that stood in lieu of a stairway, its stones so uneven and slick that I clung to him to keep from slipping. The dark passage went to an upper gallery, turn after turn at hard right angles leading to the top, but Colin stopped before we reached it, pushed me against the wall, and gave me a kiss that tempted me beyond all reason. As soon as I began to pull away, he lifted his hand to the back of my neck and began tracing circles with a single finger, sending the most delicious darts down my spine.

"You're terrible," I said. "You can't kiss me here."

"This is supposed to be our honeymoon," he said, kissing me again. "I'll kiss you wherever I desire. Now tell me about the baths."

"Not a chance." With no inconsiderable effort, I stepped aside and smoothed my skirts. "I don't think I could have married you if you weren't so wholly distracting. But I shall resist you right now."

"Dreadful girl."

"It will be all the better later." Our eyes locked on each other. "Isn't that what you always say?"

"And you'll tell me about the baths?"

"Perhaps." I bit my now swollen lips. "If you're able to persuade me."

"I can't wait to win our bet."

"I can't wait for you to lose," I said. We sat, continuing to stare at each other for at least two minutes longer than any decent person would tolerate. He ran a hand through his hair, shook his head, and continued up the passage.

"Tell me about Ceyden," he said. I described for him what I'd learned about Ceyden, Jemal, and Roxelana and what I'd found, pulling out the notebook in which I'd cataloged each of the pieces of jewelry.

"Perestu all but chucked me out of the harem after she identified her ring."

"What will you do next?"

We stood near the stone rail that ran the circumference of the gallery all the way around the building. I looked across the gilded screens shielding the ladies' area. The painted designs beneath them mimicked the pattern on the window arches and ceiling, bursts of geometric flowers in blue against a burnt gold background. The beauty was breathtaking, but it troubled me to think that the women were all confined to the space, isolated from everything going on around them. Another beautiful cage. As I thought about it, however, I considered my own society. We women might be allowed to sit wherever we wanted in church, but we had no more clout than our Ottoman counterparts. Our segregation was merely less visible.

"There are any number of ways Ceyden could have got those objects. What if she was blackmailing their owners?"

"That would explain Perestu's actions. Have you any proof?"

I grinned. "Not a shred, my dear boy. If blackmail is the explanation, she must have known something horrifying enough to induce her cohorts to part with their treasures."

"I don't think I like the theory, Emily," he said, turning away from the rail and leaning his back against it. "What purpose would getting jewelry serve? She had access to whatever she wanted and didn't need money."

"Unless she was planning to escape."

"Escape? When she was doing everything she could to gain the sultan's favor?"

"I admit freely there are holes in the hypothesis. However . . ." I stepped towards him and rested my hand on the cool marble post that held a tall candelabra above the rail. "What if she knew something about the sultan himself? Suppose she was blackmailing him, and suppose he was tired of it and had someone kill her?"

"He's the sultan—she's essentially his slave," he said. "She'd have nothing on him worthy of blackmail."

"Had I even an inkling of the deficits in your imagination, I would never have married you. I feel entirely misled."

"My deepest apologies. How awful for you."

"I shan't ever recover," I said.

"I would hope not." His eyes danced. "I expect you to be despondent for at least six months."

"If you weren't such a beast, you'd have the decency to make a vain attempt at consolation," I said.

He lifted my chin and kissed me, one hand around my waist, the other on my face.

"We are in a church!" I said.

"A mosque. Was my effort not enough? Are you not consoled?"

I studied his face and suppressed a smile. "It was admirable, I suppose."

"Admirable?"

I shrugged. "I was trying to be generous. Given our surroundings, I can only assume you are operating with great restraint."

"You're kindness itself." He stepped back, warmth radiating from his smile. "So, blackmailing the sultan?"

"I convinced Perestu to let me take the book of poetry from Ceyden's desk and am hoping the marginalia turns out to be more than an analysis of the poems."

"Blackmail records? Unlikely that she'd leave something so sensitive out in the open."

"They may have been coded somehow. At any rate, they appeared to be written in Greek." I watched a group of men, bent over in prayer, kneel on the floor below us.

He smiled at me. "Anything else to report?"

"At the moment, I find myself suddenly more interested in telling you about the *hamam*."

"Perhaps you made me wait too long," he said. "I might have other plans."

"Unlikely in the extreme," I said, meeting his eyes and pulling him towards me. "And at any rate, I'm confident I can convince you there's nowhere you'd rather be."

"I can be awfully stubborn."

"Not as stubborn as I am," I said.

He tipped his head back and laughter spilled out of him. "Truer words I have never heard."

I am pleased to report that when we did at last return home, he did not prove stubborn in the least.

The next morning, I headed across the Bosphorus to Stamboul— the old section of the city, a peninsula jutting into the Golden Horn and the Bosphorus—hoping to see Bezime at Topkapı. Meg had sliced a piece of gingerroot for me, expressing veiled concern at having seen me return home ill day after day and telling me that chewing it would prevent seasickness. Lovely though the gesture was, it had little effect on the overwhelming nausea that hit the moment I stepped into the boat and felt the waves churning beneath me. By the time the crossing was over, I was sweating and cold at the same time, my stomach lurching every time I drew breath.

"My dear Lady Emily, please let me assist you!" Mr. Sutcliffe called to me from the far end of the palace dock. He reached the boat in a few short strides and gripped my arm, steadying me as I rose to my feet. "Are you quite all right?"

I doubled over and was sick all over the wooden planks, then sank to my knees, tears stinging my eyes as mortification burned my cheeks.

"Do you need a doctor?"

"No, I'm—it's just seasickness. I can't believe it's affecting me so severely."

He passed me a handkerchief. "Come. Let's get you inside."

"I did not expect to see you here," I said, accepting his arm to help me up.

"I was calling on an old friend." We'd reached the gates of the palace, where Mr. Sutcliffe explained to the guard that I was ill and expected by Bezime. The sentry admitted us at once, shouting to a colleague to alert the former valide sultan before taking us to a place I could rest.

We crossed the marble pavement of a terrace surrounding a large rectangular pool, in whose center stood a square fountain, its tiered stone sides cut in a lacy pattern. In front of us was open space with sweeping views of the Golden Horn, broken only by a small pavilion with a golden peaked roof, a single bench under it, perpendicular to the Baghdad Pavilion, which Mr. Sutcliffe informed me had, in the past, served as a library. After passing under a series of tall arches, decorated with blue and burgundy paint that complemented the colored stone, we entered the Revan Kiosk, a small and utterly charming building. Blue floral tiles lined the walls to the ceiling at least twenty feet above, light streaming through stained-glass windows at the halfway point as well as from openings in the domed roof. I dropped onto the usual low red divan tucked under windows, these shuttered with wood panels inlaid with mother-of-pearl and tortoiseshell.

"Shall I send for your husband?" Mr. Sutcliffe asked.

"No, thank you, I'll be fine. I'm already better just from being on steady ground." A servant appeared with apple tea, but its sweetness made me cringe and I abandoned it on the table in front of me. I inhaled until my lungs hurt, blew the breath out slowly. "I'd no idea how I would suffer for insisting on taking a house across the Bosphorus. I had such romantic visions of crossing the water every day."

"You're not the first to have been defeated by its currents." He sat at the opposite end of the sofa, brushing its bright silk with his hands. "Are you quite sure you don't want me to send for your husband? I know what a comfort family can be in times of difficulty."

"You're very kind, thank you, and right as well," I said.

"Nothing more important than taking care of those you love. It's something I'm afraid I was never able to do well enough."

"I've no doubt you did as much as any man could."

"I could not live with myself if I did not agree." His eyes glinted as if he might cry, but instead he smiled. "The color's come back to your face, so it seems the worst is over. We shan't need to disturb Hargreaves."

"No, that won't be necessary. I wouldn't want to alarm him."

"Very good. You look much better now," he said. "I'm glad to have run into you. I was planning to call on you later today, and this saves me the trip. I have something I'm afraid may prove to be evidence in Ceyden's murder."

"*Afraid* is a strange choice of word."

"It points in a most unwelcome direction, which is why I didn't bring it up earlier. But I kept thinking of what Hargreaves said about physical evidence, and, well . . ." His voice trailed off, and he looked at the ground. "I don't like to cause unnecessary trouble."

"Justice sometimes requires trouble," I said. "But it's important to uncover the truth."

He reached into his pocket and pulled out a glittering object. "I found this that night after the opera in the courtyard where Ceyden was killed."

"It's beautiful." I fingered the object he'd handed me, a golden Byzantine cross, three inches long, hanging from a broken gold chain.

"It belongs to Benjamin St. Clare. I was with him the day he bought it."

"Why didn't you give this to the guards?" I asked.

"I—I suppose I should have, but I was scared."

"It's surely not the only cross of its kind in Constantinople, and even if it does belong to Benjamin, it's entirely possible he lost it weeks before the murder. He could have been invited to the opera on a different night and dropped it then. After all, it's not as if we've a witness who saw him at the palace."

"Quite right. No witness. Still, take it with you and ask your husband his opinion—I don't like having it in my possession. There's something else as well. I had gone to visit him at the dig the day before Ceyden's death—I've always been fond of the boy. Reminds me of my own son, I suppose. It was an unplanned trip, he didn't know I was coming, and it turned out he was not there. His compatriots said he had business in Constantinople and was visiting his father. Which, of course, he was not."

"He told us he came to Constantinople as soon as he'd heard the news. My husband sent a message to him at the dig."

"And the messenger reported back to the embassy that he was unable to deliver his epistle in person, as the man to whom it was addressed was not in camp."

"Does Sir Richard know this?" I asked.

"No. It is fortunate that I was the one who spoke to the messenger, and I've kept all of this to myself. I saw no reason to alarm him in case I'm misinterpreting what I've seen. He's shouldering so much at present—I've no desire to increase his burden."

"Of course not. But if—"

"He's always said he would support me, offered me every kindness. I will do anything I can to protect him. This is why I was concerned when I learned there would be a wider investigation. I do hope that if you find—"

He stopped speaking when light spilled into the room as the door opened. "Ah! Emily! You don't look sick in the least!" Bezime glided into the room and took my hands in hers. "It is quite another thing, I think."

"Seasickness," I said. "It breaks my heart that the Bosphorus doesn't agree with me."

"Yes, I imagine it would." She turned to my companion. "I did not expect to see you again so soon, Mr. Sutcliffe."

He'd leapt to his feet the moment she entered and now bowed to her. "It is a pleasure, m'lady."

"Of course it is. Why have you returned to me?"

"I saw Lady Emily ill on the dock and brought her—"

"I see. Thank you for your kind services. They are much, much appreciated."

Mr. Sutcliffe turned red at her abrupt dismissal but otherwise maintained his composure. "I shall leave you to your conversation."

"I do appreciate it," she said.

"And I am indebted to you for your assistance, Mr. Sutcliffe," I said. Another bow, and he exited the pavilion.

"He is a kind man," Bezime said. "But troubled. He lost his family to disease years ago and is still plagued by nightmares. I worry for him. He does not sleep well."

"It's very sad," I said. "He told me he'd lost a child, but I was unaware of the details."

"Two children, during some dreadful epidemic. His wife, too, all a very long time ago. This sort of wound, though, does not heal well. I still mourn my own son."

"The sultan, Abdül Aziz?"

"Yes," she said. "I will never forget when they took the throne from him. The minister of war came to the palace to drag him away. I fought that dreadful man off—scratched his face, pushed him to the ground—but there was no stopping him. He took my son and imprisoned him."

"I had no idea your son was deposed."

"Yes. And he died not long after. Cut his wrists with a scissors I'd given him to trim his beard."

"I don't even know what to say. I'm so terribly sorry."

"It was my fault. I killed him."

"No, no. Of course not. You couldn't have—"

She stopped me and placed a cold hand on mine. "Enough of this. I tell you only so you know I am familiar with the pain shared by both Mr. Sutcliffe and Ceyden's father. There is no grief worse than that from losing a child."

"I can only imagine," I said.

"Yes, for now. You, Emily, blame your troubles on the Bosphorus?"

"Seasickness is—"

"You are not seasick. You are with child."

"I . . . well . . . it may be, but I—"

"I am already certain. Your own confirmation will come soon enough. But it is most disturbing to me. Nothing good will come from this situation."

"Why would you say such a thing?"

"I have read your charts, chanted for you, done all that I can to see your future. You are not on the right path."

I hardly knew how to react. I was stunned that she would say such a thing, horrified she would address so delicate a subject with someone she knew only slightly, and I was more than a little scared, for she seemed to know definitively the answer to a question I'd been afraid even to pose. "I don't think you should—"

"No, of course you do not. You are unused to people speaking directly about this topic, and the terror in your eyes would be readable even to a fool. Does your husband know of your condition?"

"I don't know that I even have a condition," I said. "There have been some signs, but—"

"There can be no doubt. I have much experience in these matters."

"I'd prefer not to discuss it. I'm here to talk about Ceyden."

"I have no interest in that subject today."

"Then it seems I have wasted a trip." I rose from the sofa.

"You will go from me now, but when you want to come back, it will be too late," she said. "Think carefully, Emily, before you cross through those doors. I have looked into the future."

"I don't believe in any of this. You can't possibly know—"

"I know what the future holds at this moment. The choices you make from now on may change your course, but you must walk with trepidation and make no mistakes if you're to have any chance at escaping your current fate."

I stood up, stormed across the room, but could not quite bring myself to leave. I turned back towards her. "Why would you tell me something like this?"

"I like you, Emily. You deserve the warning."

Rather than wait for my husband on the steps of the Archaeological Museum, as we'd planned, I paced the perimeter of the first court-yard at Topkapı, looking for him on the path that led to the museum. Bezime's words had sickened me. My temples throbbed, my stomach would not stop twisting around itself, and my mind was full of fear. I saw Colin as he walked through the gate, arms crossed, tension in every calculated step he took. He called out when he caught sight of me and waved, but as I reached out for his hand when he stood before me, his eyes flashed a combination of concern and anger.

"Did you omit anything when you told me what happened at Yıldız yesterday?"

"No, of course not," I said. "You're awfully accusatory."

"I can't say I much liked receiving a visit from the British consul telling me that you and I have been banned from there."

"From Yıldız?"

"Yes."

"Heavens," I said, rolling my eyes and starting for the museum's steps. The neoclassical building had opened not more than a year earlier, and although it was not so large as the British Museum, I'd looked forward to viewing the collection from the moment I'd read about it on the train. "If I've given that much insult, I'd certainly like to have known at the time I was doing it. I might have rather enjoyed it."

"This isn't amusing, Emily. Did you promise to help someone escape from the harem?"

"I—how—" I closed my eyes, sighed hard. "I didn't say I would help her escape."

"But you spoke to the sultan about it?"

"I asked him in general terms if he would consider arranging a marriage for her."

"And this is why you were removed with such force? Why you had bruises on your arms?"

"Yes," I said.

"And you conveniently neglected telling me that particular detail," he said. "How could you think broaching such a topic to the sultan would be appropriate?"

"She's living like a slave."

"And a loveless marriage would be an improvement?"

"I don't know. She's converted to Christianity, Colin, and is living in a state of mortal sin. She's embraced the work of St. Thomas Aquinas."

"Aquinas? The same who said, 'Drink to the point of hilarity'?"

"It's not a joke. She's very serious about her faith and is tortured at not being able to walk away from sin."

"I cannot believe this." He turned away from me, walked towards the museum entrance, put his hand on the door, then turned back. "This is not some diversion. We've been granted access—unprecedented access, I might add—to the sultan and his harem because both the

British and Ottoman governments want to avoid an embarrassing diplomatic situation. You don't have the right to take advantage of that to forward your own interests."

"How can you speak to me like this?" I asked. "I've done nothing wrong."

"You are acting as an authorized representative of the British Crown and are to operate in a very specific and limited manner."

"I had no idea the Crown was so little interested in—"

"In what, Emily? In the romantic concerns of persons not British?"

"It's not romantic, it's theological!" My mouth hung open, and I could not breathe. "I never thought you of all people would recriminate me for—"

"For stepping completely out of bounds? I consider you my equal, and I will always tell you when you've gone too far."

"Gone too far?" I could not keep my voice from trembling.

"Come inside," he said.

He bought our tickets and ushered me into the museum. We did not speak again until we'd reached the Alexander Sarcophagus, the stunning and enormous object that had inspired the building's architecture. It had not belonged to the great king, but its white stone showcased his strengths. On one side, he sat, wearing a lion's head for a helmet, astride his horse, Bucephalas, fighting the Persian army, his enemy near defeat. The opposite panel showed him hunting lions. I leaned close, irritated at finding myself so distracted when before such a significant piece, but wholly unable to concentrate.

"Don't be outraged," Colin said. "I would have said the same thing to a man."

"And I hope that he would ... would ..." I was losing my temper, and fast, despite the fact that I knew he was not being wholly unreasonable. I should have discussed Roxelana's situation with him before I broached the topic with the sultan. I wondered if she had taken it upon herself to speak to Abdül Hamit. I looked at my perfectly handsome husband and felt nothing but anger. My tenuous grip on control was slipping fast; it was taking all my focus to keep from stomping my foot in petulant indignation and storming across the gallery. This, coupled with unwanted tears filling my eyes, was too much to be borne. It was as if I were no longer myself.

"You hope he would call me out." He smiled. "Pistols at dawn? Or do you prefer swords?"

"I'd never be so dramatic," I said, pretending to be fascinated with the detail on the face of a lion, Alexander's prey.

"I imagine not." He pressed his lips together, pushing them to one side, what he always did when he was trying not to laugh. Much though I hated to admit it at the moment, it was an irresistible maneuver.

"If I must, though, I'd pick swords," I said. "More elegant."

"Is that so? Rather messy in the end, don't you think?" He walked back to me.

"You've been very firm about denying me my Derringer until I learn to shoot, so I assumed it would not be a wise move at this juncture to choose pistols."

Now he did laugh. "I apologize if my frank manner of speech was too much. I should have couched my criticism in softer terms."

This was not at all what I wanted. "No, no, you shouldn't have. I don't want to be coddled. I'm sorry if my actions have made things more difficult."

He touched my face, his rough hand cool on my cheek. "I shan't coddle you. Not now, at any rate. But there may come a day—a happy day—on which you require an extended period of coddling. Beyond that, however, I shall be as hard on you as I am on anyone."

I did not like this talk of extended coddling, particularly as I had a strong suspicion he was referring to the probable cause of my would-be seasickness. Every dreaded emotion swirled through me, but I forced them away. "I want that treatment—that respect from you always. Regardless of whatever happy day we may reach."

"Some circumstances—"

"Please." I had to interrupt. "Not now. Let's discuss the matter at hand."

"Of course." He paused, just for an instant, flashing my favorite smile. "We're in a tricky situation. Tell me about your afternoon."

"There's so much, I hardly know where to start." I took Benjamin's cross out of my reticule and recounted Mr. Sutcliffe's story.

Colin frowned. "It shall be easy enough to confirm whether it does belong to him. We are, however, going to need to get back into the harem. Do you think you can work your charms on the sultan and regain your access?"

"I shall have to find a way. We got along famously at first. I may have overstepped my bounds speaking to him about Roxelana, but that doesn't seem enough—particularly as it's not connected to the murder—to cause our expulsion. Something else had to be a contributing factor, and I'm convinced it has to do with Ceyden's collection of ill-gotten jewels."

"I've no doubt you can ferret out the truth. I'll see where this leads us." He took the chain from me and stopped in front of a small, glass-fronted case.

"Is this all that remains of Troy?" I frowned at the uninspiring grouping of broken pottery. "There must be more—all that gold. I've read about it."

"Schliemann took it all to Berlin." Heinrich Schliemann, the German archaeologist who'd found and excavated the site, had published pictures of his wife draped in the gold he called the Treasure of Priam. "Smuggled it."

"We must go to the site of the excavation before we leave Turkey," I said. "I will not sleep well again until I've seen the ground upon which Hector's blood spilled."

He pressed my hand to his lips. "You're so dramatic."

I smiled, but my thoughts had already returned to our purpose. "Do you think there's a chance Benjamin killed his sister?"

"There's always a chance, Emily."

"I don't even want to imagine what that would do to Sir Richard."

"Or to Benjamin," he said. "If he did it, did he know who she was?"

"Could he have killed her to save her from the shame of being in the harem?"

Colin laughed. "You and your fiction. When we're old and gray and full of sleep, I'd like nothing more than to see you turn your talents to writing the worst sort of sensational novels."

"'Old and gray and full of sleep.' What a lovely phrase. Poem?"

"Yeats. It's to be in his next collection. He showed it to me last time I was in Dublin."

"Well, I've no intention of ever being full of sleep. Old and gray, however, is unavoidable."

Colin had gone in search of Sir Richard, leaving me to wait for his return at a tiny tea shop, where over perfectly crispy baklava I repeated again and again in my mind what Bezime had told me. Her words had sliced through me, ripping bright holes in the shaded hollows of my soul from which I'd been hiding since my marriage. The prospect of having a child terrified me. I'd never been able to shake from my memory the sound of screams echoing through the halls of my parents' estate when I was eleven years old. The noise had wakened me, and I'd slipped out of the nursery, my bare feet cold on the marble floor as I sought the source of the disturbance, more than a little confident I had at last found a ghost, something my cousin James had tried and failed to do every time his family visited us. But as the cries grew louder, I recognized the voice. It was James's mother, my aunt Clarabelle. We'd been told there would be a new baby in time for Christmas; instead there was a funeral.

Death was something to which we were all accustomed. My older brothers, twins, had both fallen to the influenza when they were thirteen years old, and James had lost a sister to rheumatic fever. Until that December, however, I'd viewed death as something that, while sad, was peaceful. Those ragged cries changed my opinion forever. My mother, tears streaming from eyes I'd never before seen cry, found me in the hallway, shivering on the floor. She marched me back to my room, told me not to be confused by what I'd heard, that this was commonplace, that it couldn't always be avoided, that childbirth was a dangerous thing.

I don't know that I've better remembered any of her words. And in the years that followed, I saw their truth borne out, most recently when an acquaintance from my school years died fewer than two years after her marriage, leaving behind a grieving husband and a sickly infant.

I disliked weakness, and my fear of so natural a process could be described as nothing else. This revelation disturbed me. The procreation of children, after all, was intended to be a primary purpose of marriage, and for every woman who died in the process, hundreds succeeded. Could it be a thousand? Or more? I wondered if knowing the true odds would offer me consolation. I placed my palm flat on my abdomen and wondered if Bezime's words had contained any bits of truth. When we returned to England at the end of the following month, I would see my physician. If he confirmed what I suspected, I would share the news with Colin and let him coddle me, if only for the period of my confinement.

An intense sensation of heat rushed through me, followed by a wave of dizziness and a wash of fear, each of which dissipated as the call to prayer started, drowning out all my thoughts. I closed my eyes, let the sound vibrate through me, and found my head much more clear when it stopped. Relieved, I turned my attention to Ceyden's book of poems. A quick glance told me they'd be best read at home, not because of nefarious undertones, but because I feared them likely to throw me too much into the honeymoon spirit. I was not at the *yalı* and so had to contain the emotions coursing through me as I devoured page after page.

"Satisfactory reading?" Colin asked, slipping into the chair across from me. I'd no idea how much time had passed since he'd left me. Poetry, it seemed, was an undeniable distraction.

"You have no idea."

"Ceyden's book?" he asked. I hardly looked up, nodding in reply. "Are the notes useful?"

"I have not yet read them. They seemed to be written in Greek, but closer examination proved that wrong."

"A code?"

"I'm afraid so," I said.

"I doubt it's a difficult one. What have you tried to crack it?"

"Nothing. I'm entirely distracted." I flipped pages and read to him:

You've so distracted me,
your absence fans my love.
Don't ask how.

Then you come near.
"Do not . . . ," I say, and
"Do not . . . ," you answer.

Don't ask why
·this delights me.

"Ah, Rumi. How far have you got in the book? It gets even better."

"Rumi, yes, you're right," I said. I had not been, before now, much familiar with the works of the famous thirteenth-century Persian poet. "Is there anything you don't know?"

"Sadly, yes. All too much, in fact."

"How does it get better?"

"Let the lover be disgraceful, crazy, absentminded. / Someone sober will worry about things going badly. / Let the lover be."

"Lovely, but a bit tame," I said, smiling.

"Keep reading, my dear. Keep reading."

"Can't you just recite the good parts to me?"

"Maybe later, if you're well behaved." A waiter placed a glass cup of tea nestled on a bronze saucer in front of him. "Don't you want to know what I learned from Sir Richard?"

"Of course," I said.

"The cross is Benjamin's. He recognized it at once. Furthermore, he had noticed his son hasn't been wearing it of late and asked him about it."

"Oh, dear."

"Quite. Benjamin said he'd lost it when the bandits attacked him en route to Constantinople after he'd learned of Ceyden's death."

"This is dreadful," I said. "Did you tell him about the messenger?"

"I felt it the right thing to do. He was deeply concerned, but convinced that his son could not have been involved in the murder."

"That's hardly surprising. What do you think?"

"I've no idea yet."

"Did you talk to Benjamin as well?" I asked.

"I didn't," he said. "He passed through as I was speaking to his father, and I thought he might respond better to you. He seems to consider me as someone on Sir Richard's side."

"I'll go to him as soon as I can."

"Thank you. I do adore your competence. I never have to worry that you'll flail." He smiled and bent his head to look at the book in front of me. "May I?"

"Of course." I passed him the tattered volume. It was a pleasure to watch him work, his dark eyes exuding confidence, his wavy hair tumbling over a forehead knotted with concentration. He reached for a piece of paper and pulled a pencil from his pocket. "Surely it can't be this easy."

I leaned across the narrow table, craning my neck to see what he wrote.

"If all she did was replace each letter . . ." His voice trailed as he scrawled the alphabet across the top of the paper. "Of course, we'll run into problems if she was writing in Turkish, but given that the book's in English and Turkish would be too obvious for someone living in the harem . . ." He fell silent again, flipping pages and writing notes, his lips tugging towards a smile. "I can't believe it."

"She didn't change the letters?" I asked, looking at the Greek letters he'd written beneath the Roman alphabet, α under "a," β under "b," and so on.

"It appears not."

"She must not have been trying very hard to hide what she was doing."

"English is not the first language of the harem. She probably thought she was being exceedingly clever."

"It must have been difficult for her," I said. "She had such trouble with it."

"Let's transcribe. No sense getting excited only to find it's useless and uninteresting."

Useless and uninteresting were not, perhaps, the right words. Confusing and intriguing, more like. She'd written a record, documenting time she'd spent following someone she did not name, someone who left the harem at seemingly regular intervals with groups of other concubines and who spent no small number of nights with the sultan.

"Simple jealousy?" I asked. "She wanted his attention, he was giving it to someone else? She might have been studying her rival."

"But there's nothing that would be of use in that way—no descriptions of clothing, no notes on what this person reads, what her interests are."

"Is that what one should take account of when considering a rival?"

"Well, if this other woman captured the sultan's interest, would it not make sense to imitate her in an attempt to draw his attention away?"

"Not at all," I said. "Imitation is at best a faded effort. She'd need to find a way to shine in her own right. This feels more nefarious—as if she were stalking this other woman."

"Stalking her?"

"And perhaps stealing her jewelry. So far, I see nothing that suggests blackmail."

"We know at least one piece of it belonged to Perestu," he said.

"Who was obviously not spending nights with the sultan."

"She keeps referring to someone and *his special meetings*," I said, handing him my paper. "Could it be Jemal? She might have been jealous if he had a close friendship with another concubine."

"Roxelana," he said. "Transcribe the rest of what's written in the book, see if there's any clue in them."

"We should also take note of the poems by which she wrote. There may be some significance to them."

"I think you should read them all aloud to me," Colin said. "I might catch something you miss."

"Or distract us both from our purpose."

He reached across the table for my hand and kissed it, his lips too soft and insistent for public decency. "Precisely my intention. Must I remind you again that this is our honeymoon?"

"You might, instead, show me. Is there any reason we can't go home now?" I asked.

10

The speed with which my husband ushered me to the docks was topped only by the effort expended by our boatman, who'd been inspired by an egregious tip. Colin swung me onto our patio when we'd reached the *yalı*, then swept me into his arms and carried me into the house. But no sooner had he pushed open the door than we were greeted by the sound of a voice, its American accent unmistakable.

"It's beastly, I know, to have three on a honeymoon, but you'll simply have to forgive me."

"Margaret!" I cried as Colin put me down. I rushed over and hugged my friend.

"What a delightful surprise," he said. His voice was sincere, but I read the disappointment in his eyes. There was no question he adored Margaret, but I knew he'd have been more welcoming had she arrived even two hours later. "I have a suspicion that you wouldn't object to a glass of whiskey while you explain to us your motives for crashing our honeymoon."

"Can't say I would," Margaret said. "I've made a narrow escape from Medusa. She's napping at the hotel and expects me to be doing the same. *Expects.*"

"She'd be horrified if she knew you were here," I said. "I remember all too well how much her former employer dislikes me. Remember when you were staying with Mrs. Taylor and she told her butler not to admit me to her house?" Margaret had spent the previous Season staying with friends of her mother's. During that time, it had been more than difficult for me to gain admittance to most homes in London because of a series of despicable rumors savaging my reputation. And while most of society had forgot the controversy, Mrs. Taylor was still cutting me dead when last I saw her.

"That's all forgotten now. You've been deemed respectable as a result of your most excellent marriage." Margaret flopped onto a settee. "I know it's awful of me to show up like this, but I couldn't resist. I'm going all the way to Persia and couldn't imagine being so close to you and not stopping. Tell me about Constantinople. Is the moonlight on the Bosphorus everything I hope it to be?" She grinned at Colin as he handed her a glass of whiskey.

"That is all the signal I need to make a speedy departure," Colin said. "I'll leave you two to catch up." He ducked out of the room, pausing only to give me a quick kiss.

"It's good to see you," Margaret said the instant the door closed behind him. "I hope I haven't completely overstepped my bounds by showing up unannounced. I wanted it to be a surprise."

"No overstepping at all. You know you're always welcome."

"I'd so hoped we could take a trip like this together. Can you imagine the fun we'd have? I admit—with great reluctance—that your honeymoon must take precedence. But I couldn't bear the thought of not seeing Turkey with you. Have you been to Ephesus yet?"

"No. Our plans have been more than a little derailed." It did not take long to update her on the situation, and she responded exactly as I expected.

"For once I'm around in time for the action," she said, choosing a cigar from the box Colin had brought with us. "What can I do to help?"

"There is something I've been avoiding because I didn't want to face it alone. Could you stand for a bit of sightseeing? It will require waiting to smoke, but not for long."

A little more than an hour later, Margaret stood, gasping, as we entered what had been an imperial reception room in the harem at Topkapı. The enormous chamber in the sixteenth-century building was styled in rococo, with gilded scrollwork and Venetian mirrors. Not an inch of space was left undecorated.

"Amazing," Margaret said, her eyes drawn to the high ceiling and heavy crystal chandelier. The bottom twenty feet or so of the walls were covered with tiles made in Delft—no doubt a gift to some earlier sultan—set in patterns of tall rectangles a yard wide, narrow strips of dark red wall highlighted with delicate gilding between them. A wider strip of this same red and gilt ran above and below the ceramic, and on top of that was another band of tiles, these decidedly Ottoman, covered in Arabic script. The rest of the wall to the domed ceiling was plaster, painted with scrolls and intricate designs reminiscent of those found on the most stunning Turkish carpets, done in pale blue, pink, and two shades of sage green, all with accents of gold. Against one wall a long divan for the sultan sat empty beneath a gilt canopy supported by marble columns. Next to this was a fountain—necessary in any room where one wanted to frustrate eavesdroppers.

Margaret sighed. "It's the most wonderfully exotic thing I've ever seen. Everything you'd want a sultan's palace to be. I'm awestruck."

Bezime was seated, smoking, on a couch tucked under the large balcony that ran the length of the wall perpendicular to the canopied sofa for the sultan. She motioned for us to join her, and I introduced my friend. "The space above you was where the women of the harem would stand to watch the sultan. I am sitting in the valide sultan's spot, where favorite concubines were also allowed."

Ornate arches supporting the gallery above separated the area from the rest of the room, and it was raised a step higher than everything except the sultan's settee. Leaded-glass windows lined the wall behind the sofas, and a brazier stood in the center of the stone floor in front of them, bringing the section a surprisingly cozy feel given the enormity of its surroundings.

"Why would anyone abandon such a place?" Margaret asked.

"The empire needs to earn the appreciation of the West," Bezime said. "And this place is not the sort of luxury expected by Europeans."

"Then they're fools," my friend said.

"I've never had much fondness for them."

"Yet you are kind to us," Margaret said.

"You're fortunate. My temper regarding the subject was put in check many years ago when the empress Eugénie was brought to me. I was valide then and greeted her with a slap. I did not want foreigners in the seraglio."

"I'm relieved not to have received such a welcome myself," I said.

"You, Emily, are different. You do not understand our world, but neither do you fit well in your own."

Margaret shot me a glance, and I knew she could read the flash of anger in my eyes. "Is it true the sultan wears shoes with silver soles?"

Bezime laughed. "Not anymore. In the old days, yes, so the concubines would hear him coming. They were not allowed to face him without permission."

"And the poor girls up in the gallery?" Margaret motioned above us.

"Most of them would never have got any closer than that to him." She looked at Margaret, studying her. "You like to smoke."

"Yes," Margaret said. "How did you know?"

"I know many things." She passed her pipe to my friend and then looked at me, her face revealing no emotion. "Emily is upset with me because I tell her hard truths."

"We're not here to discuss that," I said. I'd not told Margaret of my earlier conversation with Bezime and had no interest in revisiting it at the moment. "I'm curious about Jemal. Why was he sent back to Yıldız?"

"I arranged it," she said. "It suits my needs."

"Is he spying for you?"

She laughed. "Perhaps."

"You have the power to send him on such an errand?"

"I am not so far out of favor with the sultan."

"Jemal was sent here to get him away from Ceyden. As that's no longer a concern, why wouldn't the sultan summon him back?" I asked.

"If Jemal had caused the sultan concern, he would have removed him from his position altogether. You doubt that I have any remaining power?"

I pushed a hand against my forehead. I wanted to trust Bezime; I'd liked her from the moment I met her. It was unfair of me to change my assessment simply because she'd made wild and certainly inaccurate predictions about my personal situation. Inaccurate. They had to be inaccurate, but the burning sensation overwhelming all my nerves suggested an appalling lack of faith in my silent protests.

"You question me because you do not like other things I've told you," she said.

"I don't want to discuss that now. I—"

"You wish to avoid the subject because you have not told your friend. A foolish decision, as she will offer you much comfort in the dark hours. But we both know you are not here to speak about a eunuch guard."

"What are you talking about?" Margaret asked.

"Please. Another time," I said. "Right now I want to know about Jemal. Does this reassignment have something to do with the bowstring? Is he trying to figure out who is threatening you?"

"Strange things are happening at Yıldız. I need to know if my interests are being protected."

"Ceyden was one of your interests, was she not?" I asked. Bezime nodded. "And she was killed. What is going on? You know more than you're telling me."

"My intentions with Ceyden went no further than attempting to help her catch the sultan's eye. Not the sort of thing people are murdered over in ordinary times. Something else is going on."

"A power struggle in the harem?"

"Not precisely. A struggle that goes further than that. Do not forget the sultan's brother, Murat, is still alive. It is entirely possible that he would like to return to the throne he was forced to abandon."

"And have only a low-level concubine help him?"

"She would not be noticed by anyone; no one would give her a second look or thought. She might have been spying, she might have been sent to do something far worse."

"Assassinate the sultan?" Margaret asked.

Bezime shrugged. "It is possible."

"Possible, perhaps," I said. "But have you any proof she was involved in such a scheme?"

"Suffice it to say, I know there are some at Çırağan who think the harem is the way to power."

"No, Bezime, that does not suffice. Besides, Murat would have to be crazy not to find someone in a better position."

"My dear child, Murat *is* crazy. Why do you think he was forced from the throne?"

"So a crazy man sends an incompetent girl to assassinate a sultan? If this is harem intrigue, I'm painfully disappointed," I said.

"Make no mistake. She was not incompetent. Remember that I helped raise her. She was skilled in many arts, deception one of them."

"So what is Jemal doing at Yıldız?" I asked again.

"Watching, listening. Deciding whether I am in danger. The bowstring was a strong message. If Ceyden was involved with Murat—and I don't know that she was—her connection to me could prove problematic. The easiest way to deal with problems is to eliminate them."

"You're so very confident about my own future. Can you not see yours?" I asked.

"I cannot." Bezime met my eyes. "And it is why I have befriended you, Emily. I know that you, too, have the gift of prophecy."

"She is absolutely marvelous," Margaret said, pacing in front of Colin, puffing on a cigar, glee filling every bit of her voice. "I've never seen anything so wonderful in my life. Is everyone in the harem like this? I'm nearly ready to sell myself to the sultan."

"Yıldız is a different world from Topkapı," I said. "If you're going to be a concubine, you want it to be the height of the empire, when you've risen to power over thousands of others and are the political ally and most trusted confidante of the sultan—"

"Who never wears his silver-soled shoes when he thinks he might see you, because he doesn't want to scare you off."

"Stop." Colin, amusement in his eyes, his cheeks tight with repressed laughter, clipped the end of a cigar. "You're both diverting in ways I could never have imagined, but we must maintain some sense of focus here. Bezime essentially lives in exile. She's got no power. The sultan did not give her a position in his harem, remember? She does not get to decide which eunuchs are sent to his palace."

"She's very clever," I said. "I agree she's without direct power, but she may have orchestrated the situation."

"How? Abdül Hamit was very clear with me on this point: Bezime has no contact with anyone who, for lack of a better word, *matters* in his court. She may seem an impressive figure—and I've no doubt she once was one. But that day has long since passed."

"So she's scorned," I said. "And hell hath no—"

"Yes, yes, fury, I know my Shakespeare. But you cannot plan assassinations, train spies, or have them assigned if you've no power."

"You can, however, take advantage of circumstances. Not having been responsible for getting Jemal to Yıldız doesn't preclude her from using him as a spy."

"True enough," Colin said.

"What do you make of her claims about Murat?" Margaret asked.

"I've spent loads of time combing through everything at Çırağan," he said. "There's an unquestionable mood of discontent in the palace, but it does not come from him or his harem. There are a handful of men who, if Murat were still sultan, would undoubtedly be his aides—his former vizier, for one. They're not happy."

"Would they enlist the aid of one of the sultan's concubines?" I asked.

"In theory, they might," he said, lighting a cigar and handing it to me.

"But do you think Ceyden?" The tobacco tasted rich, all nuts and moss and spice and oak.

"It would surprise me," he said.

Margaret paced. "Why would he choose Ceyden? How would anyone at Çırağan know of her existence?"

"They wouldn't," I said. "Someone with status would have had to refer her."

"Bezime could have done that," Colin said. "Still, I'm not sure. I'm afraid she's trying to manipulate you."

"I would think that she, more than anyone we've spoken to in either palace, would want to know the truth about Ceyden's death," I said. "She's the only person who seems to have felt anything approaching real affection for her."

"Is there a solution to the crime that would harm her?" Colin asked. "Is she protecting someone?"

I swirled the whiskey in my glass. "I don't know. But your idea that she's manipulating us is striking. What if it's for the most simple of reasons?" I asked. "What if it's nothing more than her trying to seem once again important?"

"An excellent hypothesis, my dear," Colin said. "Keep it near you as you continue your work. You'll find that people are often not complicated in the least."

Every inch of my body hummed; never had I known such delight. To be sitting with the man I loved, engaged in a lively discussion of our work—work in which he considered me an equal—my dear friend at my side. There are moments when all in life seems right and good.

Meg stepped into the room and announced Sir Richard, who followed close behind her. He looked a mess, fatigue darkening the already deep circles under his eyes. Margaret leapt up and poured him a whiskey after Colin had introduced her and she'd offered him her condolences for Ceyden.

"I have heard so much about you," she said, handing him the glass. "Your life fascinates me. What stories of adventure you must have."

"Adventures that didn't turn out well in the end," he said.

"I understand, and I'm terribly sorry about that," Margaret said.

"But do you ever consider the good parts now that the bad can't be changed?"

Sir Richard froze, looking at her, and I all but cringed for him, wishing there were something I could do to change the subject, reverse her words, anything. But my angst was unnecessary. He smiled.

"A wise question, young lady," he said, his words almost slurred. I wondered if he'd been drinking before he came to us. "And I'm afraid my answer is no, although it shouldn't be. I thank you for pointing out this shortcoming."

"You can't stay forever mired in sadness," Margaret said. "At some point, you have to let yourself live again."

"It seems I'm not doing a particularly good job of that."

"Has something happened?" Colin asked. "Forgive me. You don't look well."

Sir Richard thanked him, shot a questioning look in Margaret's direction. She stood up at once.

"Will you excuse me?" she asked. "I've been away far too long. Miss Evans will be beside herself with worry, and if I don't hurry, I won't have time to dress for dinner. Lovely to meet you, Sir Richard. I do hope that when I see you next, you'll share a story about your travels."

And she was off, winking at me on her way out of the room.

"There's been another incident with papers from the embassy," Sir Richard said, rubbing his forehead. "More missing. Papers that were in my charge."

"Sensitive in nature?" Colin asked.

"More so than those taken on the train, but nothing of vital import."

"From where were they stolen?" I asked. "Your home or the embassy itself?"

"That's the odd part—I'm convinced beyond all doubt that I had not removed them from my offices in the embassy. But they're gone, and there's been no security breach."

"Who can access your offices?" Colin asked.

"The door's never locked. What's awkward now is that this, being the second time it's happened, is placing me in a bit of jeopardy. I was reprimanded rather severely and fear that I may lose my position."

"Does the ambassador think you are stealing documents?" Colin asked. "Is he accusing you of espionage?"

"Nothing so iniquitous. He's afraid I've grown old and forgetful and incompetent. I admit that I have not been entirely myself of late—"

"Which is completely understandable in your circumstances. You're dealing with enormous stresses," I said. His eyes were clouded, his face gray.

"But Sir William took no disciplinarian action?" Concern crinkled around Colin's eyes.

"Not officially. But as ambassador he will not tolerate another mishap."

"Who would be doing this to you?" I asked.

"I very much appreciate, Lady Emily," he said, "the fact that you do not question my mental stability."

"Of course I don't." I didn't, did I? He'd been through a terrible tragedy; no one could recover from that immediately. "Have you any suspects?"

"Sadly, no."

"Are you quite certain there were no other problems at the embassy? No one else is missing anything?" Colin asked.

"No. I made loud and outraged demands that everything be gone over—I was all but accused of mania for having reacted so severely. A search was conducted, and nothing was out of place."

"To what did the papers pertain?"

"Employment issues. Notices of staff reassignment, that sort of thing, which often include comments on performance. London had shipped an enormous batch to us some months back, mainly addenda to files, records of things going far back, to be added to what we have. It was a terrible backlog. Should have all been forwarded ages ago. Poor Sutcliffe was swamped organizing it all."

"Had anyone received bad reviews?" I asked.

"Not bad enough to merit stealing the notes. And doing so wouldn't accomplish anything regardless—it's not as if it would change the person's position. The authors of the reports wouldn't have altered their opinions."

"True enough," Colin said. "Although if they were old, it might be the sort of thing no one would miss if they were to disappear."

"I go back to my original thought when you were robbed on the train," I said. "Someone is deliberately targeting you, and I'm convinced that all of these events—the robberies, the attacks on Benjamin, and Ceyden's murder—are connected."

"We can't discount the possibility." Colin stood up and crossed his arms. "There's a party tonight, given by the wife of the consul. We'd not planned to attend, but I think it would be beneficial to do so. I'd like to talk to your colleagues away from their offices."

"I am deeply indebted to you for your assistance," Sir Richard said, closing his eyes. "I don't know how I shall ever repay you."

"Seeing you through all this to a point where you can, as Margaret said, remember the good will be payment enough," I said.

"Just promise me, Lady Emily, that you especially will be careful. I couldn't live with myself if I brought harm, even indirectly, to another person."

Colin had sent a message to the consul's wife—she replied at once, saying she was delighted we could join her. Instead of dinner and dancing, she'd decided to stage a séance. And so, after a light supper (during which Colin expertly gathered as much information as possible about the trouble at the embassy), we retired to her sitting room, where a medium called Madame Skorlosky, a Russian, sat at a special table she'd brought for the occasion. She called us to join her, and we each took a seat, mine between Mr. Sutcliffe and Sir William.

The ambassador leaned over to me. "Do you believe in this rot, Lady Emily?"

"I've never given it serious consideration," I said. "I will confess to being fascinated, however." Mr. Sutcliffe tugged at his collar, shifting in his chair. "What about you, Mr. Sutcliffe? Have you great hopes for this experience?"

"I do, actually. I've not attended a séance before, but have wanted to for years."

Colin, sitting across the table, was watching me the way he did when I first met him, his eyes never leaving mine. I smiled at him, feeling myself blush, wishing we were home. He did not return the smile, only stared.

Madame Skorlosky rose from her chair. "We will now begin. I ask that you all close your eyes and focus, sending from your thoughts any hints of doubt or confusion. The spirits will be with us tonight. I can sense them already." I could hear her blowing out the candles on the table. Everyone was still and silent. "Place your hands flat on the table. Concentrate, and you may now open your eyes."

We all did, finding ourselves in a room now shrouded in darkness. Next to me, Mr. Sutcliffe was breathing hard. I could see nothing save a vague hint of white shirt trembling against black.

"Are you all right?" I whispered, leaning close to him.

"I—I will be fine," he said. I could hear him move his hands off the table. He wrapped his arms around himself.

"As we begin our journey—" Madame Skorlosky's rich tones filled the room with a pleasantly eerie chill, but my neighbor was anything but enchanted. All at once, he stood up, knocking over his chair and sending the table rocking.

"I can't do this," he said, his voice cracking. "Please, someone strike a lamp."

There was a general commotion as he grew more and more upset, pleading for light. He was crashing about now, unable to see, slamming into furniture. I cringed at the sound of shattering porcelain, remembering a lovely vase that had graced an end table at the far side of the room. A match flashed, and Colin lit first the candles on the table and then a lamp, which he carried with him as he went for our friend, who had retreated to a corner, where he was crouched, trembling uncontrollably.

The party broke up soon thereafter, an uneasy feeling settling over the room. Colin took Mr. Sutcliffe home, then returned for me, finding those of us left drinking tea and barely talking. The scene had been a disturbing one.

"He's embarrassed more than you can imagine," he told me as we set off for our own house. "His son, who died of typhoid when he was four, had always been afraid of the dark. The fever caused some sort of hallucination, and he thought, as he lay dying, that no one would bring even a candle to him. Sutcliffe lit twelve lamps, but the boy couldn't see any of them. He was hysterical—crying and thrashing about—and remained so until his last breath. Ever since then, Sutcliffe has faced nothing but demons of his own in the dark."

"I can't imagine anything more dreadful. To be unable to soothe his own child at such a moment."

"He'd come tonight hoping to contact his family and didn't realize the room would be dark."

"Such awful pain," I said. "Poor man. How does one come to terms with such torment?"

"I don't know that it's possible. It . . . forgive me, Emily, if I sound harsh. But it suggests a weakness of the mind. A degree of instability."

"He's suffered an incalculable tragedy."

"And now must deal with the rest of his life. The dead are gone." We sat in silence as the carriage rattled towards the docks. Eventually, he took my hand. "I have a confession. I'm glad the séance did not go on."

"Why?" I asked. "I knew something was bothering you. You were looking at me in a way I haven't seen you do in years."

His head was lowered, but his eyes lifted up to mine. "I thought you might want to try to speak to Philip."

"Oh, Colin." I pulled his head onto my lap, combed through his hair with my fingers. "Whatever would make you—"

"I know you must still think of him."

"Yes, but not like that."

"I know," he said. "It's foolish."

I bent over and kissed his head. "Not at all," I said. "We've reconciled with each other's pasts, but can't expect that they won't occasionally creep up on us. But you must remember, all that matters now is they served to bring us together."

We slept far later than we had planned the following morning, scrambling to prepare to leave for the archaeological site to which Benjamin was attached, barely having time for breakfast.

"I do think it's a pity the site's not farther away," I said as we rode, side by side, on horses Colin had arranged for us. "I should have liked for us to spend the night in a tent."

"If you recall, our original plans for this excursion included you waiting in town until I determined whether the site was safe."

"Which you did last night. I saw the reply to your wire sitting on the breakfast table."

"Touché," he said. "According to the director of the excavations, there's been no trouble for some time."

"You'll make me positively lackadaisical if you insist on protecting me without my even knowing it," I said.

"But you do know it. You're clever enough that there's no need to alert you. You'll find out on your own." He pointed to a dot on the horizon. "It's there. Only about fifteen minutes more. Why don't you tell me what else you've learned from Ceyden's book of poetry?"

"Reason has no way to say / its love. Only love opens / that secret. / If you want / to be more alive, love / is the truest health."

He smiled. "I meant her marginalia."

"I'm making my way through it. Forgive me the occasional distraction."

He stopped, and I did the same so he could lean over and kiss me. The sun hung high above us, but the air was cool and sweet, the wind bending the fields of wildflowers that surrounded us. Red poppies and vibrant hyacinths and a host of others I did not recognize— yellows and whites and bright oranges. "You know I never doubt you," he said. "I'm sorry for what I said last night."

"No more of that," I said, kissing him back, flooded with a desire to never see anything change between us. "But I do fear we're losing our focus. Come." I urged my horse forward, quickly pulling away from him until he raced to catch me. At such a pace, we arrived at the site in short order, my excitement palpable. Although I'd seen innumerable ruins during my time in Greece, I'd not had the opportunity to visit an active dig and speak to the excavators. I hoped that once our business was finished, we would have time for an academic discussion.

Dr. Cartwright greeted us the moment we'd entered the camp, ushered us into chairs set up under a large square of canvas held up by tall poles, and offered us tea.

"We do manage to be civilized, even in the wilderness," he said.

"Thank you for agreeing to see us," Colin said. "I'm hoping you can tell us about the troubles Benjamin St. Clare has had here."

"Sporadically over the last several months he appeared to be the target of snipers—you see the hills around us." He motioned to the mounds, littered with boulders. "Shots would come from them, seemingly out of nowhere. They were never close enough to put him in harm's way. More of a threat than anything, I thought."

"And you've no idea why he would be singled out in such a manner?" I asked.

"Not in the least."

"Has anything been stolen from the site?" Colin asked.

"No. Nothing. We haven't suffered from that sort of misfortune here—largely because Roman baths are not the sort of sites where one is likely to find trinkets of value. Gold, of course, is what people want."

"So there's been no disruption of your work aside from the attempted attacks on Benjamin?" I asked.

"None at all. I can't begin to imagine how stressed the poor boy must be—and now with the terrible news about his sister. So sad."

"I understand that he was not here when the messenger came," I said. "How were you able to get in touch with him? It couldn't have been easy, but I'm sure he very much appreciated the effort."

"Much though I wish I could take credit, I'm afraid I can't," Dr. Cartwright said. "He'd left us the week before to pursue other interests. This life isn't for everyone."

"Left permanently?" I asked.

"Oh yes. I don't think the decision was an easy one, but I had the impression there was a lady involved and that he was planning to get married. Given his family history, I couldn't fault him for wanting to embark on a more traditional path."

"Have you heard from him since the murder?" Colin asked.

"No. We've all sent condolences to his father. I'm sure he'll respond when he's ready."

"Have you any idea as to the identity of his fiancée?" I asked. "We had no idea he was engaged."

"I think it was quite secret. Perhaps her family didn't approve. One never can tell with these situations. But I'm sorry, I've no idea who she was."

"Was he close to any of his colleagues?" Colin shielded his eyes from the sun that was making its way under the edge of the canvas roof.

"We're a collegial group, as you might expect given the proximity in which we live and work. You're certainly welcome to chat with any of the boys—I know they'll offer any assistance they can. If you'll come with me, I'll introduce you."

While the information we gleaned from Benjamin's compatriots did not complete our picture of the man, it was not without use. He was, evidently, a meticulous excavator with infinite patience who was never daunted by a task.

"I never saw him frustrated," a young Englishman fresh out of Oxford told us. "His dedication inspired me. He considered nothing impossible. Which is, I suppose, why it didn't much surprise me that he fell in love with an unattainable woman."

"Unattainable how?" I asked.

"He never elaborated. Held his private life close, didn't much talk about it, and when he did, never gave details."

"Do you think she was married?"

"I assumed, naturally, that she was attached to someone else."

"But he thought they were going to be together?" I asked.

"I can't say that with any conviction, Lady Emily," he said. "All I know—as did the rest of us—was that he'd decided to take a new direction in his life and returned to Constantinople."

"He told you he would be living in the city?"

"No, I believe it was only to be a stopover. He didn't intend to stay in Turkey."

"Did he speak of returning to England?" I asked.

"No. He never made mention of that. Said something about France once—some small village in the south. But I don't know that he intended to live there. Surely his father could fill you in on the details? I thought they'd patched things up after their latest falling-out."

"We weren't aware there had been a problem," Colin said.

"From what I've seen, there had always been problems. He was tense whenever his father visited, and they inevitably descended into argument."

"Do you know about what?" I asked.

"Benjamin's choice to work here. Not here specifically. I suppose it would have been the same at any site. Sir Richard would have preferred that his son pursue something more civilized—or simply live the life of a gentleman. He did everything he could to put him off archaeology. I know the attacks worried him, but on some level, I think Sir Richard welcomed them. Benjamin never got hurt, but they went a long way to shattering his nerves. And now he's moving on." He shrugged. "So you can well imagine it did not surprise me to see them getting along better after Benjamin had decided to leave."

"So his father knew of this plan?"

"I thought so. Sir Richard's last visit ended more cordially than usual. I drew what I thought to be the obvious conclusion."

After thanking him for his help, I turned to my husband. "What now?"

"You spend the rest of the day perusing the ruins," he said. "You've earned a little amusement. I'm going to the village. There's no doubt I'll find our sniper there."

He returned hours later, his face tanned, eyes flashing. I'd persuaded Dr. Cartwright to put me to work after he'd given me a thorough tour of the site and was bent over a pile of dirt, sifting it through a strainer. I stood to wave to Colin as he rode towards me.

"I don't think archaeology is for me," I said, placing the strainer on the ground. "I'm afraid I haven't the patience for it. Did you have any luck?"

"I did. I talked to a man whose son had been hired by an elderly Englishman to shoot at a man at Cartwright's dig but never hit him. He was emphatic about it, apparently—said if Benjamin was hurt, there'd be no pay."

"Did he give you any further description?"

"Only that he was tall."

"Like Sir Richard," I said with a sigh. "This is not moving in the direction I hoped it would."

12

The next morning, my husband set off for the embassy and I for the St. Clares' house in Pera, where I planned to speak with Benjamin. I knew all too well the pressures that could be exerted by parents with strong opinions and hoped that I might be able to get him to open up to me. Colin and I crossed the Bosphorus together, sitting side by side in our small boat, the European shore opening up in front of us.

"You're turning green," he said. "I'd no idea you were so prone to seasickness."

"It comes as a complete surprise to me as well."

"I wonder—" He stopped.

"What?"

"No, it's silly."

"I don't know that I like you stopping and starting with me," I said. "We've always spoken freely to each other, have we not?"

"Forgive me. Yes, of course we have. But there are some subjects best left alone by . . ." He laughed, shook his head. "I'm a man, after all, and that guarantees there will be certain topics with which I will never be entirely comfortable."

I knew, of course, with absolute precision to what he was referring, and I cursed my nausea, feeling ambivalent about the entire situation. I stared into his eyes, debating confessing to him my fears, my suspicions. Something dark tugged inside me, reminding me of what I stood to lose by telling him too soon. Not only my independence and his support of my work, but I would also risk disappointing him. Regardless of Bezime's ridiculous insistence of her certainty on the matter, I did not know if I was with child. Part of me longed to share with him my thoughts, but while he would be excited—that was clear by the way he was looking at me, eyes bright as he shot me a crooked smile—my own reaction would not be so simple. And that was bound to disappoint him.

"Heavens! I shall do all I can to avoid the topic for as long as possible," I said, removing my gaze from his and focusing on the horizon. "Did you ever think I would so easily fall prey to something as diabolically simple as seasickness?"

"I confess I didn't."

"Nor did I. I've decided it's a punishment for past hubris. I've been too confident in my abilities, physical and otherwise."

"So you're quite sure it's seasickness?"

I gave him my brightest smile, my heart breaking just a little at the deception. "Unless the cook has been poisoning my food," I said. "How are you feeling? Dizzy? Hint of queasiness hitting you?"

"I've never been better." He was watching me with an intensity that all but made me squirm.

"The food must be safe, then. And you are the picture of health, as always," I said. "Since you're so smug and superior, why don't you take a practice swim right now? We're halfway to the European shore. It would be good training for your inevitable fate."

He smiled. "You're glowing beneath the green, do you know that?"

Benjamin greeted me with warmth, and when I'd explained what I wished to discuss with him, he begged to leave the house, not trusting his father's servants to resist the temptation of eavesdropping on the prodigal son. Delighted at the prospect of seeing another part of the city, I agreed at once, asking only that we go on foot—the day was a glorious one, the air full of the green, floral scent of spring but not having lost entirely the final hint of winter's crispness. We made our way to the Golden Horn, crossed the Galata Bridge, and proceeded to the Spice Bazaar.

Fashioned from long, tan bricks and with three moderate-size domes on the roof, the bazaar was located across the street from the bridge, next to a mosque. The plaza in front of the holy building was so full of pigeons, I thought for a moment I was back in London at St. Paul's, at least until I began to listen to the voices around me. I'd been in the city long enough to distinguish Turkish from Arabic and heard two women speaking French as they passed me. What was most amazing, however, was the number of languages I could not recognize, and I wanted them to be all things exotic: Berber dialects, Farsi, or some ancient, nearly dead tongue.

We'd entered the bazaar through the front, central arch and then, ducking between stalls brimming with brightly colored spices— scarlet peppers, purple sumac, golden curry—Benjamin guided me through mazes of covered streets until we'd come out a side exit, climbed a stone staircase, and reached a small restaurant, where the owner stepped forward at once to greet us.

"Mr. St. Clare," he said, pulling out a seat for me at a tiny table tucked into the corner of his room. "You have been away too long."

Benjamin murmured something in reply, speaking Turkish and drawing a sigh from the other man, who shook his head and replied in kind before disappearing into the kitchen.

"Ali is an old friend upon whose sympathetic ear I have relied too many times," Benjamin said. "He did not know about Ceyden."

"I'm sorry. I know well how grief creeps up everywhere when you've lost someone you love."

"My father tells me you were widowed."

"Yes, only a few months after my first marriage."

"I offer all my condolences," he said. "Though they're far too belated to be either meaningful or welcome. I must confess that losing Ceyden again has torn me up in ways I wouldn't have dreamed possible."

"Were you close as children?"

"All we had was each other. We traveled so much, we never had time to make other friends, but didn't feel the need for them. We were perfectly suited playmates. Of course, as young as she was, she'd go along with nearly any game I invented."

"What happened after the attack?"

"I was shipped back to England, where I stayed with a less than congenial aunt. My father had lost his own parents years before, and there wasn't anyone else to care for me. I understand why he did it—it was crucial that he try to find Ceyden, and he insisted I be packed off to somewhere safe. But even after five years, when it was clear there was no hope, he didn't come for me. I went to school, and then to

Cambridge, and by the time I was done found I had little use for him."

"Did he ever go to England?"

"He visited me twice. Sent letters once a week and always gave me a generous allowance. We never had any arguments up to that point, but then we didn't have any real conversation, either."

"And he continued in diplomatic service?"

"Yes. I've tried to never fault him for any of this. He lost my mother in the most brutal way possible and failed to stop Ceyden's kidnappers. I can sympathize with his desire to keep me away from harm. But what little boy wouldn't prefer that his father provide the protection himself?"

"He loves you very much."

"Yes, I suppose he does in his way." He rolled his eyes and stared at the ceiling, pain etched in the clenched muscles of his jaw.

"Do you think he could have stopped the kidnappers?"

"Yes, I do. If he'd let me run for cover by myself—which I could easily have done—he would have been able to catch up to them."

"They might have killed him," I said.

"Or he might have been able to pull her out of her abductor's arms."

"Do you blame him?"

"Sometimes. It's not reasonable, I know. But then, neither is standing over one's mother's brutalized body."

"Useless words, but I'm so very sorry," I said.

"Thank you."

We sat in awkward silence until Ali appeared carrying a great, puffed circle of bread and three dishes, one of hummus, one of something that resembled eggplant, and one brimming with tiny chopped vegetables. "For you to start. I will bring you all the best things," he said. Two steps behind was a boy with tall glasses filled with red liquid.

"I feel as if we shouldn't eat given the conversation we've been having," I said.

"Not at all," he said. "These things happened so long ago, there's no freshness to the wounds. I've gone over it in my head countless times and blathered on about it to anyone who would listen for far too long. I've made my way to the position of accepting all of it."

"That's no small feat."

"I thank you." He poked at the dishes in front of us. "Now eat."

I spooned some from each platter onto my plate, ripped off a piece from the bread, and dipped it into the vegetable mixture. Sweet tomato and onions burst into my mouth, unable to compete with the surprising combination of mint and hot pepper. I sighed, delighted.

"You like it?" Benjamin asked.

"If you want to understate my undying love for this dish, yes," I said, taking another bite.

"Try the aubergine. It's spectacular."

I scooped a bit of the eggplant concoction from my plate. "Delicious," I said. "Not a hint of bitter."

"Ali's got the best food in Constantinople."

"I don't doubt you. Forgive me, but I must return to our previous topic."

"I understand."

"What was your father's reaction when you took up the pursuit of archaeology?"

"He was angry. In that quiet and infuriating way of his. No storming about or yelling from him. Just silent disapproval, all the while making it clear he would do anything he could to convince me to stop."

"You must have been horribly frustrated."

"He could not understand that I was doing something different from embarking on a life like the one he'd abandoned. I'm not dragging a family around with me, not recklessly off in search of adventure."

"You view him as reckless?"

"In hindsight, yes. And he'd be the first to agree. I understand and respect the choices he made for us all. What I can't forgive is his inability to accept the consequences of his decisions. He knew he was taking risks, but he wasn't prepared for them. And I'm the one still suffering for it."

"Dr. Cartwright tells me you've resolved to abandon archaeology."

"You've spoken to him?"

"My husband and I visited the site yesterday."

He shifted in his seat, pushing his hands down on his chair and twisting. "It was an agonizing decision, but I'm not walking away from the work, just the location. I'm going to try to find a position on the continent. Italy, perhaps. Working with Cartwright planted in me the urge to pursue things Roman."

"Italy? Lovely. Will you be in Rome?"

"I—I don't have any specific plans yet."

"What inspired this decision?"

"Nothing in particular. A touch of boredom, I suppose. The desire to travel. A wish to put some distance between myself and my father."

"Was anyone else planning to go with you?"

"Go with me?" His mouth hung open and he stared at me, then tossed his head and bit a piece of bread slathered with hummus. "Who on earth would go with me?" I could feel him tapping his foot beneath the table.

"I wouldn't have the slightest idea, of course. Don't fault me, though. I'm a lady and therefore more than a little prone to leaping without thought to romantic conclusions. I'd half hoped you'd tell me a story of forbidden love and a dramatic escape and a fresh start in a new land."

"What a ridiculous thing to say." His voice caught in his throat as he began, but in the end was full of nails. "Why would you think that?"

"I'm a newlywed, Benjamin, and as such bent on seeing those around me as happily matched as I am myself." I wanted to give him a chance to come clean on his own.

"An astonishing position."

"Not really," I said. "Particularly given your colleagues were all under the impression you were getting married."

He waited before answering, and I could see him summoning calm—blowing out a slow breath, dropping his shoulders, closing his eyes. "I—" He sighed. "I have not had good fortune in love."

"Does she live here?"

"More or less."

"Were you with her the night of the murder?"

"Of course not," he said. "I was at the dig."

"No, you weren't." I stopped for a moment, giving him what I hoped was a piercing look. "I've been to the dig, I've spoken to your colleagues. You had already left."

His body was agitated, foot tapping, his hands playing with the tines of his fork. "Yes, I had left. But I hadn't gone far. I wanted to spend a few days alone in the wilderness."

"Where did you sleep?"

"I had my tent."

"Did anyone see you? Can anyone vouch for you?"

"Unfortunately as I did not know my sister was being murdered, I had not arranged for a companion to provide an alibi. I needed some time to myself before setting off on the next part of my life. Particularly as it's one that seems so impossible."

"What is the impediment?" I asked. "Does your father not approve?"

"He certainly wouldn't, given the opportunity to pass judgment. But the lack of his blessing would only have been one in a series of stumbling blocks."

"Her parents?"

"They're dead."

"Is she attached to someone else? Married?"

"Not married, no," he said. "But there is . . . an understanding."

"Can she not break it off?" I asked. "Surely there is some way for you to be together, and she's doing her fiancé no service by staying where she knows she cannot be happy."

"We both know these situations are never so simple." He pulled off another piece of bread. "And at any rate, it's too late now."

"Too close to the wedding?"

"Too close to everything."

After finishing with Benjamin, I moved from one bazaar to another, meeting Colin in front of the Grand Bazaar—Kapalıçarşı—at a stone entrance reminiscent of a crusader's fortress. This was infinitely larger than the Spice Bazaar, but I couldn't see that from the outside. It was only after stepping through the pointed archway and into the labyrinthine maze of covered streets that I was overwhelmed. The number of stalls was astonishing, and the paths through them, some wide, some narrow, seemed endless. In every direction were stacks of cloth, shawls, dried fruits, lanterns—nearly anything imaginable.

"Sir Richard knew nothing of it?" I asked as we made our way through the dense crowd walking along the expansive main street, jewelry shops on either side of us, gold chains and bracelets all but spilling from their windows.

"He was entirely ignorant of his son's plans to leave the country," Colin said. "Will you forgive me for changing the subject, just for a moment? I have a gift for you."

"Of course," I said, smiling.

He pulled his hand out from behind his back to show me a bottle of port. "Not vintage, but all I could find here on short notice."

"Port! Oh, I do adore you!" The kiss I wanted to give him would have left no question of my burning affection for him, but the public location forced restraint. I squeezed his hand and smiled at him, leaving him in no doubt as to what would come later. "I had the most divine luncheon today with Benjamin. But don't let me distract you from either your purpose or your own story. Finish telling me about Sir Richard."

"Turkish delight?" A man holding a platter stepped in front of us as we turned a corner. "You try?" Colin took two pieces, handed one to me, and thanked the man before continuing on.

"You don't feel guilty not buying any?" I asked, biting into the powdery softness.

"No, it's not expected," he said. "The approach seems aggressive to us, but it's meant to suggest nothing but warm enthusiasm. And there are no hurt feelings if you don't buy. Here—let's go this way. I want to look at carpets."

"Did you learn anything interesting today?" I asked.

"Fished around at the embassy—as I said, it's clear Sir Richard had no idea his son was planning to go to France."

"Today he told me Italy."

"Italy? Which do you think is the lie?" he asked.

"I've no idea—he's clearly hiding something. You didn't tell Sir Richard his plans, did you?"

"No, though I hope you encouraged Benjamin to," he said.

"I'm afraid I didn't," I said. "I'm less than pleased with the entire situation, and don't see that Benjamin, who has suffered his entire life, should be forced to reveal something he'd prefer to keep private."

"You don't think his own father has the right to know where he plans to live?"

"No, I don't. Benjamin's a grown man—he deserves the freedom to make his own choices."

"I am well aware of your passion for freedom. But you must admit, Emily, it has to have its limits."

"I will give you that. Begrudgingly," I said. "But I can't agree in this particular incidence. This is a boy who witnessed terrible things as a child and was, for all practical purposes, abandoned by his father thereafter. If he now, as an adult, chooses to cut himself off from that relationship, I don't see there's any cause to interfere."

"What if the relationship could be healed?"

"For that to happen, both parties would have to desire it."

"Sometimes your lack of sentimentality scares me," he said. "Where is your maternal instinct?"

His eyes told me he was joking, but the words struck me like a slap. "Perhaps I don't have any." I stopped in front of a stall of brass goods—*hamam* bowls, goblets, candlesticks.

"That's an awful thing to say."

"What if it's true?" I picked up a bowl, pretending to examine it.

"My dear girl, it's not true. It's a silly thing to even discuss. You couldn't avoid maternal instinct if you tried. It's the most natural thing there is."

I raised an eyebrow. "Have you already forgotten my own dear mother?"

"She's fiercely devoted to you in her own way." He leaned forward, put a hand on my cheek, and took the bowl away from me, setting it down. "You're sensitive today."

"Yes, forgive me. I'm tired."

"I shan't tax you, then," he said. "Let's get to Hasan's and sit in his shop and find at least ten carpets you can't resist." Hasan was the best-known, most respected carpet dealer in the city, and had come highly recommended to us by no fewer than six people at the embassy.

"That sounds lovely," I said. "Did you learn anything else of use from Sir Richard?"

"He admitted the relationship has been strained for some time, but credits it to Benjamin's stubborn insistence on deliberately going against every bit of advice he's received from his father, right down to choosing Cambridge over Oxford."

"Do you have sympathy for this position?" I asked.

"To a certain degree. A man wants his son to respect him, of course. But only a fool gives advice expecting it to be taken. I know I caused my own father more sleepless nights than he perhaps deserved. But that's part of hammering out one's independence."

"Exactly," I said.

"Here—this way." He steered me through a passage into an older section of the bazaar. Here the ceilings were lower, supported by curved arches and pillars, and the smell of spicy lamb and onions drew crowds to a kebab stand.

"My day was somewhat more productive than yours sounds,"

I said. "In addition to having a spectacular meal, I did confirm that Benjamin is in love. He would not admit to planning an elopement, but there is a lady. An unavailable lady."

"Married?"

"No."

"Engaged?"

"What other option would there be?" I drew in a quick breath, shocked by the thought that had stolen into my head. "I have a theory."

"I am all eagerness to hear it," Colin said.

"He was in love with a concubine." We passed a shop full of glistening lamps, their shades—some round, some teardrop shaped—formed by mosaics of colored glass, sending candlelight dancing from them.

"When would he have had opportunity to even see one, let alone speak to her and fall in love with her?"

"They take excursions from the palace," I said.

"Carefully guarded excursions." He followed my eyes. "Do you want one of those lamps?"

"No, I'm just looking. It's possible, you know—he could have met a concubine."

"You're letting your love of the dramatic color your judgment. I like *Abduction from the Seraglio* as much as the next chap, but that's not what's going on here."

"What if Ceyden was killed because she was trying to escape? Her hoard of jewels could have financed quite an expedition."

"Are you suggesting that Benjamin had inadvertently fallen in love with his sister?"

"It's beyond terrible, I know. But consider it: She was a beautiful girl and reminded him not only of his childhood playmate, but also his mother. He saw her out, somewhere in town, and was instantly captivated."

"Do continue," Colin said. "You know how I enjoy your forays into fiction."

"He could have bribed someone—one of the guards—to tell him her name. And then to deliver messages. What more revered way is there to fall in love than by being seduced by beautifully written letters?"

"I've always been a great supporter of intelligent conversation, but far be it from me to question the value of a well-written missive."

"And then they began to plot their escape." I breathed in the most delicious scents—bergamot, ginger, vanilla—as we walked in front of a display of olive oil soaps. "An escape that would never happen because it was discovered, and Ceyden, rather than being allowed to stay alive and shame the sultan with her deviant thoughts, was silenced, to be forever forgotten. Benjamin's Byzantine cross, which he'd given her as a token of his affection, was torn from her neck as she struggled against her executioners."

"Deviant is a bit strong, don't you think?" he asked.

"But you agree that, in theory, it's possible?"

"We're not in a position to dismiss any reasonable hypothesis," he said.

"So you admit it's reasonable?"

"I may not be ready to own it as reasonable, but will admit to possible. It would explain the strange reaction we've had from both the sultan and the government. On the one hand, they want to cooperate with the British, but on the other, they'd very much prefer that this all go away."

"So they let us into the harem, assuming we'll find nothing."

"But you stumble upon the jewelry—"

I cleared my throat. "I did not stumble, my dear. I analyzed the situation and determined the best course of action."

"*Mais oui*," he said.

"*En français?*"

"There are times, Emily, when you so capture my imagination that I can only speak in French."

I reached for his hand, brought it to my lips, and kissed his thumb. "Once Perestu saw that I was close to discovering too much, she notified the sultan and we were summarily denied all further access to the harem."

"This is the part, my dear, where things begin to fall apart. Perestu's countenance changed when she realized a piece of her own jewelry was in Ceyden's cache. If your speculations are correct, shouldn't that reaction have come the instant you found anything sewn into the gown?"

"Not necessarily," I said. "There must be something about that particular piece. Perhaps it's a clue of even more significance than we'd previously thought."

"How so?"

"It may be the object that links Perestu directly to the murder."

"Or to Murat's discontented vizier," he said. "Perhaps she's the link between his discontented associates and the harem."

"So you believe there is a link?" I asked.

"I cannot deny it. Where did Benjamin tell you he was the night of the murder?" I recounted for him our conversation, and Colin shook his head. "I'd hoped he'd have a firm alibi."

"Do you think he needs it?"

"Let's hope not."

A distinguished-looking man stepped out of the shop in front of us. He bowed.

"Mr. Hargreaves, the ambassador told me to expect you. I am Hasan. Welcome. Please, come in. You will have tea?"

Six hours later, we emerged. Colin was wrong about my finding ten carpets. I was not able to narrow my selections below thirteen.

11 April 1892
Darnley House, Kent

My darling Emily,

I must confess that your letter left me full of melancholy. I do so wish you and Colin might have had at least a few weeks to yourself without any work. I know how you adore it, but I've found myself looking back on my own wedding trip with such fond memories of perfect bliss that I want you to have it as well, my dear. Things change so much as a marriage progresses, and although I've more happiness than I deserve, I still can't help wishing, sometimes, to go back to those early days.

These sentiments are no doubt brought on by my current condition. The doctor has confined me to my bed—I'm told it's a mere precaution because of some pains I've suffered in the past week and that I ought not be alarmed. It is not as if I'd been accustomed to gallivanting about—your mother would never allow that. But even under her strict regimens I was able to sit outside every day, and I find I miss the fresh air keenly.

To be quite honest, I'm terrified. The doctor says almost nothing to me, but I can hear the whispers in the hall. Your mother is more worried than I've ever seen her, and I feel as if everyone knows some dreadful secret about my condition but won't tell me. Darling Robert is on his way here, news that at once delights and distresses me. I can think of nothing better than having him beside me, but he can only be coming because he is aware of how serious things have become. Do you think he will warn me of the horrors I'm to face? If I'm truly ill, I'd rather know than be left in ignorance.

They're all being so kind and indulgent, it's as if they hope to make my last days pleasant ones. I'm not supposed to know, but I overheard talk of own dear parents being sent for. Can you fathom the gravity of the situation if they're being summoned from India?

Do please send me more letters—reassure me, Emily. Because although everyone tells me not to worry, I know you of all my friends can best understand the fear I'm hiding. I miss you very much and wish desperately you weren't so far away.

I am, your most devoted friend,

Ivy

13

"I wish we weren't so far from her," I said, pacing in front of Colin, waving Ivy's letter as I walked the terrace where we'd been having breakfast, having to force myself to breathe, fear creeping through my skin. "She needs me."

"I will contact Robert," Colin said. "Find out what he knows. If things are serious enough, we can, of course, return home at once."

I pressed my hands to my temples. "But what of Ceyden?"

"The dead can wait," he said, wrapping his arms around me. "We can come back after the child is born." He rested his cheek against mine. "I've never seen you upset like this. You're trembling. Try to put your mind at ease. The most likely scenario is that Robert's response shall relieve all your worries."

"I want more than anything to believe that," I said, having little faith it would happen. Ivy was the least alarmist person I'd ever known. Writing such a letter—one that so directly addressed both her condition and her fears—would have mortified her. If anything, she would let me believe things were not so dire as they truly were.

"I don't think I could survive if anything happened to her. She's been beside me my whole life."

"You would. I'd make you."

"I'm not sure I'd thank you for it."

"You forget how persuasive I can be." He put his arms around me, but I stiffened instead of relaxing against him. "We must distract you. Worry accomplishes nothing."

"I don't want idle distraction," I said. "Let's focus on our work."

He pulled back from me, searched my face, his lips closed but pulled in a firm smile. "You're quite certain?"

"Beyond doubt. I don't know any other way."

"Come with me to the embassy, then. The ambassador has asked to see me."

Even before we'd reached the entrance to the British embassy in Pera, it was evident that we'd stumbled onto a scene. The door swung open as we approached, and Sir Richard stalked out, a feverish glint in his eyes.

"This is an outrage!" Sir Richard turned to face Sir William, the ambassador, staggering as if he might keel over. "I've done nothing but serve my country and will not tolerate being treated like a common criminal."

"Richard, you know that shall never happen," Sir William said. "No one is suggesting such a thing. But you must understand that given the circumstances, I cannot allow you to remain in your position. Now, when you are exonerated—"

"Outrageous," Sir Richard said, slurring the word and interrupting the ambassador. "And I have nothing further to say." He continued his unsteady march in the direction of the gates, barely pausing to raise his hat to me.

"What on earth?" I asked, grabbing his arm and stopping him. "More missing papers?"

"Yes, but it's gone beyond that," Sir Richard said.

"What happened?" Colin asked, his firm voice the sort that would always elicit a reply.

"I'm sure William would be all too happy to fill you in. My opinion seems to have been rendered irrelevant."

"I want to hear your side, not his," Colin said.

Sir Richard sighed and pressed his hands together. "When I arrived for work this morning, he was waiting in my office. Two of my colleagues' desks were ransacked overnight, and I was the last person to leave. There were six files stolen. One of them was found in my safe."

"And the other five?" I asked.

"Were sitting on a table in the library at my house," Sir Richard said.

"How were they discovered?" Colin frowned.

"I had already looked in the safe," Sir William said. "And asked to be allowed to search Richard's home."

"As I knew I'd taken nothing, I of course gave him permission."

"It's not that I don't believe you, Richard." Bags hung heavy under the ambassador's eyes. "But you must understand that I cannot allow you to continue in your position until we've sorted all this out. I've a responsibility—"

"I have spent nearly all my life in the Consular and Colonial Service. To be forced out now, under such circumstances, is unconscionable."

"It's only temporary," the ambassador said. "You'll be back in no time."

"If you were confident of that, you wouldn't be pushing me out at all." He looked at me. "Will you excuse me, Lady Emily? I'd like very much to go home." He staggered off the embassy grounds, nearly tripping over his own feet.

"What more is there to this, William?" Colin.

"I spoke to his son, who confirmed there was a stack of files on his desk last night. I don't suspect Richard's being intentionally deceitful—but he's been so careless of late. Not paying attention to the details of his job. I've had to rebuke him several times, and I'm afraid this was simply a botched effort to make everyone else around him look incompetent—to prove he's not the only one misplacing things."

"So his position is in peril?" I asked.

"Honestly, Lady Emily, I think he's coming unhinged with grief. He hardly acts like himself anymore. I'm trying to give him time to recover. If he does, and regains his competence, I'd happily have him back. Until then, however, I can't have on my staff a gentleman in his condition. It appears he's even begun drinking in excess. Sutcliffe found him asleep at his desk earlier in the week. Too much Scotch."

I'd been looking through the gate as he spoke and was distracted by the sight of Jemal striding along the street outside, his posture more impossibly erect than usual. Stunned to see him outside of the palace, I turned to Colin and murmured to him what I'd seen. He looked at me with serious eyes.

"Follow him," he said. "I'll take care of things here and meet you back at the *yalı*."

I excused myself at once and set off after him, barely able even to keep him in view. He was moving quickly and had a considerable head start. He passed through the streets of Pera, in front of fashionable shops and beautifully appointed homes, gradually making his way down a steep hill to the waters of the Golden Horn and the Galata Bridge. As I crossed in front of the train station, I remembered arriving with Colin, full of newlywed bliss and a different plan for these weeks than reality was prepared to offer us. Going uphill again, Jemal climbed towards Topkapı but did not enter the palace grounds, instead continuing in the direction of the spires in the distance.

I'd now closed enough ground between us that I could have called for his attention, and considered doing exactly that until I watched as he turned into the park between Aya Sofya and the Blue Mosque, headed directly for a bench on which sat Benjamin St. Clare. I stepped behind a palm tree (a pathetic hiding place, but my options were beyond limited) to observe them. Jemal did not sit, nor did Benjamin stand. I could not hear anything they said, but saw more than enough. The eunuch pulled out from his jacket a velvet bag that looked familiar, all the more so when he removed from it a bowstring.

I took in every detail I could. The velvet was similar to but not an exact match for that containing Bezime's bowstring. Hers had been a deep blue, this was black. Benjamin blanched as he looked at it and threw up his hands. Jemal bent over, pointing in the Englishman's face, his arm shaking. Shaking his head, Benjamin pushed away the bowstring and rose from the bench before running in the direction of the Bosphorus.

Jemal remained standing, stationary. I debated only for an instant before walking towards him. "What's going on?" I asked.

He did not look surprised to see me, did not miss a beat. "Nothing, Lady Emily."

"Why aren't you at the palace?"

"You think I'm a prisoner? You think I cannot leave?"

"No, of course, but I saw—forgive me, I saw your exchange with Mr. St. Clare. You have a bowstring. Why were you showing it to him?"

"Bezime showed it to you. Why should you care with whom I decide to share it?"

"Surely it's not the same one," I said.

"Of course it is." His sharp voice snapped.

"But why has the velvet changed?"

He leaned close to me. "Not everything is pertinent to your inquiries."

"But—"

"If you'll excuse me, I'm late for a funeral. A friend of my sister's died in childbirth. A sad story, as I'm sure you can well imagine. They'd been inseparable since they were girls. A terrible tragedy."

His eyes danced too much to lend any hint of veracity to his statement, and my stomach turned as I wondered why he would say such a thing to me. He might have overheard us speaking, or Bezime must have told him about my condition—*alleged* condition—but that he'd managed to hit upon my one real fear stunned me. Could he know something about Ivy? Did Bezime know something? It couldn't be possible, but the coincidence was too much to bear.

I claimed to put no stake in anything magical or psychic, but all at once I was gripped with terror. Jemal took his leave from me before I could speak again, and I found myself standing alone in the park, wrestling with unsettling emotions and trying to forget the hideous sound of my aunt's dying cries. Tears pooled in my eyes, and I looked to the sky, brilliant azure, hoping they would disappear. Instead, inevitably, they streamed down my face, stinging. Desperate to find some sort of comfort, I looked at the two magnificent buildings within my sight and headed for the Blue Mosque.

Aya Sofya might have proven a more reasonable choice. It had, after all, once been a Christian church. But so out of my element was I that I knew, absent of conscious thought, listening only to instinct, that solace would come only from something removed from all that I'd previously known. When I reached the courtyard of the imposing seventeenth-century building, constructed on the foundations of what had been the city's Byzantine palace, I pulled a scarf over my hat, draping the soft cloth around my neck, covering the bottom of my face and all of my hair.

Signs pointed me to the visitors' entrance, and I sat on a bench to slip off my shoes. My breath caught in my throat as I entered the building, my eyes drawn to the high, domed ceiling, a space that seemed to pull you up to heaven. I stood next to a thick column, bracing myself against it with a shaking arm before sinking to my knees and starting to pray.

First I turned to the words I'd known all my life. The prayers I had learned as a child, in whose familiarity I had always found comfort. But I knew it was not enough, so I leaned back on my heels and started again. I pleaded. Pleaded that she would be safe, that her child would bring her years of joy, that it would be the first of many, that she would know the pleasure of grandchildren. And then I began to bargain. I would never step beyond the careful bounds Colin placed on our work. I would better respect my mother. I would reach out to those less fortunate than I and give them whatever they needed. I would welcome eighteen children of my own. This thought stopped me, but only for a moment. My eyes closed, and I held my breath, trying to feel every bit of my body, searching for some sign of another life inside me, but feeling nothing. And that gave me the courage to offer my final bargain. Me instead. If one of us had to be taken, it couldn't be Ivy.

No sooner had the thought formed than I knew my offer was tainted, as it had been made only after finding no sign that I was with child, and I struggled at once for some way to prove my sincerity, to convince God or Allah or whoever was listening in this tiled sanctuary, watching me in the light filtering through stained glass, that my prayers were worthy of consideration. I was too numb and terrified for tears to form, and my mouth was dry, my lips beginning to chap. But I stayed on my knees, determined to stop what felt like inevitable tragedy.

When at last I rose, I felt no better than when I'd begun. The low-hanging iron chandeliers swam in front of me, their votive candles throwing scattered light over the soft carpet under my stocking feet. I watched the men on the other side of a wooden barrier designed to separate the tourists from the faithful. A few knelt, prostrating themselves, heads touching the ground, pointing in the direction of Mecca, across the Bosphorus, which was visible out tall windows that lined the far wall. Had they found peace here?

I turned away from them and faced a wooden screen blocking off a small area in the back of the mosque. A sign was pinned next to the entrance, identifying it as the section where women might pray. No view of the water here, no spectacular stained glass to inspire them, not even a location as good as that given to visitors. Without even momentary consideration, I went inside.

As it was not a designated prayer time, there were only a handful of women present, and I knelt next to them, not looking at their veiled faces, and began again my supplication. The sound of the murmured voices surrounding me, sweet and soft, isolated in this tiny space, stirred the tears that before would not come, and soon I, too, had my forehead on the carpet, my body shaking with sobs.

Almost at once, I felt a hand on my back, and I pulled myself up as the woman, not removing her hand, began to speak to me in Turkish.

"English," I said. "I'm so sorry."

She tried a language I did not recognize, and I shook my head. The other women around us had gathered close, whispering to one another, until one voice rose above the rest.

"I speak a very little English. Why you so sad?"

A figure in black pushed her way to the front of the group, motioning for us to be silent, then taking my hands in hers. "We go outside," she said. I followed her—as did the other five ladies—to the park behind the mosque, where she sat on a bench and patted the seat next to her, gesturing for me to take it.

"You are scared," she said. "You have a lover or husband who is in danger?"

"No." My voice was little more than a whisper.

"A sick parent?"

"No."

She studied me, her eyes lingering on every part of me. "You are with child and you fear for your safety." It was not a question.

"I—I don't know," I said. One of the women around us was speaking quietly in Turkish, the words too rapid for ordinary conversation. She was translating for the others.

"You are. But I do not think you weep for yourself."

This unnerved me in no small way. My stomach clenched, then felt as if it would fall all the way through me. "I do not. It is my dearest friend."

"We will pray for her, too." Again she took my hands in hers, pressing hard on them. "It is a danger that cannot be avoided," she said. "But we are all sisters in this and must always take care of one another. Even if you are not with her, you will watch over her and keep her safe."

And for just an instant, I believed her. I smiled—and they all smiled—and we laughed, all tension dissipating. They left me, waving as they went, and I had the peace I'd sought in the mosque. But it did not last. As suddenly as it had come, it flew away, and I knew that I would need more than fleeting moments of comfort to get me through these next weeks.

14

Although my calm did not last long, at least the edge was gone from my fear. Colin had beat me back to the *yalı* and was toying with chess problems on the terrace when I stepped off the boat. I flung myself onto the chair across from him.

"Are you well?" he asked, meeting my eyes. "You don't look like yourself. Have you been crying?"

"I'm tired, that's all," I said, not wanting to talk about my time in the mosque. "I followed Jemal all the way to the Blue Mosque." I briefed him on the situation.

"Another bowstring?"

"I don't believe it's the same one."

"Why would he show it to Benjamin?" Colin asked.

"I don't know. He looked angry, but I couldn't hear what he said."

"Bezime believes hers came from Yıldız, correct?" I nodded as he continued. "What if it's from Çırağan?"

"And Bezime and Jemal are connected with Murat's advisers?" I asked.

"It didn't take long to finish up at the embassy—there wasn't anything else to learn. So while you were following your man, I finished the interviews I needed to conduct at Çırağan. There was a suicide shortly after Ceyden's death—a servant who'd worked for Murat's vizier."

"Is there a connection?"

"Tenuous at best. But his wife insists that he'd been making frequent trips to Topkapı before he died. Said he'd been delivering letters and that Bezime gave him some concoction that was supposed to help their baby sleep. Apparently it cries ceaselessly—"

"Colic," I said.

"And you claim to have no maternal instinct."

"Hardly relevant at the moment," I said. "I shall ask Bezime about him as soon as possible. At the moment, though, I'm going to finish with Ceyden's notes."

I dashed inside to grab the volume of Rumi's poetry, my heart pounding. It infuriated me that the mere mention of a baby could send me into such a panic, and the state of my emotions being so wholly beyond control made me worry all the more about my condition or lack thereof. Gripping the book, I returned to the patio and forced myself to focus on the task of transcribing Ceyden's marginalia.

Colin watched me, paying better attention to my facial expressions than his chessboard.

"Emily—"

"Mmmm?" I didn't look up, afraid to meet his eyes.

"Is there something you're not telling me?"

"Of course not."

"You seem distracted."

"It's only worry about Ivy," I said, reaching for his hand and continuing my transcription. He sat quietly, still not touching his chess pieces, for some time before speaking again.

"Is there anything I can do?"

"Distract me."

"Finish your work and I promise I'll drive every bad thought out of your head."

I returned to Ceyden's notes and he to his chess, solving no fewer than four problems when at last I found what we needed.

"I think I've finally stumbled upon something of use." I read aloud to him. "'It was he there who saved all of us when the boat turned. Must not forget that, nor what he gave thereafter.'" I nearly tipped over my chair hopping out of it and shoved my transcription of the sentences into Colin's face, taking out half the chess pieces on the board in front of him.

"Your enthusiasm is admirable," he said. "But I'm at a loss to understand the meaning."

"Where would she have been in a boat that capsized?" I asked. "The Bosphorus, of course. We have to find out who rescued them."

"How do you know that she was in the boat? We've no idea—"

"Yes, you're quite right, I'm sure." I smiled. "Keep thinking that way. And so long as you do, you'd best give serious consideration to improving your swimming skills. I'm aeons ahead of you in figuring all this out." I gave him a firm kiss on the mouth, then spun around to go inside.

"Dare I ask where you are going?"

"Topkapı. It's time I get some answers from Bezime."

I collected Margaret on my way—or rather, out of my way—to Topkapı. I'd told her, as we walked across the Galata Bridge from Pera to the palace, all the things Bezime had predicted and confided in her my fears of childbirth. She'd proven once again a sympathetic friend and did all she could to reassure me that the former valide sultan's words did not merit serious consideration. She'd very nearly convinced me, even if only temporarily, and I much appreciated the vigor with which she argued against their truth. Bezime received us as soon as we'd arrived, meeting us in one of her pretty sitting rooms.

"Do you remember any such event?" I asked, sitting across from her as she passed her pipe to Margaret.

"Who could forget?" She stretched her elegant arms in front of her, golden bangles clinking together. "It led to a pretty scandal."

"Don't make me beg you to tell," I said.

"You are quick to forget your anger at me."

"I have not forgotten," I said. "But I've chosen to overlook it at the moment. This is too important."

"Denial and avoidance will not change your fate."

"I do wish you wouldn't provoke her," Margaret said. "I rather like it here and don't want to feel I can't come back and visit you."

"You will return, but not when I am here," Bezime said.

"You'll be restored to a position of greatness at Yıldız?" Margaret asked.

"No. I will simply be gone."

Frustration crept up my spine, and it was with great effort that I stopped myself from either making a biting remark or leaving the room. "When did this boat tip, and who was on board?"

"It was more than half a year ago, and I don't know all the passengers—it was concubines and their guards, on their way to an excursion in Stamboul. They may have been going to the Blue Mosque, I don't remember."

"Was Ceyden one of the party?" I asked.

"She was."

"Who rescued them?" Margaret asked.

"Most of the eunuchs panicked, and the captain of the boat proved useless. Two men saved everyone: Jemal, your old friend, and a foreigner who'd witnessed the accident from another boat. I do not know his name."

"I saw Jemal earlier today," I said. "He was carrying a bowstring. I watched him show it to Benjamin St. Clare."

"Ceyden's brother?"

"Yes." I studied her carefully, but her face remained like marble. "Do you know anything about this?"

"Jemal is back at Yıldız," she said. "I wouldn't have any idea what is being sent to him."

"But you said he's spying for you," I said. "Surely he would report having received such a thing."

"Perhaps he's not so loyal as I thought."

"Could he be the one sending them?" I asked.

She jerked to attention. "No. Never."

"You're certain?"

"There are things I know," she said.

"Could you please elaborate?" I asked.

"Not now." She looked in my eyes, cocked her head slightly, and touched my hand. "Your friend at home will suffer no harm."

Much though I hated to admit it—primarily because I felt that believing any one of Bezime's prophecies required giving credence to all of them—I felt lighter than I had in days when I recounted for Colin, on our way to a reception at the British embassy, my visit to Topkapı. Lights shone from all the windows of the building, and the sounds of a Mozart divertimento filtered through the grounds as we made our way to the entrance.

"You're confident she's talking about Ivy?" he asked.

"Of course she is. Who else would it be?"

"Perhaps I'm in terrible danger and don't even know it."

"Somehow I find that most unlikely."

"No hope that you'll rescue me?" he asked.

"As if you'd ever need it," I said. We stepped inside, and it was like being back in England—everyone dressed in the latest fashion, familiar accents, routine gossip everywhere I turned.

"I don't know when I've seen you look so tired," Colin said.

"Hardly a comment that will make me flush with confidence for the rest of the evening."

"Fatigued or not, you're still the most breathtaking beauty here—or anywhere—tonight."

"Is that meant to improve my mood?"

"Of course. But the motive does not detract from the sincerity of the statement."

"You're good." I squeezed his hand.

"And I rather like you tired. Makes it all the easier for us to duck out early and go home."

"If only we could go now," I said, the sentiment growing to an emphatic crescendo as he grazed the back of my neck with his hand. It was too late, however. We'd reached the front of the line, made our greetings, and joined the crush in the reception room. Before long, waiters in smart white dinner jackets had pressed into our hands tall flutes of champagne, and we were pleasantly engaged in exchanging stories of Constantinople with fellow travelers.

"You've seen so very little!" exclaimed the wife of a career diplomat as I sipped my wine. "But I suppose that's the sign of a happy honeymoon. You're spending all your time reading poetry to each other while gazing at the Bosphorus."

Would that our tourist deficiencies could be explained by such a reason. "The Blue Mosque is spectacular," I said. "And I have every intention of returning to Aya Sofya before the week's end. I don't think my previous visit did it justice."

"I have heard, Lady Emily, that you've been in the harem. Is it true?"

"It is," I said.

"Bad business, this murder. It's deplorable that you should be forced to embroil yourself in the investigation. I suppose there's no one else, and the poor girl—bless her half English soul—deserves justice. But what a burden for you!"

"I do what I must." I had no desire to embark on a philosophical discussion of my work.

My companion made no move to stay on the subject. She dropped her voice. "And have you been to the *hamam*?"

"I have."

She nodded. "I am most impressed."

"Have you visited one in your time here?"

"Never. But I have read Lady Mary Wortley Montagu's *Turkish Embassy Letters*. Fascinating!"

"I read it on the train. She's absolutely right about the baths."

"Hundreds of women?"

"Not nearly so many when I was there, but all, as she said, 'as exactly proportioned as ever any goddess was drawn.'"

"I quite liked the bit when she said the women thought her husband had locked her into her stays."

"Yes, that was amusing," I said. "You should go see for yourself. It's an extraordinary experience, and I'm told the Cağaloğu Hamam is the finest public bath in the city. It's not far from the Blue Mosque—I'd be happy to accompany you if you'd like."

"To be honest, Lady Emily, I think I'd be more comfortable were I safely anonymous. Don't think I could begin to relax if anyone I knew might see me."

"I understand completely. I must say it astonishes me that Ottoman society, which in so many ways is more oppressive than our own, is dotted with pockets of enlightenment."

"The Ottoman culture is more liberated than ours in many ways," she said.

"But the women are veiled."

"That they are. Yet I've never seen an instrument of oppression that gives such freedom—it hides their identities and enables them to move about the city visiting whomever they wish—if you understand my meaning." She glanced to both sides before continuing. "They can meet their lovers wherever they like."

"Is that so?" My face was hot with embarrassment. I was not yet quite so enlightened as I longed to be.

"I was at least as horrified as you when I first heard the stories. But now I'm rather used to it." She leaned in, close. "Makes me feel almost French. The Ottoman women keep control of their money after they're married, you know. And should they find themselves divorced, the husbands must continue to support them."

"Not at all what I would have expected," I said. I was about to inquire whether she'd befriended many Ottoman women during her time in the city when we were interrupted by the sound of an ugly altercation at the entrance to the room.

"I will not be accused!" Sir Richard, his hair wild, pushed his way towards the ambassador.

Sir William stepped forward. "No one is making charges. I merely wanted to know—"

"I will not have it!" He lunged as if to shove the other man but lost his footing and tripped. Colin, who had been standing several feet away from me, conversing with a group of gentlemen, reached him in a few swift strides and stopped his fall.

"What's going on here?" he asked as the partygoers all stood, silence spilling through the room.

"I think it would be best to take this conversation somewhere more private," Sir William said as Mr. Sutcliffe stepped from the on-lookers and made his way to Sir Richard.

"Surely public mortification is unnecessary," he said. "I will not see my friend humiliated."

Colin and Sir William stepped aside, speaking quietly before turning back to Sir Richard. "Come with me . . . ," Sir William began, but Sir Richard shoved him away and stormed through the crowd, his eyes bulging.

"This is unconscionable," he said. Mr. Sutcliffe, a beat behind, called after him. With a quick look at the ambassador, Colin caught up, took Sir Richard by the arms, and steered him to an antechamber off the hall. I excused myself to my companion and followed at once.

"What is going on?" I asked.

"We've had a rather strange incident," Mr. Sutcliffe said. "A young man from the hinterlands appeared here this morning asking to see Richard and demanding money."

"It's outrageous!" Sir Richard looked on the verge of apoplexy, veins pulsing, sweat building, his color darkening. "I've never seen that person before in my life."

"He claimed he was the one causing trouble at the archaeological site where Benjamin was employed," the ambassador said. "Wanted us to believe Richard had hired him to scare his son off the job."

I paused a moment too long before I spoke. "But—"

"I've lost even your confidence," Sir Richard said, looking at me through glazed eyes. Colin put a hand on the older man's shoulder, steadying him, and led him to a chair.

"I think we need a doctor," he said.

"No," Sir Richard said. "My health is of no concern."

"Your health ought to be of concern. Who will take care of your son if you become infirm?" Mr. Sutcliffe's face was smooth as marble. "No one can do for him the things his father would."

"You hear what they accuse me of," Sir Richard said.

"It might be a good idea to see a doctor—" Sir William was not allowed to finish.

"I said no." Sir Richard's voice, full of venom, shook as he spoke. "I'm not ill, I'm upset."

"Of course you are," I said. "Will someone get him a drink?"

"Do you understand the implications of this?" He leaned forward, speaking low. "That they would suggest, even for a second, that I would threaten the life of my own son?"

"Where is this man now? My husband can speak to him. I've no doubt there's some other explanation."

"He's disappeared," Mr. Sutcliffe said, coming close. "Made his accusations, and when it became clear he would get no money, he left. I doubt we'll see him again."

"It's not that I don't believe you, Richard," the ambassador said. "But you see, don't you, that I had to ask you questions?"

"I don't see anything decent in it," Sir Richard said.

I stepped to my husband's side and pulled him away from the group. "What do you think of this?" I asked.

"It proves nothing. If Richard had hired the man, he wouldn't have been so careless about paying him."

"You think it's someone else?"

"If it is, we're unlikely to find the man again. He's sure to have been paid off for doing this." He touched my arm. "I should think you'd be relieved at the possibility that Richard isn't responsible."

"I'd like to believe that. But he's so scattered of late, so upset. What if he did forget to pay the man?"

"Then it's best we forget it all," Colin said. "The man has enough troubles, and no one was hurt in this scheme."

"But what if he tries again?"

15

"Do you think," Colin asked, "there has ever been a more badly interrupted wedding trip in the history of matrimony than ours?" We were sitting on our terrace after a late breakfast, watching the water turn steel gray as clouds careened across the sky.

"It seems unlikely," I said, turning my attention to the chessboard in front of my husband. "How many moves to mate?"

"Two," he said, staring at me instead of his pieces. "I'd wager we've the worst luck ever."

"Try your bishop to b3," I said. "I'm of the opinion that you should refrain from entering into any more bets at present. You're already going to be swimming the Bosphorus."

"Funny you bring that up. I was just speaking to a seamstress yesterday about diaphanous robes for you."

"What a shame I won't get to wear them."

He knocked over black's king. "At least you're good at chess."

"I do appreciate the compliment," I said. "Anything new on Sir Richard this morning?"

"Nothing good, I'm afraid. He's being recalled to England."

"His behavior since we first met him has deteriorated more than I would have thought possible."

"He's under no insignificant amount of stress," Colin said, then shook his head. "We've gone over this too many times."

"I know. I keep hoping there's some other answer. Do you think he will ever recover?"

"I've no idea."

"And what about Benjamin?" I asked.

"Have you given any thought to the possibility that he was at Yıldız the night of the murder?"

"No. He didn't kill his sister."

"You believe his alibi?"

"I think there are many times a person would be hard-pressed to prove where he'd been at a given moment," I said.

"What do you think happened to Ceyden?"

"Are you inviting me to speculate?"

"I am." He smiled and set up the chess pieces again.

"I can't believe I'm going to say this, but I don't want to," I said. "I've no idea where we're headed at the moment. None of it fits yet."

"When has that ever stopped you?"

"Never until now."

"You, my dear, may just turn out to be a first-rate investigator."

"You mean I'm not one already?" I asked. "I'm crushed."

"Don't be. I've got something for you." He handed me a sheath of papers. "I've compiled all I have pertaining to the situation at Çırağan. It's not enormously compelling, but if you put it all to the sultan properly, you might convince him to allow you back into Yıldız. I've got our vizier friend to admit that he was corresponding with Bezime, though he insists it was for nothing more than medical advice."

"If that's so, why did his messenger commit suicide?" I asked, reading through the papers while listening to him. "I shall confront Bezime at once. I'm not pleased she's withheld this from me."

"I still believe Murat is blameless, so do not let the sultan believe otherwise."

"You don't want to take this to him yourself? It's your work."

"I trust you to handle it."

I leaned across the table and kissed him, then pulled away. "Thank you. I shall ask for an audience with him immediately," I said. "I would never have thought it possible to adore someone as much as I do you. Are you real?"

"I certainly hope so," he said. "If not, I'll have a terrible time appreciating you in your diaphanous robes."

Colin and I left the *yalı* together, later than we'd planned, neither of us willing to pass up what turned out to be an inspired interlude of not working. The mere thought of diaphanous robes has an extraordinary effect on gentlemen, but I think we may be forgiven the distraction. It was, after all, our honeymoon, and we weren't too dreadfully late. My husband was off to the embassy, and I to Topkapı to confront Bezime about her correspondent from Murat's camp. I was eager to see her reaction to Colin's evidence. We parted company when the boat dropped me at the palace dock, and I waved to him as he pulled away towards Pera, across the Golden Horn. When I arrived in Bezime's quarters, I was caught in a whirlwind of chaos. The sultan was coming to Topkapı, and the former valide was preparing to meet him.

"There's a matter of no small importance that we must discuss," I said, watching as a maid draped her in a gold satin dress woven with silver thread. A second servant came forward to fasten a heavy necklace of emeralds.

"This is not the time," she said.

"It concerns the sultan." I told her what Colin had learned at Çırağan, expecting her to show some measure of concern. Instead, she threw back her head and laughed.

"This is insignificant. Yes, this former vizier or whatever he was wanted my assistance, but I never offered him anything beyond a salve to treat an eye infection."

"Do you have his letters?"

"I burned them."

"Can you prove you never encouraged him?"

"I don't need to. He's accomplished nothing, and regardless, the sultan would never doubt me."

"Do you think, perhaps, you're overconfident?" I asked.

"Never. Come with me. You shall see."

"You should be careful about this, Bezime. The sultan is paranoid, by all accounts, and if he suspects, even for a moment, that you've been in contact with someone connected to Murat who—"

"I've done nothing wrong and hence have no need for fear."

"Did you tell him the former vizier is trying to hatch a plot?"

"He does not need to know everything when I know it."

I was not as sure of this as she appeared to be, and I struggled to follow her through the halls of the palace—she was walking so fast, I could barely keep up—passing through the harem gates and into a broad courtyard in which stood Arz Odası, the Audience Hall, where Abdül Hamit was to meet with a group of foreign diplomats. The building had been restored after a fire nearly forty years ago, but now its white walls gleamed. More than twenty columns supported the flat roof that stretched over a splendid porch on three sides. We climbed to the entrance, passed a fountain next to the door, and stepped inside.

The walls were simple, white and without ornamentation, but the ceiling was painted in gold and green. Most magnificent, however, was the enormous gold canopy over a throne that did not resemble a chair—it was more like an enormous couch, large enough and deep enough to be a bed. Hundreds of years earlier, those who entered this room hoped their words would please the sultan. If they didn't, his guards might execute them on the spot. Although this was no longer a concern, nerves twinged through me.

The sultan was standing in a corner of the room, talking to an adviser, his back to us. Bezime hardly paused before gliding over to him and prostrating herself before him.

"Stand up," he said, a half-smile on his face.

"My son," she said, standing, stretching her arms to embrace him. "You know I will always consider you that."

A terse nod sent the adviser scurrying away. "What are you scheming now?"

"When have you known me to scheme?"

"Is there a time when you're not scheming?"

Her laughter echoed through the chamber. "You are too hard on me. I've brought you a friend whom you have been persuaded to treat with disdain."

His eyes passed over me with no hint of interest. "Lady Emily is treated precisely as she deserves."

"I understand your feelings, Your Majesty," I said. "And I did not come here expecting to see you. I'd planned to set an appointment at Yıldız."

"But instead you interrupt my time with Bezime."

"It is urgent," Bezime said. "And concerns Murat."

He winced. "What is it?"

I paused, thinking Bezime would want to tell him, but she did not speak. "My husband is confident the former sultan is perfectly content with his situation. My husband has, however, confirmed that an associate of his is in the process of attempting to stir up trouble."

"How so?" He crossed his arms and peered at me, his eyes all intensity.

"I can give you this—it details all he's learned." I passed the papers to him, thankful I'd brought them to show Bezime. "But Bezime can tell you better than anyone his approach."

"Bezime?" His muscles tensed, and he spun on a heel, facing her and then taking a step closer. "You know something of this?"

"He'd written to me, prodding to test my loyalties." She shrugged. "I disregarded him."

"And you did not tell me?" His voice shook.

"It was irrelevant. I have read your chart. You have nothing to fear from him."

He slapped his hand against the wall next to her. "That is not a decision for you to make. I should have been informed at once."

"Forgive me. It is not always easy to reach you."

"It would be in this sort of situation."

"I need it to be all the time," she said.

"Please," I interrupted. "What's important now is that we ensure that no one else in the harem—here or at Yıldız—has received letters from him."

"It is all irrelevant," the sultan said. "He will be arrested at once."

I shuddered at the thought of the man's fate. "But you need to know if there's anyone else with whom you should be concerned."

"I could—" Bezime started, but the sultan stopped her at once.

"I will deal with you later," he said. "Leave us now." Without the slightest hint of worry on her face, she bowed and retreated from the room.

"I do apologize for springing all this on you," I said. "I had wanted to reach you through the proper channels."

He nodded. "I have, perhaps, acted in haste when banning you from Yıldız. I sometimes let others have too much influence on me."

"It was Perestu, wasn't it? She was upset at my finding the jewelry."

"I don't know what troubled her and don't suppose it matters now. Do you think I am safe?"

"I do, and my husband agrees. I hope you know that if we felt you were in the slightest danger, we would alert you at once." I remembered Bezime's story about them coming for her son and better understood the paranoia of the man standing before me. He was at once supremely powerful and grotesquely vulnerable.

"I expect nothing less."

"I do think, however, that if you allowed me to return to Yıldız, I could determine fairly quickly whether this man had contacted any of the concubines there."

"He will tell his captors after he's arrested."

"How can you believe him?"

"They are persuasive men and settle for nothing short of the truth."

I hoped I hadn't visibly cringed. "But Ceyden. What if there is a network of connections in the harem? What if he does resist your men? Is it wise to depend entirely on the confessions of one man?"

"No, Lady Emily, it is not." He stood, watching me, silent for so long that I started to fidget. "You may return to Yıldız, but only so long as it pleases me. And you are not to foster the traitorous wishes of any of the concubines. Roxelana will not leave the harem. Is that understood?"

"Yes, yes, of course."

"And if Perestu asks that you walk away from certain questions, you are to respect her."

I wanted to protest but bit back the words. I was in, and for now that would have to be enough.

"You look happier than I've seen you in I don't know how long," Margaret said. She was waiting for me on the terrace at the restaurant in Misseri's, where we planned to have tea with Colin. "Where have you been?"

"I, my dear, have triumphed," I said, recounting for her my conversation with the sultan.

"Wonderful! That's fantastic, Emily."

"I must admit to being rather pleased," I said, pouring milk into my tea. "I wonder what's keeping Colin? He should have been here by now."

"Do you think something's wrong?"

"No, he's undoubtedly detained questioning someone."

I didn't begin to worry until we'd finished our tea and talked the afternoon away. As the sun started to set, I grew anxious and went to the hotel desk to see if he'd sent a message that had somehow not made it up to us on the terrace. There was nothing, of course, but when I returned, Margaret had ordered for me a glass of port.

"Dare we speculate?" she asked.

"There's no point," I said. "Any fiction we write would undoubtedly be worse than reality. It will not serve to make us feel better."

It was not until the last shards of colored light were fading from the sky that my husband appeared. He squeezed my hand and kissed my cheek but did not sit down, his face all tense muscles, his mouth tight. I looked up at him, afraid, as he spoke.

"Bezime is dead."

16

We went to Topkapı at once. The trip across the Golden Horn was short, and the boat dropped us right at the palace docks. Inside the gates, all was quiet, as if nothing had happened, until we reached the entrance to the harem, where Colin handed Margaret and me off to Jemal. Colin could not accompany us but would interview the palace guards, search the outer courtyards, question servants and anyone who might have seen or heard something unusual.

"I didn't expect to see you here," I said to Jemal, numbness temporarily replaced with surprise. "Has your assignment been changed again?"

"Not permanently," he said. "A brief mission only."

I thought I might crawl out of my skin. "Did you kill her?"

"Don't be absurd. What century do you think it is?"

"I heard the sultan say he would deal with her later."

"And now he'll never have the chance. More's the pity."

I wondered about the bowstrings and revisited the possibility that Jemal had not received one but was instead the person responsible for sending them. If that was the case, who was to get the one he'd shown to Benjamin?

The silence was oppressive as we came closer to the valide sultan's apartments, but Jemal did not take us into the rooms, instead continuing to walk until we'd reached the Courtyard of the Favorites. Bright moonlight bounced off the white plaster walls of the wood-trimmed building that contained apartments occupied by sultans long ago. The rows of wooden shutters were tightly closed, and the only sound apart from our steps on the cold stone floor was that of water pouring into the pool that edged one side of the courtyard.

Sprawled beneath the elegant oval arches of the path running along the sultan's rooms was Bezime's body, surrounded by a ring of guards and a handful of silent women. The color drained from Margaret's face in an instant, and unable to offer much in the way of consolation, I took her shaking hand in mine as we approached the group. Violent death—the thin, reddish purple bruise on her neck identified it as such—offered those looking at the body no reassurance, no hint that a soul had found peaceful rest.

"How was it done?" I asked.

One of the guards bent down next to her and lifted a familiar object from the ground: a white, silken bowstring. I closed my eyes, tried to control my breath, knowing there was nothing that would still my heartbeat. "Did anyone witness the attack?"

Of course no one had. Nor had anyone seen or heard anything remotely suspicious. I questioned everyone present—Margaret by my side, unable to speak—but did not expect answers full of enlightenment. Could I doubt, even for a moment, that Bezime's death had been sanctioned at the highest levels? Part of me wanted to run from the palace, not stopping until I'd found Colin and was safely ensconced in a compartment on the *Orient Express*. But at the same time, I felt the slight beginnings of a sensation I'd not known in many months: the unmistakable titillation that held firm its place next to the deepest fears.

Forcing myself to focus, I struggled to find anything of significance. After combing every inch of the courtyard and finding it devoid of anything that could be construed as evidence, I asked Jemal if I could question the other women in the palace. He did not object. Margaret hovered behind me, her hand pressed hard over her mouth.

"I'm sorry, Emily," she said as we waited for him to begin sending them in to speak to us. "I'm all but useless. I had no idea this would be so difficult."

"It's appalling. There's no other word. But if we are to find justice for Ceyden—and now Bezime as well—we cannot allow ourselves the luxury of mourning right now. Push aside what you've seen as best you can and help me. When we get home, we can collapse."

Jemal stood over us as we questioned the girls. Not surprisingly, no one admitted to seeing or hearing anything out of the ordinary. And none of them met my eyes during the interviews. That futile exercise complete, I turned back to the eunuch.

"Where are the police? Have they already been through?"

"No. This is a simple harem matter. No use troubling the police."

"So it's an ordinary day in the harem when someone is murdered?" I asked. "Come, Jemal, I'm not so naïve. This was an execution, was it not?"

"You've been reading too many books, Lady Emily."

"Is there no interest in finding out who killed her?" I asked. Margaret, still quiet, was methodically tugging at her gloves.

"The sultan will come here tomorrow, and the killer will confess," Jemal said.

"What assignment were you sent here to do?"

"It is not for your ears."

"Where was your loyalty? To Bezime or Perestu?"

He laughed. "You believe those to be the options?"

"Then tell me who has your allegiance," I said.

"The sultan, of course. Do you not understand who he is? That he rules all of us?"

"Of course I do, Jemal, but I find I no longer believe anything you say." Our search had yielded nothing of interest, leaving only one thing to be done. "Has someone searched the body for clues?"

"Was it not obvious how she died?" he asked.

"Not to determine the manner of death, but to see if she had with her anything of interest. May I look for myself?"

We returned to the site of the murder, and with great effort, I forced myself to go through Bezime's clothing. It sickened me to disturb her ill-used body, but I had no choice in the matter and began my search. She had no pockets, no jewelry with hidden compartments, and had dropped nothing near where she fell, at least nothing that remained. I expected her skin to have lost its warmth but was surprised and horrified by its almost inhuman smoothness. She was like a polished stone, and I fought back tears as I patted her sleeves and bodice until I felt something strange against her abdomen. With trembling fingers, I opened the front of her gown; she'd been dressed for bed. There, stitched to her camisole, was a slim pouch. I pulled an embroidery scissors from my reticule, cut the seam, and removed the superfluous fabric. Inside were five folded sheets of papers—letters.

"What have you found?" Jemal asked. "Hand it over, please."

"Absolutely not," I said.

"You will give them to me now," he said.

"No. I will read them myself and determine whether they are pertinent to the case. And as there's nothing more to be done here tonight, I'm going home to mourn Bezime. Will you please keep me abreast of funeral arrangements?"

"Stunned. I'm stunned," I said, stacking the letters in a neat pile next to Ceyden's book of poetry. "I expected them to be from Murat's vizier."

We had returned to the *yalı,* and much though I wanted to collapse and weep, I pushed myself to work instead, not wanting to miss a detail that might lead us to capture the man who had killed Bezime and, no doubt, Ceyden.

"Who, then?" Colin asked.

"They were all written in English—perfect English—in the handwriting of a gentleman. And Ceyden's notes refer to events cited in the letters."

"Benjamin?" Margaret asked.

"I did confirm with him this afternoon that he was involved in the rescue of concubines following a boating accident in the Bosphorus," Colin said. "I've not had the chance to update you."

"Did he admit to falling in love with one of them?" I asked. "Or say anything that gives a clue as to the identity of his lover?"

"No, nor did he admit to noticing that Ceyden was among the girls he helped."

"He's trying to hide it, of course," I said. "He's mortified that he didn't know it was his sister."

"That's possible. Margaret?" My friend was sitting, arms wrapped tight around her, her face gray. "Are you all right?"

"It's cold out here, isn't it?" she asked.

The night had grown chilly, and the air off the water biting. I rang for a servant, and within moments we had steaming cups of *salep*, a thick, white drink made from the dried tubers of orchids that reminded me of tapioca.

Margaret looked as if she were suffering from shock. Colin draped a soft blanket over her shoulders and asked her if she wanted to go to bed; we had plenty of room for her. She declined, insisting that she wanted to sit with us.

"I will manage to make myself useful," she said.

"What do we have?" Colin asked. "Perestu's reaction to finding her ring in Ceyden's room. Notes in Ceyden's hand and letters possibly—most likely—in Benjamin's."

"And what of Sir Richard?" I asked. "Am I really to believe that all the strange happenings around him are coincidental?"

"I'm afraid we're beginning to diverge here, Emily." Colin warmed his hands around his glass. "It's becoming increasingly difficult to believe that Sir Richard's troubles—minus those connected with Ceyden's death—are due to anything but his own mental decline."

"How can you say that? He has lost his daughter," I said.

"Don't forget the attacks on Benjamin," Colin said. "Perhaps he did order them. We may be dealing with a man losing his grip on reality."

I slept only sporadically that night, dreaming of Bezime, waking up sweat-soaked and gasping for air, clinging to Colin. Sadness I had expected, along with fear and horror. But the anxiety consuming me was unlike anything I'd previously experienced—for it came with a feeling of dread that shouted to me, putting me on notice that Bezime had been right, that I was on a bad path, and that a terrible outcome was inevitable.

Not wanting to wake up my husband, I buried my sobs in my pillow, trying to lie as still as I could. Realizing sleep was not going to come, I slipped out of bed and into the hallway. I would go downstairs and read where the light would not disturb Colin. Before I'd reached the sitting room, however, I heard a rustling noise at the end of the corridor. I froze, listening. The *yalı* was not laid out like a typical European house, and my dressing room was not connected to the bedroom but attached to the *hamam*-like marble bath on the ground floor. The noise was coming from there.

I debated my options, distracted only by the sound of my heart leaping out of my chest. My knees trembled, my stomach churned, and sweat dripped down the back of my neck. Moonlight filled the hall, and something sparkled on the floor—glass from a shattered window. I heard the *swoosh* of wood against wood as drawers opened, more rustling, then dull steps. I looked back to the stairs, wondering if I could reach them before whoever was inside found me. There was nowhere to hide, and I was not about to confront a stranger in my house. Holding my breath, I gathered the skirt of my nightgown in my hand and sprinted back upstairs, praying I'd been quiet enough.

Colin woke at once and stormed out of the room without hesitating. He called for me to come down only a few moments later. Our intruder was gone, and with him all my jewelry, the lock on its case forced open. We sent for the police at once. They were apologetic and embarrassed and assured us the city was generally safe, but admitted the chances of recovering any of the stolen goods or the culprit were slim at best.

I was unnerved, more so than my husband, who ushered me back to bed and held me until he fell asleep. I'd been the victim of theft before and knew well how vulnerable the experience would leave me. This was another most unwelcome distraction for a honeymoon.

I wanted it all to stop; to have a moment of peace. Feelings of fear and violation kept me awake the remainder of the night, leaving me with nothing to do but pray for respite, repeating my silent words over and over until they were met by the sound of the muezzin singing the morning's first call to prayer.

14 April 1892
Darnley House, Kent

My dear daughter,

I write not to alarm you, but to keep you informed on the topic regarding which I am certain you are keenly interested. The physician saw Ivy today, and is concerned by her lack of strength—particularly as she seems to be growing weaker with each passing day. I pray that she will manage and come through this as well as possible.

This is something about which we must speak plainly, as it is a part of life that cannot be avoided. At present, there is no need for you to think of coming here—I know from Colin's wire to Robert that you were considering it. I will, of course, send you word at once if the situation grows more serious.

Do all you can to enjoy your wedding trip. It won't be long until you're going through a confinement of your own. And as you are as obstinate and stubborn a person as I have known, there is no question that you will sail through it with an ease that borders on indecent.

I am, your loving and devoted mother,

C. Bromley

The terse calm of my mother's letter did nothing to relieve the anxiety that had poured over me after the robbery. If anything, it brought back every fear I'd known since childhood of the subject at hand, and I felt as if I'd been slammed against the steel door of a vault. Inside, of course, unable to unlock it. Colin and I had taken two days of rest—he'd hoped it would calm my nerves. We'd picnicked on the Asian shore, explored the most beautiful mosques in the city, and hired a boat to take us all the way up the Bosphorus to the Black Sea.

My mental condition may have improved, but physically it was becoming more difficult to ignore that something was changing in my body. Dizziness had become my frequent companion, and I'd begun to notice other symptoms as well. All of my maladies might just as easily be explained as the effects of the stress under which I was operating, and I had no evidence that could give me solid confirmation. It was maddening not to be able to know the cause.

"Are you certain you're ready to get back to it?" Colin asked. He was to call on Sir Richard—whose state of mind had not improved in the least—after walking me to Yıldız. We'd spent the morning wandering the gardens at Topkapı, then gone to the Blue Mosque, and were now making our way across the Hippodrome, where an ancient Egyptian obelisk rose from the site where Romans had raced their chariots. "I don't want you to push yourself."

"It's time," I said. "Though I shall mourn the loss of my jewelry forever. I'm only glad they didn't take my ring." I fingered the band he'd given me when I'd accepted his proposal. Formed in the shape of a reef knot, it was an ancient piece, from the Minoans on Crete, gold inlaid with lapis lazuli. I treasured it more than all the diamonds and precious gems in both our families.

"The only benefit was getting two days of you all to myself. In the previous week I'd spent more time with Margaret than you."

"Should I be jealous?" I sneaked a sideways glance at him, warming at the sight of his smile.

"Exceedingly. She has proposed that we all run away together and live as nomads. Convinced me that I'd look rather well in the robes of a Bedouin. And, if I recall correctly, you've something of a propensity for men in such attire." It was almost a year ago that an exceedingly charming thief dressed in such an outfit had drugged me. The incident left me embarrassed but unharmed, the recipient of a hazy sort of illicit kiss whose occurrence I'd never admitted to my husband.

"That you would," I said, feeling an automatic lightness as we began to flirt. "It's something we ought to make use of after you swim the Bosphorus for me."

"I'll swim the Bosphorus, scale the house, climb through your bedroom window, throw you over my shoulder, and take you away to my camp."

"You'll need to stow the robes on the terrace. They wouldn't achieve the proper effect if they were wet."

"Excellent point."

"I'm glad you've come to terms with the fact that you're going to lose our bet," I said. "It speaks highly of your masculine security."

"Darling girl, I'm humoring you. You'll be the one in robes—diaphanous, remember?"

"I don't see why one ought to exclude the other. Can't you kidnap me regardless of the outcome of our wager?"

"Look how quickly you back down!" he said. "Just a moment ago you were brimming with certainty at the prospect of victory. Now you're making contingency plans?"

"Don't be silly. I'll win. That goes without saying. But now that I've got the image of you as a Bedouin in my head, I'll do whatever I must to ensure the vision becomes reality."

"I haven't seen so real a smile on your face in days," he said. "I've missed it."

"I propose a second wedding trip when we've finished here. Three months, at least, somewhere no one will find us and where there's no possibility of being embroiled in any sort of intrigue beyond that necessary when searching for Bedouin robes in a Western country."

"Where would you like to go?"

"Surprise me," I said, meeting his eyes. "I trust you implicitly."

It had grown later than I'd expected, so we hired a carriage to take us to the docks. My enterprising husband took advantage of the quiet surroundings, and as the door was closed, he distracted me in a most pleasant fashion, thoroughly improving my state of mind, at least superficially. But on occasion, a superficial boost can carry over into something deeper, and in this case, it gave me the confidence to tackle the remaining tasks at hand. We parted company in Pera, heading for our separate appointments.

Roxelana was waiting for me in a courtyard landscaped in the style of an English garden: Rows of neatly trimmed boxwoods lined gravel paths, bright flowers peeking out at intervals. We sat on a stone bench, side by side, in silence. I'd hoped that by waiting for her to speak, she might be persuaded to divulge some pertinent secret. It might have seemed a reasonable strategy, but it accomplished nothing.

"I'm glad to see you," I said.

"Have I any hope of being freed from this purgatory?"

"Can we talk candidly?" I asked. I'd hoped to discuss Ceyden before turning to this topic, but there was some merit to be had in addressing her concerns first.

"I hope so. 'Reason in man is rather like God in the world.'"

"Aquinas, I assume?" I asked; she nodded. "You may not like what I have to say. I've given this no inconsiderable amount of thought, and your options for leaving are limited. If you're unwilling to consider marrying someone the sultan deems suitable—"

"I will not consider it," she said.

"I respect your position. But it leaves us only with incredibly risky alternatives."

"I want to escape." She was leaning so close to me, I could feel her breath on my cheek.

"If you're caught—"

"I know perfectly well what will happen if I'm caught. You think I have not considered this? All earthly punishment pales in the face of damnation."

"Yes, of course," I said. "But you must not think of this lightly. And before we can discuss it further, we must address another topic.

I understand that someone from the harem was meeting with an Englishman in the palace gardens. Do you know anything about this?"

"An Englishman wouldn't be allowed to speak to anyone from the harem," she said, her ivory skin losing its creamy warmth.

"I suspect that Jemal was instrumental in arranging the meetings."

"He would never allow a man in."

"You're wrong, Roxelana," I said. "He did. I've the letters to prove it. I can see you know something. Whom are you trying to protect?"

"No one." She looked at me. "There is no one in the harem I would care to protect."

"This is serious," I said. "Two people are dead. What if the murderer acts again?"

"Surely you don't think the same person killed Bezime and Ceyden?"

"I think it's extremely likely," I said.

"It's impossible. No one has access to both harems."

"Jemal does."

"Jemal is not a killer," she said.

"You're certain of that?"

"He's as corrupt as anyone, but he'd never harm any of us."

"Corrupt how?"

"Oh, nothing serious. He's always willing to help us if we ask—bring books, sweets, organize entertainments."

"Is any of that forbidden?"

"No, but he has ways of expediting things. If, that is, you make it worth his while."

"He takes bribes?"

She shrugged. "Why not? It's tedious here. Ennui has a funny effect on people. We learn to make our own intrigues so as not to go mad from boredom."

"What sorts of intrigues?" I asked.

"Nothing pertinent in the ways you'd like. It's all trivial. Trivial, but diverting. I'm not going to detail it for you—that would be nothing more than idle gossip."

The way she set her jaw suggested it wasn't all trivial. I changed the direction of my questions. "Tell me again about the night you found Ceyden's body. I want to know every detail."

"You already know. I had gone outside for a walk—it was a beautiful evening. The courtyard in which she was murdered has always been a favorite of mine. I say the rosary there every night I can. I'd gone straight there and nearly tripped over her. It was horrible."

"Did you hear anything on your approach?"

"Nothing at all."

"No one talking? No sound of footsteps or someone running?"

"I remember vividly being struck by how quiet it was."

"Did you touch her body?"

"Of course not!"

"Not even to make sure she wasn't alive?"

"No. Should I have? I was scared out of my mind and ran for help without even thinking."

I thought back to the scene as it was when Colin and I arrived. Ceyden's body was facedown, and given the atmosphere in which we found it—alerted by Roxelana's screams—I admit that I assumed she was dead. But had I come upon her in quiet peace, I would have thought she'd fainted or fallen ill and would have turned her over to see.

Roxelana shifted her jaw. "At any rate, that hideous bruise on her neck was wholly unnatural. I knew something was wrong at once."

And now I knew she was lying. Misremembering, perhaps, but I did not believe that. No one could have seen the bruises without first turning her over, and Perestu had taken Roxelana away before Sir Richard touched the body. Ceyden's long hair was covering her neck until her father swept it out of the way, and even then, there were no visible marks there. The bulk of the bruises were on the front and sides.

"Have you heard what Perestu and I found in Ceyden's room?" I asked.

"You were in her room?" Now she came alive. Her shoulders pushed back, hands clenched into fists, pupils constricted.

"That surprises you?"

"I hadn't given it any thought." She closed her eyes, mashed her lips together. "Was there anything of interest there?"

"As a matter of fact, there was. Do you mean to tell me there's been no gossip about this in the harem?"

"Everyone had already been through her room—no sense letting her clothes go to waste."

"There was a lot of clothing still there." I studied her face. "I think you'd like me to believe you're callous about her death. But the truth is, it's frightened you. Why is that?"

"What did you find?"

"Notes. Trinkets."

"What kinds of notes?" she asked.

"I'm sure you could tell me."

"Why would you say that?"

"Because you look worried," I said. "Did she know you wanted to leave the harem?"

"No one knows that."

"Even Jemal?"

This gave her pause. "Of course not."

"You're certain?"

"Absolutely," she said. "What else was in Ceyden's room? You said trinkets?"

"Yes. Some lovely jewelry that apparently did not belong to her."

All the color drained from her face; her lips were almost blue. "Whose was it?"

"That's what I'm trying to determine."

"I—I—I cannot discuss this any longer." She stood, walked a few paces, turned back to face me. "Some secrets are too dangerous to play with."

Following this conversation, I sought out Jemal. Much to my relief, he was back at Yıldız, so I would not have to make my way across town yet again. We sat in another courtyard—this one on the opposite side of the grounds to the one in which I'd met Roxelana—full of roses not yet in bloom and lilacs whose scent filled the air with sugar.

"We cannot be overheard here," Jemal said, standing close to me, directly in front of the tall fountain at the center of the garden.

"Water, yes," I said. "It reminds me of Topkapı."

"I am to talk to you. So says the sultan." He pursed his full lips. "I do not like it."

"Why not?"

"You do not understand our way of life."

"I understand very well that two women have been murdered on palace grounds and am confident that no one's way of life views such events as acceptable. I'm most interested in your relationship with Roxelana—"

"Relationship?" I could see a mask fall over his eyes. "An odd choice of word."

"I can't say I agree," I said. "I think you're closely connected to her in ways that might cause trouble for you with the sultan."

He drew in a deep breath, held it, then turned away from me. "I'm afraid there is nothing I can help you with today, Lady Emily. I will inform the sultan that I am, of course, full of regret not to have been of more use."

"Don't do this."

"You know nothing."

"What about Bezime? Do you want no justice for her? Isn't she the one who arranged for you to come back here? Wasn't she your champion?" I didn't want him to walk away and hoped that any or all of my hurried questions would cause him to stop. I was not so lucky, however. He stared at me before going, shaking his head.

"No good will come of the path you are on."

His words stung me, so well mimicking Bezime's. I walked past the sultan's workshop as I made my way out of the palace grounds. He was inside—I could hear the sound of his plane through the window—but I did not pause to speak to him, instead continuing on and contemplating his position. When not angry, Abdül Hamit was gracious, exceedingly polite, cultured, Western, and enlightened when it came to education, particularly for women. He loved music, wrote poetry, and had even penned an opera of his own. How did one reconcile all that with his multiple wives and concubines and slaves and mutilated guards?

There was a certain amount of wisdom in what Jemal had said. I did not understand this sort of life. And although I did not doubt my ability to solve the murders, I wondered what my ignorance and naïveté led me to overlook. It was essential that I recognize the limitations I carried with me. With this in mind, once back at the *yalı* I sat down again with the letters I'd found on Bezime's body, imagining that I was the concubine who had received them. That I was a woman in love with a man forbidden to me, someone who by loving me put himself in danger—who could neither address nor sign his declarations. Reading them this way made them far less romantic than they'd appeared at first glance. The tenderness was heartbreaking, the yearning hurt my soul.

When I'd finished, I carefully folded them and put them in a small compartment in one of my trunks. To leave thoughts so intimate out in the open was wrong, and I already knew all I needed to about them. Someone, most likely Benjamin, had written them to Ceyden. Whoever in the harem discovered their dalliance—too flighty a word for the depth of emotion it was clear they shared—put a stop to it by silencing the disobedient concubine. And at the moment, one person struck me as the most likely candidate: a eunuch with too much information and a grand sense of importance.

18

"I need your absolute candor, Benjamin," I said, once again sitting across from him in Ali's restaurant near the Spice Bazaar, this time hearty plates of İskender kebabs in front of us. I swirled a bite of chicken in thick yogurt sauce as I spoke. "The complications of your situation have become more clear to me, and I want to help you. I understand how dreadful all this is, particularly after learning what I have since Bezime's death. She had the letters."

"What letters?" Every inch of his body sagged.

"The ones you wrote. The love letters."

"No. It's not possible."

"She raised Ceyden. They were in close contact. Perhaps she gave them to her for safekeeping," I said.

"There is no proof of any of this. None." He ripped off a piece of bread and slogged it, all false nonchalance, through the sauce on his plate.

"But you don't deny it?" I asked. "There's no need to protect her anymore, Benjamin."

"I never—"

"You did not know who she was. How could you ever have suspected the truth?"

"The truth? What do you know about the truth?"

"No one can fault you," I said. "But it's critical now that we press forward and find the person responsible for her death. Jemal delivered the letters for you, did he not?"

He closed his eyes. "Yes."

"And you met him when the boat capsized?"

"Yes." His rough voice trembled.

"How did you persuade him—"

"I bribed him, Lady Emily. I paid dearly for it—not only in money, let me assure you. My conscience has suffered no small amount."

"All that jewelry. Was it to finance your escape?"

"It would have helped."

"I need you to help me to better understand what was going on. Everyone says—forgive me if this is cruel—that Ceyden was desperate to earn the sultan's favor. There are rumblings of political unrest, rumors that Murat is planning a coup. Was Ceyden attempting to get close to him to forward some sort of plot? Or was she merely doing whatever she could to cover her true intentions? To ensure that no one would suspect her of plotting to flee the harem?"

"I don't know anything about politics," he said.

"Do you know how she got the jewelry?"

"Ceyden?" he asked. "She stole it."

"I'm sorry. I know this is painful. The fact that she's your sister—"

He stared at me, eyes steady but lacking focus. "You have no idea."

"We will find justice."

"I don't see the point. All I want is to go as far away from here as I can."

"Are you still planning to leave?"

"I don't know," he said. "I can't abandon my father, can I?"

"He doesn't seem well."

"He isn't, and I don't see him getting better unless we remove ourselves from Constantinople. There's nothing left for him here but more misery."

"You don't think he'll be reinstated at the embassy?" I asked.

"Have you spoken to him lately? He's barely coherent and can hardly keep on his feet. He's coming completely apart."

"Where would you go? Italy?"

"Italy?" His eyebrows shot to his hairline. "No. Wouldn't want to go there. France, maybe. But my father belongs in England."

"I thought—" I stopped, going over the conversation we'd had on our previous visit to Ali's, certain he had told me he'd taken a position on a dig in Italy. We'd discussed his interest in all things Roman. "France. Yes. I have a dear friend in Paris—I should put you in touch with her."

"Thank you," he said. "I would appreciate that. But not quite yet. I don't want to alarm him. It's not going to be easy to persuade him to leave, especially after he buried my sister here. Better that I have everything arranged and present it as a fait accompli."

"How long do you think that will take?" I asked.

His expression changed, his eyes lightening, the color returning to his face—but there was a hint of effort in it, a strain in his features, as if he were pushing too hard. "No hurry, I suppose. Much though I'd like to go at once, I'd be sure to regret not setting everything up carefully. Are you still hungry? Ali's baklava is incomparable."

Benjamin had not exaggerated about the baklava, and I so indulged myself that I was unable to down even a single cup of tea when I met Margaret on the terrace at Misseri's that afternoon.

"I do wish I could meet the sultan," Margaret said, slathering butter on a scone. "The master of the seraglio. A figure who has fueled the romantic dreams of untold Western gentlemen for thousands of years."

"Well. Not Abdül Hamit himself," I said. "He can't be more than fifty or so."

"You know perfectly well what I mean."

"I do. I just wish he were willing to fuel the romantic—or, rather, religious—dreams of one of his concubines."

"But Roxelana refuses to marry, correct?"

"Yes. She wants us to help her escape."

"Is such a thing possible?" Margaret asked.

"I don't know," I said. "If it is, it's full of risk. She can't walk out of the palace—we'd have to bribe guards who most likely would turn on us."

"What about helping her slip away when she's away from the palace? I saw a group of concubines picnicking along the Golden Horn," Margaret said.

"How many guards were with them?" I asked.

"More than I could count."

"Colin would not like any of this," I said. "And it would be difficult, to say the least. If she were to go on an excursion and in some legitimate way be separated from the group—I don't know how—if she could get out of the building—"

"She could climb out a window," Margaret said.

"And change into a common dress and common veil," I said. "But as soon as the guards realized she was gone, they would tear the city apart looking for her."

"And she would be caught."

My mind was zooming. "Which is why," I said, grinning, "she would walk, slowly, to the nearest tea shop and sit there, unfazed by any commotion, reading a novel. They'd never notice her."

"You're brilliant, you know," Margaret said. "We have to find a way to do it."

"But this sort of thing simply cannot be organized by someone with ties to our government—and my decision to work with Colin has put you firmly in that camp." I frowned. "I don't need a diplomatic incident during my first assignment."

"Which is why we would have to be extremely careful."

"You're a terrible influence."

"The worst. But it would be possible to pull it off—and think of the accomplishment, Emily—to free a woman enslaved to satisfy the base needs of a man who treats her with no honor."

"The risk is enormous. What if they executed her if she was caught? And what would happen to Colin? And us?"

"I do wish there were a simpler way," Margaret said. "She's being stubborn. You could satisfy your obligation to both her and the Crown if you were able to arrange a suitable marriage. It would be easy enough for her to leave that situation on her own—even if all she did was demand a divorce, which I'm told is not unheard of here."

"I'd merely move her from one master to another," I said. "Would you have me do the same to you?"

"No, but—"

"But what? Should she suffer for having been born in a different society? And what are we, morally, if we don't intervene? How can I willingly stand aside when I see someone forced to live with injustice and the fear of mortal sin?"

"Her quality of life is far better than that enjoyed by most of the population of England," Margaret said. "I know that doesn't make it right, but—"

"So she doesn't deserve help? Because her circumstances come with certain measures of comfort? How can I ask to be treated as my husband's equal, to be valued as fully as a gentleman in our own society, if I let my fellow women be used in a most abominable fashion?"

"Truth is, the harem doesn't sound half-bad," Margaret said. "But if Roxelana doesn't want it, she shouldn't be forced to stay."

"No. She shouldn't." I rubbed my forehead. "We must find a way, Margaret. To leave her there makes us complicit with her captors. We're worse than them, in fact, if we do nothing in the face of a situation we know to be wrong."

19

Two days later I went to Yıldız, the skeleton of a plot in hand. Roxelana fell to the ground in front of my feet, her head buried in her hands, joyful prayers flowing from her lips, when I told her what Margaret and I were scheming.

"You understand how risky this will be?" I asked, pulling her to an upright position before sitting on the bench in front of a fountain. I silently praised the Ottomans for being so good at placing running water everywhere to avert eavesdroppers. Before this trip, I had never considered how useful this could be and wondered now if perhaps I should adopt the practice in our country estate.

"There's no fate that could be worse to me than staying here and risking my immortal soul," she said. "'Three things are necessary for the salvation of man: to know what he ought to believe; to know what he ought to desire; and to know what he ought to do.'"

"This isn't romantic nonsense. We don't sit back after the curtain falls and have a good cry before going home to a snug bed."

"I know perfectly well what is at stake. No punishment on earth could compete with what I might suffer for all eternity." Her religious fervor was certainly focused.

"Assisting you is not a decision I make lightly," I said. "I don't trust you entirely, Roxelana. I don't believe for a second that you've been candid with me."

"I have told you everything I can."

"I'm not convinced. But I shall help you regardless because on principle I don't believe that it's right to enslave anyone. It's barbaric."

"Thank you," she said. "I cannot begin to express my gratitude. You've no idea what it is like for me in here. I have to hide even my prayers."

"I'm so sorry. Sorry that you've been subjected to any of it." I met her eyes. "I do hope, though, that if there is anything else you can tell me about Ceyden's death, you will not hesitate. I'm working to get you your freedom. Don't deny the same to an innocent man."

"There's still no evidence against the guard? No one's come forward as a witness?"

"No."

"Then he'll be released. Even if there's a trial."

"Not necessarily," I said. "Please, do the right thing. If there's something you know, you must tell me."

"There's nothing more. I wish there were."

"As do I." I didn't believe her, but knew no way to force the truth from her. She was scared and weak and deserving of my help despite her imperfections. "How difficult is it for you to arrange an outing in town?"

"It's not the slightest trouble."

"How often do such excursions take place?" I asked.

"Every week or so."

"When the time comes, don't plan one yourself. Go at someone else's suggestion, and alert me to the details as early as possible. I'll arrange everything from there."

"You will find suitable clothing for me?"

"Yes, and as for the timing of all this, I think it's best if we—"

"Lady Emily Hargreaves?" The voice, full of force, came from the entrance to the courtyard. "The sultan has summoned you. You will come at once."

Roxelana shot me a look full of panic and gripped my hand so hard, I feared it would be crushed. "It's the *kızlar ağası*," she said. "The chief black eunuch. Nothing good can be happening. I should have already run."

"Don't panic. He can't possibly know what we're discussing."

"How did he know we were here?"

"There are only so many places to look, dear," I said. "Hold your head up and try to look bored. I'll go to him. You've no need to be involved."

"And you, Roxelana. Perestu wants you immediately."

Stricken, she stood, holding my hand as we followed the *kızlar ağası*, as imposing a figure as a eunuch could be—tall, with elegant bearing and proud features—towards the palace, splitting off when we reached the entrance to the harem. The sultan, apparently, was waiting for me in a public section of Yıldız. We made our way through long, narrow corridors, made claustrophobic by their ornate decoration: enormous porcelain urns on one side, rows of giant crystal candelabras on the other, stretching from the floor almost to the ceiling, their heavy bases reaching almost to the edge of the runner in the center of the hall. After passing through a pair of inlaid doors, we reached a reception room that might have been found in any aristocratic residence in Western Europe. Heavy curtains hung from tall windows, silk covered the walls, and the furniture was perfectly ordinary. Velvet-covered settees stood along side chairs with gilded arms, and in the center of the chamber was a round sofa, in the center of which was another huge candelabra. It was on this sofa that Abdül Hamit was sitting.

"I bear no good news," he said. "But felt you should be informed at once. Ceyden's murderer has been identified. I've ordered his arrest and expect him to be taken into custody within the hour."

"Who is it? How—"

"An Englishman. Benjamin St. Clare, the son of a man I have entertained here—a man you know."

"Yes, Sir Richard." I could hardly speak. "I'm more than stunned. What led you to this conclusion?"

"One of the eunuchs came forward. He saw Mr. St. Clare fleeing from the direction of the courtyard and followed, but was not able to catch him. When he heard Roxelana's screams, he gave up the pursuit, fearing that she had been violated by the intruder."

"And he's certain it was Ben—Mr. St. Clare?"

"He recognized him from a previous encounter."

"He'd been to the harem? How is that possible?"

"No, nothing of the sort. That would not be possible. There was a mishap on a boating excursion. Mr. St. Clare assisted with the rescue and spoke at some length to Jemal after the matter was settled."

"Why did he wait so long to come forward?"

"He was afraid St. Clare would come after him. I don't understand how any of this came to pass. I can only imagine that there was some sort of connection formed between this young man and Ceyden—she was one of those he rescued."

"It's understandable."

"It's unacceptable. But it does prove him to be of weak character."

"Jemal did not actually see him in the courtyard," I said. "You said he saw him running near it. How can any of us be certain Mr. St. Clare killed her?"

"He found this near her body."

I knew before he handed it to me what I would see: the cross Mr. Sutcliffe had given me. Benjamin's cross. The sight of it sent my head spinning. Of course. It had been taken when my jewelry was stolen. I'd been so upset, I'd not considered it as more than one more casualty along with the rest. There hadn't seemed to be any connection between the theft and Ceyden's death.

As I considered what I believed the couple had intended to do the night of the murder, images of the jewelry sewn into Ceyden's gown returned to me. If she had planned to flee, she would surely have been wearing it. But if she'd changed her mind, telling Benjamin only when he arrived to spirit her off, she wouldn't have worn it. His reaction to her news might have been violent. And much though I did not want to believe him capable of murder, I knew all too well that when desperate, people turn to terrible things.

"I—I don't know what to say," I said, stalling. "I find it impossible to believe."

"As do I, Lady Emily. I must find out how this criminal gained access to my harem. I begin to wonder if this palace provides any measure of safety." He creased his forehead. "And I feel I owe you some sort of apology. Had I not stopped you from pursuing your investigation, albeit temporarily, we might have learned this earlier."

"Thank you, Your Highness," I said. "Do you suspect there is a connection to Bezime's death?"

"I cannot doubt it," he said. "I do not think we have two murderers running rampant through my palace. I cannot forgive myself for not doing more to prevent it."

"Do not be so hard on yourself," I said. "We all can only make the best decisions possible in a given moment. I, too, wish I could have done something."

"He must have known she had the letters you found on her body," he said. "And killed her in a vain attempt to recover them lest his sins be discovered. I regret having cut her so thoroughly out of my life. I should have listened to her better."

"She knew you loved her."

"I did not pay attention when she told me she was being threatened."

"Truly, do not be so hard on yourself," I said. "All you can do now is ensure that her murderer is brought to justice. May I speak to Mr. St. Clare when he's in custody?"

"It is not necessary."

"I want to be certain that—"

"There can be no doubt of his guilt."

"But what of Bezime's death? There's no hard evidence to implicate him. We can't prove he knew she had the letters."

He nodded, satisfaction streaming from his eyes. "You think you can persuade him to confess?"

This was not at all what I had in mind—at least not in the way he meant. My desire was to learn the truth, regardless of the outcome. If Benjamin was guilty, I would accept that, but if he was not, my task would be to prove his innocence. For now, I could not believe his guilt a foregone conclusion. My body began to ache and my head to throb as dizziness coursed through me.

"It is worth a conversation," I said, my mouth dry.

"Yes, I can allow that."

"Thank you."

"I must know," he said, crossing his arms and pressing them hard against his chest. "I must know what happened to Bezime."

Footsteps sounded in the corridor outside, and the *kızlar ağası* started for the door. He opened it to find Colin, who stepped forward, bowing to the sultan before crossing to me and kissing my hand.

"Benjamin is gone," he said, his voice low as he looked into my eyes. "He's taken all his field equipment and disappeared."

20

"He's in bad shape," Margaret said, greeting us at the door of Sir Richard's house in Pera. "The doctor's given him a sedative. There was no other option."

I embraced her. "I don't know what I'd do without you here."

"Not have to worry about me being completely undone at the sight of my first body."

"Your first?" I asked. "So you've not sworn off the whole business?"

"Not all the way. But I couldn't pursue it as you do. I've not the strength, and at any rate, Mr. Michaels would be too horrified by it all. I'm rather fond of him, you know, and would hate to drive him to an early death."

"An excellent policy when considering how to treat one's spouse," Colin said, bending to kiss her on both cheeks. "Where's your chaperone? I must say, she's not doing much of a decent job keeping an eye on you."

"Back at the hotel. She had a fit of the vapors as soon as she heard about Benjamin."

"Not, I'm sure, because she feared he was unjustly accused, but because you'd been socializing with his father," I said.

"Precisely."

"I spoke to the ambassador," Colin said. "If Benjamin is located and stands trial, he's agreed to be his diplomatic representative in court."

"Does he believe he's innocent?" Margaret asked.

"That's unlikely," Colin said. "But regardless, it's important that our government provide him the best possible support. In the case of a guilty verdict, there will be less chance of a feeling of unfairness."

"You think he will be found guilty?" I asked.

"I don't see how he could not," he said.

"But you don't believe he murdered his sister?" I didn't like the look in his eyes—half-hard, half-questioning.

"I'm afraid I do," he said. "And don't—Emily, I know you—don't take that as a gauntlet. There's no need to set off on a quest to prove his innocence."

"How can you say that?" I asked. "The sultan has Benjamin's cross, which had been with my jewelry. Whoever stole it could have planted it as evidence."

"I admit it doesn't all fit together, but the fact is a witness has placed him on the palace grounds the night of the murder. He had no legitimate reason to be there."

"That does not mean he murdered Ceyden. Did you find anything of significance in Benjamin's room? Any indication of where he may have gone?"

"Nothing," he said. "But I'm going to try to find him."

"How?" I asked.

"The same way I'd track anyone," he said. "No time to explain it now. When this is all done, I'll teach you."

"You'd better."

"It shall be difficult to contact you while I'm gone—I'll be passing through undeveloped areas without telegraphs. No need to worry if you don't hear from me."

"Be careful," I said, fear and hesitation in my voice.

"And you," he said, taking me in his arms. "I do believe there's little chance someone other than Benjamin is responsible for Ceyden's death. But I could be wrong, and if I am, I've no idea what may be in store for you while I'm gone. Take care to invite no unnecessary danger."

And with that, he took his leave from us, heading back to the *yalı* to prepare for his trip. I felt more empty than I ever had before.

"Are you all right?" Margaret sank onto the sofa next to me. "Your face is gray."

"I'm worried," I said.

"Of course you are. He is, too. I don't know when I've seen a man so stricken. Have you any idea what it takes for him to allow you to pursue this sort of work? It can turn dangerous without the slightest warning, and that must torment him."

"You know well my feelings about anyone *allowing* me to do anything."

"Oh, it's appalling—you know I agree. But the fact is, Emily, he would be perfectly within his rights to stop you."

"Yet he doesn't."

Tears pooled in my eyes, and I did nothing to stop their fall. "It means more to me than anything he could ever do. To be treated as an equal, to be given one's freedom . . . what is a greater sign of love and trust and every good thing?"

"What about when it comes your turn to give something back? What if the thing he needs most is for you to refuse some of your independence?"

"You mean if I am . . ."

"Perhaps then. Perhaps some other time. Do you love him enough to do it?"

"I do," I said, my voice shaking.

"You don't sound convinced."

"I'm not. Not about loving him, but about ever having to forgo my freedom. I don't want to believe it will ever be necessary."

"That's not reasonable," Margaret said.

"I am not so worthy as he."

She rolled her eyes. "You had all my sympathy until that statement. Now I know you're nothing better than the average romantic fool. And here I thought you were being profound."

I laughed. Nerves again, but it helped dissolve the tension knotting in me. "You've succeeded in distracting me enough that I shall be able to focus my efforts. I think we should begin by giving Medusa a useful purpose. Can you bring her here?"

"You're joking," Margaret said. I didn't reply. "You're not."

It took her nearly two hours to convince her extremely displeased chaperone to follow her to Sir Richard's house. I'd nearly given up hope when Medusa—no, Miss Evans—stormed into the room. Within minutes of her seeing how much the poor man needed assistance, she'd begun organizing the household and directing the cook to make soup. That settled, Margaret and I set off for Yıldız.

"Who do you think took the cross?" Margaret asked as our carriage sped towards the palace.

"I don't know. Do you think Benjamin murdered Ceyden?"

"No," Margaret said, not a shred of hesitation in her voice. "I think it was Jemal. She was trying to escape—he would have caught trouble if she had. So he stopped her."

"But why, then, did he wait until now to come forward?"

"For that question, I have no answer."

"I think he's in love with Roxelana," I said. "And I think she was afraid and persuaded him to stay quiet lest her own attempts to escape would be thwarted."

"More security at the palace if the sultan knew what Ceyden had planned?"

"Precisely," I said.

"Do you suspect a servant?"

"Let's not theorize. I'd prefer firm answers."

Jemal kept us waiting for nearly three-quarters of an hour before joining us in the courtyard where Ceyden had died. I'd wanted to see him in this setting, to note any changes in his behavior, any discomfort at being back at the site of the murder.

"You've chosen an inconvenient time to appear," he said, folding his arms and standing in front of the bench on which we sat. "I'm in the midst of moving into larger rooms. A reward for my service to the sultan."

"How fortunate for you," I said. "What particular service merited such a payoff?"

"That is not your concern. Why are you here?" he asked. "There's nothing left to discuss."

"We both know that's not true," I said. "How did you get the cross?"

"I found it in the courtyard."

"No, you didn't."

"Of course I did."

I sighed. "You did not find it in the courtyard."

"I can go like this all afternoon, Lady Emily. Have you nothing better to do?"

"You, Jemal, don't place enough value on your time," I said. "If you found it in the courtyard, it was only after you'd placed it there yourself. I know this beyond doubt."

"How so?"

"I know that a mutual acquaintance of ours brought it to you."

"Then I don't see why you're talking to me," he said. "Perhaps you should take the matter up with him."

"Why are you trying to make it look as if Mr. St. Clare committed this crime?"

"Trying?" He tossed his head back. "Ridiculous. I saw what I saw. There's no lie in it."

"But what about the cross?"

"Sometimes, Lady Emily, justice needs a little help. That doesn't mean the truth isn't being served."

"How can you be so confident you are right?" I asked.

"It is my job," he said. "This conversation is finished."

21

Finished with Jemal—or rather, him finished with us—we made our way to Topkapı. I wanted to search Bezime's quarters to see if we'd overlooked anything the night of her death. Margaret was quiet as the boat reached the dock below Scraglio Point. "I must admit I'm not filled with joy at returning here," she said

I linked my arm through hers as we stepped onto the shore. "Understandable. It needs to be done, though. For Bezime. Take what slim comfort you can from the fact that we've come in daylight this time."

"I've not before been tempted to offer to pop back and check on Medusa, but I came close when you told me where we were going."

"I'm glad you didn't," I said. "I need you here."

"I'm useful, you know. Just so long as you keep me away from corpses. I don't know how on earth you survived finding your anarchist dead in Vienna."

While embroiled in an investigation the previous winter in Vienna, I'd discovered the body of a man who'd been at once my nemesis and my ally and doubted I would ever erase from my mind the image of dark, pooled blood and the jagged slash across his neck. "It was hideous and changed me in ways I do not embrace."

"I never thought I'd say this, but in the end, I'm going to leave the adventure to you and retire to a quiet, academic life."

"You and Ivy can live on neighboring estates," I said.

"And have fourteen children apiece. God willing." She looked at me. "I'm sorry."

"She's going to be fine," I said, knowing my words did as little to convince her as they did me. The further along Ivy went in her confinement, the more danger she would face.

We'd reached the gate and in short order were standing in Bezime's rooms. Once again, I relished the distraction of work.

"Forty rooms," I said, stepping into a dining chamber. "Where do we even begin?"

"I wouldn't even bother, Lady Emily." Perestu stood in a doorway at the opposite end of the room, leading to what had been Bezime's bedroom. "You're on a dangerous path."

"Why would you choose those words?" I asked.

"Isn't that what the witch told you? I know all about it, of course. Nothing that goes on here escapes my notice. Yıldız is my domain, but I must keep abreast of any threats that might come from here. The eunuchs are a marvelous resource. So knowledgeable about the palace. Know every nook and cranny, every secret passage."

"Why are you here?" My spine felt like rubber. Something in her eyes—a fierce determination—frightened me.

"I have private business."

"Regarding Bezime?" I asked.

"She was my rival," she said. "And Abdül Hamit could have elevated her at any time. No one's position in the harem is ever secure. I spied on her, she spied on me."

"What did you learn?"

Perestu lowered herself elegantly onto a divan, placing her trim arms on the top of the backrest. "Bezime did not like losing her power, her influence. So she opened avenues of communication that should have stayed closed."

"Do you refer to Murat's vizier?" I asked.

"The sultan has already taken care of him, so it is no longer relevant. My son is indebted to your husband for discovering the unrest."

I cringed at the thought of what must have been done to the man, traitorous or not. "That is not what brings you here," I said. "What is your business?"

"It is none of your concern."

I went through the catalog of conversations I'd had with her, searching for a time when she'd been less than candid. As I did this, I realized she'd been, in general, direct with me with one exception. "Why were you so upset at finding your ring amongst Ceyden's stash of jewels?" I asked.

"Because I had given it, years ago, to someone I thought would forever treasure it."

"But there's no reason to think that person gave it away to Ceyden. Much though I hate to speak ill of the dead, it's clear that Ceyden stole it all."

"Ceyden could not have stolen my ring. It was no longer in the harem."

"Who had it?"

"I thought perhaps Bezime managed to get it, and I can't think of anything that would pain me more."

"You gave it to someone you loved?" Margaret asked.

"I have known no love or affection since my husband died," Perestu said. "But I was fond of a man after that. Someone I saw on rare state occasions. We became friends, in the most appropriate fashion—never acknowledging the weight of our stares. I would never have involved myself with him. We shared much in common; both understood loss all too well. When the friendship became too difficult, too painful, we parted, and I gave him the ring to remember me by."

"Is this man still in Constantinople?" I asked.

"Yes."

"You must tell us who he is," I said.

"No, Lady Emily. There is nothing I must do. Perhaps you do not understand my rank."

"There must be some connection—"

"It is impossible. The only explanation is that he lost the ring or it was stolen from him and somehow wound up in the hands of that trollop," she said. "I reacted the way I did when I saw it because it hurt me to know that my friend no longer had it."

"Don't you want to speak to him? To find out how he came to lose it?" Margaret asked.

"If he wanted me to know, he would have sought me out and told me. Sent me a letter. As he did not, I can only conclude the subject is as painful for him as it is for me. And I have no desire to further pursue it."

"But—"

"Was there something in particular you were hoping to find here, Lady Emily? I've been through it all and saw nothing that struck my interest. I burned Bezime's diaries, of course. It would not do to have the sanctity of her most private thoughts violated."

"You burned them?" The air rushed out of my lungs.

"It is what we do for one another," she said. "For all that I feared and disliked her, we both lived in the harem, and were, for a period, friends. We come from the same world, and I will not see her dishonored in death."

There was nothing left for us at Topkapı. I searched every inch of the valide's apartments to no avail. Not that this was a surprise. Done, Margaret and I trudged to the embassy, where I'd agreed, in Colin's absence, to make regular reports as to the status of my investigation. The ambassador ushered me into his walnut-paneled office that looked straight out of a London club. I sat in an overstuffed leather chair that was too hard to be comfortable and accepted a cup of tea.

"First Flush Darjeeling," he said. "Arrived today. Perk of the job. My colleagues keep me well stocked in foreign delights."

"It's delicious," I said, hardly tasting it, the hot liquid burning my throat.

"I am pleased that your husband has gone after young St. Clare. Terrible scandal, this. Don't know how much of it we'll be able to bury."

"I wish I had more to tell you today," I said. "I spoke with Perestu and searched Bezime's rooms, but found nothing further of interest."

"I do appreciate your agreeing to these little meetings. It's a bit unusual. . . ." He hesitated. "We don't ordinarily have ladies involved in such things."

"I understand, Sir William. If there's nothing further, I think I shall return home."

"Nothing else here. I shouldn't worry too much about any of it. Hargreaves will find the boy and this will all be wrapped up soon enough. You might focus on sightseeing. I fear you've not seen enough of Constantinople."

I thanked him and stepped into the hall, where Margaret, who'd been waiting for me, was talking to Mr. Sutcliffe.

"I was just saying to Miss Seward how much I've been looking forward to seeing you again," he said.

"Thank you," I said. "You're well?"

"I am, thank you. A spot of trouble with one of the families I'm working with—the mother turned out very unworthy indeed."

"Unworthy?" I asked.

"Her daughter fell ill with influenza, and she refused to send her son to the country as I suggested to keep him well."

"Did he get sick?" Margaret asked.

"He did and he died, and it's his mother's fault. I can afford no tolerance for such people." He frowned, shook his head. "Is there anything I can do to help Benjamin?"

"I wish I knew what any of us could do."

"Is there any chance he's innocent?" His eyes were so full of eager hope—bright and clear.

"I believe so, but I can't yet prove it."

"Do you think you'll be able to?"

"The truth always comes out in the end."

"Have you told his father anything encouraging?"

"Not yet," I said. "I want to wait until I have something of substance to share with him."

"Is he at home?" Mr. Sutcliffe asked.

"He is," Margaret said. "We've left him in the care of friends."

"Perhaps I will call on him. He undoubtedly needs the support, and I feel awful I've not been around more. Things have been terribly busy here; another belated load of records has come in and overwhelmed me. But that's no reason to let down a friend in need."

"I'm sure he would appreciate a visit," I said.

"No one understands his loss better than I," he said. "If you'll excuse me, I must go to him."

22

My nausea returned almost as soon as we'd left the embassy, and I'd decided to go home, hoping that rest would restore my health. I was exhausted, the trek from one palace to the next and then to the embassy taking every ounce of my energy. I found no respite in sleep, suffering a painful night, plagued with vivid dreams of the most awful sorts of destruction. They came in flashes—no narrative connection. I saw Colin falling, heard terrible screams in a dark room, and could not escape water pressing down on me, heavier than lead, but not reaching my mouth or keeping me from being able to breathe, simply crushing me.

So I was far from restored when I set off for Pera the next morning. Margaret had sent a message saying that Miss Evans, concerned about Sir Richard, had moved their things to his house so that they could stay there and she might keep a closer eye on him. I set off as soon as I'd refused breakfast—not even the thick yogurt that usually settled my stomach looked appealing—and braced myself for what I knew would be an unpleasant trip across the Bosphorus.

"I'm afraid he's not well at all," the doctor said moments after I'd arrived at the St. Clare house. "He's suffering from terrible tremors and has started to hallucinate."

"Have you any idea what's causing it?" I asked, my head beginning to hurt again. "It must be more than worry for his son."

"I'm afraid so, Lady Emily. I can't be certain, but if pressed, I'd guess that he's become dependent on chloral hydrate—he's exhibiting symptoms of withdrawal, including severe gastritis. I'm very concerned."

"What can be done?"

"If my diagnosis is correct, I should be able to treat him. I assume that since he's been under the care of Miss Evans, he's not had the opportunity to take the drug."

"I would imagine not. Did you find a supply of it?"

"I've not looked, but I can't imagine what else is causing this. It also explains the erratic behavior he's exhibited over the past weeks."

"Is there anything more we can do to assist you?" I asked.

"No. I shall continue to check on him daily and will keep you abreast of his condition."

I thanked him and rang for Sir Richard's valet. "Where does your master keep his medicines?"

"Everything's in his dressing room," the man replied. "Would you like me to show you?"

I spent more than an hour with the valet and Margaret, searching the house. None of us found even a trace of chloral hydrate. I crossed the street to the embassy, asked for and was granted permission to search his office. Again, no chloral hydrate. This absolute lack of physical evidence told me one thing: Sir Richard was not a man addicted to a drug; he was a man being poisoned. I needed evidence, and I needed to determine if what was happening to Sir Richard was separate from the murders in Constantinople.

I rushed to the embassy and straight into the ambassador's office, hardly waiting for him to answer my knock. "Is there any way to get a message to my husband?" I asked. "I've information he needs."

"I have not had word from him—and I'm certain he'd be in touch with you before me."

"Unless he had news of Benjamin," I said. "He would inform you first of that."

"Have you uncovered something new?" Sir William asked.

"I'm quite certain now that this case is far more complicated than we'd initially believed. We need to revisit everything that's happened from the moment Sir Richard collapsed on the *Orient Express*."

"I of course offer you whatever services in the embassy's power. But I don't see how his collapsing during dinner on a train relates to two murders in Constantinople."

"These crimes are not about Benjamin. They're about his father. Would it be possible for me to look through his service files?"

"What do you hope to find?" he asked.

"I'm not sure. Something that links all these events together."

"You're unlikely to find that in his employment record."

"If I'm wrong, I've wasted nothing but my own time," I said. "Please, Sir William?"

"It's an irregular request, Lady Emily. Those files are confidential. The clearance your husband obtained for you did not extend to this sort of thing. He, on the other hand, would be allowed access. Perhaps when he returns . . ."

"I fear that may be too late."

"It's the best I can do," he said. "Unless you'd like me to look through them for you? I could alert you if I noticed anything glaring."

"No," I said, the skin on my neck beginning to crawl as I started to question his sincerity. I shook off the feeling; he was being honest. Why would I be given access to sensitive information? Nonetheless, something tugged at me, made me balk at his offer, as if he might remove and destroy something crucial from the file. "That won't be necessary. I wouldn't know what to tell you to look for. It's undoubtedly a foolish idea."

"If you change your mind—"

"Thank you," I said. "I shan't bother you again with such a silly request."

I stepped through the embassy door, greeted by a sublime spring day, the air heavier than in winter but fresh and breezy, not a hint of the oppressive humidity that would come with summer. I went up the hill, in the direction of Yıldız, where I planned to meet Roxelana, but before I'd walked more than a few blocks, I turned east towards the Bosphorus. Following the path along it would require scaling the hill again, but I could not resist the beauty I knew awaited me. The wind blew stronger near the strait, gulls riding currents of air, bobbing between the boats crowding the water. The sun burned on my face, and I pulled down the brim of my hat to better shield it, a gesture that caught me entirely off guard.

It made me feel like my mother. My mother, who would have scolded me without mercy at finding me in the sun without a parasol. I ground my teeth and sighed, keeping my eyes open only so that I would not trip as I was walking. Had I unwittingly entered a new stage in my life? Unwitting was perhaps not the correct word, as I'd known marriage would inevitably lead to it. But the reality—if reality it was—struck me hard. I was short of breath by the time I reached the gates of the palace and grateful for the glass of cold, tart cherry juice Roxelana offered me when I met her in a sitting room in the harem.

"I would be more comfortable if we discussed this somewhere private," she said, glancing in the direction of the other women, gathered in small groups scattered around the large chamber, which, like the rest of Yıldız, was furnished in Western European mode. The concubines might have been debutantes chatting at a garden party in London. So much for the exotic.

"It's important now that no one thinks we're skulking off to talk alone," I said. "We can't afford to draw any attention to ourselves."

"I understand, but it makes me nervous."

"So you've opportunity for an excursion?" I asked.

"Tuesday. A group is going into the city to shop at the Grand Bazaar."

Visions of opportunity flew through my head. The chaos of the bazaar would make it simpler than I could have hoped for Roxelana to vanish. "This is perfect. The bazaar—"

"I won't be in the bazaar itself. We go to the sultan's private section of the Nuruosmaniye Mosque, next to the bazaar. The merchants give their goods to the eunuchs, who in turn show them to us."

"Will there be opportunity to escape from the building?" I asked.

"There must be," she said. "But I've never before had occasion to consider it."

"I shall go look this afternoon and come back to you tomorrow. Do not tell anyone of this—not even Jemal."

"I promise." Her eyes were dark, serious. "Is it true they've arrested the man who killed Ceyden?"

"Not yet," I said. "A suspect is being apprehended, but he'd fled before the police came for him."

"There—there are rumors it is an Englishman."

"Yes, I'm afraid so."

"Will they find him?"

"My husband's looking for him, and Colin never fails. He'll be found, don't worry."

"I've heard it said they seek the wrong man. Do you think—" She stopped, looked out the window, then back at me with a smile that could have charmed Alexander into handing Greece over to the Persians. "I'm excited about Tuesday," she said, her voice louder now. "I'm told we shall see fabric more beautiful than any made in history. I want at least four new dresses."

My reconnaissance at Nuruosmaniye was fruitful. I was able, by pressing the right amount of money into the right hands, to be admitted to the sultan's lodge, pleading that an enthusiastic tourist not be denied the pleasure of seeing the space. A partition had been set up to shield the ladies of the harem, behind which, Roxelana had told me, they would be measured for their dresses. Wooden grilles covered the windows, and I had to determine whether they could be opened with ease. The caretaker who'd let me in was staying close to me, his eyes darting to the door every time he heard a noise, as if he feared Abdül Hamit would come in unannounced and find me violating his room.

I slipped into the ladies' section and fell to my knees, hoping that if he thought I were praying, he would leave me in peace. He stood at the opening of the screen, watching me; perhaps my effort was not sincere enough. I closed my eyes, pressed my hands together, and murmured an "Our Father" under my breath. Even without looking, I could feel he was still there. I tried to summon the focused energy I'd felt in the Blue Mosque, not believing it would come, surprised when it did. All of my fears, my worries, were so close to my skin that it took almost nothing to coax them to surface. I remembered the sounds of my dear aunt's dying cries, then imagined Ivy's voice replacing hers, then mine. I pictured Colin standing over me, his face fading, and tears streamed down my cheeks.

I looked up, and as I met the caretaker's eyes, he turned his back, blushing to his fingertips, then walked away from where I knelt and stood sentry in the main doorway to the building, his back to the interior. Fortunate and desired though this outcome was, I found that I could not readily cast away the emotions I'd summoned. Sinking farther down, dropping my head onto my clasped hands, I prayed as I had before, this time not undercutting my bargain: me for Ivy.

Finished—and shaking—I struggled to my feet and went to the windows, inspecting the grilles. They were held in place with latches, like shutters. Checking over my shoulder to ensure I was not being watched, I opened one. A simple task. Even the hinges, smooth-moving and silent, cooperated. Shooting another glance behind me, I tried to open the window. This took more effort, and I nearly lost my balance trying to push the sash, but eventually I managed. The drop to the ground was not terribly far and would set a person in a gallery that led from outside to the mosque.

I closed the window, but not fully, leaving enough room for me to slip my hand in and open it from outside. It was not the best plan, but I saw no other immediate way to escape the building. We would have to consider ways to improve upon it—distractions or something. I wished Colin were not gone. His suggestions would be invaluable, and he would be able to look at this space and see six safe but hidden routes to safety. Then I remembered that he would not approve of any of this in the least, and a sinking, twisting feeling in my stomach told me I would have to do this on my own and apologize after it was done.

After taking a careful study of the rest of the room, I thanked the caretaker, pressed another coin into his hand, and walked the perimeter of the building until I reached the part-open window. Margaret was tall enough that she'd be able to reach it without problem. I planned to give Roxelana a set of simple clothes and a veil that she could hide under her skirts, switching into them when she was supposed to be dressing after her measurements had been taken. She would wear traditional Turkish clothes to the mosque—garments that would not require assistance to put back on—and take them with her when she went, so that as the eunuchs searched for her, they would be looking for someone in the wrong outfit.

Once outside, she would have to make her way down the ramp that led to the building. The main risk she would take was being seen dropping from the window. The area outside was not crowded like the mosque's main courtyard, but another diversion here would be helpful. If she could reach the Grand Bazaar without being noticed, she would have her freedom.

Cataloging ideas about how we could draw attention away from the building, I walked to meet Margaret, who was waiting for me outside the courtyard—we'd thought we'd make too much of an impression if we both went into the sultan's lodge—and keeping her away meant she stood no chance of being recognized should I call on her to organize a distraction.

"Do we have a viable strategy?" she asked, leaning against a stone wall.

"The beginnings of one," I said. "You will be instrumental in pulling it off."

"I like that kind of plan." We walked towards the Grand Bazaar, crossing through its entranceway and into the labyrinthine streets of stalls. "How will you get her out of the city?"

"I'll hire a coach—closed—to meet us. We'll figure out the best place. First, though, let's decide where she should sit and wait for things to calm down." Within minutes, we'd found a stall that sold baklava and tea. The chairs and tables set up in front were filled with both men and women, so it seemed as appropriate as any other spot. "I'll wait for her here."

"Veiled, of course," Margaret said.

"I shall consider it. There's nothing wrong with having a bit of fun in all this, is there?"

I went to Yıldız after finishing our work at the bazaar. Perestu had sent a note asking to see me. She was waiting in an elegant sitting room and was, for someone who had requested a meeting, surprisingly silent. Her quiet stillness teemed with elegance; even the way she breathed was full of grace, and I could not help staring at her.

"Your careful study of me unnerves me," she said.

"Forgive me," I said. "You are unlike any woman I've met before."

She let out a long breath. "You are kind not to press me for the reason I wanted you to come today. I appreciate it, and it makes me think that you are trustworthy. I have two problems and wonder if you can assist me with them."

"I'm of course happy to try," I said.

"The first is something that I've debated taking to the sultan, but if it's possible to eliminate the threat without aggravating him, the outcome would be preferable for everyone involved."

"What is it?"

"There are rumors that someone is trying to flee the harem."

My breath caught in my throat, and I willed myself to freeze, wishing I could channel Perestu's grace. "How could such a thing be possible?"

"It isn't," she said. "It will be stopped, and the offenders will be punished in the most severe ways."

"How severe?"

"That is for the sultan to decide. But I can assure you he would show little mercy."

"Have you any idea who is forming the plot?"

"Not the slightest," she said. "You've spoken with some of the girls and have become closer to a familiar figure here than any foreigner has in the past. I do not ask you to betray a confidence, only that you let it be known that you've heard the rumors and have reason to think what's being planned is a bad idea—that might be enough to stop the ingrate organizing this offense."

The emotions pummeling me at this moment were as thoroughly unpleasant as any I knew: guilt, embarrassment, anxiety, fear. Not a litany of favorites. I considered what to say, what to do: Should I warn Roxelana and cancel our plans? Force her to continue to live in a circumstance so abhorrent to a woman of her faith?

I realized I'd been quiet too long. "I shall do what I can," I said, confused and conflicted. "What is the other matter?"

"I want to know how my friend came to lose my ring." Her voice was soft, quivering.

"Whom did you give it to?" I asked.

"Mr. Theodore Sutcliffe," she said. "He's compassionate, full of sympathy. A man whose soul has been so deeply touched with grief that he's capable of emotions that terrify most of us."

"I know him," I said.

"I assumed as much. Do you think you could find out what happened to my ring?"

"Of course," I said. "That's no trouble at all."

"Thank you, Lady Emily. You are more capable than I first thought. I admire your strength."

19 April 1892
Darnley House, Kent

My darling Emily,

I've been doing nothing of late but reading, and have devoured all the books you'd hidden in your dressing room—I told Robert to look for them, remembering it had been an old habit of yours to spirit the raciest volumes off to safety there. Your mother was, as I need hardly tell you, out of her mind when she saw them. Madame Bovary *near drove her to swoon. The only thing that saved the poor book from the fire was my own dear husband insisting it was an especial favorite of his. A statement you know cannot possibly be true, but a testament to his love for me. He saw the comfort the novel brought and could not bear to see it taken away.*

Other than that, I'm consumed with weakness and more exhausted than I would have thought possible. The doctor is so kind, but tells me nothing of substance, and Robert, try though he may, cannot hide his fear. I pray all his suffering will be erased by the sight of an heir, and that I shall survive to see him.

Apologies for a bleak letter. I'm so very scared—terrified, Emily. I couldn't bear to let anyone but you know that. I've never felt so bad in my life—physically or emotionally. Forgive me, my friend, for so burdening you with my troubles. I've nowhere else to turn, as the only thing that could make my plight worse is knowing that I've caused Robert more worry.

I send you all my love and miss you very, very much.

I am, your most devoted friend,

Ivy

I could not stop the tears as I read Ivy's letter and was consumed with panic at the thought of what she still had to face. How desperately I needed Colin's support. I wished there were some way I could contact him, prayed that he would return soon. Loneliness filled every corner of our *yalı*, and I had no intention of coming out of our room. I curled up on the bed in a ball around his pillow, breathing in the scent of him lingering on its surface.

My throat burned from sobbing, and when I'd cried so much that no more tears would come, I forced myself up and rang for Meg. There was nothing more I could do for Ivy from here. The best course of action was to focus on my work, finish it as efficiently as possible, and return to England. I only hoped that Colin would be back soon.

Meg fawned over me, pressed a cool cloth to my swollen eyes, refusing to let me dress until I approached something she considered presentable. She went about her work in a fashion much gentler than her usual manner, insulting my scalp with not a single hairpin.

Once dressed, I set off for Pera. The Bosphorus, as if sensing my dire condition, played sweet as well, its waters as placid as I'd seen them since arriving in Turkey. Upon docking, I took a carriage to the embassy, too tired and heartsick to walk, and shortly was admitted to Mr. Sutcliffe's office.

"What a surprise to see you, Lady Emily. What can I do for you?"

"I've come on a strange errand," I said. "Perestu asked me to do it on her behalf."

"The valide sultan?" He tugged at his shirtsleeves, adjusting his cuff links.

"I understand that you shared a close friendship. She speaks very highly of you."

"She is an excellent woman."

"I do not doubt it," I said. "She told me that, years ago, she gave to you a ring as a token of her friendship. Strangely enough, that same ring has turned up in the harem—in the possession of Sir Richard's daughter."

"Impossible," he said. "I keep it under lock and key in my house."

"You can imagine how upset she was to see it—at first she feared that you might have given it away—"

"I would never," he said.

"Of course not. But I'm sure you can imagine she was devastated to see the ring back in the harem."

"I—I—" He stammered but formed no coherent words. "The ring is in my house," he said, tugging again at his sleeves, this time so hard that I feared for his cuff links. "Follow me there now. I will show you."

It took us fewer than ten minutes to reach his residence, and he marched into his study with me tailing behind, barely able to keep up with him. He pulled down a wooden box from a high shelf on a bookcase and placed it on his desk. "It's in here," he said, pulling out a set of keys from his jacket, fumbling until he found the right one. He placed one hand on the side of the box and was about to push the key into the lock when the top sprang open.

"I don't understand," he said. "I know it was locked. I can't bear to even look. Please. Will you?"

Inside, resting on a blue velvet lining, were an engraved silver christening mug, a piece of faded ribbon that looked as if it might have once been pink, and an ivory comb. I held out the container to him. "There's no ring."

"This cannot be," he said. "Who would do such a thing?"

"Do you have any ideas? Who knew you had it?"

"I—I—" His voice choked. "I can't bring myself to even say it."

"You must, Mr. Sutcliffe."

"I showed it to Benjamin. We were talking one day—he was remembering his sister. How they used to play. I told him about my children and showed him these souvenirs I keep. The ring was in the box as well."

"But why would he take it?"

"He must have needed money for his elopement. Why didn't he ask me?" He pressed the palm of his hand hard against his forehead. "I suppose I wouldn't have given it to him. And he didn't know me well enough to ask."

"We don't know that Benjamin took it," I said. "What of your staff?"

"They've all been with me for years."

This, of course, meant very little, but I saw no reason to mention it at the time. He was clearly distraught. Regardless of the identity of our thief, I could at least put to rest Perestu's fears that her friend had knowingly abandoned her gift.

"There's no question that Colin will locate Benjamin. And when he does, we'll be able to ascertain whether he took the ring."

"He took it."

"We must remember, Mr. Sutcliffe, that he has not been proven guilty."

"You suspect someone else?"

"I'm only saying we should not leap to conclusions."

"I will ask that you forgive me, Lady Emily, but I cannot think of him as anything but a thief and worse."

"What's obvious is not always right," I said. "Real life is not as simple as the sultan's operas. Like the performance of *La Traviata* we saw at Yıldız."

"Ended neatly, to be sure, but so much tragedy," he said. "And I can't stand more tragedy. Truth is, I much prefer something more lighthearted, with a happy ending. Particularly when I consider what we all faced when we left the theater."

I stood quiet, stunned, and then took my leave from him, wondering how he could have forgotten the end of the opera. I could picture him in the courtyard with the rest of us, standing over Ceyden's body. But if he'd been in the theater, he wouldn't have thought the show had been a tragedy. I began to wonder if I needed to think in another direction entirely.

"What does the doctor say?" I asked when I returned from Mr. Sutcliffe's, my head spinning. "Is he progressing as expected?"

Sir Richard's health had been improving, but he was not yet well enough to leave his bed. Miss Evans had given the cook urgent suggestions as to appropriate recipes to help him regain his strength—

again reminding me of my mother—and was convinced they would make all the difference in his recovery.

"Yes," Miss Evans said. "He stopped taking the drug so suddenly, it was a terrible shock to his system."

"If he was deliberately taking it, I cannot understand why it's impossible for us to locate the bottle," I said.

"He must have hidden it somewhere," Miss Evans said.

"But why? It's a common enough sleeping aid. His servants wouldn't have thought anything of him keeping a bottle around. It doesn't make sense." I stood up, unable to keep still. "I'm going back to the embassy to look through his office again."

Margaret threw on a hat and started for the door with me. "Any more from Ivy?" she asked. I told her about the latest letter.

"Oh, Em, don't you just want to go home?" she asked. "There's no shame in it, you know."

"I think I shall, when Colin returns." The pain of missing him had moved from dull to sharp, more of a stab than an ache. Wanting only to move forward, I opened the door to let us out of the house. On the step was a young Englishman, out of breath, his face bright red and covered in sweat.

"Lady Emily, the ambassador sends me with urgent news. I'm afraid there's been another murder at Yıldız, and . . . well . . . that Mr. St. Clare was involved yet again."

I did not wait to hear another word. We hailed the first available carriage, paying triple to motivate the driver to rush. Once through the palace gates, we were admitted to the harem, where there was none of the usual clamor of voices and laughter. Perestu received us in a small salon in her apartments, her face drawn, no spark in her eyes.

"It is good of you to come. We've suffered more tragedy today."

"Who? What happened?" I asked.

"Jemal. The same as the others, with a bowstring."

"And because the method has not changed, Mr. St. Clare is suspected again?" Margaret asked.

"We are not so unsophisticated. The guards searched Jemal's room and discovered a bundle of letters—written to him by Mr. St. Clare."

"May I see them?" I asked.

"If you wish, but there's no need. They prove that Jemal was letting him into the palace to meet with a concubine—Ceyden, obviously. And that he was accepting regular payments for granting the privilege."

"And there's no question they were written by Benjamin?" I asked.

"None. The first is signed—it came shortly after Mr. St. Clare had assisted in rescuing the ladies whose boat capsized in the Bosphorus. The handwriting on the others is a perfect match."

This was disheartening, and I could feel myself taking it harder than perhaps was reasonable. Too many troubling thoughts tugging at already fraught emotions; never before had I felt so scattered. I hardly knew Benjamin, had no reason to take more than a professional interest in his situation, yet coming to a point where his guilt seemed inevitable stung me, and not only because it would prove my instinct wrong. A wave of nausea hit me, and I clung to the arms of my chair to steel myself against it, unaccountably feeling as if I were about to burst into tears.

"Where was the body found?" I asked, my voice strong despite my spinning head.

"In one of the gardens. I'll have someone take you."

There wasn't much to see. I searched the area—not looking at the body, which had already been covered with a makeshift shroud—

and then went to the eunuch's room. Beyond the letters, there was nothing of interest. The ordinary possessions of a man. As for his correspondence with Benjamin, there could be no question of the relationship between them. Jemal was taking bribes.

"What do you think?" Margaret asked, whispering as we walked through the palace gates, headed to the docks on the Bosphorus.

"There's still no absolute proof, of course, but . . ." The water's beauty eluded me entirely. "I'm afraid it doesn't bode well."

"Motive?"

"He could have killed Ceyden because she'd decided not to run away with him, and Jemal because he'd decided to stop accepting bribes."

"Poor Sir Richard."

"Although . . ." I stopped walking. "Why, if Ceyden was already dead, would he need continued access to the harem?"

"Maybe it wasn't a question of bribes," Margaret said. "What if Jemal had threatened to blackmail him?"

"Jemal had already given evidence against him. Killing him would have made little difference at this point. And why, if Benjamin fled after suspecting he'd be arrested, would he have returned to Constantinople?"

"Jemal might have had further proof—something more solid."

"And tested Benjamin by coming forward with just a bit of it first?" I considered the possibility. "Maybe. But it doesn't sit right, somehow."

"What, then?"

"What if Benjamin wasn't in love with Ceyden?"

24

Fired with new enthusiasm at this revelation—for I considered it nothing short of just that—I turned on my heel and went straight back to Yıldız.

"Roxelana?" Margaret said as we walked to the harem. "In love with Benjamin?"

"She found Ceyden's body and may have even witnessed the murder. Think on it—if she was the one trying to escape, with her lover, and Ceyden happened upon them. Ceyden, who wanted more than anything to gain the sultan's attention?"

"So do we confront Roxelana?"

"I'd wager she knows where he is," I said. "That's why she's so keen to make her escape right away. She wouldn't be doing it if she had nowhere to go. What a fool I've been!"

"I thought you were going to send her to London?"

"I was. I told her I'd help her in any way I could, assuming that she had no other options."

"So you think Benjamin is somewhere, skulking about, waiting for her?" Margaret asked.

"It wouldn't surprise me." For an instant, I was horrified by my thoughts, because I realized that more than a small part of me was hoping they could pull it off. Escape. Find happiness together. Had my moral compass gone completely wild? We'd reached the sitting room in the harem. Roxelana came through the door only a few minutes later and sank next to me on a settee.

"I did not expect to see you until—" Her skin had lost its glow, her eyes were dull. "Is something wrong?"

"There are many things wrong," I said. "I need you to start being honest with me. You were the one meeting an Englishman in the harem. Benjamin."

"I—I—"

"Spare me denials. I have a great deal of sympathy for you, but I cannot tolerate deception. You have misled me at every turn and in doing so may have destroyed Benjamin's chance at exoneration."

"Please, Lady Emily." She had started to cry. "I will tell you anything—"

"Yes, you will," I said. "Starting with Ceyden and her cache of jewelry. Where did she get it?"

Roxelana was crying too hard to answer.

"You must stop," Margaret said, passing her a handkerchief. "You'll draw attention to yourself."

"You're right." One last sob spilled out of her as she dried her eyes. "The jewelry was mine. All of it, so far as I can tell. I saved every piece I got—much of it was given to me by the sultan. Ceyden hated that he favored me. She used to follow me, torment me. Thought it was unfair that he would choose me when I didn't want him."

"She was jealous," I said.

"Terribly," she said. "When I met Benjamin, the world opened before me. I never lived before the day he pulled me from the waters of the Bosphorus. He paid Jemal to deliver letters to me, and when we could stand that no longer, he paid more for Jemal to sneak him into the palace so we could see each other."

"And Ceyden discovered this?"

"Yes. I caught her in my room. She told me a pretty story about coming to me for advice—flattered me. I fell for it until later that night when I realized all the letters Benjamin had written me were gone."

"She took them?"

"Yes, and she admitted it when I confronted her. Said she'd given them to a friend who would hold them for her, someone who wasn't in the palace. That she would use them against me."

"But the jewelry?" I asked. "You were planning to use it to finance your escape?"

"Yes."

"Where did you get Perestu's ring?"

"I had nothing of Perestu's."

"It was a large sapphire in a round bezel encrusted with diamonds."

"I do remember it. Jemal gave it to me. He told me it had been a gift to him from a friend."

This gave me pause, but I could not stop to think. "Why would Ceyden take your jewelry? I'd think she wouldn't do something to hinder you."

"She stole it the day I was planning to leave," Roxelana said. "I'd sewn everything into a gown—that's what you found—thinking I could wear it and arouse no suspicion. But when I went to get dressed that evening, it was gone. I was in tears when I went to meet Benjamin, unsure if we'd be able to carry out our plan. She followed me that night, stood in the shadows as we spoke. We didn't know how we could go without the jewels, and that's what she counted on. She stepped forward and laughed at us. Said that she'd taken them in case I slipped out too easily—she didn't want to miss her opportunity to catch us in the act. And then she started to call for a guard . . ."

"And Benjamin stopped her," I said, a terrible weight descending onto me.

"Yes." Her voice hid her sob. "He was afraid that if we were caught together, I would be executed. He panicked."

"What happened then?"

"He—he lunged at her throat and strangled her. She fell to the ground, and I told him to run, which he did. Once I thought enough time had passed for him to be well away, I went for the guards. She wasn't dead then, you know. She spoke to me after he left—" Now her tears could not be stopped.

"What did she say?" I asked.

"That the sultan would never want me again. She must have died when I was on my way to get help." She held her head up high. "I suppose you won't help me now."

"What of your Aquinas?" I asked.

"'Love takes up where knowledge leaves off,'" she said.

I met her eyes. "I gave you my word. This is all unspeakably awful, but does not change the fact that I don't agree with the way you are being forced to live. Our plans will not change." What I did not say was that I could not abandon her because I feared what might happen should she still be in the harem when the full truth of the situation was revealed.

When we'd returned to the *yalı,* Margaret went straight for the decanter and filled two glasses with port. Before she'd crossed the room to hand me one, Meg came in with a small envelope.

"A wire for you, madam."

My stomach clenched, fearing bad news from England, but the words surprised me less than their author would have expected. I looked up, meeting Margaret's eyes, reading her concern. "No, it's not Ivy," I said. "It's from Colin. He's found Benjamin at Ephesus."

"That's wonderful," Margaret said. "More or less."

"He's made a full confession. He admitted to killing his sister. They'll be in Constantinople within three days, sooner if he can hire a boat." I felt ill. "We must go to his father. I don't want someone from the embassy breaking this news."

Of all the unpleasant trips I'd taken across the Bosphorus in the past weeks, this was by far the worst. I looked at Seraglio Point, far off in the distance, hazy in the sun, and rehearsed what I would say, knowing there was no magic to it, no particular set of words that would lessen the blow. Margaret took my hand in hers.

"I never thought this trip could have turned out so badly," she said, a forced brightness in her voice. "Do you think, perhaps, it's a sign that I'm to marry Mr. Michaels as quickly as possible and settle into an ordinary life?"

"You're beginning to worry me," I said. "That's at least the second time you've made such a comment."

"Do you ever wonder if we're too set on being independent and fierce?"

"Are you joking? Is this meant to distract me?"

"Well, yes, it's meant to distract," she said.

"But not to be a joke?"

"No." Now her gaze moved in the direction of Seraglio Point. "Forgive me, Emily. Are you happy? I know you adore Colin and don't doubt for an instant that you have found the man for whom you were designed. But this is your wedding trip . . . It's bad enough that I invaded your privacy—and I hope you'll forgive me for that—"

"Don't be absurd," I said. "Honeymoons go on for months and months. Besides, haven't you read *Can You Forgive Her?* Didn't Glencora keep Alice close to her for most of her wedding trip?"

"An entirely different circumstance, my dear."

"Quite." I could not help but smile.

"I cannot help but consider things differently now," Margaret said. "I wouldn't want my honeymoon interrupted as yours has been—"

"No one wants to contend with murder."

"Obviously. But you do enjoy it, Em—not the murder part, but the rest. You've gotten to cavort about Constantinople with more freedom than anyone since Lady Mary What's-her-name. Some days I think you thrive on it, but lately it seems to be taking a toll."

"I'm just worried about Ivy. It's nothing else. This is how I want my life to be, Margaret. I wouldn't have it any other way. I want to do this work. It's important to me."

"I'm afraid I'm becoming a hopeless romantic," she said. "It's rather disgusting."

"You really do want to hole up at Oxford, don't you?"

"I think I do," she said.

"You don't think it will become claustrophobic?"

"No. Have you any idea how much Ovid I have left to translate? And then there's Virgil. That is the work I need. This trip has made me realize that I want Mr. Michaels by my side all the time. Gallivanting about isn't much fun without him."

"I would hope not," I said. "Otherwise what would be the point in marrying him? I miss Colin dreadfully every moment I'm not with him." As we came closer to the European shore, Topkapı looming above us until we'd passed it after turning into the Golden Horn, my nerves took firm hold of me, my heart pounding in my chest. From the dock, it did not take long to reach Sir Richard's—we took a carriage, wanting to get to him as quickly as possible.

Miss Evans greeted us at the door. "He's feeling much better today," she said. "Has been receiving visitors. Even came downstairs."

"Did he?"

"For a while," she said. "But he started to get tired and went back up. Still, an improvement."

"I fear that we'll only make it worse." I left Margaret to explain to her and found my way to Sir Richard, propped up in bed on a mountain of pillows, a copy of Jules Verne's *From the Earth to the Moon* beside him.

"Lady Emily, it is good to see you, but I'm afraid Miss Evans should not have let you come up. I'm not so well as I was earlier." His voice slurred and his head bobbed. "Even the coffee Sutcliffe brought up to me didn't help. Of course it was as bad as that I get at the embassy. Too bitter. Expect better at home."

"I'm so sorry to disturb you," I said. "And wouldn't have were the matter not of the greatest urgency."

"What has happened?" He sat up straighter. "Is it my son?"

"I'm afraid so. Colin has found him—don't worry, he's safe."

"Thank heavens. Where was he?"

"Ephesus. They're on their way back now."

"This is joyous news," he said. "I cannot begin—"

"No, please. Wait. He's admitted to Colin that he was responsible for . . ." I hesitated.

"Not for Ceyden?"

"Yes. I'm so sorry."

"It's not possible. My son would never . . ." His voice faltered, then failed altogether. His head nodded forward, then dropped back against the pillows. I thought at first he was stricken with grief, but then his jaw went slack and his mouth hung open.

"Sir Richard? . . . Sir Richard?"

He did not respond. He was breathing—I could see that—but he was not conscious. I pulled the bell cord, then ran to the hallway, shouting for Margaret. The ensuing chaos should have woken the dead, as Miss Evans came into the room and gave a shriek, horrifying and inhuman.

"Has he gone? Have we lost him? Oh, it's too, too dreadful!" she said.

Margaret appeared almost at once and, proving she had not lost her ability to keep her wits about her, did the reasonable thing. She sent for the doctor, who arrived in short order.

"It's more chloral hydrate," he said, coming to meet us in the corridor outside Sir Richard's room after examining his patient.

"He couldn't possibly have taken anything," Miss Evans said. "I've followed your orders to the letter. He's had no access to it."

"While I do not doubt your sincerity, madam, I know of what I speak. The man has taken an overdose. Not enough to kill him—but his breathing is dangerously shallow. I will do what I can."

"Will he survive?" I asked.

"I cannot say."

"Whom did he see today?" I asked, turning to Miss Evans.

"Oh, all kinds of people. Half the staff of the embassy called on him."

"The coffee," I said. "It was the coffee."

"What—"

I did not linger to hear the rest of her sentence but rushed back into the room, grabbed the cup from the nightstand, and brought it to the doctor.

"You'll find it in here," I said. "Mr. Sutcliffe brought it up to him, correct?"

"Yes," Miss Evans said. "I poured it for him myself. But you can't think—"

The physician sniffed at the contents of the cup, then dipped a finger in it and cautiously touched the tip to his tongue. "That's chloral hydrate."

"Do excuse us," I said, taking Margaret by the arm and dragging her down the steps as fast as I could, nearly tripping on my skirts. I slid across the marble floor as I tried to stop when we'd reached the front door.

"I take it we're going to the embassy?" Margaret asked, grinning.

"I do love not having to explain things to you," I said.

We were there in almost no time, breathing hard as the ambassador came to us in the hall—for our arrival was not without commotion.

"Lady Emily, Miss Seward, are you quite well? Do sit down. Let me get you some tea at once," he said, ushering us into his office.

"I have news," I said.

"Yes, I've heard from your husband. I'm terribly sorry that—"

"No, Sir William, it's all wrong," I said. "All of it. Sir Richard has been poisoned and—"

"What?"

"I need to speak to Mr. Sutcliffe at once."

"He's not here. He left yesterday on holiday—he's going to Rome."

"No, I don't think he is," I said. "Could you please let me search his office?" I explained to him what had happened at Sir Richard's.

"I can't imagine that this dreadful conjecture of yours is true," Sir William said. "And even if it were, would he be foolish enough to leave evidence at the embassy?"

"I think Mr. Sutcliffe was dosing him here," I said. "Please let us look."

"I suppose there's no harm, but it seems a useless endeavor," Sir William said.

He brought us to the records room on the ground floor of the building and opened the door to a small office. A quick search ensued, but to no avail, which disappointed but did not surprise me. "Do you think there's any way we could get permission—a warrant, whatever the appropriate thing would be—to search his home?" I asked.

"Absolutely not," Sir William said. "Sir Richard has had difficulties for some time now. And people with troubles like that are, well . . . I'm sorry, Lady Emily. I let you look in Sutcliffe's office only because you're so very enthusiastic about your detecting, and I do appreciate what you've been doing. But a lady such as yourself couldn't begin to comprehend the lengths to which those afflicted with this sort of madness will go to satisfy their cravings. It brings to mind opium houses and the like. I understand your desire to find someone other than Sir Richard to blame for these problems. It is admirable that you revolt at the thought of an English gentleman destroying himself, but in this case, it's precisely what is happening."

"There's more," I said. "I've discovered a connection between

Benjamin and someone else in the harem—not Ceyden. I think we're mistaken altogether about what—"

He held up his hand. "Please, Lady Emily. I understand how upsetting all this must be to a person of such delicate sensibilities. But the truth is now known. There's nothing further to be said."

"But who killed Jemal?" I asked. "If Benjamin's in Ephesus, he couldn't have done it."

"He could have gone there immediately afterwards."

"He wouldn't have had time. Please, Sir William, let me look into this further. Will you at least tell me more about Mr. Sutcliffe?"

"I'm sorry, Lady Emily, there's nothing more to be done. If, as you say, Benjamin was not involved in Jemal's murder, then the entire matter's of no concern to the embassy."

"Of no concern?" I asked. "How can you say that?"

"We became involved in Ceyden's case because she was the daughter of an Englishman. Jemal's death will be investigated by the Ottomans, as it should be."

"I think, though, that Mr. Sutcliffe—"

"No, Lady Emily. You're wrong. There's nothing further to be done. I thank you for the services you provided your country—I've no doubt you did thorough and excellent work. The sultan himself has spoken highly of you. But now the business is done."

I opened my mouth to protest, but he had already stood and opened the door. Margaret rose to her feet and waited for me, urgency in her eyes. Feeling defeated, I followed her out of the room and then the building.

"This is a disaster," I said.

"What can we do?" Margaret asked. "Do you believe that Mr. Sutcliffe is on his way to Rome?"

"Not for a second."

"But, Emily, you know that Benjamin is guilty."

"Probably," I said. "But I'm slightly less convinced of that fact than I was an hour ago. I want to get into his house. I suspect we may find the chloral hydrate there."

Mr. Sutcliffe's butler, a sullen man with no sense of humor, assured us that his master had left on holiday, with plans to go to Rome.

"I'm so sorry to have missed him," I said. "Could I leave a note?"

"Of course, madam." He held out his hand.

"Oh," I said, frowning. "I'll need paper."

"Follow me." With no enthusiasm, he took us into a small, bright sitting room at the front of the house. "You'll find paper on the table."

I pulled out the chair in front of a delicate ladies' desk, picked up a piece of paper, flipped open the inkwell, and dipped the pen, flashing Margaret a look I hoped she would interpret correctly. She sighed heavily and lowered herself onto the nearest chair.

"Would it be possible for us to have something to drink? The walk here completely exhausted me," she said. And just like that, we had the room to ourselves.

"I want to get into his study," I said. "It's the most likely place for him to have hidden something."

"Where is it?" Margaret asked.

"Two doors farther down the hall. It's where he showed me the box that was supposed to house the ring."

"Do you want me to go?"

"No, I will. You pretend to be ill. If I'm caught, I'll say I was looking for help."

I ducked into the hall after satisfying myself that there was no one in the corridor, walking on the balls of my feet so that my heels would not click on the hard floor. I laid one palm flat on the door and slowly turned the knob with the other, opening it just a crack, then looking behind me, making sure I was still alone. As confident as I could be with trembling legs, I pushed further, until I could see into the room.

Mr. Sutcliffe was sitting at his desk.

"Lady Emily!" He leapt to his feet.

"Oh, I'm—I'm so sorry," I said. "I was leaving a note for you and Margaret fainted. We've been walking too much today. I was looking for someone to—"

"How dreadful. Did you ring for help?"

"I—I wasn't even thinking. Just ran out, hoping to— I'm not even making sense." I met his eyes and for the first time saw depths of coldness in them. "Will you please help me?"

He stood there, staring for long enough to terrify me. With no time to evaluate options, I did the only thing that sprang to mind: I forced myself to cry. The effort was not entirely successful, but a well-placed handkerchief can hide many things, the absence of tears only one of them.

"She wanted to take a carriage, and I insisted . . . I love to walk, you know—it's all my fault—"

"There, now, she'll be fine."

He put a hand on my back and guided me to the sitting room, where, to her credit, Margaret was sprawled out, half on her chair, half on the floor. To anyone with experience, it was clear her pose was far too elegant to be authentic, but there are moments in which artistry cannot be resisted. Mr. Sutcliffe pulled a bell cord, and the butler appeared almost at once. As soon as he saw Margaret, he stepped out again and returned with a bottle of smelling salts that he handed to his master. She flinched admirably when he placed them beneath her nose—although that would not have required much acting—opened her eyes, and looked at our host.

"Mr. Sutcliffe," she said. "You are like a vision of an angel."

"I . . . well, yes. Thank you, Miss Seward."

"I'm so sorry for disturbing you," I said. "I know you're off to Rome and in the midst of the last-minute rush. We picked a terrible time to call. For all practical purposes, you're already gone." I almost felt sorry for him. It was embarrassing to have been caught claiming not to be home, although everyone does it to avoid unwelcome callers. My sympathy was more than limited, however, as first, I strongly suspected Mr. Sutcliffe of murder, and second, I did not like to include myself in any list of unwanted visitors.

"Yes. Apologies. Had I known I would have two charming ladies calling, I should not have said I wasn't at home," he said.

"Especially if you knew one was about to faint," Margaret said, picking herself up off the floor.

"The subject we came to discuss is not urgent. It can wait until you return from your trip," I said.

"Will you be in Constantinople that long?"

"I wouldn't dream of leaving without seeing you again," I said. I had moved close to the door and then realized I was about to make an exit that lacked even a shred of grace. "Will you dine with us your first night back? I'd so love to hear about your trip."

"It would be my pleasure. And I must insist that you allow me to call my carriage for you. We can't have Miss Seward walking any further today."

Margaret, theatrically serious, looked at him with wide eyes. "I cannot thank you enough. You have rescued me today without making me feel even the slightest tinge of embarrassment. How ever will I make it up to you?"

"I would be distressed if you felt even the slightest need to try," he said.

And with that, we left, both of us silent until we'd exited the carriage at the docks.

"That was a debacle," I said, stretching out across the foot of Margaret's bed. Instead of returning to the *yalı*—and intent as I was on getting some much-needed privacy—we had gone to my friend's suite at Misseri's after checking in with Miss Evans. Sir Richard had awakened and was doing much better. The doctor had assured us he was in no danger and would make a full recovery.

Margaret and I made our exit as quickly as possible. Back at the hotel, we had dinner sent to the room, and following long baths, we both pulled on nightgowns, poured glasses of port, and sat on the balcony outside her bedroom, watching the city's lights below us.

"Thank heavens you were prescient enough to think of having me faint," Margaret said. "If you hadn't suggested I be on guard before you left the room, you would have come in to find me rummaging through the drawers of that desk."

I sipped the tawny liquid, loving the warmth it sent through me. "That would have been a disaster. But I'm worried. He's on to us."

"'On to us'? What does that even mean? We don't know what

we're doing, do we?" She laughed. "For all that it was a debacle, it was awfully fun. You've very nearly convinced me to reconsider the benefits of detecting."

"Tired of the settled life before you've even started?"

"Maybe."

"Whatever will Mr. Michaels say?"

"I'm afraid even to consider it," she said. "I had such a lovely letter from him today. He's taken to writing in Latin, which is a great improvement. His words flow much better, and he less frequently relies on academic phrases to persuade me to believe the depth and breadth of his passionate admiration for me."

"You're terrible."

"No, I'm not! I love him more than anything, but the man is an awful writer. It's tragic, really."

"Doesn't seem to be keeping him from getting his heart's desire," I said.

"Well, perfection would be boring. And I don't mind being better at something than he is."

"So you write good love letters?"

"The best," she said.

"Show me."

"Never." Her grin was two shades from evil and made me laugh. "What about Colin?" she asked. "How are his letters?"

"Every delicious thing," I said. More laughter; the space around us was warm with it. I wondered how many more nights we would have like this. So much changed after marriage. But, no, it was not marriage that concerned me. It was my old fear, taking me back to that December night so long ago, when my aunt had died.

"You've grown dull," Margaret said. "What is it?"

"Ivy. I'm scared for her."

"I am, too. We all know well what can happen. But we can't let it paralyze us."

"You're right, of course. I just never thought it would be so hard." I swirled the port in my glass and pressed my lips together, feeling the early sting of tears. "Everyone else seems to be able to reconcile herself with the risk. I don't know why I can't."

"Does there have to be a reason?"

"I suppose not. But if there were, I might be able to understand and then overcome it."

"You're so strong, you'd never have a problem."

"Maybe." I smiled. "I would like to give Colin an heir. It would bring him great joy."

"Of course it would. And you as well."

"Yes." My face was growing hot. "It would."

She took my hand. "Whatever happens, I shall be there with you. You won't be alone, and you won't have to pretend to be anything other than terrified."

"Thank you, Margaret. I don't know what I'd do without you."

We embraced, finished our port, began to strategize, and by morning had a more than reasonable plan as to how we could learn more about Mr. Sutcliffe.

The sun hit our more than reasonable plan with a harsh and unforgiving light, but we were undaunted. Phase one would be simple enough; it was the second half that could prove tricky. We started by making the rounds in Pera, calling at the home of every British expat we could think of. Thankfully, as the daughter of an earl, my rank enabled us to do this without introductions.

"In fact," I said, ringing the bell at our fifth house, "my mother would say this is my social obligation. A lady of rank, she always tells me, has a responsibility to call on those around her. To not do so is rude."

"We can't have that," Margaret said.

In the space of a few hours—exhausting hours that left us over-full of tea and biscuits—we learned that Mr. Sutcliffe's career had taken him to Vienna (his first post, where he served with the gentle-man who was now one of the top aides to the consul here in Turkey), Canada, Portugal, and the West Indies. But it wasn't until we met with a Mrs. Hooper-Ferris that we stumbled upon anything of use.

"Oh, the West Indies were awful!" We'd spent a pleasant half hour with our hostess, the wife of one of the embassy's top officials. "We were there at the same time as the Sutcliffes—terrible epidemic of typhoid—people were dropping everywhere. It's when he lost his entire family, but I'm sure you knew that already," she said.

"Yes," I said. "I'd heard that. Terrible."

"Terrible tragedy. His wife—Cate—beautiful girl. And so young. They had two children, a boy and a girl. Must have been six and four years old, if I remember. All gone in the space of twenty-four hours."

"How dreadful," Margaret said. "The poor man."

"It marked him forever, beyond the way you'd expect grief to. To make matters worse, he'd balked at the assignment in the first place—had asked to stay . . . well, I can't remember where he'd been before. Didn't want to take his children because he knew all too well the is-lands were rife with fever. But there's no arguing these things. You go where you're told to go."

"Is it never possible to request a change?" I asked.

"You can, of course, request anything. But it's unusual for it to come to fruition. I believe he'd lined up a colleague who had agreed to switch with him, but then there was some change in plans. I don't recall the details."

"It's terribly sad," I said.

"That it is. But of course it did spur all his charity work—good, that. Although I have heard said that he's more than a little obsessed with it all. Thinks he knows better than anyone what it means to be a decent father."

"Understandable, I suppose," Margaret said. "How did you find the West Indies? I've heard it's beautiful there."

"Hideously hot," she said. "Unbearable mosquitoes. I'd say do all in your power to keep as far away as possible."

"How disappointing," I said. "I've always had such a dreamy vision of the islands."

"Don't mistake me," Mrs. Hooper-Ferris said. "From behind a good mosquito net, it's a lovely, lovely place."

By four o'clock, I was certain of two things: It would be too soon if I ever saw another biscuit, and the loss of Mr. Sutcliffe's family was connected to all that was swirling around Sir Richard.

"We need to find out more about his request to get a different assignment," I said. "But I'm afraid the ambassador won't be of any help."

"Do you know anyone else in the diplomatic service we could contact?" Margaret asked.

"No."

"What about Jeremy?" she asked. Jeremy Sheffield, Duke of Bainbridge, was my childhood friend who had declared his love for me last winter in Vienna. "He can be useful when he wants to be."

"More than useful," I said. "But I hate to trouble him, given the circumstances."

"I think he'd adore rescuing you while you're on your honeymoon."

"That's exactly the problem," I said. "I wonder if my father could help?"

"It's worth trying," Margaret said.

"I can send him a wire, but it would be days before he'd be able to learn anything. He's not in London." We were winding back through the streets of Pera, stepping carefully over uneven cobbles.

"Could we just confront Mr. Sutcliffe?"

"Of course, but I want some proof—something substantial. If he finds out we're on to him, he may run," I said. "I have an unorthodox suggestion."

"My favorite kind," Margaret said. "I think I'm beginning to get my nerve back."

"You'll need it if you're to agree to this scheme. I wouldn't suggest it if I could think of any other option—preferably a more reasonable one—but I can't seem to do that. How do you feel about calling on the ambassador?"

"You said he won't help."

"He's not going to realize that he is," I said. "First, though, we have to find a shop. I need to buy candles."

Two hours later, I was hiding in a broom closet in the British embassy, having slipped away while Margaret and I were ostensibly waiting to speak to Sir William. An earnest clerk led us to a small reception room. We spent a quarter of an hour discussing elephants with a gentleman newly arrived from India, who was hoping this posting would be as exciting as his last, but once he'd been summoned away, we were alone, and I dashed to the first reasonable hiding place I could find.

So far as closets go, this was not an uncomfortable one. It was neither overly crowded nor musty smelling. I had crammed myself into the far back, sunk to the floor, and sat there, wishing I'd had the sense to remove my corset before this endeavor, until all the ambient noise had disappeared from the corridor. Despite my attempts to stretch my legs, both were cramped, and returning to my feet was prickly painful. I managed, then fumbled in the dark to open the door. Once in the hall, I pulled from my reticule one of the candles and matches I'd purchased and soon had enough light to keep me from tripping over any ill-placed furniture.

I made my way to the records room, figuring it as the most likely spot to find employment files. I pulled open drawer after drawer in the cabinets that filled it, eventually reaching the one I sought and flipping through folders until I saw the two names I needed. My heart racing, I took them both, held them to my chest, and started towards a table where I could read them. But before I could spread them on the surface, I heard a terrible crash on the other side of the door.

For a moment I was frozen, forgetting even to breathe. Then sense returned to me, and I blew out my candle, snuffing the glowing ember of wick with my fingers to stop its swirling smoke. Now unable to see, I dropped to the floor and scooted under the table, terrified. Nothing happened. I started counting seconds, to see how much time was passing, but could hardly keep track of the numbers. All I wanted was to get out as quickly as possible. I strained to listen but heard no further sound, and decided to get up. As soon as I had, however, I heard a second noise—not so loud as the first—followed by a hollow thump.

Not being foolish enough to open the door and see what was there, undoubtedly ready to confront me—I was having visions of Mr. Sutcliffe with a sword, not that *that* would make the slightest bit of sense—I knew it was time to take sudden and decisive action. Not hesitating, I crossed the room as quickly as I could in the dark, unwilling to risk relighting my candle, and pushed open the first window I reached. I had not planned to leave with the files, but at this point, saw no other option. Hiking up my heavy skirts, I sat on the ledge, flung my legs over, and hopped to the ground.

Once there, I stayed close to the building, not wanting the guards to see me skulking around. I knew there'd be no avoiding them eventually but had come up with what I considered a better than average strategy for dealing with them.

"Good evening, gentlemen," I said, hugging the files close to my chest, my arms wrapped tight around me as I walked down the path to the gate. "The grounds are so beautiful, even in the moonlight, I simply couldn't tear myself away."

"You—when—" the younger of the soldiers stuttered incomprehensibly.

"I assume Miss Seward left ages ago. Was she with Sir William, did you see?"

"No, madam, I believe he left alone."

"Very good, then. I'll catch up with her now. Thank you, and have a lovely evening." I breezed past them, a brilliant smile on my face, and looked for the carriage I knew Margaret would have waiting for me at the end of the block. She opened the door as soon as she saw me coming.

"I've been beside myself," she said. "It's more awful than you can imagine sitting here and having no idea what's going on."

"I can assure you it was nothing but invigorating excitement inside." I handed her the files as I stepped into the coach and told her what had happened.

"Do you think someone's in there?" she asked.

"I haven't the slightest idea," I said. "And wasn't about to find out. I wish I hadn't had to remove anything, but I had no choice."

We returned to Misseri's, where we could peruse our purloined letters at our leisure.

"Port," Margaret said, handing me a glass. "Cigar."

I lit it, but the smell turned my stomach. "I can't," I said, snuffing it out in the crystal ashtray on the table.

"Are you ill?"

"Let's hope." I looked at the folders in front of me. "Which would you prefer? Mr. Sutcliffe or Sir Richard?"

"Sutcliffe, please. I want to be the one who finds whatever it is we're looking for."

"Go forth and conquer." I pushed the file to her and opened Sir Richard's. It was dull reading, but that came as no surprise. Records of his assignments, comments about his performance, letters praising his skills and efficiency and dedication from a series of well-heeled ambassadors filled the folder, but nothing suggested any connection between him and Mr. Sutcliffe.

"Anything of note?" I asked Margaret, filling her glass with more port.

"So far just a letter about this West Indies business," she said. "Terrible. He was granted an extended leave after the funerals, but served out the rest of his tour there. Other than that, though, a re-markably uninteresting record. No sign of trouble yet, however."

"All right. Let's compare their postings. Were they ever together?" A quick assessment showed us they had crossed paths in Vienna—on that first assignment of Mr. Sutcliffe's. "Mrs. Hooper-Ferris men-tioned that he'd tried to arrange something with a colleague, someone who'd agreed to switch with him. I'd bet anything the colleague was Sir Richard."

"Is there reference to such a thing in his file?"

I flipped through the pages, skimming as I went. "There's this—when he requested assignment in Constantinople, it was noted that he had never before asked for a specific post."

"Does that signify?" Margaret asked.

"Only if Mr. Sutcliffe thought he'd asked for the West Indies." I closed Sir Richard's file. "May I?"

"Of course." Margaret leaned back in her chair, blowing rings of smoke. "I have to admit I liked feigning swooning better than going through papers. My dedication is suspect at best."

"I love you regardless," I said, and kept reading. "Here, here it is. A letter he wrote asking to be allowed to have a colleague, Mr. Richard St. Clare—pre-knighthood—be assigned to the West Indies in his place. 'Mr. St. Clare has assured me he would happily take this post and has already submitted the appropriate paperwork to arrange the details.'"

"But he never did?"

"It seems not." I took a long breath, rubbed my forehead, and went back to Sir Richard's file. "Yes . . . Yes. This is enough, Margaret, it's enough. Look." She stood beside me, reading over my shoulder. "The page here that says he never made any such requests was stamped as received here only six months ago."

"Why the delay?"

"Who knows? Perhaps it was misfiled, or never sent from wherever he was posted when he applied to come here. The point is that Mr. Sutcliffe is the one to whom it would have gone to be filed—he's the one who would have stamped it. And when he did, if he read it, he'd know that Sir Richard never tried to help him avoid the West Indies."

"And hence, let his family die from typhoid."

"Which to a man thoroughly devastated by loss—so grieved that he never remarried and became fixated on others suffering a similar loss—might be sufficient to inspire him to seek revenge."

"So he poisons Sir Richard?" Margaret asked.

"But doesn't kill him—makes him look incompetent to the point he loses his job. And he hires thugs to harass his son."

"But Ceyden?"

"I don't know yet how or if she fits. Can you doubt he'd find it sweet revenge to kill the daughter of the man he holds responsible for the deaths of his own children?"

"We don't know that's what he's thinking," Margaret said.

"Agreed," I said. "But it's decent conjecture. And suppose he killed Jemal—the man who knew of Benjamin's dealings at the harem. He might have been bribing Jemal as well and decided it was time to make sure he'd keep quiet about something."

"Is this enough evidence to take to the ambassador?" Margaret asked.

"It should be sufficient to at least get his attention and persuade him that the matter requires further investigation. It shows Mr. Sutcliffe had a powerful motive. Now we need to find some evidence of him possessing chloral hydrate—and more about his friendship with Bezime. Let's not forget she liked to play at being a physician."

26

As it was too late to confront Bezime herself, I had to settle for talking to the only person left who might have the answers I sought. Perestu started pacing almost as soon as I asked my first question. The lines in her forehead deepened, and her brown eyes clouded. "I don't know how to answer you," she said. "I have not had contact with your Mr. Sutcliffe in months. I told you that before."

"What was his relationship with Bezime?"

She closed her eyes. "How could I possibly know that?"

"You read her diaries, didn't you?" I asked. "You must have. How could you have resisted? Didn't you want to know what her relationship with him was?"

She did not answer.

"He loved you. I've no doubt of that. You should have seen his reaction when he realized your ring was gone." I hated the knowledge that he'd been putting on an act, but I had no reason to doubt his feelings for Perestu and even less reason to want to see her more hurt.

She turned, tears hanging heavy in her eyes. "You must not speak of love between us. There was none."

"Friendship, then. Whatever you want to call it. He cared for you. Any woman in your situation would have read those diaries."

"He came to her frequently, but I do not think they were lovers," she said.

"Did she say anything about discussing Ceyden with him?"

"Nothing at all."

This was unfortunate, but far from a shock. "What can you tell me about the loss of his family? I know it affected him deeply."

"Of course it did. You've no idea—what it is to lose a child. Two children. And his wife. He loved her."

"I know."

"And to then have found out that a man he called his friend lied about the one thing that might have prevented all of it. . . ."

She paused, and I dared not even breathe. But when she didn't continue, I had to say something. "It might have been a mistake, you know. Sir Richard could have filed the request and all those years later it could have been lost."

"You know the story?" She smiled, a slim, halfhearted effort. "That makes me feel less like I'm betraying him."

"I don't know the details, but I'm not convinced it was anything more than a misunderstanding."

"No, that's not possible. When he saw the paper, he confronted Sir Richard, who admitted everything. He apologized, but what good was that? Said that he couldn't leave at the time because he was following some new lead as to where his daughter might have been. It all amounted to nothing, of course, and poor Theodore lost everything."

"Sir Richard knows all this?" I asked.

"Yes. There can be no doubt. The last time I saw Theodore was when he came to me immediately following their conversation. I'd never seen him so upset, so . . . ragged."

"And it was that day that you broke off your friendship?"

"Yes. The timing was appalling, I admit. But something in him scared me that day—the intensity of his hurt, his anger. And I knew that I was in danger of getting too drawn in to him. I didn't want that, so I cut it off."

"That takes no small measure of strength," I said.

"Not nearly as much as it should have," she said. "I'd been pulling away for months without him even knowing. Otherwise I couldn't have done it."

"I'm sorry," I said. "It must have been terribly painful. I would never broach such a subject if I didn't think it of critical importance. What did Bezime write about Mr. Sutcliffe?"

"She knew of his anger, that was clear, and it concerned her. He wasn't sleeping well—nightmares. He had suffered from them for years. She gave him something to help him, but didn't think he was taking it, as he never seemed to her more rested." Tears choked her voice. "I wish I could have given him something solid like that—something that might actually have helped."

I felt as if I were standing on the edge of a very tall cliff, about to plummet to an unthinkable and inane ending if I did not choose my words with absolute precision. I walked over and stood in front of her, placing my hands on her shoulders. "The sort of friendship you gave him was far more substantial than some sort of medicine it sounds like he never even took."

"Yes, but she gave him more every time he called. She must have had reason to think it was important."

I tried to sound as casual as possible. "Do you remember what it was?"

"Some sleeping aid . . . chlor . . . chloral . . ."

"Chloral hydrate?"

"Yes," she said. "That was it."

"Not the best choice, I'd say. Highly addictive and can have dreadful side effects."

"Is that so?"

"Yes. Far better that he have a friend who understands him," I said.

"Thank you," she said. "It brings some measure of comfort."

"He doesn't have to be lost to you altogether, does he?" I asked.

"Yes. There's no other way. I will not let myself fall in love again, especially in such impossible circumstances."

I could not argue with the wisdom of that.

I rushed from the palace to meet Margaret, who had taken care of arranging the final details for Roxelana's rescue. The time had come at last to pull off our plan. Excitement and fear surged through me, my nerves thin, and I prayed we were doing the right thing in the right way. I could not let myself think of the fallout that would come should our plans be exposed. We'd been careful, and I was confident her escape would be successful. Hubris is a dangerous companion.

"You'll find this amusing," Margaret said as we raced to the Nuruosmaniye Mosque. "A friend called on Medusa yesterday, all full of ex-pat gossip. Apparently, the night of your adventure in the embassy one of the stray cats that lurk about the city got in through an open window and knocked over a vase."

"That was the crash that terrified me?" I laughed.

"Yes. The poor creature was still inside in the morning, and the staff have adopted it."

"Well, it does make for a good story. I must tell you what happened at Yıldız this morning." We were walking quickly, and I struggled to breathe evenly as I recounted my conversation with Perestu.

"What a shame that she burned the journals," said Margaret. "Do you think she would testify?"

"I could not say. When faced with the truth of what he's done—"

"Are we even sure what that is?" she asked.

"Yes, we are. He poisoned Sir Richard, sabotaged his career, possibly made threats of violence against his son—"

"We can't prove that last."

"That will undoubtedly be the most simple part of all this. Colin can go back to the village and pay enough to get the full truth."

"Fair enough," Margaret said, walking faster. I could not match her pace—I was feeling more winded than I should, and it was all I could do to keep from letting her gain too much distance ahead of me.

"He must have been following Benjamin—I'm convinced Jemal alerted him to the planned escape."

"He might have even witnessed the murder."

"And then taken the evidence to give to the proper person when the proper moment arose," I said. "He wanted to be sure Benjamin was held accountable." I stopped, dead in the center of the street. Margaret had to pull me out of the way of a delivery cart.

"Emily! Pay attention."

"I didn't see it before," I said. "But now I do. Remember, she spoke—"

"They're already inside," Margaret interrupted, looking at the line of carriages in front of the building. "Hurry."

She hurried towards her station while I turned into the Grand Bazaar, taking a table at the café we had chosen and ordering tea and baklava. Ideas blazed through my head, but I kept settling on a single one: Benjamin hadn't killed Ceyden. Sutcliffe had. The scenario played out easily enough. He'd followed Benjamin, watched Roxelana flee screaming. Ceyden may have heard him, called out for help, seen him—and he'd killed her to keep her silent. Not only to ensure no one knew he'd been in the harem, but because he knew he could frame his nemesis's son for the murder.

I admitted to myself, as I crunched another bite of baklava, that the story was as yet incomplete. But another few days of work and I'd have uncovered the rest. Bezime was a threat because she knew about the chloral hydrate. She could have asked Sutcliffe about it. And Jemal—he'd been both dispensable and dangerous. I thought it very likely he'd witnessed Ceyden's murder.

A slim glint of satisfaction passed through me, which led me to be filled immediately with concern. This was always the most dangerous stage—the part when you begin to map out the solution but don't know enough to see the holes that leave you vulnerable. I checked the watch on my lapel—newly purchased to replace the one stolen from the *yalı*—and tore a piece of paper from the small notebook I carried in my reticule. On it, I wrote everything I knew, suspected, or felt was reasonable conjecture pertaining to the case. Then, moving on to a second sheet, I put down the unreasonable conjectures of which I was fond as well as a full detailing of our plans for Roxelana, cringing at the thought of my husband reading this.

I asked my waiter if it was possible to get an envelope and within a few moments had in my hands a set of smooth linen stationery. After sealing my missive, I addressed it to Colin in care of the embassy, and my enterprising server found a boy to deliver it almost before I'd asked. Having taken this precaution, I felt better protected. Not in the classic sense. I had no desire to see Colin swoop in and fix any of this; I wanted to do that myself. But it was as if I'd bought insurance against needing him—he'd know where to find me, what to do if something went wrong. Undoubtedly, I'd require his assistance only if it was impossible for him to offer it.

Satisfied, I finished my tea and looked again at my watch. My stomach churned; too much time had passed. Roxelana should have been here by now. I looked around, growing more nervous with each passing second, wondering if she could somehow have been confused by the maze of the bazaar's streets. I wanted to search for her but knew better than to leave my post. What would she do if she arrived and I was gone?

But after another half hour, I saw little choice. I paid my bill, deciding to go to the mosque, where I would find Margaret. I hoped more than anything that Roxelana had not been caught—that she hadn't come because it was too risky, because she wasn't able to get the privacy required for her escape. As I walked, I began repeating, barely under my breath, a simple prayer.

"Lady Emily Hargreaves?" The small voice came from behind me, and I turned to see a boy, no more than nine years old. "Are you Lady Emily Hargreaves?"

"I am," I said.

"This is for you." He handed me an envelope made from thick, creamy paper and disappeared into the crowd around me. With shaking hands, I tore it open, almost afraid to read.

My dear Lady Emily, the game is up. You've gone too far and I've had to take actions I did not wish to. I have Roxelana. She will be alive for thirty more minutes unless you present your-

self to me in exchange for her. She is easily frightened, not at all like my own brave girl who complained not once during the final hours of her illness, and I find myself already tired of her crying. How would you like me to silence her?

I am at the Basilica Cistern, the Yerebatan Sarayı. You will have to figure out how to get there. Just be sure to come quickly and to come alone. If there's anyone else with you, it will end badly for us all.

I felt short of breath, and my throat ached as I gulped for air. I was not foolish enough to believe I could pull this off alone—it was worse than any situation I could have imagined. I'd thought any danger Roxelana faced would come from the sultan. There was little time to consider options, so I took the first reasonable one that sprang to mind. I asked my waiter to point me to the police—he located an officer patrolling the bazaar and stopped him at once. Not wanting to waste even a moment, I pressed the note—which was obviously from Mr. Sutcliffe—into the man's hand and explained as efficiently as possible that he must send help and get word to the British embassy at once.

He looked at me as if I were insane, and I could not pause long enough to convince him otherwise. Instead, I ran to the nearest exit, hired the first carriage I saw, and made my way to the cistern. It was only because I'd read so extensively about the city that I was even aware of it, finding it described in the travel memoirs of an Italian gentleman. Near the Blue Mosque and Aya Sofya, it had been built in Roman times to bring water to the city, and families living above it still used it—taking its water from well-like openings in their basements.

Having no time to collect De Amicis's book from the *yalı*, I had to rely on my memory. He'd described coming to the cistern through the garden of a nearby house. I'd reached the neighborhood and knew I was in the right general vicinity, but it was not apparent which house's garden contained the entrance—so I could do nothing but knock on doors and hope someone could help me. On my third attempt, a veiled woman answered. She did not speak much English, but I kept repeating "Yerebatan Sarayı" over and over, and at last she nodded and pointed me to the house across from hers. I raced there, only to find no one home.

I made my way around the building, hoping to find a way into the garden, through which I could reach the cistern, and my heart soared when I saw a green door, in dire need of new paint, in the wall. I pushed it open and rushed through it. Across from me was a stone arch, below which were steep stone steps, slick with water and moss, descending deep into darkness. Pleased that I had not bothered to empty out my reticule after last night's adventure at the embassy, I pulled out the candle and matches I still had with me and lit them before making my way with great care down the stairs.

Every nerve in my body was shaking when I reached the closed door at the bottom. I opened it and stepped into an enormous domed underground chamber, its vaulted ceiling supported by arches above row after row of columns, hundreds of them. Water filled the room below the wooden platform on which I stood—and my candle reflected green in it, the color eerie, almost unholy. There was no sound but that of water dripping from the roof, pinging into the pool below, echoing relentlessly.

No sound, that is, until the door shut behind me, and I heard the unmistakable click of a bar latch snapping into place. I turned around, wanting to test it at once, only to find my fear all too real. The lock had fastened; I could not get out. Panic rose through me as the darkness of the space enveloped me, but there was nothing to do but move on.

I took a step forward, testing the wooden planks over the water before putting my whole weight on them, wondering at what point I'd face Sutcliffe. Was he behind a column? Waiting for me just beyond the light of my candle? I was sweating despite the coolness of the space and had to force my feet forward.

"I did say thirty minutes, did I not, Lady Emily?"

His voiced bounced around me; I could not tell where he stood.

"You're using up all your time. Might want to hurry."

And then I heard a muffled sob that fueled me to move forward with greater speed. "Let her go," I said. "You can well see that I'm here and alone."

"This is not a time for you to be making demands," he said.

I bit back the reply on my lips and continued walking, trying to determine where Roxelana was. "What is it you want from me?" I asked.

"You should have left things alone," he said. "There was no reason to interfere. All those deaths after Ceyden's are on your conscience."

"I have not killed anyone."

"They would all be alive still if it weren't for you."

I wanted to keep him talking, to distract him while I came up with a viable strategy. "I know you killed Ceyden," I said, wanting to test my suspicion.

"It doesn't matter what I did so long as St. Clare thinks it was him."

"You did kill her."

He laughed. "I never dared hope my revenge would be so complete. The boy made it easy."

"Roxelana?" I asked. "Where are you? Are you next to him?"

More muffled sobs, with a greater urgency this time. "Quiet!" he said.

I heard footsteps. He was on the walkway, not in the water. I looked over the edge of the path, gauging the depth. Fish darted, startled by the light, and their reaction inspired me. I could see clearly the bottom of the green pool, not more than three feet below the surface. I broke the top third off my candle and then tilted it so that the wax pooled on the wooden rail next to me, until there was enough to hold the luminary upright. Sticking it hard into the middle of the melted mass, I held it in place until the wax had cooled. I backed away, wanting to distance myself from the light. Then, hiking up my skirts to my knees, I ducked beneath the rail and stepped into the water as quietly as possible and stood, perfectly still.

"Are you waiting for me to come to you?" he asked. The light from his torch—much stronger than that thrown by my candle—bounced between walls and water as he spun around, looking for me. Moving in silence, careful not to splash in the water, I walked away from the door across the open expanse of the pool, keeping far from the space illuminated around him.

Every time I reached a column I would pause, resting against it, wishing I could slow my heart, that my legs would stop shaking. And then I would continue on, moving in a wide half circle until I'd come almost close enough to see him from behind.

"I am not amused, Lady Emily," he said, still watching for me. "I can kill her now. Come to me at once."

A metallic clicking told me he was readying a gun. My breath was coming too fast now, my eyes stinging from the sweat dripping down my brow. I could not let Roxelana die. A few more steps and I could see her. He'd been holding her by the arm but had to let go to pull the pistol out from his belt, keeping the torch held high, looking all the while in the direction of my candle.

I knew better than to think I could get the gun from him. There had to be another way. As I watched my candle's flame in the distance, it came to me. Stepping back, I crouched behind a column, the base of which was a hideous head of Medusa, inverted so as to be upside down. I reached under my skirt and pulled off one of my petticoats, holding it under the water to flood every fiber of the cotton. Bundling it up into a loose but heavy ball, I wrapped it in my skirts and again moved towards them.

I somehow needed to will my arms to stop trembling, lest my plan be ruined altogether, but I seemed wholly incapable of controlling them. I held my breath, for it was too ragged and too loud as I continued to move towards them, away from my candle, disturbing the water as little as possible.

And then I waited. The stub of my candle did not take long to burn out, but it seemed like hours before its light was gone.

"What have you done?" he asked. "Blown out your candle? Do you forget I have something better?"

I resumed my journey through the water. Terror struck with full potential once I'd reached the flickering circle lit by his torch. He was holding it in his left hand, his right firm on the pistol pointed not towards Roxelana, but where he thought I was standing. I could see now that the columns were not identical. Some were Corinthian, some Doric, and one not far from me was covered with carvings that looked like tears.

"I've grown tired of your games," he said. He raised the gun to the ceiling and fired. Roxelana screamed as the shot ricocheted, but it hit nothing of consequence. Acting out of pure instinct, I knew this was the moment and flung my soaking petticoat onto the flame of the torch. The water doused it at once, and we all stood in absolute darkness.

"Roxelana, run!" I said, silently thanking whoever had decided petticoats should have enough yardage in them to give them a serious heft when wet. "Follow the railing and get to the door."

I'd figure out some way to unlock the door when I reached it. I heard scrambling feet—it sounded as if she tripped but managed to right herself and set off. Mr. Sutcliffe, however, was still. Not wanting to go near him, I tried as best I could to retrace the way I'd come, no easy feat in an underground room devoid of all light.

"What have you done?" His breathing was hard, irregular, too fast, his voice quivering as he spoke. "Light your candle again. At once."

I kept moving, hoping I was headed for the door, hoping that the police in the bazaar had taken my direction seriously and that soon we'd have reinforcements. And then, despite myself and despite the hideous circumstances, I almost laughed, realizing that if Colin were there, he'd be bent on rescuing me, and this made me all the more determined to escape on my own.

Roxelana was moving, her steps steady but not fast, but Sutcliffe had still not summoned whatever it would take to make himself move. A whimper escaped from his lips, his fear and panic palpable. I prayed he would not be able to conquer it.

"You must light the candle. Please!" He was shouting now, desperate. "I can't stand it—you must help me."

And then I heard a terrible sound. A match. I turned to see the quick flash of brightness. He tried to light the torch, but it was too wet, and he struck a second match and started walking.

"I will kill you," he said. "You should not have done this to me."

I had somehow wound my way back to the boardwalk, my hand,

which I'd held out in front of me, rubbed against a post of the rail, a splinter sliced into my palm. Undaunted, I continued on, using the rail as a guide. The second match burned out, and he lit a third.

"I can't open it!" Roxelana had reached the door and was banging on it, her voice full of tears. "Help me, Emily!"

We were so close now. If I could get to the door, I could figure out some way to open the latch. I moved more quickly, then slowed my pace, not wanting to give him audible clues as to where I was. I wished Roxelana would stop pounding on the door but could do nothing about it. I was nearly to her.

The dim match light died, and I braced for him to strike another, but he didn't. "Light your candle! You do not understand what you are doing to me. Light it!"

He was crying now—heaving sobs—and I let myself move more quickly. No sooner had I started than he began shooting. He was aiming at the ceiling again, trying to frighten us. Great chunks of plaster or rock or something crashed into the water, setting Roxelana screaming again. I pulled myself out of the water, held both sides of the railing in my hands, and ran as fast as I could.

"Emily! Please! Help me!"

I did not mean to reply, but the words came out almost before I realized it. "I'm coming!"

My voice bounced through the chamber, but the echo didn't confuse him enough. The direction of his bullets was more pointed now, and I dropped to my knees, determined to crawl the rest of the way, a dull pain in my side as I pulled myself along on my elbows. It was only when my corset, already damp, started to grow warm that I realized he'd hit me. The wound itself did not hurt much, but I felt woozy at once, scared and sick. Rescue no longer seemed a dreadful proposition.

I had no choice but to keep moving, and now it seemed that he had regained some nerve. I could hear his heavy footsteps, far behind me on the turn-filled walkway. He was screaming, knocking against the rails, even fell into the water once with a great splash. This spurred me on as a flash of heat coursed through me, and I began to wonder how badly I was hurt. I put my hand to my abdomen, feeling blood, tears streaming from my eyes as I realized that whatever my condition, as Bezime called it, had been, it certainly wouldn't be any longer. And just then, I knew with certainty that I did welcome it, that I could manage to conquer my fears. But the chance was gone. All I wanted was to stop, to lie down, to sleep, to ignore Roxelana's voice, which sounded farther and farther away.

I kept crawling.

When I reached the door, I could hardly stand, not only because I was weak, but because I was shaking so violently. Roxelana pulled me to my feet, and together we began wiggling the latch of the door. I could tell by touch that the mechanism was the same as that on the barn door of my father's estate in Kent. It was a type that, in theory, could be opened from the inside but in fact stuck easily and was almost impossible to manage. As a girl, I'd become an expert at undoing it from both inside and out—spending more time than my mother liked in the barn with my horses. The memory overwhelmed me, dizziness with it, and I nearly lost my entire train of thought until Roxelana shook me. I remembered where I was and tried again and again but was unable to generate the right force at the right angle on the lock.

And then Mr. Sutcliffe's steps grew heavier, his cries more savage. He could not have been more than thirty feet from us. Summoning every bit of strength I had, I jammed the latch as hard as I could and felt the door give. Roxelana and I tumbled out of it, slamming it hard behind us, cramming the latch hard into the locked position but knowing that if we could force it, he would be able to as well.

"Find something heavy," I said, doubled over in pain, trying to drag myself up the slippery steps. "Block the door with it."

"I don't see anything. I don't know what to do. I can't—" Roxelana's face was ashen, her eyes sunken.

"One of the stones from the edge around the stairs," I said.

"I don't want to hit you."

"You won't," I said. "I'll keep moving."

"Let me help you first," she said.

"No, it will take too long. Push it over."

She stood behind one of the rectangular blocks stacked in haphazard fashion on either side of the top of the stairwell, serving as a sort of barrier to keep people from dropping down the steps from the side. She strained against it, and it moved, only slightly.

I could hear Mr. Sutcliffe fiddling with the latch, clawing at the door. "Let me out! Please! Please!" His voice broke into sobs.

"He's here. You must hurry."

She pushed again, harder, I think. I could no longer see her. My vision had become hazy. But I heard her groaning and then heard the scraping sound of rock, followed by a crash, followed by sobs.

"Is it in front of the door?" I asked, the words almost impossible to form.

It sounded as if her answer were yes, but the only thing I heard with clarity was fingernails digging into wood.

POST OFFICE TELEGRAPH

May 2, 1892

Handed in at: Canterbury at 1:37 PM
Received here at: 12:13 PM

TO: Mr. C. Hargreaves
c/o British Embassy Constantinople

Mrs. Brandon having great difficulties. Send prayers and prepare my daughter in case things turn worse. Will update at regular intervals.

Bromley

27

Forgetting flowers is the easiest thing in the world. They're there, in the background, and you almost don't notice at all until you start paying attention, cataloging the colors, gauging the sweetness of their fragrances. I loved irises, their grape scent filling the garden in spring, and roses, of course, climbing over walls and trellises. It had been such a pleasant night's sleep, full of blooming fields and sparkling sunshine. Warmth radiating from me, I reached for Colin, wanting to pull him to me.

My arm, however, felt only cool sheets, rumpled blankets. I started to turn on my side, to see if he'd already awakened, but was stopped by a shooting pain that sent a cry from my lips, which I realized, as I woke further, were cracked and dry.

"Colin?" My eyes were so heavy that it was hard to open them, but as soon as I spoke, I heard sounds all around me. Footsteps, sharp breaths, rustling skirts.

"My dear girl." His voice was like liquid heaven, and I felt his weight next to me now. I turned my head and forced open my eyes.

"You look dreadful," I said as he sat on the edge of the bed. "When's the last time you shaved? I won't have you with a beard. I simply won't."

He laughed—relief and nerves—and kissed me on the forehead. "My dear girl." It was all he could say, apparently, and he kept repeating it.

We weren't alone. Margaret was on my other side. "Good heavens," I said. "Is it a party? What have I missed?"

And then I started to remember. I felt the heavy bandage on my abdomen under my nightgown and started to cry. "Did they catch him?"

"They did." Colin wiped my tears with his hands. "You set everything up without a flaw. The police arrived within ten minutes of your losing consciousness. Roxelana was tending to your wound."

"How did Sutcliffe get her?" I asked.

"I never even saw her," Margaret said. "He must have been waiting outside the window. He followed us because he was suspicious that you were on to him, and as soon as he saw us stationed near the mosque and then saw the caravan with the concubines, he knew what we were planning. You were right that he'd been tailing Benjamin. He'd arranged for the shootings at the dig to make Sir Richard worry—he wanted to drive him crazy. And from following Benjamin, he knew all about Roxelana."

"Is she—" I could hardly bear to think what must have happened to her.

"The sultan has forgiven her, but will not allow her to leave the harem," Colin said.

"And Benjamin? He didn't kill—"

"I know," he said. "He did try to strangle her, but she wasn't dead when he fled from the palace. He twisted his ankle making his escape and invented the bandit attack to explain it. He's not having an easy time with any of this."

"It's all so awful. He must be heartbroken to lose Roxelana as well."

"He is, but I think he considers it a fitting punishment." He brushed the hair off my forehead. "You did it, darling. Sutcliffe confessed to everything. Ceyden, Bezime, Jemal—your speculation about him finishing Ceyden was dead on. Being able to frame Benjamin for the murder brought an extra measure of revenge, though at a price— Jemal demanded additional payment for implicating him to the sultan. Sutcliffe was willing to part with the money, but decided Jemal had proven too demanding to be trusted any further."

"And so he killed him," I said.

"Yes. He spared no detail when he spoke to the police. You so terrified him by locking him in the dark, he was like a wounded child when they removed him."

"Sir Richard?" I asked.

"Will be reinstated at the embassy as soon as he regains his health. And, yes, Sutcliffe was slipping the chloral hydrate into his coffee every day at the embassy."

"What about the train?"

"Sutcliffe was two cars away from us."

"And Murat?"

"The former vizier has been charged with treason, and I got him to admit his messenger's death was not suicide."

I wanted to sit up, but the pain stabbed again as I tried. I fell back on my pillows, then opened my eyes and looked to the far side of the room. "How long have I been unconscious?"

"The doctor's kept you sedated for more than a week," Colin said.

"And what of Ivy?" I asked. "Has she had her baby?" I couldn't breathe as I looked at them. They'd both gone gray and were staring at the floor, their silence thick like tar.

"Would you excuse us?" Colin said, and I wanted to tear at his arms and beg Margaret to stay, if only to stop him from telling me—to give me even another hour of ignorance. When the door had closed, he took my face in his hands and leaned in to kiss my lips. "So much has happened."

"I don't even want to know," I said, sobs choking me, tears stinging my ragged lips, as pain cut through my abdomen. "Don't tell me. I won't let you. I don't want to know."

"Darling." He kissed the tears, wiped my face. "You've been through so much. It's not what you think. Ivy is fine. She has a daughter who is healthy as anything. The birth was extremely difficult, and we all feared for her. But she came through all right."

I wanted to slap him. "Why, then, would you set me up like this? Have I not been through enough? I thought she was dead. I—"

He took my hand. "Things have not turned out quite so well for us."

The sinking feeling returned to my stomach, and I knew what he was going to say. "I wasn't sure," I said, more tears coming. "I would have told you if I were. But it was too early—"

"I know, darling. The doctor said as much."

"I'm so sorry. I would never have—"

"Stop," he said. "You had no choice. He was going to kill her. It was necessary danger." His eyes were heavy with sadness, red-rimmed.

"I just wish—"

"Don't." He kissed my eyelids. "You must rest now."

"When I'm well, I'm sure we can—"

Now he squeezed my hand, hard. "Maybe. Your injuries have made it so that it's not clear . . ." His voice faltered, and I felt my heart shredding into pieces. "My dear girl, I'm just so glad you're all right. You've no idea what I've been through. I can't lose you. Ever."

I laid my palms against his rough cheeks. "You won't."

"You don't know that," he said. "What we do is dangerous."

"Do you want me to stop?"

"You wouldn't be you if you stopped," he said. "And I wouldn't adore you the way I do if you were anything less."

I closed my eyes—it was so hard to keep them open—thinking how fortunate I was to have him, a man who saw me for who I was and loved me without questioning any of it. And then I remembered his words and considered that I might never be able to give him an heir. Panic and fear flooded me at an intensity at least a hundred times greater than that I'd felt when I was trapped with Mr. Sutcliffe.

"Don't," he said. "I see exactly what you're doing to yourself and won't stand for it. We'll face it when the time comes—if the time comes. It's not the worst adversity there could be. We have each other, Emily. Isn't it greedy to want more?"

"Maybe I'm greedy." My voice was raw.

"Forgive yourself for that," he said. "When you're well enough to travel, I'm going to take you away to somewhere safe and prove to you beyond doubt that you, my dear girl, are everything to me. But in the meantime . . ." His voice trailed off and he kissed me, his tongue coaxing my lips apart.

"Yes?" I asked when he pulled back.

He stood and picked me up, cradling me in his arms, and stepped to the balcony, where he gently set me in a chair. Ducking back into the bedroom, he grabbed a blanket and tucked it around my shoulder, then my knees, then under my feet.

"There is a boat downstairs waiting to take me to the European shore. It's been there from the moment I knew I'd lost our bet. Prepare yourself, darling wife. I am about to swim the Bosphorus for you."

Author's Note

While I've tried to stay true to the history of the twilight days of the Ottoman Empire, I have chosen to take a few liberties. My character Bezime is based on an actual person, the valide sultan who eventually came to be called Pertevniyal. Deciding it might be confusing to have two valides whose names started with "P," I kept her as Bezime. I have further played with history by letting her stay alive some years longer than she actually did. How could I resist having such an extraordinary character avoid death long enough that Emily might meet her? The real Bezime slapped the empress Eugénie, was extremely interested in astrology, smoked a pipe, and attacked the minister of war when he came for her son, the sultan. She was not, however, unceremoniously murdered by an unruly Englishman.

Reading
Group
Gold

TEARS OF PEARL

by Tasha Alexander

About the Author
- A Conversation with Tasha Alexander

Behind the Novel
- *Tears of Pearl*: A Timeline of Events

Keep on Reading
- Recommended Reading
- Reading Group Questions
- "Emily and Colin's Wedding"

A
Reading
Group Gold
Selection

For more reading group suggestions,
visit www.readinggroupgold.com

 ST. MARTIN'S GRIFFIN

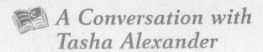 *A Conversation with Tasha Alexander*

Could you tell us a little bit about your background, and when you decided that you wanted to lead a literary life?

Stories have always been a central part of my life. My parents are both university professors, so I grew up in a house full of books and spent many wonderful evenings listening to my father reading out loud to us over an enormous bowl of perfect, buttery popcorn. He'd read Thurber, Saki, and Frank O'Connor and have us all in stitches laughing. We also made weekly trips to the library, where I was allowed to check out as many books as I wanted (often stacks far too tall for me to carry). By the time I was five, I was a devoted reader and writing stories of my own. Bad, bad stories of my own. My parents were very kind about them.

Is there a book that most influenced your life? Or inspired you to become a writer?

The first book that was truly significant to me was Laura Ingalls Wilder's *Little House in the Big Woods*— it's what my mother was reading to me when I realized I could read on my own. Talk about life changing. I was astonished to find that books didn't require a grown-up; it was as if the entire universe had opened itself up to me.

Who are some of your favorite authors?

Jane Austen, David Mitchell, Anthony Trollope, Jeanette Winterson, Arthur Phillips, Elizabeth Peters, Anne Perry, Dorothy L. Sayers.

What was the inspiration for your heroine, Lady Emily?

Having spent much of my life devouring every book dealing with the Victorian and Edwardian eras, fiction and non, I knew I wanted to write about the period. Real-life women inspired me—Gertrude Bell, Lady

> *"By the time I was five, I was a devoted reader and writing stories of my own."*

Meux, Jennie Churchill, and even Queen Victoria herself. But what really appealed to me was thinking about how, in the midst of a period wrought with rules and etiquette, women managed to embark on adventures and stake out their independence.

I didn't want to write about someone too radical. Instead, I was interested in creating a character who had the opportunity to grab her freedom, but to keep her true to the period. I wanted to bring her to enlightenment gradually. Emily starts off as the pampered (though obstinate and intelligent) daughter of an earl. She wants for nothing, but is bored with society. From there, she undergoes an intellectual awakening that in turn sets her up to take a broader view of society and the world around her.

You have already authored three books in the Lady Emily mystery series, *And Only to Deceive*, *A Poisoned Season*, and *A Fatal Waltz*. What was the inspiration for *Tears of Pearl*?

Tears of Pearl was always going to be a honeymoon book, and I knew the setting would have to be exotic—Emily would require nothing less from a wedding trip. But I also wanted it to be a novel that dealt with some difficult facets of Victorian marriages. The loss of an infant was extremely common during the period—about 150 babies died per 1,000 births (for context, the current rate in the UK is estimated to be 5 per 1,000). This was something women of the period had to face and deal with, and something I didn't feel right ignoring in the series, particularly as Emily is now a happy newlywed. Childbirth was a dangerous prospect, both for mother and baby, and I wanted to give serious thought to how women must have felt about this, particularly given they had no real control over the situation.

About the Author

Reading Group Gold

Do you scrupulously adhere to historical fact in your novels, or do you take liberties if the story can benefit from the change?

I'm fanatical about accurate details (although admit freely that no one can get everything right all the time). I don't like to be sucked into a story only to find out the background or key events weren't correct. In my first book, *And Only to Deceive*, everything Emily looks at in the British Museum (minus the novel's fictional vase) was an object already on display in 1890. Clothing, food, and transportation, as well as everything significant to the books' settings, are accurate. I try to be careful about how I portray real historical figures— I do my best to keep their personalities true to what they actually were, and to stick to the basic facts of their lives (for example, Abdül Hamit II's first daughter did die after being burned while playing with matches).

And to what extent did you stick to the facts in writing *Tears of Pearl*? How did you conduct your research?

When I first started working on the ideas for the book, I had expected there would be strict limits to what I could have Emily do in Constantinople. Like most contemporary Americans, I assumed women—particularly Western European women—wouldn't be able to move effortlessly through the city, wouldn't have any access to the sultan or the harem. Lady Mary Wortley Montagu, whose husband was the British ambassador to the Ottomans in the early eighteenth century, wrote a series of letters that radically opened my mind. She visited with the sultan, bathed with his concubines (and revealed that the Turkish baths were not, in fact, lascivious and degenerate), and became familiar with the city and its culture. Her letters were greatly influential to

> "I was interested in creating a character who had the opportunity to grab her freedom, but to keep her true to the period."

subsequent English women travelers, who followed her example and explored the Ottoman capital with abandon over the next two centuries. In the nineteenth century, Lady Layard, another British ambassador's wife, became close friends with the sultan, dining with him and his family, watching him play with his children in the harem, and making frequent visits to the palace. As accuracy is of vital importance to me, I was thrilled to see there was historical precedent that made it possible for me to send Emily into these places without having to stretch credulity.

In the end, though, I did decide to take some liberties in *Tears of Pearl* when it came to one character—the first time I've done such a thing in any of my books. The character Bezime is based on an actual person, the valide sultan who eventually came to be called Pertevniyal. Deciding it might be confusing to have two valides whose names started with "P," I kept her as Bezime. I further played with history by letting her stay alive some years longer than she actually did. How could I resist having such an extraordinary character avoid death long enough that Emily might meet her? The real Bezime slapped the empress Eugénie, was extremely interested in astrology, smoked a pipe, and attacked the minister of war when he came for her son, the sultan. She also, as described in the book, gave her son the scissors he used to kill himself. She was not, however, unceremoniously murdered by an unruly Englishman.

As far as research, along with reading about a time and place, travel is an essential component. It's impossible to get a real sense of a location without visiting it. I spent weeks in Turkey working on the book. It's an extraordinary place—a gorgeous meeting of East and West. The architecture and scenery is stunning, the food delicious, and the people some of the most friendly, helpful, and generous I've ever met. One of my favorite experiences came on my third visit to Topkapı Palace. I was sitting on the floor in the Imperial Hall, scribbling notes after having taken countless pictures. The guards couldn't believe I was spending so much time in each room and asked why I wasn't rushing through like the other tourists. When I explained I was researching a novel, they were delighted, and took me through the harem, telling me stories and pointing out details I would have missed otherwise. It was fantastic.

In your research of the Ottoman Empire, the Sultans, and their harems, what was the most interesting/surprising/shocking thing you learned?

Two things surprised me equally. First, when reading Lady Mary Wortley Montagu's letters, I learned that Ottoman women used their veils to give themselves a measure of freedom. Her identity disguised, a woman could meet anyone she wanted—including her lover—in public. I'm fascinated by the idea of something that can be an instrument of repression can also be used to gain freedom.

Second, although I knew the sultan's concubines came from all walks of life, I did not know that even those from the most humble positions outside the palace had an equal opportunity to gain power and influence within the harem. In *Tears*, I tell the story of the sultan seeing Bezime carrying laundry through a square in Constantinople and deciding at once he wanted her in the harem.

"As much as society has changed over the centuries, humans are human."

Why do you think readers are so drawn to historical fiction?

It's an escape into an entirely different world with novel clothing, rules, and politics—but one where the same fundamental things matter to the characters. As much as society has changed over the centuries, humans are humans, battling difficult choices, searching for love, caring for their families.

Who are some of your favorite historical figures?

Cleopatra, Elizabeth I, and Georgiana, Duchess of Devonshire.

Are you currently working on another book in the series? And if so, where is Lady Emily going next?

Dangerous to Know is set in France, where Colin has taken Emily to recover from the injuries she suffered at the end of *Tears of Pearl*. They divide their time between his mother's house in the Norman countryside and visiting friends in Rouen. I spent a great deal of time last summer in Normandy doing research. It is a spectacular place: rolling fields of barley, cloud-filled skies that look straight out of one of Monet's paintings, the rugged coastline. And the food! I'm getting hungry just thinking about it. Gorgeous cheeses, perfectly flaky croissants, sole cooked in brown butter sauce, beautifully tart cider.

Please find an excerpt from Dangerous to Know *following this Gold guide.*

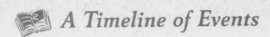 *A Timeline of Events*

1466–1478	Topkapı Palace built
1837	Victoria becomes Queen of England
1861–1876	Abdül Aziz reigns as sultan
1875	Ottoman Empire goes bankrupt
1876	Murad V reigns as sultan; Victoria named Empress of India
1876–1909	Abdül Hamit II reigns as sultan
1882	Married Women's Property Act in UK expanded. "All married women are . . . rendered capable of acquiring, holding, and disposing of any property as their separate property..."
1887	Queen Victoria's Golden Jubilee
1901	Queen Victoria dies
1922	The last sultan, Mehmet VI, sent into exile. End of the Ottoman Empire.

 # Recommended Reading

Reading
Group
Gold

Inside the Seraglio

John Freely

This book's subtitle gives a hint at the stories of intrigue found inside: *Inside the Seraglio: Private Lives of the Sultans of Istanbul*. It reads more like a novel than nonfiction, and is full of mesmerizing details about the personalities of the Ottoman rulers.

Lords of the Horizons

Jason Goodwin

Goodwin's beautifully written history of the rise and fall of the Ottoman Empire is a delight to read. Carefully researched and utterly engaging.

Keep on Reading

The Imperial Harem of the Sultans: Daily Life at the Çiragân Palace during the 19th Century

Leyla (Saz) Hanımefendi (translated by Landon Thomas)

This slim volume is an absolute treasure —the memoirs of a concubine who lived in the sultan's harem from the time she was four until she was released to be married. An unmatched account of what life in the harem was really like.

In the Palaces of the Sultan

Anna Bowman Dodd

Dodd, an American travel writer, visited Abdül Hamit II at Yıldız Palace in 1901 and wrote this memoir about her experiences. A fascinating and entertaining read.

The Turkish Embassy Letters

Lady Mary Wortley Montagu

Lady Mary's letters are a gold mine for anyone interested in learning about the lives of women in the Ottoman Empire. As the wife of the British Ambassador, her time in Constantinople provided her with the opportunity to bury herself in Ottoman culture—which she did with much pleasure. Her smart, insightful commentary enlightens and educates.

Lady Enid Layard's Journal

www.browningguide.org

Lady Layard, the first woman to dine at the sultan's table, became a close friend of Abdül Hamit II while her husband was ambassador to the Porte in the late nineteenth century. The royal children visited her home for tea, and she was a frequent guest in the harem. Her journal catalogs her experiences and provides detailed descriptions of the sultan's character.

Reading Group Questions

1. What did you know about the Ottoman Empire
    before reading *Tears of Pearl*?

2. Take a moment to discuss your perceptions
    about harems. How are they portrayed in popular
    film/television adaptations? In previous novels? In
    this novel? How, if at all, did this book inform you
    about harem culture and/or women's rights in
    Victorian-era Turkey?

3. As the author noted in the Conversation, Victorian
    women faced extreme danger in childbirth. How do
    you think this affected their views on motherhood?
    How does it affect your own?

4. How do women, in the past and today, find ways to
    be independent in restrictive societies?

5. Compare the ways in which Bezime and Perestu
    handle their power. Do you think Perestu will main-
    tain her influence once she's no longer valide?

6. Do you think the concubines would be better
    off outside the harem? Why or why not? Discuss
    the types of challenges they might face in the
    "real" world.

7. Why do you think modern readers enjoy novels
    about the past? How and when can a powerful
    piece of fiction be a history lesson in itself?

8. We are taught, as young readers, that every story
    has a "moral." Is there a moral to *Tears of Pearl*?
    What can we learn about our world—and our-
    selves—from Emily's adventure?

*Now that you've experienced
their honeymoon you can attend the
occasion of their marriage...*

"Emily and Colin's Wedding"

I'd never given the slightest consideration to the implications of being a drenched, mud-splattered bride. The rain, cold and heartless, had not daunted us in the least. Its contrast to the warmth of our urgent kisses only increased the bliss that surged through my trembling body after I agreed to abandon convention (as well as my mother's—and Queen Victoria's—carefully orchestrated plans for a grand society wedding) and marry my dashing fiancé, Colin Hargreaves, at once, as we stood on the cliff path on the Greek island of Santorini.

I had assumed, in the moment, that we'd take our vows rain-covered and rumpled, though I'd not worked out the mechanics of how such a ceremony would be managed. Logistics rarely have a place at such times. What could be more jarring than to worry about details in the midst of a grand romantic gesture? Colin told me he had a license; the rest could only be trifles. If Buckingham Palace relied on him as one of its finest agents, capable of bringing any mission to a satisfactory conclusion, I had no need for concern. I slipped my arm around his waist and nestled my head below his shoulder as he pulled me close. We turned away from the Aegean Sea, its foamy grey waves crashing into the rocks far below us.

**Please visit
us.macmillan.com/tearsofpearl
to find the rest of this exclusive FREE story!**

Turn the page for a sneak peek at
Tasha Alexander's new novel

Dangerous to Know

A Novel of Suspense

Available November 2010

1

Although a stranger to the Norman countryside, even I knew a dark pool of blood under a tree was not something a tourist should expect to see during an afternoon ride. Sliding down from the saddle, I put a calming hand on my horse's neck, then bent to investigate more closely. Had I been able to convince myself the congealing liquid was something less nefarious, the sight of a pale hand, blue fingertips extended, would have changed my mind at once. Without stopping to think, I rubbed my abdomen, the remnants of dull pain still present after my own encounter with violence, and took a step towards the body.

Only a few months ago, during what was meant to be a blissful honeymoon, I'd been trapped in a cavernous cistern deep below the city of Constantinople with the villain who shot me in an attempt to keep quiet my discovery that he was guilty of murder. His efforts were, of course, in vain. But although I succeeded in exposing the odious man and saving the life of the sultan's concubine whom he'd held as a hostage, I'd lost something more dear. I did not know when I stepped into the gloomy bowels of the city that I was with child. Now, instead of preparing for an heir, my husband and I were no longer sure we could ever have one.

Colin Hargreaves was not a man to be daunted, even in the face of such tragedy. He insisted that nothing mattered but my recovery and packed me off to France the moment I was well enough to travel. His intentions were the best. His choice of location, however, fell something short of perfection. Not Normandy itself—the lush countryside was stunning, the rich, cream-laden food magnificent—but our lodgings at his mother's house left something to be desired. Although that, too, is not entirely precise. There was nothing wrong with the manor, a sprawling, comfortable building constructed primarily in the seventeenth century by an aristocrat whose descendents did not fare well during the revolution. Rather, it was I who was the problem. At least so far as my new mother-in-law was concerned.

I'd heard nothing but complimentary words about Mrs. Hargreaves, who had fled England after the death of her husband some ten years before. Her own father had been left a widower early, and encouraged his daughter to remain at home—not to take care of him, but because he, not much fond of society, felt she should be allowed to lead whatever sort of life she liked. His fortune ensured she would never need a husband for support. Free from the restraints of matrimony, Anne Howard passed nearly twenty years traveling the world while her girlhood friends married and had children. It was only when she reached her thirty-sixth year that, halfway up the Great Pyramid at Giza, she met Nicholas Hargreaves. By the time they were standing again on terra firma, the couple were engaged. Three days later they married, and afterwards, never spent a single night apart.

I had hoped Mrs. Hargreaves would shower me with the warmth she showed her son—that she would rejoice to see him so happily matched. But after a fortnight of her cool detachment, I determined to spend as much time as possible away from the prickling discomfort of her disapproving stare, and it was this decision that led me to the unhappy resting place of the girl sprawled beneath a tree, her blood soaking the ground.

Bile burned my throat as I looked at her, my eyes drawn from her fingers to her face, framed by hair so similar in color and style to mine we might have been taken for twins. There was no question she was dead, no need to check for any sign of life. No one could have survived the brutal gashes on her throat. The bodice of her dress was black with blood and had been ripped at the abdomen, revealing what seemed to be an empty cavity.

I could look no further.

I wrapped my arms around my waist as my stomach clenched. I wasn't sick, but only because I was too horrified, too stunned even to breathe. Closing my eyes, I tried to focus, to move, to think, but was incapable of anything. I spun around at the sound of a sharp crack, like a branch breaking behind me, then turned back as my horse made a hideous shriek and reared. Realizing I'd neglected to tie him to the tree, I started towards him, but was too late. He'd already broken into a run.

Which left me six and a quarter miles from home, alone with the murdered girl.

Trees and grass and flowers spun around me as I tried to regain enough composure to take stock of the scene before me. I should have been better equipped to deal with this. In the past two years, I had become something of an investigator after solving the murder of my first husband, Philip, the Viscount Ashton, whom everyone had believed died of fever on a hunting trip in Africa. Since then, I'd thrice more been asked to assist in murder cases, the last time while on my wedding trip in Constantinople. Colin, my second husband (and Philip's best friend), worked for the Crown, assisting in matters that required, as he liked to say, more than a modicum of discretion. Because no man could gain entrance to the sultan's harem, he had asked me to work with him in an official capacity when a concubine, who turned out to be the daughter of a British diplomat, was murdered at the Ottoman palace.

Successful though I'd been, none of my prior experience had prepared me for the sight before me now.

I squinted, blurring my vision so the field of poppies beyond the tree and the body melted into a wave of crimson buoyed by the wind. My boot slid on slick grass as I stepped forward and forced myself to look, memorizing every detail of the gruesome scene: the position of the girl's limbs, a description of her dress, the expression on her face. Simultaneously confident and sickened that I was capable of giving a thorough report of what I'd seen, I turned and started the long walk back to the house, my stomach lurching, my heart leaping at every sound that came from the surrounding fields, my legs shaking.

For the briefest moment, I wanted to pretend that I'd seen nothing, wanted to abandon myself to fear. Tears, ready to spill, flashed hot in my eyes, and I dug my fingernails into my palms. Which was when I heard a twig snap. I stopped long enough to see a rabbit scurrying across the path in front of me. And all at once, my fear turned to anger—anger that I no longer felt safe in this place that was supposed to offer respite. Pulling myself up straight, I marched back to the house, ready to tell Colin we had work to do.

It had taken me more than two hours to reach Mrs. Hargreaves's manor, nestled in a tree-filled grove deep in the Norman countryside northwest of Rouen, but as long rides had become my daily habit, I had not thought my absence would strike anyone as unusual. Hence my surprise when my husband rushed to greet me almost as soon as I'd opened the door. Overcome with relief at the sight of him, I collapsed into his arms, hardly pausing to breathe as the story tumbled from my lips.

"You're not hurt?" he asked, patting my arms and taking a step back to inspect me.

"No," I said. He looked me over again and then, seemingly satisfied, took me inside, sent the nearest servant to get the police posthaste, and sat me down on an overstuffed settee in the front sitting room. His mother, who had been reading, set aside her book and rose with a look of horror on her face.

"What has happened?" she asked.

"Emily has found a body," Colin said, pacing the perimeter of the room. Mrs. Hargreaves remained perfectly still, her face serious, as he recounted for her all that had transpired.

"The police?" she asked.

"Are already on their way," he said and directed his attention back to me. "You're quite certain of the location?"

"I'll have to show you. I don't know that I could explain how to get there," I said. "I hadn't followed a specific route."

"I was frantic when your horse came into the garden without you," he said. "I wanted to look for you but had no idea what direction you'd gone."

"I can't imagine you frantic. You're beyond calm—infuriatingly calm—in the face of danger."

"Not, my dear, when it comes to you. Not anymore." He sat next to me and took my hand, rubbing it with both of his.

"I will not stand for you going all protective," I said. "Next thing I know you'll be sending me to bed early and censoring the books I read."

"I know better than to try to influence your choice of reading material."

"You do have excellent taste," I said. "I might consider taking your advice."

His mother sighed loudly and all but rolled her eyes. "I wish you would let me send for my physician to look her over, Colin," she said. "Do you think, Lady Emily"—she insisted on addressing me formally, her voice full of sharp scorn, to remind me of her disapproval of the use of the courtesy title to which I, the daughter of an earl, was entitled—"that you'll be quite able to bear the sight of the body again? I can't help but worry about the constitution of such a delicate and sheltered girl."

"I'll be perfectly all right," I said, feeling my cheeks blush unpleasantly hot. "Anyone would be upset by what I've seen, but that doesn't mean I'm incapable of doing the work necessary to ensure justice for the victim of this unspeakable crime."

"And am I to believe you are better capable of achieving such a thing than the police?" she asked. I had no time to reply as the butler announced Inspector Gaudet, a towering man, tall and broad, with a beard and handlebar mustache that made his face resemble George, newly-created Duke of York, younger son of the Prince of Wales. His size, however, would have dwarfed the duke.

"I assume," he said, crossing to me, "that you are Madame Hargreaves, who found the body."

"*I* am Madame Hargreaves," Colin's mother said, stepping forward. "I believe you want Lady Emily."

"I'm afraid my own lack of a title puts me beneath my wife in rank," Colin said, shaking the policeman's hand. "Hence the confusion. But I must say, there's no other lady I'd rather have precede me."

"Yes, of course," Mrs. Hargreaves said. "At any rate, Lady Emily is the one who found the murdered girl."

"Investigation will determine the cause of death," Inspector Gaudet said.

"There can't be much of a question," I said. "She was brutalized." Before I could stop them, tears sprang from my eyes. I pressed a handkerchief to my face and tried to compose myself.

"I do not need you to describe for me what had been done to her. I've already summoned a doctor to analyze the state of her body. He can't be more than ten minutes behind me. What I need is for you to show me the precise location of the scene. Do you feel able to do that?

I understand how difficult all this is." His voice was full of sincere worry.

"I appreciate your concern," I said. "But I'm prepared to do whatever is necessary."

Within a quarter of an hour the doctor and another policeman had arrived, and we were all mounted on horseback, Colin keeping close to my side. Mrs. Hargreaves had debated joining the party, but in the end was persuaded by her son to stay behind. We set off, and it quickly became apparent retracing my route was not quite so easy as I thought it would be. I had followed a path from the house beyond the road that led to the village, but then diverted through fields on whims in search of flowers, or to follow the sound of a particularly fetching birdsong, or hoping to find the peace that had eluded me since the day of my injuries in Constantinople.

"I know it wasn't much farther," I said, frowning. I'd made a habit of timing the length it took me to reach the beginning of the village road—exactly half a mile from the house—and I knew how long I'd been riding at approximately the same speed. Six miles in any direction was not so easy to find, and I made enough missteps—mistaking one field of poppies or flax or wheat for another—that the others began to doubt I would be of any use to them. In the end, I managed to recognize from afar the twisted limbs of the tree that stood over the body.

My horse reared as we approached, sensing, I suppose, my own tension as much as it did the smell of blood that hung in the air. We all slowed, then stopped, no one moving for several minutes. I could not bring myself to look again at the hideous sight.

"I can't believe it," Colin said, dismounting, his voice gruff. "I never expected to see something like this again."

"Again?" Inspector Gaudet stood next to him.

"It's as brutal as the murders in Whitechapel," he said. The collective terror that had descended on all of London when Jack the Ripper stalked women in the East End was something no English man or woman would soon forget. Chills crawled up my arms at the mere thought of his horrible handiwork. "Emily, did you hear anything at all when you found her? Sounds that suggested someone was close by?"

"Only the crack of a branch," I said, hesitating. "But I can't say I was aware of much beyond her."

"She hasn't been dead long." The physician was kneeling beside her. "You're lucky not to have arrived any earlier than you did, Lady Emily."

My eyes lost all focus. I came off the horse and tried to walk towards Colin, but my knees buckled. He stepped back and moved to catch me, but I pushed him away, knowing there was no stopping the inevitable. I ran as far as I could from the tree, then doubled over and was sick.

Gaudet turned to the other police officer. "Organize a search. We must comb the entire countryside. Hargreaves, take your wife home and look after her. She's done all we need of her and ought not trouble herself with this matter any longer."

2

From the beginning of our marriage, I had taken much pleasure from sharing daily routines with Colin. Dressing for dinner, for example, had become a time during which, once we'd shooed away our servants, we could discuss, quietly and in private, the events of the day. Often my husband dismissed my maid, Meg, before I was quite done with her, so he could help me finish fastening laces or buttons or jewelry. The only area into which he would not stray was the taming of my hair. Tonight, our rituals were the same, but I could not stop my hands from shaking long enough to put on the dazzling diamond earrings he had given me for a belated wedding present.

"It's possible you've reached your physical limits, Emily. Now is not the time to be pushing yourself." He took the dangling jewels from me and pulled me up from my seat in front of the vanity.

"Don't be ridiculous," I said. "My only problem is that I'm embarrassed and disappointed in myself." With gentle hands he turned my face to him and carefully snapped each earring into place, then kissed my forehead.

"I've seen men with greater experience and stronger stomachs than yours have more violent reactions than you did today. But I do worry, my dear."

"And you worry me. You promised you wouldn't try to keep me from working when opportunity presented itself." I leaned towards the dressing room's mirror, biting my lips to give them color. I'd chosen a gown of shell-pink satin with a delicate moiré in a darker shade, hoping the hue might enhance my complexion, which looked unnaturally drawn and faded.

"I wouldn't dream of stopping you. But now is not the time—"

"How can you say that?" I asked, pulling one of my hairs from the sleeve of his perfectly cut cashmere jacket.

"First, because you're still recovering from your injuries. Second, there's no reason to think Gaudet needs any assistance. He seems competent." He stood behind me, checking his appearance in the mirror.

"How can you say so? He hardly even interviewed me."

"He didn't want to push a lady in your condition."

"I'm not in a condition anymore."

Silence fell between us. Colin put his hands on my shoulders, bent down, and kissed me. "Forgive me. I didn't mean—"

I reached up and squeezed his hand, watching him in the mirror. "I know." We did not speak much of our loss. It was too depressing and filled me with guilt.

"We don't have to go down to dinner tonight," he said. "I can have a tray sent up to us here."

"No, your mother would never forgive me for ruining her plan to introduce us to the neighbors."

"Given the circumstances, she would understand," he said.

"She would take it as further proof of my inadequate constitution."

"She doesn't mean to be hard on you."

"Of course not." I sighed, the damp air that had crept into the ancient house chilling me to the bone. "But she's certain I'm not nearly good enough for you."

"My dear girl, in her mind, no one could be good enough for me." He kissed me again. "Thankfully, I've never been one to give the slightest heed to other people's opinions. I think you're absolute perfection."

"I shall have to content myself with that. Your mother is a force nearly as unmovable as my own."

"Give her time, my dear, she'll come around. As I was the only bachelor brother, she's come to depend on me since my father died."

"I don't want that to stop," I said. "She should be able to depend on you."

"And she will, but she'll have to get accustomed to sharing me. She's used to having me all to herself much of the time. I admit I thought she'd adjust more readily and am sorry her reaction to you has caused you grief."

"It's not your fault," I said. "Come, though. If we don't head down now, we'll be late, and that will only serve to put her off me all the more."

He took me by the hand and led me to greet his mother's guests. The oldest parts of her house dated from the fourteenth century. Built in traditional style, the low ceilings and beam construction on the ground floor made for cozier surroundings than those to which I was accustomed. The space was warm and welcoming. Long rows of leaded glass windows lined the walls, letting in the bright summer sun. The surrounding gardens were spectacular, bursting with blooms in myriad colors, and enormous pink, purple, and blue hydrangea popped against the estate's velvety green lawns.

Halfway down the narrow, wooden staircase, Colin stopped and gave me a kiss. "I suppose it is for the best that you decided not to take dinner upstairs," he said. "As I do have a surprise for you. Coming, I think you'll agree, at a most opportune time. She's likely not only to cheer you immensely, but also to terrorize my mother into accepting you."

"Cécile!"

"Mais oui," he said.

I'd met Cécile du Lac in Paris, where I'd traveled while in the last stages of mourning for my first husband. An iconoclast of the highest level, she was a patron of the arts who'd embraced Impressionism when the critics wouldn't. She'd had a series of extremely discreet lovers, including Gustav Klimt, whom she'd met when we were in Vienna together the previous winter, and considered champagne the only acceptable libation. Although she was nearer my mother's age than my own, we'd become the closest of friends almost at once, brought together by the bond of common experience. Like mine, her husband had died soon after the wedding, and like me, she had not been devastated to find herself a young widow. Of all my acquaintances, she alone understood what it was to spend years pretending to mourn someone. And even when our histories diverged, it did not drive a wedge between us. When, at last, I came to see Philip's true character, and found my grief genuine, she accepted that as well, even if it was due to empathy rather than sympathy.

Had Colin not informed me of her arrival in Normandy, I would have guessed in short order, as the yipping barks of her two tiny dogs, Brutus and Caesar, greeted us at the bottom of the stairs. Cécile patently refused to travel without them. I rushed down—realizing full well the hem of my dress was about to be the victim of a brutal attack—and reached for my friend.

"Chérie!" She embraced me and kissed my cheeks three times. "It is unconscionable that you have made me miss you so much and for so long. Paris has been crying for your return."

"I'm beyond delighted to see you," I said, squeezing her hand and then tugging at my skirt in a vain attempt to remove the two sets of teeth bent on destroying it.

"They are terrible creatures, are they not?" She picked them up, one in each hand, and scolded them, Caesar, as always, receiving the lighter end of her wrath. Cécile viewed preferential treatment of his namesake the only justice she could give the murdered emperor. "Ah, Monsieur Hargreaves, is it possible you have become even more handsome?" She returned the dogs to the floor so Colin could kiss her hand while she glowed over him.

"Highly unlikely, madame," he said. "Unless you can see your own beauty reflected in my face."

She sighed. "Such a delicious man. I should have never encouraged Kallista to marry you without first trying to catch you for myself." Soon after we'd met, Cécile had adopted the nickname bestowed on me by my first husband, making her the only person who'd called me Kallista to my face. Philip had used it only in his journals, and I'd not known of the endearment until after his death.

"You flatter me," he said. "But truly, your timing could not be more flawless. I can't think when we've needed you more."

"I've been waiting for the invitation." We had not seen Cécile since our arrival in France. When the *Orient Express* dropped us in Paris, my health was not so good as it was now, and I'd been in too much pain for even a short stay at her house on the Rue Saint Germain. "You are pale, Kallista, but that's to be expected after what Madame Hargreaves tells me you've seen today."

My mother-in-law entered the corridor, a bemused look on her face. "Are you planning to stand out here all night? Do come sit, Madame du Lac," she said. "I'm longing to improve our acquaintance." She looped her arm through Cécile's and led her into a large sitting room, where the rest of the party waited for us. The furniture reminded me of that in Colin's house in Park Lane—functional yet comfortable, elegant in its simplicity. The silk upholstery on slim chairs and a wide settee was the darkest forest green, blending beautifully with the walnut wood of the pieces.

Mrs. Hargreaves made brief introductions—her neighbors, the Markhams, a handsome couple, had already arrived—and dove into eager conversation with Cécile. As they were of an age, it did not surprise me to see them quickly find common ground. I hoped their new friendship might distract her from criticizing me. Colin pressed a glass of champagne into my hand then crossed the room to bring one to Cécile and his mother. I took a sip, but could hardly taste it, still feeling more than a little disjointed, off-balance, after the events of the day. Mr. Markham came to my side.

"Do you find this all quite nonsensical?" He was English, but looked like a Viking—broad shoulders, blond hair, pale blue eyes. "Someone was murdered today and we're all to stand about acting as if nothing's happened? Drinking champagne?"

"It's beyond astonishing," I said, relieved to have the subject addressed directly.

"And you're the one who stumbled upon the body, aren't you?" he asked. "Forgive me. Have I made you uncomfortable? I've a terrible habit of being too blunt."

"There's no need to apologize. Nothing you could say now would make the experience worse." My stomach churned as I remembered the brutal scene.

"What are the bloody police doing?" he asked. "Will the inveterate Inspector Gaudet be joining us for dinner? Will he regale us with tales of his investigation?"

"George, are you tormenting this poor woman?" His wife, slender and rosy, appeared at his side and laid a graceful hand on his arm. He beamed down at her.

"You are unkind, my darling," he said. "I wouldn't dream of tormenting anyone, let alone such a beauty. Lady Emily and I were merely discussing the way everyone is avoiding the topic much on all our minds."

"I can't imagine the tumult of emotions throttling you at the moment," she said. Her English was flawless, but made exotic by her thick

French accent. "But I must admit I'm desperate to ask you all sorts of completely inappropriate questions."

"I shan't allow that," her husband said. "You, Madeline, don't need any fuel for bad dreams."

"He's beyond protective." She beamed up at him. "But so handsome I'm likely to forgive him anything."

"She requires protection," he said. "Anyone would, living where we do."

"Are you afraid the murderer will strike in the neighborhood again?" I asked.

"No, one murder does not make me believe the area's entirely dangerous—not, mind you, because I have any faith in Gaudet's bound-to-be-infamous manhunt. Protection is necessary because the condition of the château in which we live would give Morpheus himself nightmares. Half the time I expect to wake up in the moat and find the entire building collapsed. The one remaining tower has grown so rickety I'm afraid we'll have to tear it down—it's unsafe."

"My love, it's not all that bad," she said. "Structurally you have nothing to fear. Aside from the tower, that is. But that hardly matters. What concerns me is our recent visitor."

"Visitor?" I asked.

"Intruder, more like. We've received a rather unusual gift," he said. "A painting."

"And how is that unusual, Mr. Markham? Are you known to despise art?"

"Quite the contrary," he said. "And you must call me George. There's no use in adopting airs of formality this far in the middle of the country. We're all stuck together and may as well declare ourselves fast friends at once."

"A lovely sentiment," I said. "Do please call me Emily. But why do you disparage Normandy? I can't remember when I've been to such a charming place."

"It is too far from civilization," he said.

"Which is why, perhaps, a kind friend thinks you need art brought to you," I said. "After all, there are no galleries nearby." This drew laughter from them both, and their happiness was unexpectedly contagious.

"What makes it strange, though, is that it was more like a theft than a gift," Madeline said.

"A reverse theft," her husband corrected.

"How so?" I asked, intrigued.

"The painting was delivered in the middle of the night and its bearer left no evidence of his entry nor exit. He set it on an easel—which he'd also brought—in the middle of a sitting room."

"With a note," Madeline continued. "That read: 'This should belong to someone who will adequately appreciate it.'"

"And this, you see, is why I have no confidence in Gaudet," George said. "He's been utterly useless in getting to the bottom of the matter."

"What sort of painting is it?" I asked.

"A building, some cathedral. Signed by Monet."

"And what has the industrious inspector done on your behalf?"

"He questioned my servants, none of whom could afford to buy a pencil sketch from a schoolgirl, after which he declared himself sympathetic to my lack of enthusiasm for the canvas."

"You do not like Impressionism?"

"No, Gaudet is simply incapable of reading a chap correctly. I adore Impressionism," he said. "We have seventeen works in that style. I bought two of Monet's haystack series last year."

"So the thief knows your taste?" I asked.

"Evidently."

"We've no objection to the painting," Madeline said. "But how am I to sleep when an intruder has made such easy entry into our home?"

"You've every right to be unsettled," I said. "What is the inspector's plan?"

"He's concluded that there's no harm done and no point in looking for the culprit."

"Madame du Lac is great friends with Monet. She could perhaps find out from him who previously owned the work. You may find you've been the victim of nothing more than a practical joke at the hands of well-meaning friends." We called her over at once and relayed the story to her.

"*Mon dieu!*" she said. "I know this painting well. It was stolen from Monet's studio at Giverny not three days ago—he wired to tell me as soon as it happened. He'd only just finished with the canvas. The paint was barely dry and the police have no leads."

I would not have believed, a quarter of an hour ago, that anything could have distracted me from the memory of the brutalized body beneath the tree, but suddenly my mind was racing. "Was there anything else in the note?" I asked.

"Some odd letters," Madeline said. "They made no sense."

"It was Greek, my darling. But I didn't pay enough attention in school to be able to read it."

My heartbeat quickened with a combination of anxiety and unworthy delight. It could only be Sebastian.